The
PENNY
JORDAN
Collection

TITLES IN THIS SERIES

BLACKMAIL

BLACKMAIL

BY
PENNY JORDAN

MILLS & BOON LIMITED
15–16 BROOK'S MEWS
LONDON W1A 1DR

First published in Great Britain 1982 by Mills & Boon Limited

© *Penny Jordan 1982*

Australian copyright 1982 Philippine copyright 1982 Reprinted 1982 This edition 1986

ISBN 0 263 75603 3

Set in Monophoto Plantin 10 on 11½ pt 19/1286

Printed and bound in Great Britain by Cox & Wyman Ltd, Reading

CHAPTER ONE

'ARE you okay?'

Lee smiled, her eyes sparkling with anticipation. Her parents had named her, rather foolishly she sometimes thought, 'Annabel-Lee,' but she was 'Lee' to everyone who knew her, a tall, slender girl with long brown hair the colour of beechwoods in autumn, and as glossy as polished chestnuts. Her eyes were green, faintly tip-tilted and fringed with thick curling lashes—witch's eyes, her father had once called them, and her mouth curved generously. No one looking at her mouth could doubt that she had a warm, deeply passionate nature.

Below them the Channel glinted silver in the morning sun. Excitement bubbled up inside her, as frothy and tingling as champagne.

'There'll be a hire car waiting for us at the airport.' Michael Roberts, her boss, told her. 'We'll drive straight down to the Loire.'

Michael was the chief wine buyer for a prestigious supermarket chain and Lee was his assistant. She had been working for him for six weeks, but this was her first 'field trip', so to speak. Michael was in the middle of some delicate negotiations with a wine-grower in the Loire Valley, who so far had been reluctant to allow his *grand* and *premier cru* wines to be sold anywhere but in the most exclusive specialised wine shops. Michael was hoping to persuade him that while these first-class wines should quite rightly continue to be sold to the connoisseur, the English wine-drinking public was growing considerably more discerning and deserved to be able to purchase good wine.

There was considerable rivalry between the various supermarket chains concerning the quality of wines their buyers managed to secure for their customers, and to be able to add the Château Chauvigny label to their range would be a feather in Michael's cap.

After lengthy negotiations the Comte de Chauvigny had invited Michael to visit the vineyards and taste the new wines, and Michael was hopeful that this meant that the Comte was prepared to do business with them.

'At this time of the year we're likely to be the Comte's only guests,' Michael warned Lee, as the seat belt warning lights flashed up, signalling the end of their journey. 'The *grand* and *premier cru* wines will be tasted later in the year by the connoisseurs lucky enough to be able to buy them. What does that fiancé of your's think about you and me flying off to France together?' he asked with a twinkle in his eyes. 'You're quite a career girl, aren't you? How will that tie in with marriage to a Boston Brahmin with a banking empire to inherit?'

'Drew knows how much my career means to me,' Lee said firmly. She had first met her fiancé when she had been working at a vineyard in Australia. They had fallen in love almost at first sight, and there had been little time to discuss such mundane matters as the finer details of their future together. Their time had been short. Lee had already been accepted for her present job, and Drew had been tied up in delicate negotiations for the amalgamation of the banking empire headed by his father, with a Canadian associate.

Until these negotiations were completed there could be no question of their marriage taking place. Drew's family came of Pilgrim stock and their wedding would figure largely in Boston's social calendar. Lee had been a little amused by Drew's insistence that their wedding should be so formal, but had goodnaturedly agreed to all Drew's proposals. She frowned slightly as the remembered that it was her turn to phone him. Their transatlantic phone calls were a weekly ritual, and she had already warned Drew that this week's would have to be brief as she would be in France.

The aircraft was descending. Soon they would be landing. She was in France to do a job, Lee reminded herself, and not daydream about her fiancé. Butterflies fluttered in her stomach. This job was important to her and she badly wanted to do well. So far she knew that Michael was pleased with her, so why did she have this vague feeling of anxiety?

Their hire car was a dark blue Renault, and they were going to share the driving. It would take them several hours to reach Chauvigny Michael had warned her. The bright May sunlight touched her hair, burnishing it with gold, and Michael smiled appreciatively. For the journey she was wearing a soft rose-pink linen suit—smart and casual—toned with a cream georgette blouse. She moved with a natural elegance, her legs long and slender as they carried her towards the car.

By mutual consent thay had decided not to stop for a meal en route. French lunches were notoriously long-lasting affairs and they had already eaten on the plane. After Orléans Lee took over from Michael. She was a good driver; careful but with enough élan not to be panicked by the French habit of disconcerting overtaking, and soon learned to leave enough room between the Renault and the car in front to allow for any mishaps.

Michael Roberts watched her as she drove, amused by her total concentration. He had never had a female assistant before, but her qualifications and experience had been far superior to those of the other applicants for the job. A wine buyer needs a love of wine; a knowledge of its creation, and most of all that unlearnable ability to discern the superior from the very good, plus a large helping of intuition. The applicants for the job had all been requested to sample several different wines and then make their observations on them. Lee's observations had been far superior to those of the other contenders. She had what was known in the trade as a 'nose'. At first Michael had been dubious about her appointment. Above all else buying wine was a serious business, and who could behave seriously with a beautiful woman like Lee? Especially Frenchmen, by whom the buying of wine was taken very, very seriously indeed. However, he had soon discovered that his fears were groundless. As his assistant Lee took her duties very seriously; her manner towards their suppliers was as crisp and fresh as a good Muscadet. He had been both amused and pleased by the way she handled the one or two suppliers who had tried to palm her off with an inferior wine. She had given them very short shift indeed, but in such a way that they were never aware that they had been manipulated.

Lee wasn't as unaware of Michael's covert regard as she pretended. Her parents had emigrated to Australia when she was in her first year of university, mainly to be with her brother who had made his home there, and she had very quickly become independent, aware of the fine line which divided a pleasant but casual friendship with members of the opposite sex from something more intimate, and she was equally skilled in making sure that that line wasn't crossed unless she expressly wished it to be. She had been so engrossed in her career that there hadn't been time for serious relationships—until she met Drew. Her parents had been at first amused and then doubtful when she told them what she wanted to do. A school holiday spent in France had sparked off her ambition, and when they realised that she was serious they had done all they could to help her, and now, just when she was realising her first goal, Drew expected her to give it all up. And it wasn't even as though they were to be married yet. It would be some time before he was able to leave Canada, and Lee had planned to save up all her holidays so that they could spend some time together, getting to know one another properly. She glanced at the diamond solitaire on her left hand—discreetly expensive without being flashy; the sort of ring considered appropriate by the Talbot family, no doubt. Dismissing the thought as unfair, she studied their surroundings. Chauvigny was closer to Nantes than Orléans and they were driving through the Loire Valley proper now, past huge châteaux, relics of the time of François I, but it was the vineyards that captured Lee's attention.

In Saumur the valley narrowed, the hills honeycombed with caverns offering wine for sale. At one point the caverns had actually been turned into homes, but the road was too narrow for Lee to give them much attention. They drove through Angers where the Loire widened. Men were working in the vineyards, spraying the precious vines with water to create a protective layer of ice in case of a night frost.

'As soon as they think the frosts are over they'll begin spraying against pests,' Michael told her. 'The recipe for being a good vintner includes such qualities as patience, a thorough understanding of the soil and climate, its benefits and drawbacks, as well as all the complicated processes that go to making a first class wine, plus that indescribable something with which one either is, or is not, born. It can't be learned.'

'We turn off here,' he instructed, indicating a steep right fork off the main road.

They climbed steadily through gently rolling hills, flattening out in the distance to Nantes and the coast, vines growing on either side of the road; through a small, almost mediaeval village, and then the château was in front of them, the smooth cream walls rising out of the still waters of a moat, fairy-tale spires, shining pale gold against the azure evening sky, the whole thing so impossibly beautiful, like a mirage floating on a calm oasis, that Lee could not understand why she felt this renewed sensation of nervous apprehension spiralling through her.

'Well, well, it looks like the real thing,' Michael commented, obviously impressed. 'When a Frenchman talks about a château it can be anything from a country cottage to Buckingham Palace. It looks as though this one really meant it. All it needs is Errol Flynn to come flying through the window to complete the Hollywood image!'

A permanent 'drawbridge' spanned the moat; the Renault disturbed two elegant swans who had been gliding slowly below. Odd how such graceful water birds could look so clumsy on land, Lee thought absently, watching them.

The drawbridge gave way to an arched gateway, beyond which stretched an enclosed courtyard. She had seen homes equally impressive in Australia, she reminded herself, trying not to be quelled by the château's air of ancient grandeur, coupled with an aura of discreet wealth. Wisteria blanketed the cream walls, racemes of purple-blue flowers smothering the gnarled branches, reminiscent in shape and size of the bunches of grapes themselves.

The sound of the car alerted the dog who had been sleeping in front of the large double doors. Lee stopped the car and wound down the window. The evening air was clean and fresh after the staleness of the Renault. She could hear the sound of water, and as her eyes grew accustomed to the creeping shadows she saw the shallow stone basin with its fountain, a boy holding— not a water jar, but a bunch of grapes from which sprang the droplets which filled the basin beneath, sparkling like champagne.

Tubs of geraniums and lobelia added a colourful splash to the cobbled courtyard, and as she looked about her, Lee realised that they were at the back of the château in what had probably once been the stables and outbuildings. She looked up at the house. Blank windows stared back at her, the circular towers she had noticed from the road having only narrow arrow slits, proclaiming their great age.

The double doors opened, the dying sun blinding Lee momentarily as it was reflected in the leaded windowpanes. A man emerged from the château dressed in an expensively tailored dove grey suit, his black hair brushed back off a face which was stamped with the indelible marks of centuries of breeding. He spoke sharply to the dog, which was still barking noisily, a wolfhound almost as high as the lean hips encased in the pale grey mohair. Nervous tension crawled sickeningly through Lee's body, causing her hands to lock whitely on the steering wheel. Michael climbed out of the car and opened her door. She followed him on legs which suddenly seemed to have turned to cotton wool.

'Michael Roberts,' Michael announced, introducing himself, 'and my assistant,' he turned to Lee and smiled, 'Lee Raven, and you, of course, must be . . .'

'Gilles Frébourg, Comte de Chauvigny.'

He spoke perfect, accentless English—but then of course he always had, Lee thought numbly, battling against the shock that had locked her muscles in mute protest, the moment she looked into—and recognised—his arrogant features. After all, his mother *was* English.

'Lee.'

His pronunciation of her name betrayed none of her shock. The hand he extended towards her was tanned, the fingers lean, his grip powerful.

'Gilles.' She murmured his name in the same perfunctory tone he had adopted, adding carelessly, 'How is Aunt Caroline?'

His eyes gleamed, as though he was well aware that beneath her calm words lurked nerve-racking chaos.

'Very well, and enjoying the Caribbean. Lee and I share an aunt in common,' he explained to Michael, who was looking increasingly baffled. 'Or at least, she is my aunt and . . .'

'My godmother,' Lee supplied, taking a deep breath and willing herself to appear calm. Talk about coincidence! She had never dreamed when she left England that their destination was also the home of Gilles Frébourg. And if she had nothing would have brought her within a thousand miles of it, she thought with a bitter smile.

'Come inside.' Gilles' smile mocked her, as though her had read her mind. 'My housekeeper will show you to your rooms. Tonight we do not dine formally, as it is your first in my home. I am sure you must be tired and will perhaps want an early night. Tomorrow we shall tour the vineyards.'

Thin gold slats of sunshine touched precious

antiques, as they stepped into a vast square hall, its
floor covered in a carpet so soft and beautiful that it
seemed criminal to walk on it. The Chauvigny arms were
cut in stone above the huge fireplace, and Lee remembered now, when it was too late, Aunt Caroline
mentioning that her sister's brother-in-law was a
Comte.

They had all been at school together, her mother,
Aunt Caroline, and Aunt Caroline's sister, Gilles'
mother, although she, of course, had been several years
older than the other two. Lee glanced at Gilles. It was
almost six years since she had last seen him. He hadn't
changed, unless it was to become even more arrogantly
male. Did he find her altered? He must do, she reflected. She had been sixteen the last time they met,
shy, gawky, blushing fiery red every time he even
looked at her, and now she was twenty-two with a
patina of sophistication which came from living alone
and managing her own affairs. That summer when she
had met Gilles he had been staying with his aunt, following a bad bout of 'flu. He had been twenty-five
then.

The housekeeper, introduced as Madame Le Bon,
was dressed in black, plump hands folded over the
front of her dress as she obeyed Gilles' summons, cold
eyes assessing Lee in a way which she found unnerv-
ing.

There was a portrait facing them as she and Michael
followed the woman upstairs. The man in it was
wearing the uniform of Napoleon's hussars, but the
lean body beneath the dashing uniform and the face
below the tousled black hair—worn longer, admittedly,
than Gilles'—were quite unmistakably those of their
host. Even Michael was aware of the resemblance, for
he drew Lee's attention to it as they passed beneath

the huge painting. The man in the portrait seemed to possess a rakish, devil-may-care quality which in Gilles had been transmuted into a careless arrogance which Lee found less attractive, and which seemed to proclaim to the world that its opinion of him mattered not one jot and that he was a man who lived only by rules of his own making. A man whom it would be very, very, dangerous to cross—but then she already knew that, didn't she?

'You are on the same floor,' the housekeeper told Michael and Lee. 'If you wish adjoining rooms . . .'

Lee felt the colour burn along her cheeks at the manner in which the woman quite deliberately posed the question. She glanced at Michael, pointedly.

'Miss Raven and I are business associates,' he pointed out very firmly. 'I'm sure that whatever has been arranged will be admirably suitable. Adjoining rooms are not necessary.

'Not that I wouldn't want to share a room with you,' he told Lee a little later when he had settled in and come to see how she was progressing with her own unpacking. Her bedroom faced out on to the formal gardens in front of the château, although with the dusk creeping over them it was impossible to make out more than the shadowy outlines of clipped hedges, and smell the scent of early flowers. 'Always supposing you were willing, which I know quite well you're not, but it doesn't say much for the morals of our countrymen and women, does it? Perhaps they've had a surfeit of visitors with "secretaries",' he added with a grin.

It could well be that Michael was right, Lee reflected, but there had been something about the way the housekeeper had looked at her when she had spoken which had made Lee feel that the remarks had been directed specifically towards herself. Her eyes narrowed thoughtfully.

'You never told me you had connections in high places,' Michael teased. 'Had I known you knew the Comte personally we needn't have bothered coming down here. You could have used your influence to get him to agree.'

'I didn't know he had inherited the title,' Lee told him. 'As you've probably guessed, our relationship, if you can call it that, is very tenuous, and there's certainly no blood connection. I've only met him once before. I couldn't even call us acquaintances.'

But there was more to it than that—much more, Lee reflected when Michael had left her to finish her unpacking and change for dinner. Such as her foolish sixteen-year-old self imagining she was in love with Gilles. It must have been the crush to beat all crushes. A small private boarding school where many of the girls were the daughters of strict Spanish and South American parents was not the ideal place to gain an adequate knowledge of sexual matters. She had been greener than grass; completely overwhelmed by the powerful attraction she felt for Gilles. Had he asked her to lie down and die for him no doubt she would have done so. Her infatuation had been of the order that asks no more of the beloved being than merely that he existed. There had been no sexual awareness in her adoration apart from that which goes hand in glove with a girl's first love. She put it all behind her long ago, especially its grubby, sordid ending, which had done so much to sully her memories of that year.

Her bedroom was vast. Their visit to the château was to be a short one—three days—which would allow them to see the vineyards, the cellars where the wine was stored, and still allow some time for the negotiations which Michael hoped would result in them securing the Chauvigny label for Westbury's. She wondered if she ought to alert Michael to the fact that her being his assistant might seriously detract from his chances of doing so, and then decided against it. She was remembering Gilles with the eyes of a sixteen-year-old child. It was surely hardly likely that an adult male of thirty-one would bear a grudge against a child of sixteen.

Gilles certainly believed in treating his guests lavishly, she reflected, hanging the neat, understated toning separates she had brought with her in the vast fitted wardrobes which lined one wall of the room, their fronts mirrored and decorated with delicate panel mouldings to match the rest of the bedroom, which was furnished with what she suspected were genuine French Empire antiques. It wasn't hard at all to imagine a provocatively gowned Josephine reclining on the pale green satin-covered chaise-longue, waiting impatiently for her lover.

Everything in the room matched; from the self-coloured design on the pale green silk wall coverings, to the curtains and bed covers.

A beautiful ladies' writing desk was set beneath the window with a matching chair; the dressing table was French Empire, all white and gold with delicate spindly legs, the table lamps either side of the huge double bed the only modern touch, but even these might have been made for this room.

Lee wasn't a fool. The furnishing in this room—from the precious silks down to the faded but still beautiful pale green and pink carpet which she suspected must be Aubusson—must surely be worth a king's ransom; and this was only one of the château's many rooms. Gilles must obviously be a very wealthy man; a man who could afford to pick and choose to whom he sold his wine. No doubt after the vintage he would hold those dinner parties for which French *vignerons* are so famous, when the cognoscenti gathered to partake of lavish dinners conducted in formal surroundings, all carefully designed as a paean of tribute to the evening's guest of honour—the wine.

This was the first time Lee had visited such an exclusive vineyard. In Australia, where she had spent a year working alongside a grower in his own vineyards, things were much more casual, in keeping with the young vigour of their wines. Now she was grateful for the momentary memory of her teenage visit to a French vineyard which had urged her to pack a slender sheath of a black velvet dress.

Her bedroom had its own private bathroom; so blatantly luxurious that she caught her breath in bemusement as she stared first at the sunken marble bath and then the gold fittings. Even the floor and walls were marble, and she felt as decadent as a harem girl whose one desire in life was to pleasure her master, as she sank into the deep, hot water and luxuriated with abandoned delight. In London she shared a flat with two other working girls, and there was rarely time for more than a workmanlike shower, and the odd long soak when she had the flat all to herself.

Lifting one long, slender leg from the suds, she eyed it dispassionately. Gilles certainly knew how to live. Why had he not married? Surely a home and responsibilities such as his must make the production of a son and heir imperative, and Frenchmen were normally so careful in these matters. He was, after all, thirty-one. Not old ... she laughed aloud at the thought of anyone daring to think such a vigorous and aristocratic man as Gilles old. Even when he did eventually reach old age he would still be devastatingly attractive. She frowned. Where were her thoughts leading her? Surely she was not still foolish enough to feel attracted to Gilles?

She got out of the bath and dried herself slowly. Of course she was not; she had learned her lesson. She glanced towards the telephone by her bed. She would ring Drew. Michael had assured her that she might, and that he would ensure that the call was paid for.

It didn't take long to get through. Drew's Boston accent reached her quite clearly across the miles that separated them. He sounded rather brusque, and Lee's heart sank.

'You decided to go, then?'

His question referred to the fact that he had not been pleased to learn that she was due to travel abroad with Michael. In fact he had tried very hard to dissuade her, and they had come perilously close to their first quarrel. Now, squashing her misgivings, Lee replied firmly, 'It's my job, Drew—you know that. You wouldn't expect me to make a fuss because you have to work in Canada, would you?'

There was a pause, and then Drew's voice saying coldly, 'That's different. There's no need for you to work at all, Lee. As my wife you'll be expected to fulfil certain duties. You should be spending these months before our marriage in Boston. Mom did invite you.'

So that she could be vetted as to her suitability to marry into such a prominent family, Lee thought resentfully.

'So that she could make sure I don't eat my peas off my knife?' she remarked sarcastically, instantly wishing the words unsaid as she caught Drew's swiftly indrawn breath.

'Don't be ridiculous!' He sounded stiff now, and angry. 'All Mom wanted to do was to introduce you around the family. When we're married we'll be living in Boston, and it will help if you already know the ropes. Mom will propose you to the charity committees the family work for, and . . .'

'Charity committees?' Once again Lee's hot tongue ran away with her. 'Is that how you expect me to spend the rest of my life Drew? I already have a career . . .'

'Which takes you gallivanting all over the place with other men. I want my wife at home, Lee.'

All at once she understood. He was jealous of Michael! An understanding smile curved her mouth. How silly of him! Michael was in his late forties and well and truly married. All at once she wished the width of the Atlantic did not lie between them, but she had already been on the phone for several minutes. She glanced at her watch and said hurriedly, 'Drew, I can't talk any more now. But I'll write soon . . .'

She hoped he would say that he loved her, but he hung up without doing so, and she told herself it had probably been because someone might have overheard. It was too late now to regret those impetuously hasty words. She could only hope that her letter would mollify him. There wasn't time to start it before dinner, and she tried to put the whole thing out of her mind until later. The black dress set off her creamy skin, still holding the faint sheen of her Australian tan. The neckline, high at the throat, plunged to a deep vee at the back, exposing the vulnerable line of her spine, drawing attention to the matt perfection of her flesh. Long sleeves hugged her arms to the wrists, the skirt skimming her narrow hips, a demure slit revealing several inches of thigh, now encased in sheer black stockings. Her mother had been with her when she bought the dress, and it was she who had suggested the stockings. 'Something about that dress demands them,' she had insisted firmly. 'It's a wicked, womanly dress that should only be worn when you're feeling particularly female, and with it you must wear the sheerest stockings you can find.'

'So that every man who sees me in it will know just what I'm wearing underneath it?' Lee had exclaimed, scandalised. She had already realised that there was just no way she could wear a bra with the dress, and now her mother, of all people, was suggesting that she went a step farther!

'So that every man who sees you in it will *wonder* what you're wearing,' her mother had corrected. 'And hope he's right! Besides,' she concluded firmly, 'there's something about wearing stockings which will make you feel the way you ought to feel when you're wearing that dress.'

It had been impossible to argue with her mother's logic, but now Lee wasn't so sure. The fine Dior stockings enhanced her long, slim legs, the velvet sumptuous enough on its own, without any jewellery. On impulse, Lee swept her hair into a smooth chignon, leaving only a few softening wisps to frame her face. All at once her eyes seemed larger, greener, the classical hairstyle revealing her perfect bone structure. When she looked in the mirror she saw not a pretty girl, but a beautiful woman, and for a moment it was almost like looking at a stranger. She even seemed to be moving more regally. She applied the merest hint of green eyeshadow, a blusher frosted with specks of gold, which had been a hideously expensive Christmas present from her brother and which gilded her delicately high cheekbones to perfection, and then added a lip gloss, darker than her daytime lipstick. Perfume—her favourite Chanel completed her preparations and then, slipping on the delicately heeled black sandals, she surveyed her reflection in the mirror, rather like a soldier preparing for a hard battle, she admitted wryly.

Michael whistled when he saw her.

'What happened?' he begged. 'I know Cinderella is supposed to be a French fairytale, but this is ridiculous!'

'Are you trying to tell me that I arrived here in rags?' Lee teased him.

'No. But I certainly didn't expect the brisk, businesslike young woman I left slightly less than an hour ago would turn into a beautiful seductress who looks as though she never does anything more arduous than peel the odd grape!'

Lee laughed; as much at Michael's bemused expression as his words. The sound ran round the enclosed silence. A door opened and Gilles walked towards them. Despite his claim that they would dine informally he was wearing a dinner suit, its impeccable fit emphasising the lean tautness of his body. Lee was immediately aware of him in a way that her far more naïve sixteen-year-old self had never been. Then he had dressed in jeans and tee-shirts, or sometimes when it was hot, just jeans, and yet she had never been aware of his body as she was now; the muscular thighs moulded by the soft black wool, the broad shoulders and powerful chest; the lean flat stomach.

'Do you two have some means of communication I don't know about?' Michael complained. 'I thought we were dining informally?' He was wearing a lounge suit, and Gilles gave him a perfunctory smile.

'Please forgive me. I nearly always change when I am home for dinner. The staff expect it.'

Lee stared at him. From her estimation of him she

wouldn't have thought he gave a damn what the staff expected.

'It is necessary when one employs other people to make sure that one has their respect,' he said to her, as though he had guessed her thoughts. 'And there is no one quite so snobbish as a French peasant—unless it is an English butler.'

Michael laughed, but Lee did not. God, Gilles was arrogant—almost inhuman! Did he never laugh, cry, get angry or make love?

The last question was answered sooner than she had expected. They were in what Gilles described as the 'main salon', a huge room of timeless elegance of a much older period than her bedroom. Louis Quatorze, she thought, making an educated guess as she studied a small sofa table with the most beautiful inlaid marquetry top. Gilles had offered them a drink, but Lee had refused. She suspected that only house wines would be served during dinner and she did not want to cloud her palate by drinking anything else first. Neither of the two men drank either, and she would feel Gilles watching her with sardonic appraisal. He was a man born out of his time, she thought, watching his face. Why had she never seen before the ruthless arrogance, the privateer, the aristocrat written in every feature?

The door opened to admit Madame Le Bon. She gave Gilles a thin smile.

'*Madame est arrivée.*'

Who was the woman who was so well known to Gilles' household that she was merely referred to as Madame? Lee wondered. Gilles did not move, and Lee could almost feel the housekeeper's disapproval. She looked at Lee, her eyes cold and hostile, leaving Lee to wonder what she had done to merit such palpable dis-

like, and all on the strength of two very brief meet-
ings—and then she forgot all about the housekeeper as
another woman stepped into the room. She was one of
the most beautiful women Lee had ever seen. Her hair
was a rich and glorious red, her skin the colour of milk,
shadowed with purple-blue veins. Every tiny porcelain
inch of her shrieked breeding, right down to the cool,
dismissing smile she bestowed upon Michael and Lee.

'Gilles!'

Her voice was surprisingly deep, a husky purr as she
placed one scarlet-tipped hand on Gilles' arm and
raised her face for a kiss which, her seductively pouted
mouth informed the onlookers, was no mere formality.

The scarlet, pouting mouth was ignored, and to
Lee's surprise Gilles lifted her hand to his lips instead.
Perhaps he was embarrassed about kissing her in front
of them, she deduced, although she had thought him
far too arrogant to mind about that.

'Forgive me for not dressing more formally,' she
purred, indicating the sea-green chiffon gown which
Lee was quite sure came from one of the famous couture houses. 'But I have only this afternoon returned
from Paris. And these are your guests . . .'

Gilles introduced them.

'Louise—Lee Raven, and Michael Roberts. Madame
Beauvaise. Her father is my closest neighbour. Another
wine grower . . .'

Louise's lips pouted, her eyes narrowing slightly as
she scrutinised Lee, so thoroughly that Lee felt there
wasn't anything about her which had not been inspected and priced—including her stockings.

'Come, _chéri_,' she protested lightly, 'you make it
sound so formal and dull. We are more to each other
than mere neighbours, you and I. And you, Miss
Raven—you are wearing a betrothal ring, I see. Do we

take it that you and Mr Roberts are to marry?'

First the housekeeper and now this woman; there seemed no shortage of people willing to thrust her into Michael's arms, it seemed.

'No, we are not,' she said shortly, not prepared to elucidate. There had been a suggestiveness behind the Frenchwoman's words which she had disliked intensely; it had almost been that of a voyeur, distasteful though the thought was, and for the first time Lee saw the sensuality behind the redhead's elegant poise, the greedy hunger of her mouth as it parted suddenly when she looked at Gilles. Feeling faintly sick, Lee wished she could escape to her room. There was something about Louise which reminded her of a particularly deadly species of orchid, all dazzling beauty on the surface, but underneath . . . poisonous.

The meal was as delicious as Lee had envisaged— soup served with a perfect, dry rosé which cleansed the palate; deliciously tender lamb with a full-bodied red which brought out the subtle flavour of the roast meat, and finally a cheese board with a choice of Rocamadour, Picodon, and Charolles, all chosen to complement the dry, fruity white wine.

Michael was a skilled raconteur, and the talk around the dinner table was general and light, only Louise pouting occasionally as though longing to be alone with the man Lee now no longer had any doubt was her lover. It was there in every look she gave him, the constant touch of her fingers on his arm; the intimate possessive glances which said quite plainly, this man is mine.

After dinner they returned to the salon. The housekeeper brought in the coffee; like the dinner service the cups were beautiful porcelain, and had not, Lee suspected, been purchased from any store.

Louise got up gracefully to pour the coffee, but to Lee's amazement Gilles restrained her.

'Perhaps Lee will be mother?' he suggested with a slight inclination of the arrogant dark head. Lee was astounded, but such was the authority of his voice that it never occurred to her to refuse.

The hauteur with which Louise surveyed her almost made her laugh out loud.

'Mother?' she repeated disdainfully.

'An English expression,' Gilles informed her. 'I should have mentioned it earlier, but Lee and I are old friends. We have an aunt in common.' He reached for Lee's hand as he spoke, such a look of tender amusement in his face that she almost caught her breath in disbelief.

Louise seemed to share her bemusement. She was staring from Lee to Gilles with narrowed eyes, her face no longer beautiful, but hard and dangerous.

'I hope that as such an old friend, Lee will not mind sharing you with . . . newer friends . . .'

There was a warning as well as a question in the silky words, and Lee realised with a sense of shock that the redhead actually thought she might be a contender for Gilles' affections. As though she would attempt anything so foolish!

She was even further astonished when Gilles carried her fingers to his lips, an expression which in anyone else might almost have been called doting, in the slate-grey eyes, now warm and smouldering.

'Well, darling?' he enquired in tones of deepest affection. 'Will you be jealous of my old friends?'

'Darling?'

For a moment Lee thought she had been the one to say the word, and then a look at Louise's furious white face informed her that although they had heard the

endearment with equal shock, the Frenchwoman had
been the first to announce her shock verbally.

Lee glanced at Michael to see what he was making
of all this strange behaviour on the part of their host,
but he was simply relaxing in his chair, a small smile
playing round his lips as he waited for the explosion
none of them were in any doubt was imminent. Unless
of course it was Gilles, who was looking for all the
world as though there was no reason why he should
not call Lee 'darling' in front of his mistress, and none
at all why she should resent it. That look of icy hauteur
would certainly have been enough to make her think
twice about creating a scene, Lee reflected uncertainly,
but then perhaps she had more experience of exactly
how brutal Gilles could be when he wanted to than the
infuriated Frenchwoman.

'Isn't that how one normally addresses a fiancée?'
Gilles murmured smoothly.

'A . . . You mean . . .'

'Lee and I are engaged to be married,' he agreed
silkily, obviously realising that while Louise had
grasped the meaning of his words, she was, as yet, incapable of vocalising her reaction to them.

'She is not wearing the Chauvigny betrothal ring.'

'A small omission,' Gilles said coolly. 'It has been
an understood thing between us for many years that
we should marry, but on my last visit to England I
found her so grown up and . . . desirable that I could
not wait to . . . seal our betrothal. Since I do not carry
the Chauvigny emerald around with me—which I am
sure, my dear Louise, you will have already marked,
will match Lee's eyes exactly—I had to make do with
this small trifle.'

Drew's diamond was removed from Lee's finger
before she could protest, Gilles shrugging aside

Louise's impatient questions as though he found them both boring and impertinent. After a long tirade in French which Lee was mercifully relieved that she could not understand, the redhead got up and stalked over to her, eyes venomous as they stared down into her oval face.

'You may have made this innocent your betrothed, Gilles—do not think I do not know why. The woman who gives birth to the Chauvigny heir must of course be above reproach, but she will never bring you the pleasure in bed that I did. She will have milk and water in her veins, your English bride, not blood. And as for you . . .' her eyes swept Lee's pale face. Events were moving much too fast for Lee. She ought to have denied Gilles' statement right from the start, but she had been far too stunned, and he, taking advantage of her bemusement, had spun a tale around them which pointed to him being a skilled and resourceful liar.

'Do you really think you will keep him?' Louise demanded scornfully. 'How long will it be before he leaves your bed for someone else's, in Paris or Orléans, while you are left to sleep alone? Look at him!' she insisted. 'He is not one of your cold, passionless Englishmen. He will take your heart and break it as he did mine, and feed the pieces to the vultures. I wish you joy of him!'

Gilles, looking unutterably bored, held open the door as she stalked towards it, and through it, leaving a silence behind her which could only be described as deafening.

CHAPTER TWO

'AND what,' Lee asked dangerously, when the front door had slammed behind the furious Frenchwoman, and Michael had discreetly left them to it, 'was all that about?'

Far from looking ruffled, Gilles appeared enviably calm—far calmer than she was herself. He lit a thin cheroot with an expensive gold lighter, studying the glowing tip for a few seconds before replying coolly,

'I should have thought it was obvious. You are not, I think, lacking in intelligence. You must surely have observed that Louise considered her position in my life far more important than it actually was.'

His sheer arrogance took Lee's breath away.

'An impression which you of course did nothing to foster!' she smouldered, too furious now for caution. Of all the hypocritical, arrogant men! To actually dare to use her to get rid of his unwanted mistress!

'Louise knew the score,' he replied emotionlessly. 'If she decided she preferred being the Comtesse de Chauvigny, rather than merely the Comte's mistress, it is only natural that I should seek to correct her erroneous impression that she may step from one role to the other merely on a whim.'

'Her place is in your bed, not at your side, is that what you're trying to say?' Lee seethed. Really, he was quite impossible! 'She was good enough to sleep with, but . . .'

'You are talking of matters about which you know nothing,' Gilles cut in coldly. 'In France marriage is an important business, not to be undertaken without due consideration. Louise's first husband was a racing driver, who was killed during a Grand Prix; for many years she has enjoyed the ... er ... privileges of her widowhood, but a woman of thirty must look to the future,' he said cruelly, 'and Louise mistakenly thought she would find that future with me. A Chauvigny does not take for a bride soiled goods.'

Lee made a small sound of disgust in her throat and instantly Gilles' eyes fastened on her face.

'You think it a matter for amusement?' he demanded. 'That a woman such as that, who will give herself willingly to any man who glances her way, is fit to be the mistress of this château?'

'She was fit to be yours,' Lee pointed out coolly.

Hard grey eyes swept her.

'My mistress, but not my wife; not the mother of my children. And before you say anything, Louise was well aware of the position. Do you think she would want me if it were not for the title, for this château?'

'Possibly not.' Now what on earth had made her say that? Lee wondered, watching the anger leap to life in Gilles' eyes. What woman in her senses would not want Gilles if he owned nothing but the clothes he stood up in? The thought jerked her into an awareness of where such thoughts could lead. What woman would? she demanded of herself crossly. Certainly not her, who knew exactly how cruel and hateful he could be!

'I am not interested in your emotional problems, Gilles,' she told him firmly. 'What I want to know is why you dared to drag me into all this, or do you still enjoy inflicting pain just for the thrill of it?'

There was a small silence when it would have been possible to hear a pin drop, had such an elegant room contained so homely an object; a time when Lee was acutely conscious of Gilles' cold regard, and then, as the silence stretched on unnervingly, she held her breath, frightened, in spite of her determination not to be, by the hard implacability in Gilles' face.

'I will forget that you made that last remark. As to the other——' he shrugged in a way that was totally Gallic, 'because you were there, because we are known to one another; because you were already wearing a betrothal ring which made things so much easier.'

'Well, as of now,' Lee told him through gritted teeth, as she listened in appalled disbelief to his arrogant speech, 'our betrothal is at an end!'

'It will end tomorrow,' Gilles told her arrogantly, as though she had no say in the matter. 'When we marry.'

'*Marry?*' Lee stared at him. 'Have you gone mad? I wouldn't marry you if you were the last man on earth! Have you forgotten that I'm engaged to another man? A man whom I love, and who loves me . . .'

'But who does not trust you,' Gilles drawled succinctly. 'Otherwise he would not have telephoned here this morning to ask if you had arrived, and if you were to share a room with Michael Roberts. I confess I was intrigued to meet you again; you must have changed considerably, I told myself, to arouse such jealousy.'

Lee ignored the subtle insult. He had known she was coming, then. Had that scene with Louise all been planned? She didn't want to think so, but knowing Gilles, it was just the sort of Machiavellian action he would delight in.

'Sit down,' he instructed her coolly, grasping her shoulders with cool hands, tanned, with clean, well cared for nails. Hands which held a strength that bruised as he forced her into a brocade-covered chair, which alone was probably worth more than the entire contents of her small flat. 'Before you lay any more hysterical charges at my feet, allow me to explain a few facts to you.

'Louise's father is a close friend of mine, and a neighbour, whom I greatly respect. Louise has completely blinded him as to her true personality, and out of charity his friends keep silent as to her real nature. He owns land which borders mine, fine, vine-growing land, which will eventually form Louise's *dot* should she remarry, but Bernard is growing frail and can no longer tend this land himself. I should like to buy it from him . . .'

'Why don't you simply marry Louise?' Lee butted in, too furious to stay silent any longer. 'Then you'll get it for free.'

'On the contrary,' Gilles said smoothly, 'I shall have to pay a very heavy price indeed. The price of knowing that my wife is known intimately to every other man in the neighbourhood who has glanced her way; the price of not knowing whether I have fathered any children she may bear. However, I now discover that our names have been linked by local gossip—gossip deliberately fed by Louise, I am sure, for she would stop at nothing to become my wife.'

Again his arrogance took Lee's breath away, but before she could protest, Gilles was continuing emotionlessly.

'I had two choices open to me. Either I must give in to Louise's blackmail, or cause great pain to an old friend.'

'And thereby lose his rich land,' Lee commented sotto voce, but Gilles ignored her.

'However, on this occasion I was presented with a third, and infinitely preferable choice—marriage to someone else, a marriage which will calm Bernard's suspicions, silence Louise's malicious tongue, and far more important, a marriage which can be set aside when its purpose has been achieved. In short, my dear Lee, a temporary marriage to you.'

Lee was lost for words. She stared at him, her green eyes wide with disbelief.

'I won't do it,' she said positively, when she had found her voice. 'You can't make me, Gilles.'

'Oh, but I can,' he said silkily.

He walked across the room, removing a small key from several on a key ring which he returned to his pocket, then unlocked a beautifully carved eighteenth-century desk.

'Remember this, Lee?' His voice was light, almost devoid of all emotion, but Lee's sensitive ears caught the faint note of triumph, her eyes fastening despairingly on the giveaway rose pink notepaper. It had been a present from her godmother on her sixteenth birthday. She had been thrilled with it at the time, but less than six weeks later the entire box had been consigned to the fire.—All but for two single sheets of the paper and one envelope.

'I wonder what that jealous fiancé of yours would have to say about this?' Gilles taunted. 'Even in today's more lax atmosphere, it still has a certain ... something, would you not agree? Or perhaps you would care to refresh your memory?'

Lee shuddered deeply, averting her face, unable to even contemplate looking at the letter, never mind touching it.

'Alas, your modesty comes too late. Indeed, after reading this I doubt anyone would believe you ever possessed any. I read it again myself this morning, and while the vocabulary and style might leave a certain something to be desired, no one could fault the clarity of the sentiments. I believe I would be right in thinking that not even your beloved fiancé has a letter such as this to treasure from you . . .'

'Do you think I'd ever . . .' Lee burst out, goaded into answering. But Gilles stopped her.

'Perhaps not. Indeed I find it hard to equate the cool front you present to the world with the undeniable passion of this letter. Perhaps you would care for me to read you a passage or two, to refresh your mind . . .'

'No!' The word was a low moan, Lee's hands going up to cover her ears. She was shaking as though held deep in the grip of some fever, her eyes as dark as jade, and empty of everything but the agony she was experiencing.

'So,' Gilles murmured, apparently not in the slightest affected by her bowed shoulders and white face. 'It is agreed. Either you will marry me—temporarily—or I shall send a copy of this delightful love-letter to your fiancé. You have the night to think it over,' he added coolly. 'And, Lee, do not try to leave here, for that will surely guarantee your fiancé's sight of this charming epistle.'

Somehow she managed to get to her feet, to walk past Gilles on legs that trembled convulsively with every step. He stopped her at the door, his eyes raking her pale face without mercy.

'Strangely enough, you do have a certain air of breeding; a beauty that speaks of cloistered walls and untouched innocence. Be thankful that I know you for what you are and do not seek to take more from you than merely your time. Were you as cool and innocent as you appear, it would be . . . intriguing, awakening you to love.'

'To lust, don't you mean?' Lee said sharply in disgust. 'A man like you doesn't begin to know the meaning of the word love, Gilles.'

'Then we should make an excellent pair, shouldn't we?' he murmured insultingly as he held wide the door.

In her room Lee did not undress. She sat before the window, staring out into the moon-swept gardens, her eyes blinded by the tears cascading down her face as the present ceased to exist and she was once again that sixteen-year-old, trembling on the brink of life, and love.

It had all started as a joke. Aunt Caroline had a neighbour who had a daughter several months older than Lee, and when Lee stayed with her godmother, the two girls normally spent some time together.

With the benefit of hindsight, Lee wondered if Sally too had not had a crush on Gilles, just as she had done herself, but it was far too late now to query the whys and wherefores. The truth was that she had fallen deeply and intensely in love with Gilles, seeing him as a god to be worshipped adoringly from a distance, and Sally had discovered her secret and teased her with it.

That fatal day had been particularly hot. They had been lying in the uncut grass at the end of Aunt Caroline's long garden. Earlier Gilles had been cutting the lawn, muscles rippling under the smooth brown skin of his back, tanned in far sunnier climes than England's. Lee had watched him with her heart in her eyes. Soon he would be going back to France, his brief stay over, and she felt as though her heart would break.

As though she had read her mind, Sally had tempted as cunningly as Eve with her apple, 'I dare you to tell him how you feel.'

Lee had been horrified. She could think of nothing

worse than that Gilles, so supercilious and unattainable, should know of her foolhardy impertinence.

'If you won't tell him, then I shall,' Sally had threatened with relish.

Lee had, of course, pleaded with her not to do—a foolish action, she now realised, and at length Sally had reluctantly agreed.

As she had claimed later, with a pert toss of her head, writing a letter was not telling, because she had not actually spoken to Gilles.

She had used her artistic talent to copy Lee's handwriting, and had signed the letter in Lee's name, using the very notepaper which Aunt Caroline had given Lee for her birthday. With so much evidence against her, it was small wonder that she had not been able to convince Gilles of her innocence, Lee reflected soberly, but his cruelty and callous disregard of how she had felt was something she would never forget.

Lee had been in her bedroom when Gilles found her. She had blushed the colour of a summer rose when he walked in. He looked so tall and handsome in his white shirt and tapering black trousers. The dark shadow of his tanned, muscular chest beneath the thin silk had triggered off an awareness of him she had not experienced previously, tiny tendrils of fear-cum-excitement curling along her spine; the first innocent awareness of sexual magnetism, but before Gilles left her room the veil of innocence had been torn aside for ever.

His presence in her room momentarily robbed her of speech, but her heart had been in her eyes as she looked up at him.

'Very appropriate,' he had sneered, his eyes on her cross-legged pose on her bed, where she had been doing some studying. 'But I regret, mademoiselle, I have not come here to satisfy your nymphomaniac desires, but to warn you of the outcome were you to express the same sentiments to a man who is not honour bound to protect you from yourself.'

'I . . .'

'Save your breath,' he had warned her. 'These prurient outpourings say it all.'

The letter had fluttered down from contemptuous fingers to blur in front of the green eyes that read it with growing disbelief. Some of the words, some of the desires expressed were unfamiliar to her, but those which she did understand were of such a nature as to bring a flush of shame to her cheeks.

'Oh, but you can't think . . . I didn't write this!' she had pleaded with him, but his face had remained coldly blank.

'It is your handwriting, is it not?' he had demanded imperiously. 'I have seen it on your schoolbooks— schoolbooks! What would they say, those good nuns who educate you, if they were to read this . . . this lewd filth?'

'I didn't write it!' Lee protested yet again, but it was no use, he wouldn't even listen to her, and a schoolgirlish sense of honour prevented her from naming the real culprit. She felt as though she had suddenly slipped into some miry, foul pool, from whose taint she would never be clean again. The way Gilles was looking at her made her shudder with revulsion. She forgot that she had adored him, and felt only fear as she looked up into his condemning face.

'I have heard my friends talk of girls like you,' he had said at length, 'girls who use their lack of years to cloak their lack of innocence!' He spat out a word in French which she did not catch but was sure was grossly insulting, and then before she could move, reached for her across the brief intervening space and crushed her against his body, so that she was aware all at once of the vast difference between male and female, his hand going to her breast as his lips ground hers back against her teeth until she was crying with the pain, both her body and mind outraged by the assult.

'I hòpe you have learned your lesson,' he said in disgust when he let her go. 'Although somehow I doubt it. For girls like you the pain and degradation is a vital part of the pleasure, is this not so? Be thankful I do not tell Tante Catherine of this!'

Lee had practically collapsed when he had gone. Her mouth was cut and bleeding, her flesh scorched by the intimate contact with him, and although she had not understood a half of what she had read in the letter she was supposed to have sent, nor the insults he had heaped upon her head, she had set herself the task of learning—a long and arduous process when one's only source of knowledge was parents, the nuns, and gossip picked up from school friends whose practical knowledge was less than her own.

The incidents had had one salutary effect, though. It had killed for ever any desire for sexual experimentation; no other man was ever going to degrade her with insults such as those Gilles had hurled at her.

She came back to the present with a jerk as someone tapped faintly on her door. She frowned. If it was Gilles there was no way she could face a further attack upon her tonight.

'Lee, it's me.'

She sighed with relief as she heard Michael's brisk familiar tones. Her boss quirked an eyebrow in query as she opened the door.

'Well, have you been holding out on me, or was the announcement of the engagement as much a shock to you as it was to me?'

'You know I'm engaged to Drew.' She longed to be able to pour out her troubles to Michael, but his responsibility was to their employers, and his first charge was to secure the Chauvigny wine for their customers. At twenty-two she was old enough to sort out her own emotional problems, although quite how her present dilemma was to be resolved she had no idea.

'I take it it was all a plot to get rid of the clinging vine—Louise,' he elucidated when Lee looked blank. 'Neat piece of thinking.'

'Neater than you imagine,' she told him dryly. 'Gilles wants us to get married—strictly on a temporary basis, so that he can acquire some land from Louise's papa, without having to acquire Louise as part of the bargain.'

'And you being an old friend, he guessed that you would fall in with the idea,' Michael supplied, totally misunderstanding. 'Umm, well, I suppose it might work. Drew is likely to be tied up in Canada for twelve months, or so you told me when you applied for your job, and you shouldn't have any trouble getting the marriage annulled.'

Now, when it was too late, Lee wished she had told Michael the complete truth. But how did you tell a man that you were being blackmailed by a letter you had never written? In not challenging Gilles to do his worse, she had already tacitly admitted that Drew would believe she had written that letter, and why should Michael not do the same?

'In fact it could work out very nicely for us, altogether,' Michael commented, not entirely joking. 'As your husband Gilles would be sure to sell us his lesser quality wine. We've won the award for the best supermarket suppliers of wine for the last two years, and I'd like to make it three in a row, which would be almost definite if we get this wine.'

Her vague hope of appealing to Michael for some solution faded; he was, after all, first and foremost, a wine buyer, Lee reminded herself fairly, and as far as he knew what Gilles was proposing was merely an arrangement between friends.

'Well, Comtesse,' Michael commented with a grin, 'I'd better let you get some sleep. When's the wedding to be, by the way?'

'I haven't given Gilles my decision yet,' Lee protested lightly.

'Umm—well, I can't see him accepting it if it isn't in his favour,' Michael warned her. 'Your husband-to-be didn't strike me as a particularly persuadable man, my dear, so I should tread warily if I were you.'

Lee was already awake when dawn streaked the sky. She washed and dressed, then hurried downstairs. The house might have been deserted. In the courtyard where they had arrived she could hear the soft coo of doves. The clatter of horse's hooves over the drawbridge warned her that she no longer had the morning to herself, and she shrank back into the shadows as Gilles rode into the yard, astride a huge black stallion. Man and animal made an impressive picture, and Lee held her breath as they walked past her, unwilling to be found watching like a voyeur of two intensely male creatures.

The housekeeper stopped her in the hall, and Lee wondered how such a large woman managed to move so quietly, materialising almost as though by magic.

'*Le petit déjeuner* will be served in the small salon,' she told Lee in repressive tones, her eyes sliding over the slim-fitting rose linen trousers Lee was wearing with a soft cream blouse and a matching rose linen sleeveless tunic.

It was on the tip of Lee's tongue to deny that she wanted anything to eat, but to do so would be an admission of defeat, and something in the house-keeper's eyes told her that the woman would dearly love to see her humiliated.

She paused by the stairs, her eyes drawn against her will to the portrait she had noticed before.

'René de Chauvigny,' Gilles commented quietly behind her, his hand on the banister over hers, pre-venting her flight. 'He was with Napoléon at the sack of Moscow and saved the Emperor's life. For that he was given these estates, which had belonged to his family before the Revolution, but which had passed into the hands of a second cousin who hated his aristo-cratic relatives enough to send them to the guillotine without compunction. The man you see portrayed there was little better. He stole a young Russian girl away from her family, ravished her and then married her. The family legend has it that the Chauvigny be-trothal ring was part of her dowry. So much did she hate her husband that she locked herself in one of the towers and refused to come out.'

Lee was appalled, contemplating the poor girl's fate. 'What happened to her?'

Gilles laughed mirthlessly. 'If you're comparing her fate with yours then don't. My foolish relative made the cardinal error of falling deeply in love with his captive bride, and the story goes that upon learning that he loved her enough to send her back to her parents, the girl relented and came to love him in turn. What is more like it is that she discovered that lan-guishing alone in a tower can be dull and lonely, and decided to make the best of matters. Whatever the truth, she bore my ancestor three sons and two daughters.'

'She must have been very lonely and frightened.'

As she was frightened, Lee admitted, although not for the same reasons. How could she keep this temporary marriage a secret from Drew? She would have to tell him. If only she had told him about the letter, this would never have happened. But she had seen no reason—or perhaps suspected that he would not understand; that he too would condemn her for something for which she was not to blame. For the first time Lee wondered exactly how much value she put upon Drew's trust, if she was already doubting that it existed, and wasn't mutual trust, after all, a very important cornerstone for any marriage?

'Do not try to pretend that you are frightened,' Gilles taunted. 'Or is that why you hid from me in the shadows of the courtyard?'

So he had seen her! Lee turned, her eyes already darkening angrily, and found herself trapped against the banister, the warm, male smell of him invading her nostrils; his chest darkly shadowed beneath the thin silk shirt. She ought to have been repelled by such maleness. She preferred fair-haired men, men whose bodies were not so openly masculine, and yet some deeply buried nerve responded to the sight of his bared chest and long tanned throat in a way that made her lips part in soft dismay, her eyes clouding in disgust at her own reaction. Had Gilles been right after all? Was she the sort of woman who responded only to the savage maleness of men?

'Come, I have not yet had your answer; not yet heard from those sweet untouched lips that you will be my bride,' Gilles jeered. 'But then we both know that you will, don't we, Lee?'

'I don't have any choice in the matter. If I don't . . .'

'I will acquaint your fiancé of exactly what sort of female he is introducing to his correct Puritan family. Does he not care about all the men who have passed through your life, Lee, or is he so besotted that he has convinced himself that none of them matter?'

'Why should they?' Lee lashed back furiously. 'Not all men think it essential to find themselves an untouched virgin for a wife. Would you respect the academic who chooses only to debate with those of inferior intellect? Or perhaps that's why men like virgins; it prevents women from discovering their shortcomings!'

'You wouldn't by any chance be issuing me a challenge, would you, Lee?' Gilles probed softly. 'Your body is very desirable—more desirable than I remember.' He studied her with insulting thoroughness; her soft breasts, outlined by the creamy fabric of her blouse; her narrow hips and long, slim legs. 'But no, I have no wish to be landed with you permanently, although any allegations you might make would hardly stand up in a court of law. Still, it might be as well were you to sign a document stipulating that this marriage will last only so long as I decree.'

His arrogance took Lee's breath away.

'You can't believe I would want to prolong it?' she exclaimed bitterly. 'I can see no means of escaping from it, and much as it goes against the grain I shall have to agree, but make no mistake about it, Gilles. I'm not sixteen years old any longer. I'm not impressed by your chauvinistic machismo . . .'

'Marriage is a very intimate undertaking, and who is to say what you will and will not feel?'

'I love Drew, and I hate you. This farce of a marriage can't be over soon enough for me. And I should like my engagement ring back.'

'You shall have it—when our marriage is dissolved. For now, you will wear this.'

Lee gaped at the emerald ring he was sliding on to her finger. It was huge, glittering green fire through the darkness of the hallway, and as he slid it on to her finger Lee heard Gilles exclaim triumphantly, 'As I thought! It matches your eyes exactly. So, now we are betrothed.' And before Lee could stop him, his hands had left the banister to grasp the soft flesh of her upper arms, his dark head blotting out what little light there was as his lips grazed hers in a kiss which was more a stamp of possession than any tender gesture.

CHAPTER THREE

THEY were married three days later in Paris. Michael went with them and attended the brief ceremony. Lee knew it was irrational to feel so bereft of family and friends. After all, it was not a 'real' marriage. She could scarcely have asked her parents to be present, but it would have been nice to have Barbara and Pat there for moral support. The other two girls, in addition to being her flatmates, also worked for Westbury's, but in different departments, and the three of them got on exceptionally well. The Personnel Officer had suggested that Lee might like to share with them, when she explained that she had no accommodation in London. The previous member of the trio whom Lee was replacing had gone to work abroad, and the arrangement had worked out very well. She would have to write to them and let them know that it would be some time before she returned, and also to warn them about sending on her mail. They were good friends, but Lee couldn't help wondering what they would make of the situation. She could hardly not tell them about the marriage when Michael had witnessed it, but she could ask them to be discreet.

After the ceremony Gilles dismissed Michael with promises to think carefully about supplying Westbury's with wine, and as Lee saw Michael's taxi disappearing towards the airport, she felt as though she were saying goodbye to her last friend.

Why Gilles had chosen Paris for their marriage Lee did not know, unless it was merely that he wished to avoid the speculation of a local wedding, although there was bound to be that, surely, when he returned to the château with his bride?

They had been married in the morning, and now it was afternoon and she was a wife of three hours, although Lee reflected that she doubted that she would ever be able to think of Gilles as her husband. Her enemy and tormentor perhaps; but her husband—never!

They had a palatial suite of rooms in an exclusive hotel, and when they returned there after the ceremony, Lee took the precaution of checking that the communicating door between the bedrooms was locked, before stepping out of the suit she had been married in, and having a brief shower.

The blue linen suit was attractive enough, but it was a far cry from the virginal white she had every right—and desire—to wear, although of course she would wear that for Drew. But somehow it wouldn't feel the same; the ceremony would be besmirched by the memory of today; of the curt words in French; the touch of Gilles' hand as he guided hers in the register before tears had blinded her when she tried to write her name.

'Lee, open this door!'

The cold voice demanded admittance. She dressed hurriedly, staring at the locked door.

'Open it, Lee, or I shall ask the maid to come up with the pass-key.'

The threat decided her. She crossed the dove-grey carpet and unlocked the door. Giles stood there, wearing the suit he had worn for the marriage ceremony, a soft, pale grey wool, impeccably tailored, and as he strode into her bedroom and removed the jacket, dropping it carelessly on her bed, she saw the name

'Pierre Cardin' stitched neatly inside.

'Couldn't you have worn anything better than that?' His eyes swept contemptuously over her suit.

Lee refused to feel threatened by the way he was prowling round her room, like a hungry panther waiting for his next meal.

'I didn't come prepared for a wedding.'

'You need new clothes.'

Lee stared at him resentfully.

'This afternoon we shall visit some of the couture houses and see if something can be organised.' Lee opened her mouth to protest, but was forestalled. 'As my wife you will have a position to maintain. After the vintage I entertain the buyers. As my wife and hostess you will be expected to mingle with women whose clothes and jewels come only from the finest houses.'

'The vintage?' Lee went white with dismay. 'But that's six months away!'

'So?' Gilles was very cool. 'Is six months of your life too high a price to pay for your fiancé's peace of mind, and my silence? By then Louise will have turned her attentions in other directions.'

'And you will be able to search for a dutiful, virginal bride in peace.'

Gilles inclined his head.

'You appear to take an inordinate amount of interest in the chastity of my eventual bride, but as she will be the mother of my children, it is only natural that I should wish her to be pure and untainted.'

'Unlike her husband.'

'Silence! You go too far! Do you goad me because I refuse to join you in the gutter? Be careful that I do not teach you the real meaning of degradation!'

Never had she seen so many breathtakingly elegant

clothes, Lee thought in a daze. She and Gilles had been sitting on the dainty gilt chairs in this pale pink and dove grey salon for half an hour while model after model paraded in front of them, and so far Gilles had not said one word, apart from introducing Lee to the black-gowned vendeuse as his bride.

'My wife is young and has had a convent education,' he said at last, 'and I should like to see her dressed accordingly.'

The vendeuse's brow cleared instantly.

'We have an entire trousseau designed for a young South American girl, which is no longer required. An elopement, you understand, about which the family do not wish to talk. They are very proud and the girl had been reared from birth for the *grand mariage*.'

Lee's heart ached for the young South American, and she mentally wished her happiness, as the vendeuse clapped her hands and spoke rapidly to the models.

'It is fortunate that your wife is so slim, although there may need to be alteration to the bustline . . .'

Lee flushed as Gilles' eyes rested contemplatively on the gentle thrust of her breasts.

'Indeed, my wife is undoubtedly female, for all her slimness of hip and thigh. Perhaps I may see some of the gowns on her.'

The vendeuse was all compliance, and Lee was bustled unwillingly to a changing room, where she was stripped of all but her briefs as yet another black-garbed woman assisted her into a thin cream wool dress, severely plain and yet somehow softly feminine, a river of tiny pleats cascading down one side to open in a soft fan when she walked.

Lee stared at herself in the mirror.

'It is perfect!' the vendeuse exclaimed. 'Indeed,

Madame la Comtesse truly has an air of innocence and chastity which is emphasised by the gown. It is no wonder that Monsieur le Comte wishes the world to know of his wife's innocence.'

The world, or Louise? Lee wondered cynically, avoiding Gilles' eyes as she paraded dutifully in front of him.

'It is quite amazing what a difference clothes makes,' he commented sardonically, when she protested that she had enough clothes to last her a lifetime. 'Who seeing you in those gowns could disbelieve your virtue, and think that the clothes of a *fille de joie* would be more suited to your personality?'

'I'm surprised you didn't buy some for me,' Lee snapped, exhausted by the long hours of standing patiently being dressed and undressed like an animated doll. 'Just to remind me of exactly what I am, in case I get carried away by my new role!'

For a second something so cold and angry gleamed in his eyes that she wished the words unsaid.

'Perhaps I might at that,' he said softly, 'and then you can entertain me with all the tricks you have learned from your previous lovers.' He spoke quickly to the vendeuse, who was hovering several feet away, and after one dubious look at Lee the woman disappeared, to return with a dress that made Lee catch her breath in dismay.

It was jade green silk, exactly the same colour of her eyes, and she flinched as she was helped into it. She had always relished the thought of silk against her skin, but in this case it felt almost reptilian. The bodice was cut low over her breasts in the shape of waterlilies, each 'flower' moulding her flesh, the skirt slashed deeply up the front and edged with the same waterlily shape that floated round the hem. It was the dress of a woman who is either supremely sure of herself, or one who wants to make a definite statement of fact about her availability, and either way Lee hated it.

'It was designed for a television star,' the vendeuse explained, and Lee was not surprised. It had that sort of extravagant showiness about it.

She refused to look at Gilles when she modelled it.

'We shall take it,' he told the modiste calmly, one finger lightly tracing the outline of the silk against the creamy flesh of Lee's breast. To the modiste that light gesture would be the sort of embrace a new husband might give to his bride, but Lee shivered uncontrollably under it, knowing that it was Gilles' way of showing his contempt for her body.

'It will serve to remind me that while for other men my wife has the purity of the unattainable, for me, she is . . . a woman.'

Lee flushed angrily. How dared Gilles do this to her? The vendeuse was openly agog as she hurried Lee back to the changing room. Did the woman interpret Gilles' words as a hint that he wanted his new bride to himself all of a sudden? She almost laughed at the falsity of it all.

Their shopping wasn't over. After the couturier's, Gilles took her to an exclusive boutique smelling of leather, where they bought shoes and handbags seemingly for every occasion.

Lee's head was spinning when they emerged. What on earth was Gilles going to do with all these clothes when she left? Surely he wasn't contemplating giving them to his real bride? The unrestrained laughter building up inside her told her how close she was to hysterics, and she swallowed hard on it, concentrating instead on the lavish displays in the exclusive boutiques they were passing. Ordinarily walking down the

Faubourg St Honoré would have been a treat all on its own, but with Gilles at her side it was more of an ordeal.

'That should see you through for the time being,' he commented coolly, having hustled her in and out of an exclusive cosmetics house, where he had calmly instructed the gaping salesgirl to provide them with everything Lee would need to match the sophisticated glamour of the Frenchwomen with whom she would be mingling as Gilles' wife.

'Won't it rather jar the image of the innocent young bride?' she commented acidly at one point, watching the girl fill a small leather case with an assortment of eyeshadows and lipsticks.

'It will present an intriguing contrast,' Gilles told her without turning his head. 'The French are quick to pick up nuances, and they will not be slow to see behind the bride in her virginal clothes, experimenting with exotic make-up, the woman responding to the lessons of her lover.'

Lee felt sick. Everything Gilles did was designed purely to create an image which he himself believed to be false, merely to sustain his own pride of race. Of course it was unthinkable that a Chauvigny should marry a wanton, so because that was exactly what he believed her to be he had to create a mirage; a Lee whom he believed did not exist.

Lee was exhausted by the time they returned to the hotel. To her horror she discovered they were dining in their suite.

'It is expected,' Gilles told her casually. 'They know we were married this morning, and naturally no Frenchman would want to spend his wedding night with other people.' He tossed a box towards her. 'You will wear this. Louise has many friends in Paris, most of whom will dine at least once a week at this hotel. I do not want them to hear gossip that the new Comtesse de Chauvigny dined with her new husband in blue linen,' he told her suavely.

'There's nothing wrong with my clothes,' Lee began hotly. 'They may not be expensive, but . . .' Her voice faltered into silence as she stared at the contents of the box. A nightgown and negligee in pure white silk poured through her fingers with fluid sensuality. The nightgown was completely plain, what there was of it. Lee swallowed as she saw the bias cut and realised how it would emphasise her body.

'I can't wear that!' she protested shakily. 'It's . . . I can't wear it, Gilles!'

'You can and will,' he told her equably, 'if I have to put it on you myself—an exercise neither of us would enjoy. It desecrates everything I believe in to see a woman like you wearing such a symbol of purity. Put it on,' he commanded curtly. 'Wear your hair down, and very little make-up. You have an hour.'

An hour to do what? Flee? Some hope! Gilles had her passport, and her money. She had woken up this morning to find them gone, and guessed by whose hand they had been removed from the handbag she had so carelessly left in the salon.

The white nightgown haunted her as she moved about the bedroom, delaying the moment when she must step into it.

She showered, rubbing her flesh briskly until it tingled, paling when she caught sight of her pale nudity in the mirrored walls. Her skin was the colour of cream where it had not even been touched by the sun, her breasts firm and taut. She moved her hands over them, her eyes suddenly very slumbrous as she tried to imagine how it would feel if she really were married and

Drew was waiting for her on the other side of that communicating door. Her heart thumped painfully, her mouth dry, and she acknowledged bitterly that she would not have felt one thousandth of the dread she felt now.

As she had suspected the nightgown, so pure and virginal off, was anything but on. The silk caressed her skin, with soft, sinuous fingers, stroking over her breasts and outlining the nipples, falling into soft folds at her feet.

The negligee was little better. It was lined with silk as iridescent as mother-of-pearl, transferring a translucent gleam to her skin. Her eyes looked huge in her waxen face, her hair, a russet, silky waterfall on to her shoulders, shadowing her face as she bent forward to find the mules which had also been in the box. Deep bands of satin and lace cuffed the negligee and bordered the front. Every movement of her body was as fluid as water, Lee thought, watching her own reflection. It would be an enticement to any man to try to catch those fluid movements before they escaped him for ever, and she could only thank God that Gilles despised her sufficiently to be the slightest bit stirred by her appearance.

He was waiting for her as she stepped into the salon, and the look he gave her made no allowances for her modesty. He was wearing a thin silk robe, monogrammed over the pocket. She supposed it was a dressing gown and shivered as she realised that under it he was naked—another part of this ridiculous charade.

'Come here!'

It never occurred to her to refuse. Her lips were dry with fear and tension and she touched them lightly with her tongue as he studied her.

'Perhaps I ought to give you that for your real wedding night,' he commented at last. 'Seeing you in it that poor besotted fiancé of yours could be forgiven for seeing only the angel in you.'

'But you, of course, know better.' For some reason his insistence on condemning her for something she did not do, his determination to see in her only what he wanted to see, was beginning to grate on Lee. 'What makes you think that he doesn't as well?' she demanded sweetly. 'It isn't exactly unknown for couples to anticipate their marriage vows, you know.'

'Bostonians share much in common with the French. He would never have suggested marriage if he thought he could get you any other way,' Gilles retorted crudely. 'No, you have deceived him with your mock innocence, but you cannot do so for ever, unless perhaps you intend to frequent one of those clinics that deal in human cynicism and for a considerable sum of money repair that which once having been torn, could never be rendered whole again.'

Lee went as white as her nightgown, her hand leaving a vivid imprint against Gilles' skin as she raised it to his face. Never in her life had she reacted so violently, and it shamed her to have done so now, but what he had been insinuating was insulting in the extreme.

'Why, you——!'

Strong fingers circled her wrist, uncaring of the fact that they were crushing fragile bones. She was held fast against Gilles and imprisoned by his arms, his hard body uncaring of her uncontrollable trembling.

'Had you really been my bride, you would not rest until you had done penance for that vicious action,' he told her through gritted teeth. 'No one strikes a Chauvigny without reprisal!'

Lee's heart beat frantically beneath the thin silk covering. She was unable to tear her eyes away from the livid fingermarks on the tanned cheek.

'You asked for it,' she said huskily, determined not to give way to the fear spiralling through her.

'And you asked for this!' Gilles grated back, his mouth fastening on hers, as though he intended to drain her completely of the will to defy him ever again. Her heart almost stopped beating, and then started again, at twice its previous rate. She tried to move her head, but Gilles' fingers grasped her hair, pulling it viciously until her throat was arched back vulnerably, her lips crushed beneath his as he reinforced the lesson he seemed determined she must learn. His free arm had been clamped about her waist, holding her against the taut maleness concealed only by the thin silk, but as Lee tried to pull away his hand moved upwards pushing aside the negligee to fasten determinedly on the soft fullness of one breast, the nightgown ruthlessly removed to allow his fingers freer access to her flesh; to allow his thumb to circle her nipple slowly and spark off sensations which made her cringe in self-disgust. Reaction shuddered through her. Gilles' hand left her breast to tilt her face up to meet the smoky investigation of his eyes.

'You must have been a long time without a lover,' he taunted softly. 'What is it your body pleads for, Lee? This?' His hand returned to her breast, shaking her with the depth of response the single embrace culled from her. 'Or this?' His head bent, dark against the creamy softness of her flesh and her moan of mingled pain and pleasure was clearly heard as his lips took the place of his hand, sending shuddering waves of emotion washing through her. No one had touched her like this. No one had shown himself to be so completely the master of her body, of its innermost secrets and desires. Feelings she had never dreamed could exist rose up inside her to mock her earlier defiance as her flesh melted to his touch. He raised his head, and for a moment Lee thought she saw the devil himself in his eyes, and yet still her overwhelming longing was to drag the dark head back to her now aching breasts, to push aside that thin silk robe and taste the tangy male flesh.

'Or this?' Gilles said softly, lifting her in his arms and carrying her through the salon, to the rich masculinity of his own bedroom. She had not been in it before, but noticed nothing but the heavy mahogany furniture and the shadowy outline of the huge bed.

Some last remnants of sanity urged her to protest, but this was quickly stifled beneath Gilles' impatient hands as he lowered her on to the bed and deftly removed the slender wisp of silk.

Her heartbeat sounded as loud as thunder, and she turned her head, unable to bear Gilles' close scrutiny. His hands cupped her face, forcing her to meet his eyes.

'You're letting the part swamp the real you,' he goaded softly. 'I'm not the first man to look upon you like this by any means, Lee, although I suspect you have seldom looked so cool and virginal; even the first time.'

Despite the cruel words his voice held a seductive quality that lulled her fears, like a panther lulling its prey into a false sense of security.

'Did you know, that summer, I actually contemplated sleeping with you myself? You were so fresh and innocent, or so I thought. I told myself I could not be the one to so carelessly pluck such a rare flower, still only in the bud, but someone else had been before me, hadn't they, my oh, so experienced little wife? The bud is already rotten!'

Lee couldn't answer. There was a huge lump in her throat. Gilles, subduing his desires because of her innocence. Had it really been like that? Of course not. How could it have been?

His hands on her body drew a broken protest past her lips. It was silenced with a kiss, so sweet and tender that Lee felt her whole body melt into heated warmth, her arms lifting towards him, but they were held, pinioned above her head, while Gilles began a thorough arousal of her body, the kisses he stroked against her now ardent flesh punctuated by soft murmuring enquiries as to whether she was enjoying his unhurried touch. Her body gave him the answer, and shame made her eyes smart with tears as she contemplated her own complete inability to control its betraying reactions. She longed to reach up and part Gilles' robe, to feel his hard male warmth against her, and yet the very strength of her longing shocked and appalled her. She had never felt like this with Drew—but then Drew had never held her like this, his lips moving from one rosy-peaked breast to the other, and then on downwards, until her stomach muscles contracted in virginal protest at the path taken by those questing lips.

At last her arms were released, but something about the look in Gilles' eyes forestalled her immediate reaction, which was to reach up for him. They were cold, as cold and bitter as the North Sea, and already she was shivering under their impact.

'Perhaps in future you'll think twice before raising your hand to me again,' he said coolly, sliding off the bed. 'We both know you wanted to provoke me into taking you, to appease your own insatiable appetites, but I think this is a more fitting punishment, don't you?' He smiled cruelly into her aroused features. 'Much more fitting. For a woman of your experience you were a little too trusting, my dear, or did you think the sight of that sexy little body would make me forget what it conceals? Now get out of my room!'

He was reaching for the phone as he issued the curt command. Shivering with self-disgust, Lee gathered up her nightdress, trying to control the pain he had just caused her. He had quite deliberately aroused her, just so that he could throw these taunts at her, she knew that now. But it wouldn't happen again.

'If you're ordering dinner, I don't want any,' she told him bitterly. 'I'm not hungry.'

'Liar,' he said succinctly, turning to glance down the length of her still nude body. 'But I wasn't. I want to get someone up here to change the bed. I detest sleeping in soiled sheets.'

Lee went white, swaying slightly as she turned towards the door. Never in her life had she been subject to such humiliation, and for one brief second she contemplated challenging him with the proof that all his accusations were unjust. But what was the use? He would probably take her with the same callous arrogance with which he had aroused her, and then mock her for allowing him the intimacies only Drew should have been permitted.

Somehow she managed to stagger back to her room. In the sitting room was mute evidence that their meal had arrived and had been left discreetly on a heated trolley. No doubt their non-appearance for dinner was perfectly acceptable in a newly married couple, but the smell of the food nauseated Lee as she turned aside and walked blindly into her own room.

Once there she stripped off the negligee she had covered herself with, and stood in the shower, with the water beating angrily into her flesh, but when she emerged from it she still did not feel clean. The marks of Gilles' fingers stood out clearly on her breasts, which seemed to her critical and sickened eyes to be fuller, tauter than before. She retched suddenly, heaving on an empty stomach as sickness swept her. She was loathsome, depraved. She had allowed Gilles to treat her as the woman he had accused her of being; she had actually responded to his vile, calculated caresses; she had actually *wanted* them, and that was something which no amount of water could wash away.

There were no tears; she was beyond that. Gilles was right—tonight she had learned a lesson she would never forget. It was branded into her flesh and burned into her soul.

If there was any way she could have left him she would have taken it. Only twice in her life had she tasted the hell men and women make for one another, and both times it was Gilles who had taken her there. There must never be a third time; because if there was she doubted that she had the ability to return. Already the horror of what had happened threatened to overwhelm her normal common sense. Her eyes strayed to the phone and she was convulsed with a longing to hear Drew's gentle voice, to beg him to take her away from Gilles—but if she did that he would want to know why, and she could not tell him. She had betrayed his trust; she had let another man gain intimate knowledge of her, so how could she go to Drew now and plead his aid?

During the night something woke her. Her face and pillow were damp with tears, and as she lay, testing the darkness of the unfamiliar room, it came to her that the sound which had awoken her had been her own crying. She had not cried like that since . . . Since the summer she was sixteen.

CHAPTER FOUR

THEY didn't linger in Paris, but then why should they? Lee thought listlessly, watching Gilles place her brand new suitcases containing the clothes he had bought her in the boot of his gleaming silver-green Mercedes sports car; after all, they were not real honeymooners.

Remembering the degrading events of the previous evening, she shuddered deeply and found Gilles' grey eyes resting on her pale face with grim appraisal. When he closed the boot he came across to her, his fingers forcing her chin upwards so that he could study her more closely.

'A little pallor in a bride is acceptable,' he said coldly, 'but you look as though you've spent the night in a house haunted by ghosts. To everyone else this marriage is a very real one, Lee, and if you give them the slightest cause to doubt that, I shall know how to punish you.'

'How, by inflicting your repulsive presence on me?'

Instead of being annoyed he merely laughed, a soft taunting sound that set her nerves on edge.

'Oh, I'm sure I can think of something. I managed all right last night.'

Lee wrenched her chin out of his hand, her fierce, 'Don't remind me of that!' drawing his brows together in a dark frown.

'You are not required to act the part of the affronted virgin, Lee, and I have already told you this. If, by adopting this pose, you are hoping to convince me that you felt no frustration, no longing for fulfilment last night, then don't. Your body gave you away most obviously.'

Lee couldn't reply for the sudden rush of tears which threatened to blind her. Like a sleepwalker she moved towards the car, dimly conscious of Gilles climbing in beside her, but when he reached across her to secure her seat belt she thrust him aside, her fingers trembling over the stiff mechanism, her bitter, 'Don't touch me!' lost in the powerful roar of the Mercedes' engine as they pulled away from the kerb.

The route was now vaguely familiar, but she was startled when they stopped just outside Blois, and Gilles negotiated the Mercedes down an unmade, rutted road to a small manor house set amidst a walled vineyard.

They hadn't exchanged so much as a word during the journey, and pride prevented Lee from speaking now. They drove into a cobbled courtyard, far less impressive than that belonging to the château, and a sturdy dark-haired man of Gilles' age emerged from the manor house, a beaming smile splitting his tanned face as he saw the Mercedes.

'Gilles!'

The two men embraced fondly, and then Gilles turned to Lee. 'Jean-Paul, I should like you to meet my wife, Lee, the new Comtesse de Chauvigny.'

For a moment the man Jean-Paul merely stared at Lee, and then he said something rapidly to Gilles in French, accompanied by a wide grin. Lee longed to ask what was going on, but Jean-Paul was opening the car door for her, and a glance at Gilles showed that he too was climbing out of the car.

'*Un moment*, I must tell Marie-Thérèse of your arrival. You will eat with us, of course?'

He had switched back to English, for her sake, Lee

suspected. She did speak a little French, but unless it was spoken very slowly she found the language hard to follow.

'Why else do you think we stopped?' Gilles joked, suddenly looking much younger than Lee could have believed possible.

Jean-Paul disappeared towards the house.

'Jean-Paul and Marie-Thérèse are old friends of mine,' Gilles explained, grasping Lee's arm to prevent her from escaping. The movement brought her into close contact with his thigh, her body cringing immediately as she forced herself to remember last night's humiliation. Gilles appeared not to notice her distress. His eyes were fixed on the open door of the small manor house.

'Jean-Paul inherited the Clos des Fleurons from his uncle several years ago and since then he has worked hard to bring it up to scratch. His uncle bought it as a hobby and the vines had been badly neglected. This year Jean-Paul is hoping to gain an Appellation Contrôlée designation.'

Lee was duly impressed. Gilles' wine already carried this seal of approval, and as she knew, only seventeen per cent of the wine produced in France in any one year was permitted the coveted accolade.

They had only covered a few yards of the distance to the door, when a young woman hurried through it, her dark hair caught up in an elegant chignon, her entire appearance neatly elegant despite the fact that she was in the later stages of pregnancy.

Lee watched as Gilles kissed her affectionately, laughing as he complained that he could no longer get near to her.

'Just you wait, Gilles!' Marie-Thérèse threatened lightly, glancing towards Lee, who had automatically moved aside to allow Gilles to greet his friend's wife. 'Soon it will be your turn, *non*?'

Lee flushed scarlet as Marie-Thérèse's eyes studied her slender frame, shuddering as Gilles' hand descended to her shoulder, grasping it meaningfully.

'Lee is still very much a new bride, Marie-Thérèse,' he said in a low voice, enriched with sensual appeal, as though he was reminding his friends that his wedding night was not long past, and still held cherished memories. 'You embarrass her by suggesting that she might already be carrying my child. Is this not so, *petite*?'

Lee glared furiously at him, tempted to remind him in front of his friends exactly what had happened last night, but as though he sensed the direction of her thoughts, his fingers bit into the tender skin of her shoulder, his eyes like iron as they warned her of the punishment any defiance would warrant.

'We are unkind to tease you,' Marie-Thérèse apologised. 'Please come with me. You will want to freshen up before lunch.'

As Lee followed her into a huge, old-fashioned kitchen, fragrant with herbs and the delicious smell of cooking food, Marie-Thérèse added, 'We were so surprised when Gilles telephoned us from Paris this morning to say that he was married. For a moment we feared the worst, that Louise had trapped him at last.' She paused by a doorway which led to a narrow flight of stairs, her expression concerned as she saw Lee's pale face. 'Forgive me! Perhaps you did not know about Louise . . .'

'I did know,' Lee assured her with a brief smile. In other circumstances she could have enjoyed the French girl's company. She was about Lee's own age, and grimaced ruefully over the old-fashioned bathroom to which she escorted Lee.

'It is old-fashioned is it not? Oncle Henri neglected the property and for now we must concentrate on the vines. Perhaps later there will be money to spare for the house.'

'I am sure you will find a difference once Jean-Paul has been awarded the Appellation Contrôlée,' Lee comforted her. 'Gilles was just telling me how hard you had worked.'

'I no longer,' Marie-Thérèse murmured. 'Now that I am *enceinte* Jean-Paul does not permit me to work in the fields. You will soon discover that to a *vigneron* his vines are a mistress who will rival his wife all their lives. Have you known Gilles long?'

She supposed she ought to have been prepared for that question, Lee thought. It was plain that Marie-Thérèse was very fond of Gilles.

'Sort of,' she temporised, unwilling to unleash Gilles' anger upon her hapless head by saying the wrong thing. 'My godmother is Gilles' aunt, and I knew him as a child.'

'And he, seeing the beautiful woman you would one day become, has waited all these years for you! It is *très romantique!*'

Lee did not bother to disillusion her. The manor house, in direct contrast to the château, was shabby, furnished sparsely, but it did at least have the advantage of being reasonably large, Marie-Thérèse commented as she showed Lee over it. The two men were sitting in the kitchen, drinking wine from the plain glasses connoisseurs always use. 'They will talk for hours if we let them,' Marie-Thérèse complained. 'Gilles has been very good to us. It is he who has persuaded the Institut National des Appellations d'Origine to consider us. This is something he is under no obligation to do, and we are very grateful to him. But come, unless we return to the kitchen the lunch which I have prepared to celebrate your marriage will be quite ruined.'

Lee was grateful that her knowledge of French eating habits had prepared her for what was to come.

The lunch was delicious and lasted for two hours, comprising four courses, excluding the cheese. When the hors-d'oeuvres had been cleared away and the delicious lobster eaten, Marie-Thérèse served them with a chicken casserole cooked in Jean-Paul's own wine. It was delicious, and when Lee had eaten every scrap Marie-Thérèse commented wickedly to Gilles,

'Now, my friend, you will not look so smug. I have put in Lee's chicken herbs to make her fruitful, and soon too she will look like me, *non*?'

They all laughed, even Lee, who did not want to upset or hurt Marie-Thérèse, but still she could not help blushing, and Gilles who had been watching her remarked suavely,

'Excellent though your herbs may be, Marie-Thérèse, they alone will not have the desired effect, is that not so, *chérie*?'

Lee was glad of the general laughter. It prevented her from having to reply, and even though she had enjoyed the company of the young couple, she was glad when they eventually departed. Keeping up the façade of a deliriously happy bride was taxing every last bit of her mental reserves, and as Jean-Paul kissed her enthusiastically on both cheeks, she wondered anew just how she was going to endure the next six months.

The afternoon was warm, with the sun shining down hotly, and when Gilles suggested removing the hood of the Mercedes, Lee did not object.

The cool air, tugging teasingly through her hair, the warm, burgeoning smell of growing things, the blue vastness of the sky above them all helped to relax her taut nerves, and as they drove through Tours, the sleep which had eluded her all through the previous night finally embraced her, her breathing light and even as her eyelids fluttered closed.

When she awoke they were in the courtyard of the château, and Gilles' wolfhound was bounding towards the car. Still half asleep, Lee struggled to sit up, appalled to discover that she had been leaning on Gilles' shoulder, and that his arms were at that very moment intent on making her a prisoner.

As he kissed her she could taste the wine on his mouth, and the familiarity, instead of being repellent, sent waves of awareness flooding over her. The sun was shining directly into her eyes, so she closed them, lying passively in Gilles' arms, too drugged with sleep and sunshine to move.

At last he released her.

'Now you are beginning to learn. No one observing our arrival can have doubted that we are indeed truly man and wife.'

Before she could speak he was out of the car, opening her door, and bending to take her weight.

To the astounded housekeeper who met them at the door he said calmly, 'This is an English custom. Have my orders been followed?'

Without waiting for a reply he strode towards the stairs, mounting them easily, despite the burden of her weight, Lee noted drowsily. Through his shirt she could see the darkness of his hair-roughened chest, and a feeling so intensely alien that it shocked her surged up through her veins. For one moment she had actually wanted to stretch out and touch her husband, to discover exactly how that alien maleness felt beneath her fingers. Green eyes mirrored her appalled shock, her hands immediately clenching into two small fists as though to prevent any further traitorous impulses. In fact she was so intent on quelling the unfamiliar surge of feeling which had stolen over her that at first Lee was unaware of the import of the huge double bed Gilles had dropped her on to, or the fact that she had been brought to a different room from that she had occupied before.

It was Gilles, removing his shirt and discarding it carelessly to disappear into an en suite bathroom who alerted her to the truth, her sun-blinded eyes beginning to observe things she had not noticed before, such as the grandeur of the bedroom, the elegance of the beautiful antiques with which it was furnished, the careless way in which Gilles returned to spatter drop-lets of water on to the priceless Aubusson carpet, his torso gleaming like polished silk as he opened another door and disappeared into what Lee guessed must be a dressing room, to return with a clean shirt, his expression sardonic as he looked into her startled eyes.

'What's the matter? Don't you care for the bridal suite?'

The bridal suite! She had known all along, of course, but it had taken Gilles' callous words to crystallise all her fears. She stared at the bed, moistening her dry lips with the tip of her tongue as she lifted wary eyes to his face.

'You can't mean that . . .' She swallowed nervously, forcing herself to go on. 'You can't mean that we have to share this room, Gilles?'

'Of a surety I do. And not only the room, but the bed as well. The men who work for me are earthy French peasants. How long do you suppose I will continue to merit their respect once it becomes known that I sleep apart from my wife? Or were you hoping that separate bedrooms would give you the opportunity to indulge your carnal appetites elsewhere? Think of yourself as doing a penance, Lee,' he mocked. 'And how much sweeter the wine of love will taste after six months' abstinence; although I suppose that is like promising a rare wine to an alcoholic. To him the quality matters little, is this not so? It is the quantity that counts.'

Lee scrambled off the bed, her face white with shocked distaste.

'Marriage to you doesn't give you the right to talk to me like . . .'

'Like a woman of the streets?' Gilles taunted. 'She at least is honest in what she offers, Lee. In a moment they will be bringing up your cases. If at any time during the next six months you give anyone the impression that our marriage is not filled with bliss and happiness, I shall exact a penalty from you that you will never, ever forget.'

From somewhere Lee found the courage to say curtly, 'Obviously you don't hold to the theory that the donkey might respond better to the carrot than the stick!'

For a moment his eyes seemed to burn into her, and then in a voice that made her feel as brittle as fine-blown crystal he said softly,

'And precisely what "carrot" did you have in mind, Lee? Or can I guess? Your good behaviour in return for my satisfaction of those desires you have such difficult in controlling?' He laughed harshly. 'Haven't I already told you that I don't like soiled goods?'

The arrival of a swarthy man carrying her cases prevented her from replying. The housekeeper was hard on his heels, her eyes malicious and curious as she stared from Lee to Gilles.

'Perhaps when she has time Madame might care for

me to show her over the château, and there is also the
matter of the dinner Monsieur le Comte was planning
for next week . . .' She let her voice fade away, hinting
more at Lee's inability to cope with such a responsibility rather than Gilles' reluctance to go
through with it in view of his newly married state.

'Some other members of our local wine-growing
commune,' Gilles explained coolly. 'I had intended to
talk with them about their views on this year's harvest.'

'Madame Louise has acted as Monsieur's hostess in
the past,' the housekeeper interrupted in tones which
acquainted Lee with the reason for the woman's hostility. It was plain that the housekeeper considered
Louise a far better person to be the new Comtesse than
Lee herself.

Half to her own surprise Lee heard herself saying
coolly, 'I am sure we shall be able to manage. And
then of course there will be the vintage, and the buyers'
dinners to arrange. I take it the buyers normally stay
overnight?'

Gilles nodded. An idea was beginning to take shape
in Lee's mind. She knew all about these dinners and
she had it in mind to wipe the supercilious look from
the faces of Gilles and his housekeeper, by showing
them what an English hostess could do when she set
her mind to it.

'I shall be ready to look over the château when I
have changed,' Lee told the housekeeper. The woman
was already looking faintly taken aback by Lee's refusal
to be put off by her cold manner, and Lee decided that
now was as good a time as any to reinforce the fact
that she was now mistress of the château, no matter on
how temporary a basis. Immaculate and elegant the
house might be, but it lacked those little touches that

made it a home; nowhere had she seen any flowers, for instance; nowhere had she sensed that warmth that comes from a house filled with love and laughter—but then of course she was hardly likely to find *that*.

'We should like some coffee,' she told the house-keeper calmly. 'Gilles, do you want something to eat?'

If her 'husband' was surprised at this sudden show of wifely concern he did not betray it.

'Coffee will be fine.'

Lee saw the housekeeper's mouth tighten as she obeyed the command, and knew that this was but the first battle in what threatened to be a hard-fought campaign.

When she had gone, Gilles asked Lee curtly, 'What was all that about?'

'I'm surprised a man of your perception needs to ask,' Lee replied dryly. 'Surely it can't have escaped your notice that she would have preferred you to marry Louise?

'I hadn't thought about it, although come to think of it, Louise did recommend her to me. She has always fulfilled her duties properly.'

'I'm sure she has,' Lee agreed. 'If you wish her to continue to run this house, Gilles, then please say so, it makes no difference to me, although I suspect that had you actually married the shy young bride you seemed determine to have, Madame Le Bon would have lost no time in putting her very firmly in her place.'

She turned away, busying herself with the contents of the first suitcase, but she was aware of Gilles watching her thoughtfully, and when she marched towards the dressing room carrying an armful of clothes he said slowly,

'You are now the mistress of this château, but I warn you, Lee, if it is not run as efficiently as it has been in the past, I shall have no compunction in giving Madame Le Bon the right to run it once more!'

She had been warned, Lee thought half an hour later, grimacing over the half cold coffee which a blushing young girl had just brought into the bedroom. She had changed into her own linen suit, and was alone in the room, Gilles having complained that he had no intentions of waiting all afternoon for a cup of coffee when he had work waiting for him. She had heard him call to his dog as he left the house, and from the clatter of horse's hooves across the courtyard guessed that he had ridden out to inspect the vines.

When she joined the housekeeper for her tour of inspection she made no comment on the coffee.

The château was larger than she had first realised, built foursquare round the enclosed courtyard, one wing given over entirely to stables, garages and storage rooms.

Of the other three, one contained a huge ballroom, which Lee did not need to be told was almost an exact replica of the Galerie des Glaces at Versailles although on a somewhat smaller scale. The room needed painting, and from the grime on the windows had obviously not been used for a very long time.

'Every Chauvigny bridegroom has given a ball for his new bride in this room,' the housekeeper told her sourly, and Lee knew she meant to underline the fact that Gilles had made no such suggestion in *his* bride's case. Lee ignored her. She had her own plans for the ballroom, which had only come to her as she realised exactly how suitable it would be for what she had in mind.

'It needs cleaning and painting,' was her only comment, but even this was not allowed to go unremarked as the housekeeper objected acidly, 'Only Monsieur le Comte has the authority to give such orders.'

Lee lost count of the number of bedrooms the château possessed. Many were closed up, their furniture under covers, and as the housekeeper showed her the rooms in the South Tower which had once belonged to the Russian girl who had been stolen away by Napoleon's Captain, Lee expelled her breath on a delighted sigh.

The rooms were cold, and only small; there was a bedroom, the walls hung with pale green silk, a comfortable window seat covered in the same material, the bed enclosed with shimmering green silk draperies suspended from a gold circlet set in the ceiling. It was a girl's room rather than a woman's, as fresh and innocent as its owner had been before her ravisher stole her away from the safety of her family. And yet she had come to love him. For some reason Lee felt herself trembling deeply inside.

The sitting room on the floor below, connected to the bedroom with its own spiral staircase, was equally enchanting, decorated in the same soft green as the bedroom, but this time with touches of palest pink, in the Aubusson carpet, and the brocade-covered chairs. It was easy to imagine the Russian girl here, dreaming perhaps of her home, alone and forlorn, until her rebellious heart betrayed her to the man who had brought her to this silken prison.

'I shall use this room as my office,' Lee told Madame Le Bon. The woman looked less than pleased, and muttered something Lee could not catch, as she preceded her back into the main part of the house.

The kitchens were last on the agenda; huge cavernous rooms looking out on to the courtyard, fragrant as only a French kitchen can be. The cook was a middle-aged woman, dressed in black, her hair screwed up into a bun, busily commanding several giggling maids until Lee's arrival interrupted her, and Lee sensed that while the woman might be reserving judgment, she had not taken an immediate dislike to her as the housekeeper had.

'We shall need to talk about the menus for Monsieur le Comte's guests,' Lee told her, ignoring the housekeeper's disapproval. 'And perhaps some way of ensuring that the coffee is hot when it reaches our bedroom.'

The housekeeper frowned and darted at bitter look at Lee. The cook started to say something, breaking off when Lee shook her head to indicate that she was going too fast. When she spoke more slowly Lee could understand. The housekeeper had said nothing of any coffee to her, and of course Madame could have hot coffee. She would see to it herself.

They parted on amicable terms, Lee heaving a slight sigh of relief. She suspected that the cold coffee had been a deliberate attempt to make her look small on the part of the housekeeper, who had probably thought that in the interest of good relations she would not complain. Lee knew the French better than that. They would not have any respect for anyone who accepted inferior food or drink, no matter how simple it might be.

Back in her own room Lee stripped off her suit and headed for the bathroom. Many of the rooms had been dusty, and she could not change into one of her new dresses without first having at least a shower.

The bathroom was equipped with both shower and bath of such a luxurious quality that Lee caught her breath. Gilles certainly didn't stint himself on any of his creature comforts, she thought, remembering Marie-Thérèse's old-fashioned plumbing.

With the shower turned on, Lee didn't hear Gilles enter the bedroom, and her first intimation that he had returned came only when she stepped out of the shower and found him watching her in a manner that made the hot colour run up under her skin, as she stretched out a trembling hand for the towel she had placed in readiness on the small stool.

Gilles was quicker.

'Why shouldn't I look at my wife if I want to?' he mocked when she started to protest. 'I'm surprised at you, my dear. Watching you shower was quite an education. You do not touch yourself like a woman who knows the full power of her own sexuality—or perhaps you don't bother when you don't have an audience.'

Lee forgot her nudity long enough to say shakily, 'That's a disgusting thing to suggest! I . . .'

She shivered suddenly, drops of moisture sparkling against her skin. Gilles' eyes darkened and for a moment she almost held her breath, quivering under the burning intensity of his gaze. She took a step forward to re-claim her towel, and with a sudden groan Gilles hauled her into his arms, uncaring that her damp body was pressed against his clothes, his breath rasping slightly as it left his lungs.

He smelled of the open air, horses, and clean sweat, and Lee trembled with the sudden realisation that she found the combination erotic, for otherwise why would her body feel as though it had been invaded by alien emotions?

'You're a witch! Do you know that?' Gilles muttered huskily against her skin. 'Even knowing what you are, I still desire you, but that's what you wanted, isn't it, Lee? That's why I found you waiting for me so enticingly . . . God, why not?' she heard him groan hoarsely 'I'm a man, after all, not a plaster saint, and when your appetite's been sharpened like mine, even the toughtest meat tastes like ambrosia!'

His breath was hot against her skin, his eyes glazed with a desire that struck terror into Lee's heart. She tried to pull away, but her frantic movements only seemed to excite him further. The kiss that punished her defiance sapped both her strength and her will. She could feel the tautly male outline of him against her body, and trembled in mingled fear and resentment.

It was only the second knock on their bedroom door that brought his head up, anger tightening his mouth as Madame Le Bon entered without permission. His bulk hid Lee's nakedness from the other woman, although whether this was by accident or design Lee did not know.

'Will you wish dinner at the usual time, madame?' she asked Lee expressionlessly. Lee had already informed her that for now they would continue with the normal routine and she suspected the woman had deliberately waited until now, hoping to interrupt a tender moment and distress the new bride. After she had shown Lee the kitchens she had taken her down to the cellars. Since childhood Lee had had a fear of being locked in a dark room, and she had sensed the woman watching her with malicious amusement as she had given them only the most cursory inspection.

To Lee's surprise, before she could answer the housekeeper's question, Gilles had swung open the bedroom door.

'I suggest if you wish to retain your position here, madame, you exercise a little more discretion,' he told her curtly. 'We are, after all, a very newly married couple!'

Bright patches of colour stained the housekeeper's cheeks, and Lee found herself holding her breath as she stalked out of the room. She had half expected Gilles to enjoy her own humiliation of being discovered practically on the point of being made love to by him, but perhaps he considered reprimanding the housekeeper's insolence more important than mocking her embarrassment.

Whatever the truth, the moment Madame Le Bon was gone Gilles released Lee, grimacing in self-disgust.

'Perhaps I should not have been so hard on Madame Le Bon,' he said cruelly. 'Had she not arrived when she did I might have given myself true reason to feel self-loathing—something you will know nothing about,' he jeered.

If only he knew! This was the second time she had been held in his arms and felt the beginnings of those emotions which seemed to rob her of her willpower. Emotions to which she was a stranger, but which she knew instinctively were dangerous when connected with her position here as Gilles' wife—a wife he had made no secret of despising for her supposedly amoral conduct.

They dined in silence, and afterwards Gilles stood up and announced that he was going to his office.

Left to her own devices, Lee went into the library and selected a book to read. Her eye was caught by a history of the Chauvigny family and she took it down from the shelves. It was dusty—another sign of the housekeeper's neglect. Tomorrow she would draw up a plan of action, Lee decided. It didn't matter that the groundwork she did now would ultimately benefit Gilles' real wife, at all costs she must keep busy during the enforced six months of her imprisonment. She would also have to write to Drew. She had decided to tell him that she was working at the château; other explanations would have to await their reunion, and she had enough problems without dwelling on those yet to be faced.

Reading the history was a laborious process, but an interesting one. She read that the château had been built during the time of François I, by a Chauvigny who had been close to the pleasure-loving monarch, but who had eventually been banished from court for seducing a young lady François himself had had his eye on. That Henri de Chauvigny had later married the girl had apparently not softened François' heart towards him, and that incident was but one example of the Chauvignys' chequered history—a history closely intertwined with that of France itself, and clearly showing the sensual greed of the Chauvigny males, Lee thought distastefully.

At eleven o'clock she closed the book and went upstairs. This moment had been at the back of her mind since she first realised that she and Gilles were to share a room. That he intended this purely as an additional unpleasantness for her Lee already knew, and so it was, but not in the way that Gilles envisaged. He thought she would be tormented by his unattainable presence in bed beside her; Lee's all-consuming fear was that the desire she had already glimpsed once in his eyes might flare up again and totally destroy her.

The bedroom was empty. Lee switched on the light, and this time carefully securing the bathroom door, prepared for bed. She did not emerge from the bathroom until she was dressed in her nightgown and the thin silk robe that had been part of the trousseau Gilles had bought for her.

2000   She need not have bothered. There was no sign of Gilles. The satin sheets felt cold and hostile and as she slid between them Lee found herself longing for the familiar comfort of her narrow single bed, at home in London. As she lay there unhappy tears slid from her eyes as she contemplated how life might have been if she had not had the misfortune to encounter Gilles. Already he had cost her the job she loved, much of her self-respect, and innumerable heart-searchings, how much more pain was there to be before she was set free?

She didn't hear him come to bed, and when she awoke in the morning he was gone, and this set the pattern for their days. One of the maids brought her breakfast in bed. It seemed that the cook thought a newly married woman needed to build up her strength before rising from her bed in the morning, and Lee enjoyed the sensual pleasure of lying in her bed, watching the sun stroke the vines in tender caress as she ate freshly baked croissants and drank the reviving hot coffee. In fact Lee was beginning to discover many things about herself there had never been time to learn before; some of them pleasant, some of them not so pleasant, and among those that weren't was her growing awareness of Gilles as a man.

She had taken to avoiding being in their room when he arrived back from the fields late in the afternoon. There was something about the earthy scent of his flesh, the beginnings of a beard along his jaw, the exposed skin of his chest, which was opening her mind and senses to emotions she had not previously known existed. It was as though the intimacy of marriage was acting like a hothouse atmosphere, forcing into life those emotions which had been shocked into hibernation all those many years ago.

During dinner one night the phone rang. Gilles went
to answer it and came back frowning.

'That was Louise's father,' he said curtly, resuming
his meal. 'He wants to meet you. He also wants to talk
to me about selling his land. I have invited him over
for dinner tomorrow.'

Lee said nothing. Already she felt sorry for the older
man, who had perhaps cherished dreams of his daughter's marriage to Gilles. Dreams which must surely
have suffered a death blow now?

Their evenings had fallen into a regular pattern. Lee
knew she ought to be grateful for Gilles' absence, but
vague feelings of restlessness were beginning to assail
her. She had taken to spending a part of each afternoon
in the South Tower. From there she had an excellent
view of the fields, and had often, inadvertently, found
her gaze straying to Gilles, tall, and darkly handsome
on the stallion he invariably rode, the large hound at
his heels, trained not to trespass near the fragile vines.

It was June, and Lee did not need to be told how
critical this month was. Now unsettled weather could
mean uneven flowering of the vines, and a staggered
vintage; wind and rain could remove the pollen, im-
peding the pollination so vital to the production of the
grapes. It was no wonder that Gilles often stared
frowningly into the blue arc of the sky, his brow
furrowed in concentration as he listened to the weather
forecast before dinner, but Lee did not question him.
She was not going to be the one to put their marriage
on a more intimate footing. Gilles treated her as a
stranger, but in a household geared to the all-important
production of wine, this did not merit comment.

After a full stint in the fields by day, after dinner
Gilles went down to the wine cellars every evening to
check the wine levels in the vats, for with the onset of

the warmer weather there was a greater risk of evaporation. Lee took no part in any of this. Gilles had not even invited her to accompany him on an inspection of the fields, even though he must know of her interest. And she was not going to ask.

She had even grown accustomed to sharing a bed with him, although she was always asleep when he joined her in it, and he was gone long before she opened her eyes in the morning.

CHAPTER FIVE

THERE was no real need to use the priceless Sèvres china for just the three of them, but Lee sensed that their guest would be flattered and proud to be treated with such distinction. The only time she had actually felt overwhelmed by the magnificence of the château was when Madame Le Bon had unlocked the china cupboards in a grim silence and allowed Lee to gaze at the treasures they concealed. Entire dinner services in Sèvres and Meissen china, designed specifically for the Chauvignys; vessels in solid gold and silver-gilt; not one but two ornate salts dating from the time when these were in constant use and also slightly more modern épergnes; cutlery such as Lee had never seen, with a delicate tracery of vines and grapes beaten on to them, the emblem of the house and seen everywhere, from the delicate scrolled gold design set into rich Imperial purple on one of the dinner services to the carving over the main entrance to the château; Chauvignys had drawn their wealth from the land since the dawn of time. There were cupboards packed with crystal as delicate and pure as clear water, and Lee had already instituted the beginnings of a system she had seen practised elsewhere; that of listing each precious heirloom, together with every occasion upon which it was used, although this last column in her book was as yet unmarked as the housekeeper had merely shrugged dismissively when Lee had asked for such details. The linen cupboards had also revealed a vast quantity of treasure, and Lee had personally supervised the washing and repairing of many of these items. It was with a feeling of intense pleasure that she wrote carefully in her book exactly what was being used tonight; although there would only be the three of them, this would be a practice run for the dinner party they were to give later in the week, and she was anxious for everything to go according to plan.

She was dressed and ready to receive their guest when Gilles entered their bedroom. He looked tired, lines of weariness drawn on either side of his mouth which Lee had not seen before.

'Is anything wrong?' The impulsive words were spoken before she could check them and she cringed mentally, awaiting the verbal mockery which was sure to follow.

To her surprise, Gilles didn't speak straight away. 'It's this weather,' he said at last. 'It's too hot, too soon; if we don't have rain soon we shall have to start manual watering; here at Chauvigny that won't be too much of a problem, but for the smaller growers like Jean-Paul . . . And if the weather doesn't break we run the risk of thunderstorms later in the year just before the vintage.'

Lee didn't need any explanation of those grim words; she knew exactly, from her sojourn in Australia, what a heavy rain storm could do to the heavily ripened grapes.

There were no words of comfort she could offer which would not sound facile, and besides, she reminded herself, she was the last person Gilles would turn to to share his problems. The knowledge was like a knife in her breast, and before she had time to question why this should be so, Gilles was on his way to the bathroom, leaving her alone to grapple with the unfairness of the emotions which seemed to have taken root in her breast; emotions which, if she had any sense, she would smother instantly, she told herself, checking her appearance carefully in the mirror. She was wearing another of her new dresses, its elegant lines drawing attention to the slender shape of her body. She had caught her hair up in a chignon and as she examined it carefully for any loose hairs Gilles emerged from the bathroom, a towel draped nonchalantly around lean hips, the dark body hair curling and still damp. A sensation not unlike that experienced shooting upwards in a high-speed lift spiralled through Lee's stomach, followed by a lethargic weakness that had her clinging to the dressing table as Gilles frowned darkly.

'Oh come on,' he protested sardonically. 'This isn't the first time you've seen a near-nude male, and we both know it. Or is it because you've been deprived of any lovemaking for so long that you can't take your eyes off my body, Lee?'

She wanted to deny his accusations, but he had moved within touching distance, his voice faintly husky as he probed demandingly, 'Would you like to touch me, Lee? To feel a man's body beneath your fingers again? Is that what you want? Is this?'

His hand caught her wrist and her fingers brushed the damp warmth of his chest, recoiling instantly, her eyes widening with the knowledge that she had found the momentary sensation deeply stirring. This was madness, she told herself weakly as she felt Gilles' breath on her neck. She was letting Gilles force her into the mould he had made for her, letting him trap her into reactions and emotions which were essentially foreign to her; and yet for one moment, with his warm male flesh beneath her fingers, she had almost forgotten why she was in this room; why Gilles had married her and what he thought of her.

'I must go. Our guest will be here soon.'

'So that's how you're going to play it, is it?' Gilles'
savagery caught her off guard and she stared up at the
angry face above her. 'A battle of wills, to see which of
us can last out the longest? Well, it's a battle that you
won't win, Lee,' he warned her as she opened the bedroom door, flying the insidious intimacy of their bedroom, and Gilles clad only in that brief towel which
did so much to tantalise and so little to hide his very
potent maleness.

Gilles had just joined her, dressed immaculately in a
dinner suit and a crisp dress shirt, when their guest
was announced, but to Lee's surprise he wasn't alone.
Louise was with him. And as she went forward to greet
them Lee shot a covert look at Gilles to see how he
was reacting to this additional guest. Either he was an
excellent actor, or he had lied to her about Louise, Lee
thought, watching him bend to kiss the Frenchwoman
with every evidence of enjoyment.

She too was subjected to a similar embrace, the cold,
hard blue eyes that Louise turned on her making her
very much aware that she had not been forgiven for
stealing the prize Louise had thought so securely hers.

Monsieur Trouville, Louise's father, on the other
hand greeted Lee extremely courteously, his eyes so
much like his daughter's but far kinder, appraising her
thoroughly.

'You are a lucky man, Gilles, to have found such a
bride,' he said at length, refusing an aperitif. 'Her eyes
are the colour of a perfect Chardonnay grape.'

'You must be careful that they do not beguile you
too easily, *mon ami*,' Louise interposed, darting Lee a
malice-spiked glance. 'Your wife may have been known
to you since childhood, but there have been years since
then when you have been apart; when you have drunk
deeply of the wine of life, and your wife has perhaps,

without your knowledge, sipped at it too.'

'Louise! Please excuse my daughter. She is abusing the privilege of an old friendship. You would not wish Lee to think you envied her her husband, Louise,' Monsieur Trouville chided in a gentle voice, but with a note in it that made Lee wonder if he was as oblivious to Louise's personality as Gilles had suggested. There had been unhappiness as well as anger in his eyes as they rested on Louise's hard face.

The dinner passed without incident. The meal was everything Lee had hoped it would be, and she had been meticulous about asking Gilles what wines he intended to serve so that the food would complement them.

Louise might have pushed away the crêpes Suzette and fresh strawberries served with whipped cream, but Gilles and Monsieur Trouville both evidently enjoyed the light sweet, and when after dinner Monsieur Trouville thanked her for the meal and suggested that he and Gilles retire to the latter's study for a business discussion Lee sensed that their guest wished to discuss Gilles' purchase of his land. This was confirmed when she and Louise were left alone and the latter commented spitefully,

'Gilles may feel that he has pulled the wool over Papa's eyes with this marriage, but I am not deceived.'

She prowled round the room while the men were gone, eyeing Lee's attractive flower arrangements disdainfully, and then when Madame Le Bon came in with the coffee Lee had requested, they exchanged a few words of conversation which, although Lee could not hear, she was sure related to her.

When the two men returned Gilles was looking far more relaxed than Lee had seen him looking for some time. He accepted a cup of coffee and their fingers touched accidentally, Lee withdrawing from the

momentary contact as though she had been burned.
Her reactions to Gilles were beginning to torment her
even more than his disturbing presence. She looked up
and found him studying her through narrowed eyes
and her heart jolted.

'Gilles, you have not yet given Lee the earrings.'
Louise's husky voice punctured the silence.

'Of course not.' Gilles glanced to the fireplace where
the portrait of the Russian bride looked down at them.
The girl had a sweetness of expression still alive today,
and Lee noticed for the first time that in addition to
the emerald ring she was wearing on her finger the girl
was wearing matching ear-rings.

'Those come only with the first year of marriage,
and the birth of the first child, surely you have not
forgotten that, Louise?'

'Silly of me, I had. We must just hope that you are
still around to wear them, mustn't we, Lee?' Louise
commented sweetly.

'Louise!'

This time Monsieur Trouville really did sound
angry, and Lee felt extremely sorry for him as he
started to apologise for his daughter's bad behaviour.

'Don't worry about it, Pierre,' Gilles told him easily,
placing his cup on the table and coming to slide the hard
warmth of his arm round Lee's waist to draw her close to
his side. 'Lee understands, don't you, *mignonne*?'

The endearment, the look of tender amusement in
his eyes, caught her off guard, and her eyes widened
and fastened on the gently smiling male lips, murmuring such blatant untruths. 'When people have as much
as we do, they can afford to be generous, is that not
so?' Gilles nuzzled the side of Lee's neck, apparently
equally oblivious to Lee's start of surprise, and
Louise's glittering fury. Only Monsieur Trouville

appeared to regard the proceedings with any approval, his smile affectionate as he chided Gilles for embarrassing Lee in front of them.

'She is still too new a bride to accept embraces in public without thinking of those given in private,' their guest commented, further embarrassing Lee, 'and I sense by the look in your eyes, my friend, that we have already outstayed our welcome,' he added teasingly. 'I shall see my lawyer about the other business next week.'

Gilles went with them to their car, while Lee busied herself collecting the coffee cups and discarded glasses. When she heard Gilles' firm tread in the hall, her cheeks were still flushed, her pulses racing betrayingly.

'It's all right, you can drop the act; they've gone.' He was leaning against the doorway, his dress shirt a white blur in the darkness, his voice suddenly menacing as he taunted mockingly, 'Were you thinking of those embraces we had exchanged in private, my lovely bride? Perhaps I ought to reward you with some more if that is the effect they have on you. Pierre was most impressed. A beautiful, chaste child he called you.'

'I expect to Monsieur Trouville anyone under thirty is still a child,' Lee commented with more composure than she was feeling.

'He certainly is easy to fool.'

Lee ignored the taunting words.

'I'm glad you were able to settle your business satisfactorily, Gilles, but I'm tired, and if you'll excuse me, I'll go to bed.'

For once she wasn't asleep when he came into their room, and she closed her eyes, forcing herself to breathe evenly as he moved about the room, discarding clothes, showering, returning to slide beneath the sheets, and even though she had her back to him and her eyes were closed she knew instinctively that he

slept without any form of covering, and all the fears
and doubts she had had right from the start of their
'marriage' returned to haunt her. She was not indifferent to Gilles; how could she be? Her very first sexual
stirrings had been aroused by him, and although repressed and dammed all through her teenage years,
they were still there, ready to spring into new life at
his merest touch. At her side Gilles moved and a flood
of desire engulfed her. To her intense shame she knew
that if he turned to her now and took her in his arms
she would be powerless to prevent him from discovering exactly how wrong he was about her. But of course,
he was scarcely likely to do that!

The heatwave continued. Every day men were out
carefully watering and nurturing the vines. Gilles had
sent two of his own men to help Jean-Paul, and as the
earth grew dry and parched, waiting the reviving caress
of the life-giving rain, so did tension infiltrate the
atmosphere, until Lee felt as though her nerves were
stretched to breaking point.

The dinner they had given for Gilles' fellow *vignerons* had passed without comment. Most of the staff now
seemed to accept her as the mistress of the château,
and with Gilles' permission Lee had commissioned a
firm of decorators to refurbish the ballroom. They had
finished only that morning and Lee had been down to
inspect the newly painted room. The colours were
those in which the room had originally been painted—
eau de nil and palest peach—and the room glowed
softly in the afternoon sun. The floor had been stripped
and re-waxed with a non-slip polish, for Lee was
determined that the vintage dinner which would end
her enforced stay at the château would be one which
would be remembered long after she had been forgotten.
There were to be forty guests for dinner, many of

whom would be staying overnight. Gilles had already given her the invitation list and there were at least another hundred people who would be attending the ball afterwards. Gilles' position locally meant that the other winegrowers turned automatically to him for leadership.

When she left the ballroom, Lee went automatically to the South Tower. The beginnings of a headache made her feel muzzy and instead of going to her sitting room she climbed the extra stairs to the bedroom.

From here she could see for miles; the tiny bent figures of the men working on the vines; Gilles among them, working alongside his men to beat the drought which threatened to destroy the crop. The sunshine slanted oblongs of gold over the carpet, the hot early summer scents wafting in through the narrow window, and all at once Lee wanted to be outside.

Discarding her elegant linen dress in favour of jeans and thin tee-shirt, she hurried through the courtyard and through the vines, aromatic from their recent watering.

Beyond the formal gardens of the château and the fields of vines stretched a small wooded copse where Gilles rode most mornings, and without being aware of it, Lee followed the dusty, dry path until she was swallowed up by the cool green interior of the shadow-dappled sanctuary from the sun's molten glare.

The stream which fed the château's elaborate water gardens had dried to a small trickle, but it was still pleasant to lie and listen to the clean sound of the water. Drowsy and more at peace than she had been since coming to the château, Lee closed her eyes.

When she opened them again her first thought was that she must have slept for hours, it was so dark, and then she realised that the darkness was the heavy, sullen clouds which had covered the sky. She got up, brushing twigs and grass from her jeans, shivering under the cooling breeze which had suddenly sprung up. A glance at her watch told her that she was already late for dinner, and as she searched for the path which had led her into the copse the first peal of thunder sounded overhead, followed by lightning which rent the sky in two.

Her first thought was relief that now they would have rain, followed by the wry knowledge that she would be soaked by the time she returned to the château. Thunderstorms had never frightened Lee; on the contrary she found them exhilarating as though all the electricity generated by the celestial activity was mirrored in some small way by her own body.

For a moment she stood with her face uplifted, welcoming the touch of the rain as it pattered down on to the leaves, and then she turned, transfixed by the sight of the motionless horse and rider guarding the exit from the small clearing where she had been sleeping.

'Gilles!' She moved towards him, noticing the way his shirt clung damply to his shoulders, his dark hair sprinkled with moisture and curling slightly.

Another clap of thunder obliterated her voice, and the stallion reared angrily, pawing the air with rolling eyes.

'Where the hell have you been, damn you?' Gilles swore, dismounting angrily. Lee's eyes were riveted on the tanned breadth of the shoulders beneath the damp shirt. The trees had obviously protected her from the worst of the rain.

'I fell asleep . . .'

How inane it sounded, with the thunder rolling overhead and lightning stabbing the sky, and a rueful smile curved her lips.

'Don't laugh at me!' he ground out furiously. 'I've been searching for you for two hours. One of the men saw you leaving the château . . .'

'Where did you think I'd gone?'

His anger puzzled her, but his reply was drowned out by another clap of thunder, more vicious this time. The stallion reared angrily, screaming shrill defiance at the elements, and then with flashing hooves was gone, leaving them alone in the clearing.

'Your horse . . .'

'He'll be all right. He'll make straight for his stable. Satan doesn't like the rain, which is more than I can say for you. Doesn't the thunder frighten you?'

Lee laughed, 'No, I love it, it's so exhilarating. Does it frighten you?'

There was no reply. Gilles was studying her closely.

'I suppose I should have guessed that,' he muttered hoarsely. 'Anything as elemental and passion-filled as this would excite you, wouldn't it? Very well, Lee, I give in . . .'

He reached for her as he spoke, his mouth covering hers and destroying all her determinedly erected barriers; the storm and Gilles seemed to meld and become one entity before which she was helpless, and as Gilles' mouth forced hers to part in soft surrender she thought fleetingly of the mother of the Greek hero Theseus who had claimed that her son had been conceived by Poseidon, the sea-god, who had come to her in a dream; such elemental desire as she was feeling now was surely God-given, and as Gilles lowered her on to the still dry grass of the small glade she made no attempt to hinder him. Droplets of rain from his hair had fallen to his shoulders and throat and she raised herself up lightly to savour them with her tongue, tasting the cool dampness with eyes that wondered at the sudden darkening of the iron-grey ones above her.

It was as though she were lost in a dream, driven by some elemental force above and beyond the sensible

motives which had hitherto ruled her life. She felt no
shame as Gilles tugged impatiently at her tee-shirt and
jeans, even revelling in the look in his eyes when he at
last gazed at her naked body. His head bent towards
her and she knew he intended to kiss her, but instead
she placed her finger to his lips and slowly began unfastening the buttons of his shirt, following the progress of her fingers, with light butterfly kisses which
drew a hoarse moan from between his gritted teeth
and invoked a punishment which left her clinging mind-
lessly to his broad shoulders while his lips and hands
left her in no doubt of his urgent need to possess her.

Above them the thunder rolled and crashed, lightning splitting the night sky, but Lee was oblivious;
some pagan part of herself she had never dreamed
existed was driving her on towards the culmination of
all those emotions she had experienced since coming
to the château but never fully understood. Now, with
her fingers delicately exploring the hard warmth of
Gilles' flesh, she did, and for a moment she was still as
she tasted the knowledge which after the initial sweetness was as bitter as Eve's apple. She loved Gilles!
Something deep down inside her shuddered and rose
up in a tidal wave and she knew beyond any shadow of
a doubt that this moment, this passionate, almost violent culmination of a love which had begun over six
years ago, was something that nothing could stop. A
vivid flash of lightning touched their bodies, Gilles' so
male, the skin darkly tanned, her own, softly curved,
pliant, female; all around them, infusing the very air
they breathed, was the smell of the grapes, of earth
coming to life beneath the rain; the moisture touched
their skins, but Lee barely noticed. She moaned softly
in pleasure, her frantic movements against Gilles' body
destroying the last remnants of his self-control, so that

he cursed harshly against her mouth and then possessed it endlessly, breaking the kiss only when his breathing had grown harsh and ragged.

Tonight she was not Lee Raven, nor even Gilles' wife, Lee told herself hazily; she was woman, a creature who had enticed and aroused man until he was driven by the need to capture her elusiveness in the only way he could—by possessing her, and with the thunder charging the air around them she arched instinctively beneath Gilles, knowing with a knowledge that went deeper than mere experience that this time there would be no holding back.

Later she would be astounded at the intensity of her passion, at the memory of how she had wantonly caressed every inch of Gilles' taut body, mutely inciting him to repeat his earlier demanding arousal of her flesh with the hard warmth of his lips and hands. At one point he had wound his hand in her hair, pulling away from her to study the swelling curves of her breasts, the creamy skin of her stomach and the tender line of her thighs, before parting them deliberately with his own in a way that made her heart jerk on its first shaft of fear, soon lost beneath the heated possession of his kiss as he murmured that her skin possessed the bloom of grapes, and her mouth tasted as potent as the richest wine in his cellars.

He possessed her with an urgency that brought pain, shadowing her eyes as they flew open, his own shocked, and then glazing as the thunder rolled overhead, and he and the storm became one, carrying her far beyond pain to a place where nothing existed but the fierce waves of pleasure created by Gilles' touch; a pleasure which spiralled and exploded, leaving her feeling as though she was floating somewhere on a soft, warm cloud.

She could hear Gilles breathing close beside her, the

sound tortured as he dragged air into his lungs. Her body was damp from the rain and the grass and all at once she felt cold.

'You were a virgin!' The words were coldly accusing and she turned her head away. 'My God, you little bitch! If it was experience you wanted . . . Here, put these on.'

She dressed without looking at him, her earlier exhilaration swamped by the sickness which had invaded her. What had she expected? That he would take her in his arms and swear undying love? That he would say his possession of her was the most beautiful thing he had ever experienced? No doubt the caresses which had sent her into such a frenzy of delight were commonplace to him. Her clothes were damp and her fingers trembled over them. She longed to look at Gilles and yet daren't in case he read the truth in her eyes. Now, with passion spent, her body was beginning to ache, and as she pulled the tee-shirt over her head she saw the beginnings of bruises on her breast. Gilles had seen them too, and he grasped her wrist and grimaced in disgust. 'Like the grapes, you bruise easily, Madame la Comtesse. What the hell were you playing at?' he burst out impatiently as though no longer able to conceal his anger. He had his jeans on, his shirt held in one hand so that Lee's eyes were fixed on the tanned column of his throat, and the pulse beating there; a pulse she had not so long ago touched with her lips and felt burst into urgent life beneath then. She dragged her eyes away.

'Why didn't you tell me?'

'Would you have believed me? You needn't worry that this means I want to hold you to our marriage, Gilles.' He was watching her sardonically. Had he thought she had suddenly decided to force his hand in the hope that once he discovered she was a virgin he would continue the marriage? Did he think she had been swayed by the knowledge of his material possessions, or worse still, had he guessed that she had fallen in love with him?

'You condemned me years ago on a letter that wasn't even written by me,' she told him slowly. 'What happened tonight, happened, and I feel no shame that it did.' She raised her head proudly, willing her eyes not to give her away, not to betray to the waiting man exactly how she felt about him. 'What we did brought me great pleasure, Gilles,' she said bravely, 'and I see no reason why I should feel ashamed of that.'

She heard his harsh, indrawn breath, and the black fury leaping into his eyes, as he turned on his heel and said curtly, 'Well, next time you feel like experimenting with something as dangerous as sex, find yourself another partner—I don't like feeling that I'm some sort of stud animal!'

He was gone, leaving her to find her own way back to the château, her dreams lying broken at her feet, as he left her in no doubt as to how he regarded what had, for her, been the most poetically beautiful moments of her life. There had been something about their union which had struck a chord so deep and primitive that she doubted that it would ever be struck again.

Unhappily she made her way back to the château. No one questioned her absence or damp clothes and hair, but there was no sign of Gilles. Refusing any supper, she went up to their room, and although she lay awake well into the small hours he never came in. That night for the first time she slept alone.

CHAPTER SIX

LEE had just finished writing to Drew, telling him that their engagement was off. She could not return his ring as yet because Gilles still had it. In her letter she had explained that she had fallen in love with someone else. No need for him to know of her marriage to Gilles; that was not something which could be told in a letter.

Soon it would be time for the vintage; already the grapes were ripening in the hot August sun, while a harvest of another kind grew slowly inside her.

She had known within a week that she was pregnant, and after the first initial shock had come a sweet piercing pleasure that she was carrying Gilles' child; a child conceived on that one night of elemental fusing. She touched her stomach gently. As yet only the most discerning person could tell that she carried a child. It was there in the faint rounding of her stomach and the fullness of her breasts; the slightly altered shape of her face, but that was all. She had been sick several times in the morning, but because Gilles slept in the dressing room and left the château long before she was awake in the morning he did not know. And that was the way she wanted it to stay. For the child's sake Gilles might insist that they continue the marriage, and her heart, starving for his tenderness, overburdened with her love for him, could not endure that. Another month and she would be gone, and her secret with her. She had become very dreamy, spending her afternoons lazily in the South Tower, dreaming of her child's birth.

Soon the grape pickers would be with them, students

in the main, and casual labour, and Lee had already gone over the dormitories above the stables and garages to check that everything was in order for their arrival.

Jean-Paul drove into the courtyard in a battered Citroën one sultry afternoon when Lee was catnapping in her room. Although the baby had as yet made scant difference to her figure, already she was beginning to feel tired.

'It's the baby!' he yelled excitedly when Lee went downstairs, awoken by the noisy disturbance of his arrival. 'I've taken Marie-Thérèse to the hospital and I came here to ask Gilles if he could lend me Henri until the baby arrives. Our grapes are ready for picking, but if I am not there to supervise . . .' He shrugged, meaning that with the cheap labour which was all he could afford the grapes could be spoiled by ignorant careless hands if he was not there on hand.

'I'm sure he will,' Lee said impulsively. 'He's in the cellar, I think, inspecting last year's wine. They think it's ready to be bottled. I'll come with you, Jean-Paul,' she added on impulse. After all, wasn't she knowledgeable enough about wines to merit an inspection of Gilles' treasured cellars?

The cellars stretched endlessly beneath the château; huge stainless steel vats standing ready to receive this year's harvest; casks containing the previous year's wine lining the long, dark cavern where the temperature was thermostatically controlled to provide exactly the right temperature for the maturing wine. Lee shivered when they walked from the bright, hot sunshine outside into the shadowed cavernous entrance to the cellars which seemed to yawn widely like some giant maw.

'You're cold!' Jean-Paul exclaimed. 'I can find my own way, Lee.'

'No, it's all right, I want to come with you.'

Jean-Paul looked at her and smiled hugely. 'Ah, I understand.'

'What do you understand, *mon ami*?' Gilles drawled from behind them.

Lee gave a sudden start—she hadn't seen him approach, her eyes still unaccustomed to the dark of the cellars.

'I understand that your beautiful young wife is anxious not to miss the opportunity to snatch a few extra minutes of her husband's time.'

Lee's cheeks burned, and she was glad of the darkness to conceal her betraying flush. Was she so obvious? She could not deny that hidden at the back of her mind had been a desire to see Gilles, even if she ultimately was forced to endure his total disinterest in her presence.

'Aren't you going to kiss her?' Jean-Paul teased. 'Many times when we were first married, Marie-Thérèse would bring my lunch out to the fields, and for a while we would forget about the vines.' He smiled reminiscently, while Gilles arched his eyebrows and said sardonically to Lee,

'Is that why you came down here? So that I could kiss you?'

Lee laughed lightly,

'No, of course not. Jean-Paul wanted to ask for your help, Gilles. Marie-Thérèse has started with the baby . . .'

She left the two men to talk while she examined the cellar more thoroughly. It was really time that she lost this irrational, childish fear of enclosed dark spaces, she thought firmly, when she had turned for the third time to check that the door was still open behind her.

'. . . so Henry will go back with you and set the men

to work.' Gilles was saying when she got back. 'And, *mon ami*!' he clapped Jean-Paul on the back, 'this year the vintage will be a good one, fit to put down for twenty-one years, for your son's coming of age, *non*?'

'Marie-Thérèse might have a girl,' Lee protested, incensed by this evidence of male chauvinism, although she herself dreamed constantly of a child with his father's dark hair and eyes.

'And next year we shall celebrate the birth of your child, *non*? Jean-Paul teased Gilles, and for a second Lee paled, terrified that he might have guessed her secret. She need not have worried, Jean-Paul was totally concerned with his wife and his vineyard in that order, and within an hour of his arrival he was on his way with Gilles' most experienced foreman.

'You will need Henri soon yourself,' Lee commented. 'Your own grapes . . .'

'Please allow me to know the condition of my grapes,' Gilles bit out curtly, turning on his heel and leaving her alone in the courtyard. Several minutes later she heard the impatient sound of the stallion's hooves over the cobbles and glancing upwards had a momentary impression of taut, angry strength as Gilles rode past her, his face an iron mask in which only his eyes seemed to be alive, hating her with a ferocity that was like a knife in her heart.

He did not return for dinner, and Lee, knowing the tremendous strength and fiery temper of the stallion, grew worried. She could barely touch her own food, and when the phone rang she leapt up, convinced that Gilles must have had an accident.

It was Louise on the other end of the line, and Lee barely listened to what the other woman was saying until she heard Gilles' name, and then her fingers gripped the receiver until they were white as she listened to Louise telling her that Gilles was having dinner with them and would not be returning until late.

There was triumph in the other woman's voice, and Lee wondered if Gilles had changed his mind about Louise as she replaced the receiver, or did he simply think it was safe to indulge his physical needs with her now that she could not pressurise him into marriage?

Alone in the huge bed she tossed and turned. She could not continue as she was much longer. Already the strain of her love for Gilles was etching dark shadows beneath her eyes, and although her skin was tanned by the sun, she was losing weight. Her hands went instinctively to the soft fullness of her stomach and the new life cradled safely there. It was nearly three months since the night when the child had been conceived. She had visited a doctor in Nantes, supposedly to have her hair trimmed, and what she had learned from him had reassured her as to her health and that of the child she carried. She had followed his advice minutely and religiously taken the vitamins he had given her.

That weekend the pickers arrived, and life at the château centred around the vines. Heavy storms had been predicted and it would be a race against time to get the grapes in before they broke.

Lee worked hard in the kitchen supervising the preparation of meals for the pickers, often going out into the fields to help with the picking when she had a spare moment. The work was hard and hot under the merciless sun which seemed to beat down from an intensely blue sky, and like the other girls Lee took the precaution of covering her head while she worked.

Her experience in Australia had taught her the importance of swift, knowledgeable picking, and when

Gilles rode along the vines on which she was working one hot afternoon, she didn't stop working to talk to him, her fingers flying deftly from vine to basket, with the rhythmic ease of the experienced picker.

'What the hell do you think you're doing?' He had dismounted from the stallion and seized her under the armpits, dragging her away from the other workers, his face livid with rage.

'Picking grapes. What did you think?' Lee asked flippantly. He looked so angry that for a moment she thought he was going to hit her.

'My wife does not pick grapes!'

For a moment she was stunned.

'Oh, don't be so ridiculous, Gilles,' she said coolly when she had her breath back. 'Storms are forecast, and with Henri and two other men helping Jean-Paul, you need every hand you can get in the fields, and mine at least are experienced.'

She glanced at their smooth palms as she spoke, her fingers stained and her nails dirty. Gilles followed the small movement, his fingers curling round her slender wrists as he too surveyed the sunburnt flesh.

'You are determined to turn me into a monster, aren't you?' he demanded savagely. He was white under his tan, his eyes no longer grey, but the purple blackness of the Syrah grape, which according to legend had been brought to the Rhone valley from Shiraz by a returning Crusader. 'Do you want my people to say that I work you until you are ill? Have you looked at yourself recently?'

A deep flush of humiliation settled on Lee's cheeks. She knew she looked less than glamorous in her ancient jeans and checked shirt, but she had honestly wanted to help Gilles, to play her part in the gathering of the harvest so that no matter what the future might bring, the wine they made this vintage would owe something, no matter how meagre, to her.

'Oh, for God's sake!' Gilles groaned suddenly, dragging her into his arms and kissing her until she was gasping for breath. As savagely as she had been taken prisoner she was released, to stand blinking in the sun while all around them the pickers laughed and joked. She touched her swelling mouth with trembling fingers as Gilles remounted. Of course, he had had to kiss her to prevent the pickers from thinking they were quarrelling. Gossip spread like wildfire when the pickers were in evidence, and Gilles would not want Louise to suspect that their marriage was cracking up. He had made no comment about the evening he had stayed at their house, and looking into his thunderous face Lee could only think that if he had gone to Louise to relieve his frustration the remedy could not have been very effective.

She was still standing staring up at him when he leaned down and swung her up before him.

'I'm taking you back to the château,' he said abruptly. 'And then you're going to rest. The picking will be finished tomorrow and then we start the pressing. The pickers have to move on to another vineyard when they finish here, so there won't be time for the usual celebrations this year—not with the weather threatening to break, but we still have the buyers to entertain, and I don't want you making yourself ill picking grapes.'

Because he needed a hostess, Lee reminded herself. How could she ever have been stupid enough to think he was taking her home because he was concerned about her? But for a brief, ecstatic moment that was exactly what she had thought!

'Relax,' she was instructed as the huge stallion

obeyed his master's command to walk. 'Satan isn't used to carrying females. Lean back against me, that will lessen the discomfort.'

Before the animal had taken more than a few paces Lee had begun to feel distinctly queasy, and was too grateful for Gilles' suggestion to question it. It was only when one arm came round her to hold her securely against his chest and the other grasped the reins loosely that she realised just how intimately she was pressed against him. It was impossible to avoid touching him, however, and her nostrils were filled with the warm male scent of him as they rode into the courtyard and he swung her down to the floor.

'There's no need to come inside with me,' she protested when he walked with her into the shadowed hall.

'Allow me to decide what is necessary for myself, Lee.' His eyes raked her pale slenderness. 'You look as though you're starving yourself to death. Are you ill?'

'Of course not!' If one didn't count unrequited love as an illness, for that was what was responsible for her wan cheeks and lack of appetite. Even sleep was sometimes an impossibility, lying alone in a bed meant for loving while Gilles slept in the dressing room.

'Louise and her father will be attending the buyers' dinner, and in view of the number of guests we shall have staying with us, I think it might be advisable if we returned to our previous sleeping arrangements.'

The curt words caught Lee off guard. She stiffened, hope trembling through her. 'You mean . . .'

'I mean that we shall sleep together, Lee, simply that and nothing more.' He said it curtly, so curtly that Lee suspected that he was warning her not to try and divert him from his chosen path. She coloured again. What did he think she was? So depraved that she would deliberately seek his rejection?

Lee had spent many hours over the menu for the banquet to be served to the buyers. As the main purpose of the banquet was to provide a suitable accompaniment for Gilles' wines, Lee consulted with him over her final menu.

For the first course, she intended to serve merlans frits en lorgnette, a delicious fish dish which would complement their local wines, followed by casserole de cailles aux morilles, a delicacy of which Lee knew the French were inordinately fond, quail cooked with tiny mushroom-like morels; for the sweet course there would be soufflé Grand Marnier, followed by regional cheeses for those with a less sweet tooth. Gilles frowned a little over the final menu, suggesting that she might be trying to take on too much. Lee didn't tell him about the sister-in-law who ran her own restaurant and who had passed much of her knowledge on to Lee when she had stayed with them in Australia. She had already discussed her plans with the cook, who visualised no problems, and as the plans Lee had been carefully laying for the last few months were meticulously followed, she felt she had every right to feel proud of her achievements.

Beds were made up with the linen which had been washed and aired weeks before, bedrooms, already cleaned and prepared, were stripped of the coverings protecting highly polished and valuable furniture. The florists Lee had visited in Nantes arrived and potted plants and shrubs were cleverly arranged in the ballroom. Musicians had been hired and carefully briefed, and when the clothes she had ordered from Orléans arrived, she examined them in satisfaction. The idea was not new; costume balls were always a firm favourite with women and had been for centuries, but this was one with a difference, because she and Gilles would be playing parts which had been played before— by a young Russian girl and her handsome, dashing husband. Whatever hopes had been in her heart when she planned this ball, as meticulously true in every detail to that held so long ago to celebrate the marriage of that other couple, Lee now acknowledged that these were dead, but at least she could have the satisfaction of knowing that this vintage would last for ever in the memories of those who attended it.

No one was forgotten, and even the chattering girls in the kitchen had their attractive striped dresses and starched, frilly aprons.

'Oh, madame, it is all so exciting!' one exclaimed as she assisted Lee with the flowers she was arranging for the guest bedrooms.

Gilles had raised his eyebrows slightly at first when Lee told him of her plans, but he had consented easily enough; he probably had too much on his mind to concern himself with such minor matters, Lee conceded. Her one disappointment was that Marie-Thérèse and Jean-Paul would not be coming. Their new, precious daughter could not be left, and although regretful they had been adamant about remaining at home. As she too would have been in their place, Lee thought, her hands going instinctively to her stomach. It had become a reflex action these days, and Gilles who had walked into the bedroom while she was on her knees examining the costumes frowned slightly.

'Is something wrong?'

What would he say if she told him, 'Nothing, your son has just kicked me?' Lee wondered half-hysterically; instead she shook her head, refusing to give in to the clamouring longing to look at the man standing over her, to feast her eyes on his virile maleness.

'Then will you stop acting like the victim of a rape?' he demanded acidly. 'Because God knows, Lee, you were willing enough . . . you . . .'

'Please don't talk about it, Gilles,' she protested quickly. 'I'm sorry if I've ever given you the impression that . . .'

'That you wanted me?' he cursed savagely. 'Well, you damned well did, Lee . . . you damned well did!'

He had gone before she could finish what she had been going to say, which was simply that she had never wanted to give him the impression that she considered herself a victim of any type, unless it was of her ever-growing love for him. Their lovemaking, which for her had been so pleasurable and was so cherished, to him appeared to be something which he bitterly resented—hated almost, and slow tears slid down her face as she acknowledged that her love was completely and utterly hopeless.

Everything was in readiness for the arrival of their guests. Lee found her feet leading her towards the tower room which had become her own personal sanctuary. Gilles was in the cellars checking on the fermentation of the new wine, and she had several hours to herself before the first of their guests would arrive.

She was too drowsy to concentrate and the thought of the cool green bed in the room above was tempting. In the upper room she removed the cool linen dress she had been wearing. Her reflection glimpsed in the mirror showed that she would not be able to keep her secret much longer—and indeed could not have kept it this long had she and Gilles truly been man and wife. She lay down on the bed, pulling the silk coverlet over herself with a small sigh. Soon she would be gone from the château. 'Until the vintage,' Gilles had said, and with this dinner party and ball it would be over. Her eyes ached with unshed tears, her hands going protectively to her stomach. For a few moments she allowed herself to fantasise about how different things would have been were they really married. How cherished and protected she would have been then. Gilles would want to take no chances; the baby she carried might well be the heir to the Chauvigny estates. But how would he have viewed her actual pregnancy? Would he have been pleased by the evidence of his virility, but slightly remote? Yes, she was sure this would have been his reaction. She sighed again, letting sleep enfold her. Madame Le Bon had been particularly difficult lately, and Lee was terrified that the other woman would discover her condition, without really knowing why she should be; she only knew that with the discovery her annoyance at Madame Le Bon's animosity had given way to a creeping fear.

'Lee!'

Someone was calling her name, dragging her back from the dreams which were so much more pleasant than reality. She opened her eyes and looked straight into the angry grey ones of her husband.

'What are you doing here? Our guests will be arriving shortly!'

He was still dressed in his working clothes, the smell of fermenting grapes clinging richly to his skin, his jaw shadowed with the faint beginnings of his beard. Lee's throat felt dry, and she swallowed nervously, shaken by a longing to reach up and touch the stubbled skin.

'Lee?' There was enquiry as well as impatience in the word.

'Yes, I'm awake. I'll get dressed and then go and get changed.'

'Dressed?'

She had meant the words only as a warning that she

wanted him to leave, but they seemed to spark off a minor explosion. Gilles' eyes darkened as, far from leaving the room, he came farther into it, and Lee was glad that she had taken the precaution of closing the curtain as he reached for her with hard hands, pinning her on to the mattress as he demanded harshly,

'You mean to tell me you are undressed? With the door unlocked and anyone free to walk in?'

His anger bewildered her.

'No one would just walk in,' she protested. 'All the staff know that I like to be alone during the afternoons.'

'Why? So that you can dream of your fiancé? What would he say if he knew that you have given yourself to me? Or don't you mean to tell him until it's too late?'

'That's a vile thing to suggest!'

'Then you have told him? Well, perhaps I ought to give you something else to tell him,' he said softly before Lee could tell him that she had broken her engagement. His hands had already slid up from her arms, one grasping the thin silk cover while the other stroked her throat.

She opened her mouth to protest, but the scent of him filled her nostrils, and instead of repudiating him, her lips parted trustingly for his kiss. She loved him so much that she ached for his touch; longed for him to possess her with tenderness and love.

There was anger in his kiss and she tried to pull away, realisation of what he actually felt coming too late. His hands held her face, and she had to close her eyes against the anger she saw smouldering there.

'Look at me!' The harsh command jerked them open again. 'It is I who is making love to you,' Gilles told her, 'so don't close your eyes and pretend it is someone else.' She heard him swear suddenly, and then the protective cover was wrenched away completely, his mouth moist and urgent against her drowsy skin, waves of pleasure sweeping over her and obliterating her willpower.

There was something almost driven in the way Gilles kissed her and touched her; as though his actions were dictated by something stronger than the commands of his brain. Perhaps his own self-enforced celibacy was proving too much for him, she thought hazily as his hands cupped her breasts, fuller now and tender. His harsh groan was smothered against her flesh, his lips hot and dry against the coolness of her skin. An overwhelming tide of love swamped her as she looked down at the darkness of his head against her breast. His body felt damp, and drops of perspiration stood out of his forehead as he dragged himself away, his eyes almost black as he studied the shadowy outline of her breasts, the nipples hard and aroused.

He muttered something in French which she could not catch, and Lee knew that he was despising himself for wanting her body, when he felt nothing but contempt for her as a person. She moved away from him, bitterly hurt by the realisation that his desire for her sprang from man's basest instinct, but with a harsh cry he seized her in his arms, holding her against the length of a body that shook with pent-up need, his face dark and congested.

His kiss blanketed out everything but her answering desire. Her lips parted tremulously as he probed and demanded access to the sweet moistness they were concealing. With heated urgency his hands stroked her body, and Lee, almost mindless with the pleasure they were inducing, forgot that such intimacy might betray her condition. The touch of his tongue against her nipples provoked a small gasped cry, answered in the heated pressure of his body. Her nails raked the smooth flesh of his back, her lips moaning soft pleas for fulfilment, which found an answer in the heated shudder of Gilles' body above her. Their situation, Gilles' lack of love for her, all faded into insignificance, and it was only the sudden slamming of a car door in the courtyard that jerked Lee back into awareness. She froze in Gilles' arms.

'Gilles!'

'What is it? If you're remembering your untrusting fiancé it's too damned late,' his desire-drugged voice informed her.

'I think your guests are arriving. I just heard a car door.'

Her shaky words had the desired effect.

'What?'

Lee felt the cool air shaft over her body as he left the bed. He glanced out of the window, and then without looking at her strode to the door, pulling on his shirt as he did so.

'I'll go and talk to them while you get changed. Don't take too long.'

Not a word about what had occurred between them, but what had she been expecting?

It took her longer than usual to shower and dress. Her fingers felt unusually clumsy, and her brain was still clouded by the unappeased desire Gilles had aroused within her. She was wearing one of her new couture gowns, glad of its elegant, flowing lines, skimming the soft curves of her body and drawing attention to her lissom shape.

She went downstairs nervously. Gilles smiled at her as she entered the salon—a smile which illuminated his harsh features, almost taking her breath away. For a moment she was actually in danger of forgetting that this was only a charade for the benefit of his guests, and her whole body trembled as he drew her within the curve of his arm, proudly presenting her to his friends.

More guests were arriving. The women were elegant as only Parisienne women can be, the men, urbane and charming, speaking in delightfully accented English as they complimented Gilles on his choice of bride.

While the men discussed wine, Lee offered to show their wives to their rooms. She could tell that beneath the polite façade the women were curious about her, and she answered their discreet questions as ably as she could, using Gilles' story that their relationship had been founded when she was in her teens. A little to her amusement they seemed to approve of such an arrangement.

When she returned to the drawing room their guests of honour had arrived—the Junior Minister for Trade, and his wife.

'A masked ball is such a delightful idea,' Madame Lefleur commented with a smile when she and Lee were introduced. 'I congratulate you on your originality.'

Lee was immediately drawn to the soignée Frenchwoman, and as they preceded Gilles and her husband up the graceful sweep of stairs, she explained how she had got the idea from the portrait of Gilles' ancestor.

'A very dashing-looking rogue,' Madame Lefleur laughed, pausing so that Lee could open the door to the suite of rooms she had had prepared for these honoured guests. Busily talking to her companion, it was several seconds before Lee saw the chaos to which the room had been reduced, and by that time it was

too late to close the door up it, because Madame
Lefleur too had seen the disruption of the elegant sitting room—dead flowers heaped untidily on the table,
the hearth covered in ashes, furniture all awry, and
easily glimpsed through the connecting door, the
unmade bed in the next room carelessly heaped with
bolsters and sheets. Lee started to tremble. What on
earth had happened? She had been at such pains to
make sure all the rooms were immaculate, and these
important guests had been given the most luxurious
suite. She closed her eyes, half believing that she was
seeing things, then opened them again, as she heard
Gilles' deep tones behind her. He would be furious
with her!

To Lee's everlasting gratitude, before she could say
or do anything Madame Lefleur stepped smoothly in
front of her and smiled charmingly at Gilles.

'Isn't that stupid of me, I think I must have left my
handbag downstairs. Would you be an angel, Gilles,
and get it for me. Lazy of me, I know, but that staircase
of yours is so very, long! You go with him, Georges,'
she instructed her husband. 'You know where I was
sitting.'

When they had gone she smiled impishly at Lee. 'I
left my bag in the auto, but by the time I have remembered that you will have had time to explain to
me what is happening.'

'I don't know,' Lee admitted slowly. A suspicion was
beginning to take root in her mind, but surely Madame
Le Bon would not be foolish enough to put her own
security at risk in such a way?

'I think perhaps I do,' Madame Lefleur said com-
prehendingly. 'Ours is a rather small circle and one
gets to know people very well. I detect Louise's hand
behind this affair. Am I not right? She has made it

very plain in the past that she considers Gilles to be her own personal property. It was no secret that she expected to marry him. And I seem to remember her once telling me that Gilles' housekeeper had once worked for her. This sort of trick is typical of Louise.'

'I'll get one of the maids up here to tidy up this mess,' Lee began, smothering a small gasp as the door was suddenly thrust open and Gilles stood there, his eyes darkening as they slowly surveyed the carnage.

'Gilles, your wife has been the victim of a most unpleasant piece of mischief,' Madame Lefleur said quickly before Gilles could speak. 'The poor girl is white with the shock of it.' Her eyes suddenly widened with remorse as she looked at Lee. '*Ma chère*, forgive me if I have spoken out of turn. Perhaps you did not know about Louise . . .'

'Lee knows all about her,' Gilles cut in abruptly. 'But you cannot seriously be suggesting that she walked in here and did this!'

'Not her, but a certain someone who has her interests at heart,' Madame Lefleur told him wisely. 'Did you find my handbag?'

'No. Georges remembered that you left it in the car. He has gone to get it.'

'Then we shall all go downstairs and drink some more of your excellent sherry,' Madame Lefleur said placidly, 'and while we are doing so your maids can undo this mischievous meddling.' She turned to leave the room and Lee made to follow her, but the shock of discovering the housekeeper's malicious destruction, coupled with the earlier events of the afternoon, plus the rush to get ready, all combined to make her feel exceedingly dizzy. She clutched the door for support, her face so white that Madame Lefleur hurried anxiously to her side.

'*Petite*, it is not the end of the world. Tell her this is so, Gilles,' she insisted, 'instead of standing there glowering like a tyrant! The poor child is close to fainting. Gilles, where is your room?'

Once in motion, Madame was as impossible to stop as an avalanche. Lee was swept back to her room. A *tisane* was ordered, and Gilles was banished to take care of his guests, while Lee recovered.

'It is a difficult time when one carries one's first *bébé*,' Madame Lefleur commented reminiscently.

Lee's cup clattered on to her saucer, her eyes round and frightened. She had thought her secret so safe, but the knowing eyes of another woman had perceived the truth instantly.

'No wonder Gilles frowned so,' Madame continued blithely. 'You must take care, *petite*.'

'Gilles doesn't know!' Now what on earth had made her say that? Lee bowed her head, unable to hold back her tears any longer. Wisely Madame Lefleur let her cry.

'All is not well between you,' she said at last, 'but there is love, Lee, I can tell that, and where there is love, there must also be life, *non*?' she enquired gently, touching Lee's stomach lightly, 'and hope. Now, you will dry your eyes, put on your make-up and go downstairs with your head held high, and your housekeeper will be left to wonder why her little plan has provoked no response. *Non*?'

'Where there is love . . .' The words kept repeating themselves as Lee prepared for the ball. But her love alone was not enough; and besides, Gilles did not want her. She was just a screen he was hiding behind to protect himself from Louise—Louise, his spurned mistress who had quite deliberately tried to make Lee look foolish in front of Gilles' important guests. How would *she* react when she discovered that her plans had gone awry?

Lee sighed, trying to push all personal thoughts to the back of her mind so that she could concentrate on the evening ahead.

Those guests who were staying overnight were now in their rooms preparing for dinner and the ball which would follow. Lee had already been down to check the dinner table and the ballroom, anxious lest Madame Le Bon had planned any other unpleasant surprises, but everything had been in order. She could hear Gilles moving about in the dressing room. Her dress lay across the bed, a mist of sea-green chiffon, cut low across the breasts in the Regency style, with tiny puff sleeves embroidered with pearls. Pearls for tears, she thought bleakly. She had caught her hair up on top of her head in soft ringlets, pale green ribbons threaded through them, and as Gilles emerged from the dressing room, she saw him studying her reflection in the mirror, his lips curving sardonically as he glanced from her to the gown lying on the bed.

'It is almost fitting that we should take the parts of René and his Russian bride,' he murmured cynically, 'Our circumstances are very similar. He too forced his bride into marriage.'

'But he eventually loved her.' There was more pain than Lee knew in the low words. Gilles studied her downbent head for several seconds before replying coolly, 'And she loved him—or so the romantics would have us believe.'

'But you of course know better?'

His eyebrows rose, his eyes lingering on her flushed cheeks and small fists. 'Surely you aren't saying that she *could* love him? A man who ravished her away from her family and home? A man ... like me.' His voice was harsh and Lee felt her breathing constrict. What would he say if she told him the truth? That she loved him. It was not something she could think about with any degree of composure. Already her heart was thumping heavily, her eyes glittering with unshed tears.

'Well, Lee?' Gilles taunted. 'Can a woman love the man who takes her without pity or compunction, purely to satisfy his own desires?'

He was gone before she could reply, leaving her to finish dressing in a hazy blur of mingled pain and anguish.

CHAPTER SEVEN

Now at last she could begin to relax, Lee thought, expelling her breath slightly.

Throughout the meal she had been on tenterhooks lest anything go wrong, but to judge from the relaxed hum of conversation all around her, their guests had thoroughly enjoyed their meal. At the far end of the table, Gilles' dark head was turned towards one of their guests, and she could observe him without him being aware of it. In the uniform of Napoleon's hussars he looked so magnificently male that her treacherous heart had trembled with aching desire for his love. Her fingers crept to the pearls encircling her throat. Gilles had placed them there before dinner. When he left their room she had thought he would not return, but he did, carrying the small, flat jeweller's box which had held the pearls René de Chauvigny had given to his bride.

'My ancestress would have it that René gave her these as a symbol of his own tears, cried when he realised how much he had harmed her.'

'But you can't mean me to wear them,' Lee had protested.

'Why not? You are my wife. It is expected that you should have some jewellery besides your rings.'

Mention of these reminded Lee of Drew's diamond, which still had to be returned to him, and she had asked Gilles to give it to her.

'Why?' he had demanded coldly. 'You cannot wear it.'

She could not explain to him that she had wanted to send the ring back to Drew, she thought on a sigh. The man seated to her left had drunk deeply of Gilles' wine and Lee had already had to remove his clammy hand from her thigh twice. He had come alone and she remembered Gilles telling her that he was recently divorced. Lee did not care for him very much, and she was glad to be able to escape to the drawing room.

Louise had come dressed as Josephine. She had waylaid Gilles by the door, fluttering her ostrich fan provocatively as she slid her fingers along his arm.

'That one has no self-respect,' Madame Lefleur commented critically. 'She thinks only of appeasing her own desires. Gilles had a fortunate escape.'

'She is very beautiful,' Lee commented unthinkingly.

Her companion's eyes widened. 'Surely you are not jealous of her? Why, it is obvious that Gilles feels nothing but disgust for her. Why do you not tell him about the baby?' she said softly. 'You cannot doubt that he will be pleased.'

Couldn't she? If she was the pure, unsullied bride of impeccable family whom he had wanted, *then* no doubt he would have been pleased. But she wasn't. She was just the girl he had married ... Her heart jerked suddenly as though it were on strings. She *was* the girl he had married, and if her child was a son, in law it would stand to inherit Gilles' title and possessions. She glanced fearfully at her husband, still talking to Louise, his expression remote and withdrawn. No, he must not find out about the baby, otherwise he might try and take it from her.

'*Chérie*, are you all right? You look so pale. They are not easy, these first months . . .'

Madame Lefleur looked so concerned that Lee

forced a small smile.

'It's nothing, and I'm very healthy.'

'Well, may I suggest that you rescue your poor husband from Louise before she devours him completely?'

Remembering the state of the guest bedroom, Lee had to stifle a small stab of satisfaction as she saw Louise studying her covertly. Had she hoped to bring Gilles' wrath down upon her head by urging the housekeeper into the wanton act of destruction, or had it been wholly the other woman's idea? Perhaps she would never know.

'Louise.' Lee smiled coolly at her, her own fingers touching Gilles' arm lightly as she drew his attention away from the redhead and to herself.

'It is time for us to open the ball.'

Whatever else one might say about Gilles, she could not deny that he was a first-rate actor, Lee thought bitterly. His smile for her was slow and sensual, the touch of his lips against her fingers as he lifted them to his mouth and brushed them lightly that of a possessive lover. Louise glared at them, her lips thinning slightly as she looked assessingly at Lee.

'You are putting on weight, *chérie*,' she said spitefully. 'You will have to be careful,' she warned Gilles, 'otherwise you will have a dumpy wife, *mon ami*.'

'Dumpy?' To Lee's astonishment Gilles' eyebrows rose mockingly, his voice a soft purr as he murmured seductively, 'Oh come, Louise, you exaggerate. As Lee's husband, I can assure you that there is nothing about her body that does not give me the utmost delight.'

Several people had overheard them and turned to smile at Lee, who felt hot colour suffusing her cheeks.

'How would you say that!' she protested as Gilles

placed her arm through his and led her on to the newly polished parquet floor.

The musicians struck up a waltz and Lee was swung round to face the cool grey eyes, Gilles' arm resting determinedly against her waist.

'What would you have had me say?' he enquired in bored accents. 'That I did not feel the least desire for you? My dear Lee,' he told her dryly, 'our guests are sophisticated men and women of the world, they would not have believed me for a second.'

'Then what will you tell them when I'm gone?' she asked bitterly.

'We will not speak of this now.' He was angry and Lee quivered in his arms. 'Oh, for God's sake,' he demanded harshly, 'what do you think I'm going to do to you? Ravish you in front of all our guests?'

The music stopped and suddenly Lee was set free. She could see Gilles' dark blue-coated back disappearing as he mingled with the other costumed dancers and her eyes grew dark with pain. A passing waiter hovered with a tray of fluted champagne glasses. So great had been Lee's desire to repeat that earlier ball in every detail that even this touch had been faithfully reproduced, and she drank the sparkling liquid with a recklessness which was totally out of character. She didn't care, she told herself as she consumed her second glass. She didn't care what happened. Gilles was dancing with Louise and her eyes seemed to devour him. The woman was repellent, Lee thought with a shudder, unaware of how young and innocent she herself looked in her pale green gown, her hair caught up to reveal the tender nape of her neck.

'Dance with me, sweet seductress?'

It was the man who had been seated next to her at dinner, and unwillingly Lee agreed. He held her too tightly, his hot breath fanning her face.

'Gilles is a lucky devil to have a bride like you. So innocent in looks—and yet if I know Gilles he will have lost no time in initiating you into the ways of love. But now he seeks fresh pastures with Madame Louise, but you and I will comfort one another.'

Before Lee could stop him he had manoeuvred her out on to one of the small wrought iron balconies overlooking the gardens, and although she protested hotly, she was not strong enough to prevent him from raining moist, loathsome kisses on her exposed shoulders and face.

His hand was reaching towards her breast, and Lee clawed desperately to be free, falling back against the balcony, when he was suddenly pulled away from her and she was blessedly free of his unpleasant embrace.

'A thousand pardons, Gilles,' her attacker muttered thickly. 'Your wine . . . the loveliness of your wife . . .'

'And what is your excuse?' Gilles demanded coldly when the other man had hurried away.

Lee's eyes widened angrily.

'My *excuse*? You surely can't have thought that I wanted him to kiss me?'

'You didn't seem to be doing much objecting from where I was standing.'

Lee shivered, suddenly cold.

'You've already made one false assumption about me, Gilles,' she reminded him quietly. 'Don't make any more.'

'I wondered when you were going to throw that in my face.' His savagery seemed to reach out and hold her prisoner on the small balcony. 'You gave yourself to me willingly enough, for all that you were a virgin.' His mouth twisted bitterly. 'What am I supposed to think? I know too well the torment of unquenched desire, the need to slake it, no matter what the cost.' His voice had dropped; he was almost talking to himself. Lee went white and clutched at the supporting rail behind her. Was that how it had been for him with her? A desire which had to be slaked no matter what amount of self-loathing might follow?

'No!' The anguished cry burst past her lips and she took one unsteady step forward followed by another, intent only on seeking the privacy of her room to hide from Gilles before he forced her to admit the truth, but a strange grey mist seemed to be reaching out for her, all round her anxious voices, and then nothing but a sensation of falling . . . falling endlessly, until her downward swoop was stopped by something hard and warm.

'Are you feeling better now, *chérie*?'

The soft, concerned voice was familiar and Lee struggled to remember why, her forehead puckered in a frown.

'Madame Lefleur!'

She hadn't realised she had said the name out loud until her companion smiled. 'Please call me Dominique. You gave us all a fright, fainting like that.'

'Gilles?' Lee lifted her head from the pillow, astounded to find she was wearing only a flimsy nightdress.

'He has returned to his guests.'

Of course—the ball! What must everyone think of her?

'I'm afraid your secret is no longer your own,' Dominique told her, answering her unspoken question. 'Fortunately one of your guests is a doctor and he was able to soothe all the very natural fears of the father-to-be.'

When Lee gave a faint, anguished moan, she added gently, 'I'm afraid you will have some explaining to do, *chérie*. He hid it well, but he was not pleased, I think, to discover his paternity in this fashion. Your guests of course are all enchanted, and Gilles has had to endure much teasing upon the subject of his virility. I shall leave you now,' she said briskly. 'Do not be afraid. Gilles is a just and compassionate man, Lee, I cannot think he would treat you unkindly.'

'But he'll want his child.' Tears rolled down her face, and Dominique stared at her, frowning.

'Of a surety, *petite*.' Her brow cleared and for the first time she looked severe. 'You were not planning to deprive him of it? That would be unfair, and somehow I think not like you. I shall leave you to sleep and perhaps think on the advantages to your child of having both parents to watch over it.'

Sleep had never been farther away. The night was warm, balmy almost, and Lee curled up in a chair beside the window, watching the moonlight play on the still waters of the moat. How different things would be if Gilles really loved her, if this child was really wanted. There were sounds of activity in the courtyard, cheery 'goodnights' and car engines starting. Wrapped in her own thoughts, Lee was barely aware of the bedroom door opening and of Gilles surveying her fragile body, her head resting on the knees she had pulled up to her chin. He moved and she turned, her eyes widening, mirroring her fear. Without a word Gilles closed the door. Tonight he looked older, and Lee trembled as he came towards her.

Sitting down made her feel at a disadvantage and she scrambled to her feet, remembering too late the sheer nightdress.

Gilles drew in a sharp breath and mirrored in the

window Lee saw her own reflection and knew the reason for it. Without the cloak of her clothes the slight swell of her stomach was clearly visible, as was the heavy ripeness of her breasts, and as though aware of the import of the moment the new life inside her fluttered and kicked, the tiny movement suspending her breath.

'So it is true.' The harsh words brought her back to reality, her hands going instinctively to her stomach.

'No! Let me look at you.' Her hands were wrenched away as Gilles' eyes travelled the length of her body.

'My child,' he said thickly at last, 'and you weren't even going to tell me. No wonder you were so anxious to leave here! What were you going to do? A discreet operation? Or has it gone too far for that? An orphanage perhaps, or did you hope to persuade your Brahmin to accept it into his family?'

Before Lee could stop him the nightdress had been torn from her with a rage that Gilles was making no attempt to hide, and she shrank back as he reached for her. His hands were surprisingly gentle, touching the changed contours of her body, in a manner which in another man would be almost reverent. Lee trembled as he spread his fingers over the gentle swell of her womb.

'You will not harm my child,' he told her huskily, 'if I have to watch over you night and day to make sure you don't.'

Lee had expected him to want the child once it was born, but this emotion—this was something she had not visualised.

'I had no intention of harming the baby,' she told him angrily. 'What sort of woman do you think I am, Gilles? But I still want my freedom,' she told him bravely.

'No!' His hands tightened and Lee gasped as she felt the child kick protestingly. Gilles released her. 'What . . .?'

'That was your son, or daughter,' she told him lightly. He had gone very pale, and she had the ridiculous urge to comfort him, because it was plain that he thought he had hurt her. 'He or she doesn't like being squeezed so hard.'

'You mean . . .' His eyes had fastened on her body, and Lee smiled, surprised to find herself so free of embarrassment, so almost maternal.

'Babies don't just lie there and do nothing,' she told him teasingly, 'They kick. And this one kicks very hard!'

All at once she felt very tired. The evening had been a long one.

'The dinner . . . Everything went well, I hope?' she asked sleepily, walking towards the bed. 'The buyers . . .'

'Were full of compliments,' Gilles told her absently. 'Lee, this . . . this child changes everything. You realise if it is a boy he will be my heir?'

'Yes!' Her heart seemed to be being squeezed in some giant vice.

'Our marriage must continue, Lee,' Gilles told her in a hard voice. 'You must realise this?' His eyes darkened suddenly. '*Parbleu*, I have it! You knew what I would say and this was why you kept your condition secret from me!'

'You were the one who said that marriage and children were a serious matter,' Lee reminded him. 'All I want for my child is love, Gilles, not position or possessions, just love.'

There was a strange look on his face, almost darkly brooding as he turned to watch her his fingers once more tracing the outline of her stomach.

'And you think I will not give him that?' His voice was oddly low. He bent suddenly and touched his lips to her burgeoning flesh. 'On the contrary,' he muttered huskily, tracing her rounded outline with soft kisses.

His touch seemed to ignite her flesh, and flames of desire burned through her, compelling her to reach out and run trembling fingers through the night-darkness of his hair, pressing him closer to her body.

'What the hell are you doing to me, Lee?' he groaned thickly. 'Don't you know what it's doing to me, seeing you like this? My child growing inside you?'

Lee didn't reply. She could not. Was he saying that he found her pregnancy exciting? That he desired her? A terrible weakness invaded her body. Common sense told her to resist him, but how could she heed common sense when Gilles was lifting her in his arms, carrying her gently to the bed, and placing her gently on it while slowly and deliberately he began to arouse her yielding flesh.

This time there was no heated urgency, no fierce demanding clamour for appeasement. This time she was floating on a warm buoyant sea. But all seas have tides, and soon she felt the insistent pull of hers, her fingers stroking the hard warmth of Gilles' shoulders, burrowing in the hair shadowing his chest.

'Lee,' he groaned protestingly, when she touched his stomach, so lean and flat. His breath was warm against her breasts, tender now and acutely sensitive to his touch.

He was gentle with her, almost tender, and yet still arousing her to a point where nothing mattered save that he possess her, completely and absolutely, and although she was too proud to tell him so herself, her body did it for her, her response as deeply passionate as it had been that first time, only now the pleasure was prolonged, drawn out until she thought she would die from it.

'There is no going back now, Lee,' Gilles told her softly as she slid into sleep, 'so you had best make up your mind to admit that you do desire me.'

'Even though there's no love?'

The words slipped out drowsily, threaded with pain.

'There is love,' Gilles told her in a deep voice. 'For the life we have created together.'

And as she fell asleep Lee's last thoughts were envious ones of her child, who already possessed what Gilles would never give her—his love.

The moment she woke up Lee knew that something was different. For a start, she was not alone in the bed. And then the memory came flooding back, and she turned her head and saw Gilles lying at her side, his hair tousled with sleep, a dark shadow lying along his jaw. In sleep he looked curiously vulnerable. Suppressing a desire to touch him, she slid out of the bed, padding round the room quietly as she collected her clothes and headed for the bathroom.

The sting of the water did much to dissipate the feeling of languor with which she had awoken and she lingered longer than usual under the shower. Against her will her eyes were drawn to her body.

'Is it your condition that disgusts you, or the fact that it's my child?'

The harsh words held her motionless and she stared at Gilles, shock sending the blood drumming through her veins as her eyes slid feverishly over his naked body.

His eyes began to darken as he stared at her damp body, and Lee knew from the pulsating response he evoked within her that he wanted her.

'No!' Her moaned protest was ignored. She retreated into the shower, thinking that Gilles would never follow her into the small enclosed space, but he did, reaching for her with a hunger that surprised her. She knew that men could feel desire without love, but the intensity of Gilles'—especially after last night— puzzled her. It was as though what had happened then had merely been an appetiser before the main meal.

'Don't tell me you don't want me, Lee,' he ordered thickly as she tried to escape him. 'And don't tell me you're not going to let me make love to you, when every movement of your body urges me to possess you.'

'Make love?' Lee demanded hysterically, seizing on the two words which had caused her the most pain. 'How can you call it that?' Tears blurred her vision, but she could feel the heat of Gilles' anger. His hands slid over her back, moulding her against him, letting her know that she had aroused him.

'I don't want you!' She knew the words were a lie, but somehow she had to hold on to her sanity, to prevent herself from being sucked down into the quagmire of passion that would leave her physically fulfilled but mentally aching for something more than mere sexual satisfaction.

'You don't?' His voice held silky enquiry, but he released her quite readily, watching her as she reached for a towel.

She left him in the bathroom, wishing she had some means of locking him in while she finished dressing. Although he had released her, passion has still smouldered deep in his eyes. Louise had already hinted that she would find it difficult to satisfy his sensual appetite, and now Lee was beginning to think she had been right. Before, when their marriage was only to be temporary, he had held aloof, no doubt not wanting the complications that a sexual relationship could bring, but now, with her carrying his child and their marriage permanent, it was obvious that he had cynically decided that she could take over Louise's role. Well, she would not! Her fingers trembled as she dried herself quickly. Keeping one eye on the bathroom door, she searched feverishly for the oil she was using on her tenderly stretched skin. Busily engrossed in this task, she wasn't aware of Gilles standing behind her until she felt his breath stir her hair. She moved forward, but she was not quick enough; Gilles' arms imprisoned her, his chest hard and warm against her back.

'What are you doing?' His eyes lingered on the satin gleam of her skin, and looking down at her own body, Lee acknowledged with a heavily thumping heart that her actions might unknowingly have seemed provocative to an onlooker. Even so her cheeks burned. If they were to stay married she would demand separate rooms. She could not endure this intimacy for much longer, even though the thought of its cessation made her ache slightly inside.

'It's to prevent stretch marks,' she explained nervously, reaching for the bottle. 'Gilles, I should like my own room,' she added.

'Why?' His eyes were fastened on her body and she licked her lips nervously. 'You do not wish me to watch my child growing inside you?'

His words touched her with the knowledge that she did. To hide her reaction she said lightly, 'Many men find the sight of pregnant women unpleasant.'

'And you wish to save me from this unpleasantness?' His tone told her that he did not believe her, and to Lee's dismay he removed the bottle she had been holding and uncapping it poured some of the clear liquid into his palm, and holding her imprisoned against him with one hand, began slowly to massage the taut skin of her stomach with the other.

'I do not find the sight of you swelling with my child unpleasant, Lee,' he told her harshly. 'On the contrary, I find it unbearably erotic.' His hands cupped her breasts, the warm contact with his skin hardening her nipples immediately. 'Like the grapes your skin has taken on a new bloom.' He was smoothing the oil rhythmically into her body and Lee felt herself melting helplessly beneath his arousing touch. She wanted to protest that he had no right to touch her like this, but every nerve end was quivering in heated response to him. 'They always say that morning is the best time to make love,' he muttered hoarsely as he stopped caressing her and picked her up. 'Hate me all you like, Lee, but you can't deny you want me.'

It was true, she could not. Tears stood out in her eyes as she stared helplessly at the dark head fastened against her breast. There was something almost obsessive about his desire for her, something that reached out into the innermost recesses of her own soul, and yet terrified her in its intensity.

'It's obscene!' she protested hysterically. 'You're degrading me!'

His hands stilled and she was jolted upright to stare into furious grey eyes.

'My God!' he breathed angrily. 'I've a good mind to teach you exactly what that word means!'

Beyond reasoning Lee lashed back bitterly, 'You already have! You accuse me of lax morals and worse, impregnate me with your child, use me to slake your desire . . . What else could there be?'

'This!' he ground out between clenched teeth, forcing her mouth to part in a kiss that humiliated her with its ice-cold contempt, lacerating her soft flesh, and stifling her small pained moans. Even then Lee could not believe that he meant to take her; her mind could simply not comprehend that any man could use such savagery against a woman, but she was soon disabused of this foolish notion.

'The baby!' she moaned protestingly at one point, terrified by the violence she glimpsed in Gilles' face. His bitter laugh jarred on her raw nerves.

'He's safe enough, madame wife. You had the option of admitting that I could arouse you, that you felt desire, but you chose to deny it, to make me lower than a farmyard animal, intent only on slaking a primitive physical urge, and rather than disappoint you, that is exactly what I shall do.'

It was a lesson she would never forget, Lee thought hours later, aching and exhausted, unable to cry, unable to do anything but curse the day she had come to the Château de Chauvigny. Her body was bruised from the cold brutality of Gilles' hands, and it seemed impossible to believe that the man who had possessed her with such savage implacability was the same one who had touched her with such tender reverence the night before.

That she was in part to blame she could not deny. Calling his touch degrading had seen to unleash in Gilles a rage she had never dreamed he possessed. She would have to get up. It must be nearly lunchtime and heaven knew what excuses Gilles had made to their guests. Most of them were leaving after breakfast, and Lee only hoped that by the time she got downstairs they would all have gone. Her wan face and bruised eyes told their own story. Her skin had a bloom, he had told her, and he had crushed it carelessly underfoot, destroying it for ever. She shivered, despite the warmth of the room. From now on she would sleep in the tower room and Gilles could protest as much as he liked. If he wanted to slake his desires in future he could do so with someone else! All the love she had felt for him had been crushed and destroyed—or so she told herself as she dressed slowly, trying to instil some sort of urgency into her aching limbs.

CHAPTER EIGHT

'Now you hold the baby, Lee,' Marie-Thérèse pleaded. 'I want a photograph of you with her—and you too, Gilles. Put your arm round Lee,' she instructed. 'That's better.'

Lee went taut the moment Gilles placed his hand on her waist. They were standing outside the small Norman church in Chauvigny and the sun was shining mellowly on the ancient stones. Lee had been astonished and flattered when Marie-Thérèse and Jean-Paul had asked Gilles and herself to stand as godparents to little Claire-Jeanne, and now, holding the baby in her beautifully embroidered christening gown, Lee tried to dismiss the wave of anguish threatening to engulf her. In three months her own child would be born, and the trap which her marriage to Gilles had turned into would completely enclose her.

As she handed the small, warm bundle back to Marie-Thérèse, she smiled at the other girl. Motherhood had brought a soft bloom to her cheeks and no one looking at the small family could doubt their happiness. All the guests had been invited back to the house after the christening. Lee had spent most of the morning helping Marie-Thérèse to prepare a cold buffet, and as Gilles helped her into the car she glanced covertly at his set profile.

Since the night of the ball he had grown into a distant stranger. They still shared a room—he had insisted on that—but for all the time they were together in it they need not have done. His manner towards her was cold and remote. When he saw her he asked conscientiously after her health, and she responded in a similarly polite fashion, neither of them in any doubt that their marriage was a hell which had to be endured for the sake of their child.

'Are you all right?' She hadn't realised that he was watching her. 'You look tired,' he added abruptly. 'You mustn't do too much.'

'I'm fine.' Physically perhaps, but mentally she was not. On her last visit to the doctor he had commented in a puzzled fashion on her frail wrists and slender legs and had told her to eat plenty of good country food. It would take more than food to tempt her waning appetite, Lee admitted wryly; it would take something she was never likely to have, her husband's love. Tears blurred her eyes as she remembered how tenderly Jean-Paul had looked at his wife and child, and as she looked into Gilles' shuttered face she felt as though a door had been slammed in her face, and all her chances of happiness locked away behind it.

Louise and her father had attended the christening and were at the house when Gilles and Lee arrived.

'I have not yet congratulated you, Gilles,' Monsieur Trouville commented, with a smile. 'I have been telling Louise that it is time she remarried and provided me with some grandchildren.'

'Children!' Louise shuddered delicately, her eyes on Lee's body. 'They ruin your figure. No, Papa. It is a wife's duty to provide her husband with a son, of course, but these women who devote themselves to the upbringing of their children become so boring. Do you not find it so, Gilles?'

Thus appealed to, Gilles smiled. 'Certainly no one could imagine you becoming boring, Louise,' was his only comment. Nothing more was said, but Lee knew that Louise was subtly reminding him of all that he had given up, and perhaps that it was still there waiting for him, should he choose to take it.

'You must rest, *chérie*,' Marie-Thérèse ordered Lee. 'You look pale, and Gilles would never forgive me if you were to overtire yourself. You are all ready for the *bébé*, *non*?'

Lee shook her head. She had made no preparations for the arrival of the child, somehow hoping that by doing so she was leaving herself the option of escaping from the château and the unhappiness it held, but deep down inside she knew that this was impossible. Gilles would never allow her to leave, not now.

It was early evening before the party broke up, and Lee's back was aching from the constant standing. Marie-Thérèse and Jean-Paul came with them to the car, Marie-Thérèse frowning a little as she saw her pale face. She had grown very fond of Lee, but her feminine instincts told her that all was not well with her new friend, and they were not close enough for her to ask what was wrong.

'You must look after Lee, Gilles,' she instructed as Gilles opened the car door. 'She does not look well. It is a difficult time for a woman, especially when she is far from her family.'

Gilles turned and looked at her, and for a moment Lee thought she glimpsed bitterness in the steel grey eyes. Was he perhaps feeling resentment that he too was trapped in this travesty of a marriage?

'Is that true, *chérie*?' he asked softly, his fingers stroking her cheek gently. The imitation tenderness was for the benefit of his friends, Lee knew, but it was impossible to prevent herself from responding to his touch, her colour coming and going swiftly, as just for a moment she closed her eyes to the truth and let herself believe that *this* was real—the warmth of his fingers against her skin, the look in his eyes as he smiled down at her, the warmth of his body as he pulled her gently against him, his lips resting lightly on her temple. Lee let herself absorb his strength, giving in to the irresistible urge to close her eyes and relax against his hard chest.

'Lee?' There was sharp anxiety in the word, and his arm came tightly round her, his fingers under her chin forcing her face upwards so that her eyes opened reluctantly, her heart warmed by his sudden urgency.

'*Are* you feeling ill? The baby . . .?'

Her heart plummeted. Of course—his concern was all for his child, not for her.

'I'm just tired.' She pulled away from him, not wanting him to see the betraying sparkle of tears, not wanting the others to guess how much she had longed to prolong the physical contact that Gilles seemed only to anxious to bring to an end.

'Tomorrow I am going into Nantes,' Gilles announced abruptly as they drove away. 'I have some business there. You will need things for the baby. Would you like to come with me, or shall I send to Paris?'

'You won't mind?'

You won't mind having me with you, was what she had meant, but Gilles frowned. 'It makes no difference to me, I merely thought that you would wish to choose the things yourself. However, I do realise that my child can't be expected to arouse the same maternal delight in your breast that your ex-fiancé's might have done.' His voice had grown very hard during this speech, and for a moment Lee was tempted to tell him just how she felt about his child, but to do so would be to give herself away completely, and their relationship was already fraught with sufficient hazards without her adding the burden of her love to them.

'I should like to come with you,' she said quietly. 'I only meant that I might be in the way.'

'If that were the case I wouldn't ask you to come with me.'

He said nothing further and Lee sensed that the subject was closed. When they reached the château he disappeared in the direction of the cellars. The new wine was due to be racked off, and Lee knew that he would want to supervise this personally. She was feeling too tired to face a meal alone in the huge dining room, and instead asked for a tray to be brought to the bedroom.

One of the young maids brought it, staring round-eyed round the luxurious bedroom before placing the appetising tray on a small table.

There was some chicken and home-cured ham with a crisp green salad, and fresh strawberries with cream for dessert. Lee knew she ought to feel hungry, but she could only stare at the food apathetically. She knew what was wrong with her; she was sickening for Gilles' love. She pushed the table away and read the letter she had received from her parents that morning once more.

The news of her marriage had surprised and delighted them, and her mother had written that they hoped to fly to France after the baby's birth to see them all. She had never been particularly drawn to Drew, Lee's mother wrote, surprising Lee by adding that she had sensed in her daughter a deeply passionate nature which would not have found contentment with a man of Drew's essentially cold temperament.

That might have been so, but at least she would not have known the aching agony she was enduring now, longing for the impossible.

She was asleep when Gilles came in and not able to witness the look in his eyes as he glanced from her sleeping body to the uneaten food, his face taut with an emotion which could have been anger.

To Lee's surprise she found Gilles downstairs in the small sitting room where she normally had breakfast, and then she remembered that they were going to Nantes.

'They are bringing some fresh croissants,' he informed her, pulling out her chair. 'I have already eaten.'

'Oh, I don't want anything,' Lee started to protest, but Gilles swept her objections aside, practically standing over her while she ate two of the deliciously warm, flaky rolls spread with apricot conserve. To Lee's own surprise she quite enjoyed them, but then she did not normally have the presence of her husband at breakfast, and as Gilles poured them both a second cup of coffee, she admitted that this might have something to do with her improved appetite.

She put down her large coffee cup to find Gilles watching her. The cup was heavy and she had been holding it with both hands, breathing in the fragrance of the coffee.

'You look like a little girl,' he said sardonically.

'But I'm not. I'm a woman of twenty-two.'

A shadow seemed to pass over his face, but before Lee could question it he was standing up, muscles rippling under the knitted cotton shirt which bared his tanned forearms with their sprinkling of dark hairs.

He looked exactly what he was, she thought as he opened the door for her—a sensual, sophisticated man, impervious to the uncertainties which beset lesser mortals.

Nantes was a bustling city, far larger than Lee had imagined, and she was just beginning to wonder how she was going to manage not to lose herself when Gilles surprised her by announcing that he would accompany her while she did her shopping.

'But your business . . .'

'A visit to a wine shipper which will take no more than half an hour at the most. We shall go there after lunch. If I do not come with you, you will tire yourself out doing far too much. You seem to forget that you are with child. Or is it that you wish you could forget?'

'I wish I could forget everything!' Lee burst out, very close to tears. It was ridiculous, but she was growing jealous of her own child; jealous of Gilles' care and concern for it, when he made no attempt to conceal his contempt of her. 'I wish I'd never come to Chauvigny; never allowed myself to be blackmailed into this farce of a marriage; and most of all never conceived your child!'

She watched Gilles turn white and would have walked away from him, driven to escape the fury in his eyes, if he had not had hold of her wrist.

'You listen to me!' he told her through gritted teeth. 'Hate me as much as you wish, Lee, but the child is innocent of any crime, and you will never, never allow it to know that it was ever resented by its mother.'

'A mother whom its father despises,' Lee reminded him bitterly. 'Gilles, let me go home. Divorce me . . .'

'And allow my child to be brought up by another? Never!'

Lee knew that for her own sanity she ought to consider giving up the child into Gilles' custody, but merely to contemplate such an action caused her the most acute pain. Just as Gilles would not allow his child to grow up away from Chauvigny, neither could she give it up to the woman Gilles would marry in her place—a woman who could never love either of them as much as she did.

In a hostile silence Gilles directed her towards an exclusive arcade of shops.

In one of them Lee pored over beautiful coach-built prams and broderie anglaise-festooned cribs, all so expensive that she turned regretfully from them to more practical items, but to her surprise Gilles lingered, drawing her attention to a delightful cradle that rocked gently when touched.

'The baby would grow out of it very quickly,' Lee commented regretfully, but to her surprise, instead of turning away, Gilles said to the saleswoman, 'My wife likes it, although her puritan English streak will not permit her to say so. We will take it. The baby may quickly outgrow it, but there will be others.'

Lee had picked up enough French to follow the conversation, and her eyes widened at this blatant untruth. Gilles had adopted a personality she barely recognised. The nursery was going to be the most lavishly equipped she had ever seen, and eventually, when the saleswoman's arms were full of fluffy toys of all descriptions, Lee took a back seat and let Gilles get on with it.

'They are always like this with the first,' the woman told Lee with a smile, 'these proud, doting papas.'

Gilles, proud? Doting? Lee took another look at him. He seemed to be enjoying himself hugely.

'We shan't need that!' she gasped when he insisted on ordering a luxurious coach-built pram.

'You will want to take him for walks when it is fine,' Gilles argued. 'And this pram will be easier to push.'

It was two hours before they left the shop. When they stepped out into the autumn sunshine, Gilles

cupped a hand under Lee's elbow. Lee saw their re-
flections in a shop window—Gilles tall and protective,
herself smaller, frailer.

'Lee, I propose that we call a truce. I cannot put
aside our marriage, but I give you my word that there
will be no repetitions of the events which led to our
present *impasse*.'

'And what does that mean? That you're condemning
us both to a life of celibacy? Or that you'll resume your
relationship with Louise, safe in the knowledge that
she can no longer force you into marriage?'

Lee had never seen him so angry, and if she had not
been so bitterly hurt by what he had said she doubted
that she would ever have dared to speak so forcefully.

He swore angrily, pulling her into a shadowed arcade
so that they could not be overheard.

'Enough! You are determined to believe the worst of
me! All I was trying to do was to assure you that you
need not freeze like a glacier every time I come near
you. You are not eating. You look pale and ill . . .'

'And you think that telling me I needn't fear your
. . . your unwanted attention is going to change all
that?' Lee was close to hysteria. 'You're condemning
me to a life without love, to a marriage which is a
meaningless farce . . .'

'And what the hell am I supposed to do?' Gilles was
equally angry now. 'Let you bring up my son on your
own, for that Brahmin will not marry you now . . .'

'I wish to God I wasn't having your child, then I
could be free . . .'

The moment she uttered them Lee knew the words
to be false. She didn't want to be free; and anyway she
never could. What she wanted was for Gilles to love
her with the depth and intensity of her love for him.

Gilles had gone completely silent, his eyes like ice.

'Only this morning you told me that you were a woman, Lee. You lied. You're still a selfish, unseeing child.'

'Where are you taking me?'

He was propelling her along the pavement and she tried to hang back, reluctant to go with him.

'To lunch. I've already booked the table.'

'I'm not hungry.' Lee knew that she was being childish, and regretted the words when Gilles turned to stare coolly at her, before saying,

'Perhaps not, but you will eat. If you behave like a child, Lee, then you must expect to be treated as such. What are you trying to do?' he demanded harshly. 'Starve the child to death? Destroy it before it is even born?'

Lee went white, swaying slightly as she stared up at him. 'That's a hateful thing to say!'

'No more "hateful" than what you said yourself a few moments ago, but you will not have your freedom at the price of the baby's life, Lee, and if you were truly a woman you would not want it.'

There was nothing she could say. Those bitter, wild words had been born of her own aching need to be wanted for herself, but she could hardly explain that without betraying her love. If she was to survive this marriage she must learn to be as distant and clinical as Gilles, but how could she achieve that when every time she saw him she yearned to touch him, when even the sound of his voice made her melt with longing, and even in her dreams the memories of his lovemaking pursued her relentlessly?

The restaurant was in a luxurious new hotel block. The head waiter murmured something to Gilles, whom he quite obviously knew, and then Lee felt Gilles' hand on her arm as he guided her across acres of thick pile carpet to a table by the window where two people were already sitting.

The words, 'What are Michael and Anna doing here?' were trembling on her lips, but before she could utter them Michael was standing up, beaming down at her, and claiming the privilege of a friend by kissing her cheek.

'Surprise, surprise!' Anna said gaily when they were all sitting down. 'I was so intrigued by all that Michael told me about the Loire that we decided to spend our holiday here. We're only in Nantes for the one night, and when Michael rang the château to see if it was convenient to come and see you, I was thrilled when Gilles suggested we lunch together.'

Lee liked Anna and had always got on well with her, but for once she found conversation difficult. Gilles had said nothing to her about Michael's telephone call. Why had he not invited them to the château?

As though he had read her mind, Gilles broke off his conversation with Michael to say urbanely to Lee, '*Now* you know why I wanted you to come to Nantes with me. I didn't want to spoil the surprise by telling you beforehand. At one time I thought I was going to have to use force,' he joked with Michael, who was smiling at Lee. 'I've never known a woman so reluctant to spend her husband's money!'

Naturally Michael and Anna laughed, while Lee bent her head over the table. Gilles had arranged this lunch as a surprise for her? She could not think why, unless it was to reinforce his determination to make their marriage permanent. Perhaps he had wanted to bring home to her the fact that her friends already believed in the myth!

'We've spent the morning equipping the nursery,'

Gilles added, further confounding Lee, who flushed a little under Michael's quizzical smile, and Anna was immediately nostalgic about her own pregnancies, and their children, who were now almost grown up.

'Do you remember, Michael?' she asked her husband. 'When James was born you were in Scotland. He arrived two weeks early,' she explained to Lee, 'and I was all on my own. My parents were on holiday, and Michael's mother was staying with his sister.'

'And I've never been allowed to forget my error,' said Michael ruefully, but still smiling. It was impossible for Lee to envisage Gilles and herself in middle age with many years of marriage behind them, teasing one another about their shared past, and all at once tears blurred her eyes, the delicious fish she had been eating almost choking her as misery tightened her throat. She was glad that the others were too engrossed in their conversation to be aware of her own silence, and it wasn't until she felt Gilles' fingers on her wrist that she realised he was aware of her distress.

'I thought the sight of your friends would please you,' he told her in a low undertone, when Michael and Anna's attention was elsewhere. 'But instead you sulk like a spoiled child!'

It was impossible for Lee to explain that she wasn't sulking; and nearly as impossible for her to comprehend that this lunch had been arranged purely for her pleasure. She shot a look at Gilles. In fact she did not believe it. Why would he do anything to make her happy? Far more likely that he was thinking of his child's wellbeing!

It was a little after three o'clock when they left the restaurant, having said goodbye to Michael and Anna, who were leaving Nantes that afternoon. Lee was surprised to find that Gilles expected her to join him in the office of the wine shipper, who expressed deferential interest when Gilles informed him of Lee's training and career.

'But that of course is now all at an end,' the shipper commented. 'As Madame la Comtesse . . .'

'As Madame la Comtesse,' Gilles interrupted firmly, much to Lee's astonishment, 'my wife will naturally take her place at my side, running the château and the business. Why else do you think I married her?' he teased, smiling at Lee. 'She is going to be a considerable asset.'

On the way back to the car Lee asked hesitantly, 'Did you mean that, Gilles? About me helping you in the business, I mean?'

'Would you want to?' His eyes surveyed her, the dark head inclined politely, and her heart melted with love. 'It would mean that on occasions we would have to work closely together.' They had reached the car and he bent to unlock the door. 'Would you want that?'

Would she? Would she want the torture of his constant presence and constant unavailability?

'Your eyes give you away,' Gilles said harshly before she could reply, helping her into her seat. He leaned across to check that her door was closed securely, his bare arm brushing against her breasts. Her response was immediate and she flushed hotly, sure that he must have felt her betraying tremble.

Today had been full of surprises, and all at once she wanted to believe that Gilles had arranged the lunch with Michael and Anna for her; that he did want her working alongside him; that he did want . . . Here she stopped her wayward thoughts, saying instead the first thing that came into her mind,

'Do we have time to go to Chinon on the way back?' she asked him. She had always had a keen interest in history and a special fascination for the Plantagenets, whose castle Chinon was.

Gilles' expression was openly sardonic. 'My, my, you are growing brave if you're willing to extend your ordeal and spend further time in my company!'

Lee said nothing, too hurt by his bitter mockery to comment, and as they drove back along the road skirting the Loire she closed her eyes and leaned back in her seat. Gilles slipped a cassette into the car's hi-fi system and the sound of the Carpenters filled the silence. The day had taken its toll of her emotions and as the dying sun warmed the tinted car windows Lee slid softly into sleep.

When she opened her eyes for a moment she didn't know where she was. It was dusk and in the half light she could just make out the vague, shadowy outlines of the castle walls of Chinon. She felt warm and drowsy, and it was several seconds before she realised that she was leaning against Gilles, her head pillowed against his shoulder, his arm resting lightly on her waist.

'It seemed a pity to wake you,' was all he said as he removed his arm and allowed her to sit upright. To conceal the sense of loss brought on by the removal of his body heat Lee searched the darkness outside.

'We could walk round if you wish, although I'm afraid it's too dark to see much.'

He was right, and yet even looking at the remains of this once great fortress made the past come poignantly alive for Lee. Had Berengaria, the lovely but unloved wife of Richard the Lionheart, ever waited within those walls for her husband?

'You look sad.' It was impossible to see Gilles' expression in the gathering darkness, but the words were almost compassionate 'What were you thinking about?'

'About how arid life is without love to bring it alive,' Lee said truthfully.

'Love? You are clinging to a myth,' Gilles said harshly. 'Your response to me when we made love was unmistakable, Lee, and yet you persist in clinging to your outdated ideology. Do you honestly believe that your Brahmin shares your passionate loyalty?'

Lee turned away. What was the point of dragging Drew into their conversation?

'I'm tired, Gilles,' she told him emotionlessly. 'Please take me home.'

She wasn't aware of having spoken the betraying word, but at her side Gilles stared at her for a moment before starting the car.

'Home? Is that how you view the château, Lee?' he asked softly.

Her cheeks burned and she was glad he could not see the betraying colour.

'I was using the word loosely. What would you prefer me to call it? My prison?'

'You are perfectly free to leave,' Gilles replied equably, 'providing you leave my child behind.'

Lee stared straight ahead of her despite the darkness, her heart filled with bitterness and pain. The night the baby had been conceived was now only a memory, but for the rest of her life she would have to pay and pay again for those moments of shared passion.

Lee put down her pen and sealed the envelope with a heartfelt sigh. She would send the letter by registered post, just to be on the safe side. Now that Drew's ring was actually on the way to him, she felt a lot happier. She had told him nothing about the child and could only hope that her mother was right when she said he had a passionless nature. She didn't want to hurt him, and now she could acknowledge that she would never have made him the sort of wife his family would have expected.

Gilles was out, attending a meeting of the local wine-growers' association. The vintage had been a particularly good one. Would Gilles agree to supply Westbury's with some of his lesser quality wines? He had not discussed the matter with her, and she was too proud to ask.

When Madame Le Bon first announced Louise, Lee thought the Frenchwoman must have come to see Gilles. She was just about to explain that he was not at home, when Louise sank down into one of the antique chairs with fluid grace, stretching out a languid arm for the onyx cigarette lighter and applying the flame to one of the Turkish cigarettes she favoured. Only when she was sure the cigarette was properly lit did she relax back into her chair, her eyes narrowed as she exhaled slowly.

'So . . .' Her eyes swept Lee's body, and for the first time Lee felt awkwardly ungainly. The redhead was wearing a dress in dark green velvet, the fabric moulding her generous curves. As always her make-up was faultless, and Lee, who had been relaxing in a soft heather-toned pinafore dress over a matching lilac blouse, felt dowdy in comparison.

'You must have succeeded beyond your wildest dreams,' Louise drawled insultingly. 'Oh, come, my dear,' she added when Lee said nothing, 'you surely do not think I was ever taken in by that little charade of Gilles'? A charade which now he is heartily regretting, poor man.' A tinkling laugh assaulted Lee's ear-drums. 'But then Gilles always was far too gallant,'

Louise continued blithely. 'I remember that summer he spent with his aunt. I warned him that sixteen-year-old girls were apt to be trouble. He did not believe me—then.'

Lee tried not to let her feelings show. Louise was implying that she knew all about that long-ago summer, but surely that could not be true?

'It is true that Gilles wanted to punish me a little and so pretended this long-standing love affair with you, but you cannot have believed he wanted the marriage to be anything other than temporary?'

Delicately arched eyebrows suggested that Lee could surely not have been so stupid as to think that Gilles might have preferred her to Louise.

'Gilles is quite free to divorce me if he wishes,' Lee replied with a calm she was far from feeling. 'That he does not do so must surely tell *you* something, madame.'

For the first time Lee saw the Frenchwoman lose a little of her poise. Her eyes flashed warningly, her hands clenched at her sides. 'So!' she hissed venomously. 'You are not the little innocent we are led to believe. Well, you may have induced Gilles to continue this folly of a marriage, madame, but it will not last. For the moment he is besotted with the idea of this child you carry, but Gilles is a man, with all that the word implies.' She paused delicately, her lips curving in a reminiscent smile. 'Need I say more?'

Lee toyed blindly with the letter in front of her. Louise was right, her words only echoed Lee's own bitter thoughts. Gilles was a man—a man whose potent sexuality would demand an outlet, and who better to provide one than his ex-mistress? There would be no repetition of the events leading to the conception of the child she was carrying, was what he had said, but a man like Gilles could not remain a celibate for ever.

Gilles had said nothing about finding Louise unsatisfactory as a mistress; far from it.

'Think about what I have said, *chérie*,' Louise purred, coming across to where Lee was standing, her eyes on the envelope lying on the desk. 'You cannot deceive Gilles for ever. Soon he will discover your hopeless passion for him. That is not what he looks for in a wife,' she added scornfully. 'Or perhaps it is that you hope one day he will come to return your feelings?' She laughed scornfully. 'You silly little English girl with your foolish dreams! Gilles is a Frenchman, a member of the nobility, trained from birth not to expect to find love in his marriage. Leave before it is too late.'

She had reached the door before Lee spoke. Listening to Louise she had run the entire gamut of emotions, but now she knew what she must do. Something in Louise's very evident scorn had awakened her fighting instinct. If she must lose Gilles, then it would not be by default; by running away like a coward and refusing to face up to the truth that Gilles did not love her.

Lifting her head proudly, she smiled at Louise with cool disdain.

'Your concern is most thoughtful, madame,' she replied coolly, 'but quite unnecessary. You see, Gilles already knows that I love him.' Summoning all her acting ability, she permitted herself a small secret smile, touching her stomach lightly. 'And our child is the evidence that he returns my feelings. If you doubt me—ask him.'

She had the satisfaction of seeing Louise's smile freeze into a cold mask. She could only hope the other woman did not call her bluff, Lee thought despairingly, but something in the way she had confronted her with the knowledge of her love had given Lee the idea that Louise was less sure of Gilles than she pretended. Surely if Gilles cared as much for her as she claimed she would have already told him of Lee's feelings?

Ultimately, of course, Lee knew that she could not win, but Louise's threats and malice had sliced through the lethargy which seemed to have possessed her lately. When the Frenchwoman had gone Lee stared out into the empty gardens, now nearly denuded of flowers. Perhaps she could not have Gilles' love, but surely she would win his respect and trust, and who was to say what might not grow from those? They were frail foundations on which to build a future, but they were all she had. Placing Drew's letter in the hall for collection, she made her way upstairs for her afternoon rest, pausing for a moment beneath the portrait of René. A woman had found the key to his heart; if only she could find the key to Gilles'!

'I understand Louise called this afternoon,' Gilles commented abruptly over dinner. 'What did she want?'

'Nothing. It was just a courtesy visit,' Lee lied, wondering what he would say if she told him the truth. She had dressed with special care tonight, wearing one of the new maternity hostess gowns she had ordered from Paris. It was a soft rust velvet with cream collar and cuffs, and with her hair curling down on to her shoulders she had an almost childlike appeal, but when she had glanced in the mirror before coming downstairs she had seen only her bulky shape and awkward movements.

'I have to go to Paris for a few days. Will you be all right?'

Paris? Lee stared at him, her heart thumping heavily. Was this going to be the pattern of their days? Discreet visits to Paris for him while she was left at home?

'Don't you want me to go?'

Lee licked her dry lips. What could she say to that?
'I . . .'

'If you are worried about the baby—about being alone,
I could ask Marie-Thérèse to come and stay with you.'

I want *you*, Lee longed to say. That's all, just you,
but of course she could not do that.

'I've been deputised by our local growers' association
to talk to the Ministry of Trade about wine exports.'

'And Louise?' The moment the words were out Lee
regretted them. She bit her lip in vexation as Gilles
frowned sharply.

'What about Louise?'

Lee tried to shrug it off. 'Oh, nothing. I thought
perhaps she might be going—I know she spends a lot
of time in Paris.' She was babbling like an idiot. Gilles
threw down his napkin and walked towards her with
purposeful steps. He didn't touch her, but she shrank
back in her chair nonetheless, shaken by the depth of
the anger in his eyes.

'You thought I was going to Paris with Louise?' he
breathed furiously. 'After all I've told you? My God,
that's some imagination you've got there! What the hell
. . . Just what sort of a man do you think I am?'

He was gone before Lee could speak, leaving her
alone at the polished mahogany dining table, her face
as white as the damask napkin Gilles had thrown down
next to a glass of wine the rich, ruby colour of blood.

When she woke up in the morning Gilles had gone,
and the tears she had not dared to shed the night before
made her throat and eyes ache. She forced herself to
get up and go about her normal duties, the whole time
her thoughts on Gilles—and how much she loved him.

CHAPTER NINE

Lee glanced out into the courtyard. There had been a sharp frost during the night and the cobblestones were still faintly rimed. Gilles' stallion poked his head over his stable door. No doubt the animal was missing his morning ride. Gilles would not be back for another two days and Lee missed him even though their daily contact was minimal.

After lunch she walked through the gardens. The leaves were already falling, only the clipped yew hedges still green. Autumn was such a sad season, permeated with nostalgia for the dying year. A tide of melancholy swept her as she glanced up at the château walls. If she was not such a coward she would pack her bags and leave, but she could not endure the thought of never seeing Gilles again, even though she knew her love was hopeless.

She paused by the moat watching the swans, too bulky to bend down with any ease. Someone hailed her and she turned, surprised to see Madame Le Bon hurrying towards her across the velvet turf.

She was out of breath when she reached Lee, panting slightly. '*Madame*, it is the wine,' she announced anxiously. 'Pierre wishes to consult with you. He is in the far cellar. I will come with you—it is dark and you may lose your footing.'

The wine! Lee felt her heart contract uneasily. The first weeks after the vintage were fraught with tension and anxieties. But what could she do? She knew little about the fermentation process, and certainly not enough to advise Pierre, who had been making wine before she was born.

As she hurried in the housekeeper's wake she wondered if this unexpected show of anxiety about her condition meant that the cold war the woman had been waging was at an end. She certainly hoped so. Once or twice lately she had come close to suggesting to Gilles that they dispensed with her services altogether, but each time she remembered that the woman had no other home apart from the château. Now she was glad that she had kept silent.

Lee had not been in the cellars since the vintage. Even though the afternoon had been cool and she was wearing a thick cardigan she shivered convulsively as she stepped out of the sunlight into the cold murkiness within. Even the electric light the housekeeper snapped on did little to banish Lee's growing feeling of apprehension. She told herself that she was being foolish, but the moment the huge wooden door swung to behind them, she had an instinctive and overwhelming urge to push it open again and admit the daylight.

There was no sign of Pierre in the main cellar which housed the huge vats of wine. Madame Le Bon made her way unerringly past them, pausing to wait for Lee who was following her reluctantly. The cellars had once extended beneath the entire château, but many of them had been walled up for safety. Even so, when the housekeeper stepped into a narrow, arched tunnel, fear seized Lee by the throat and she longed to turn and run.

'*Madame!*'

Only the housekeeper's precise, dry voice halted her, and she shivered as she skirted dust-encrusted wine racks, barely glancing at their priceless contents, even though those same bottles anywhere else would have aroused all her professional curiosity and excitement.

Something moved on the cellar floor, and she bit back a scream.

'*Alors*, these mice!' the housekeeper commented, unmoved. 'Pierre must get himself a cat.'

Mice! Lee cringed. She wasn't really frightened of the small, furry creatures, but there was something about the combination of being so far underground, the long shadows cast by the single dim electric bulb, and the unidentifiable scuttering noises that destroyed her normal calm, good sense.

'Surely Pierre can't be down here?' she protested when the housekeeper unlocked an arched wooden door at the end of the passage and stood aside for Lee to precede her. 'I think you must have it wrong, and he's waiting for me in the château.'

'*Non*. He said you were to meet him down here,' the housekeeper assured her firmly, as Lee stepped hesitantly into the small room beyond the door.

It was completely empty, but by the time Lee's eyes had grown sufficiently accustomed to the dark to perceive this for themselves, it was too late. The huge door had closed behind her, and as she stood there, frozen with disbelief, she heard the housekeeper turning the key in the lock.

'Now, Madame la Comtesse, let us see if you still as determined to remain at the château!' Lee heard her call triumphantly, the sound flattened by the thick wood. 'You may call all you wish,' she added callously when Lee begged her to open the door. 'No one ever comes down here.'

The door was too thick for Lee to hear the sound of her retreating footsteps, but her imagination painted the picture vividly enough. Shivering with fear and horror, Lee felt the darkness press down on her, stifling her with the threat of all the unrecognisable horrors it might conceal. All her childhood fears of the dark came rushing back in a wave which made her claw frantically at the wood, even though logic told her that it was an impassable barrier. Only when her nails were broken and her fingers torn did she drop numbly to the cold stone floor of the cellar, her head cradled on her arms as she gave way to her terror. What would happen to her? Had the housekeeper gone mad? Did she intend to leave her down here for the rest of her life? Now, when it was too late, Lee remembered the untouched dust on the bottles and the passage floor. People used that passage seldom, if ever. She could die here and no one would ever know. She must not give way to hysteria. Of course she would be found. The housekeeper was just playing a cruel trick on her, thought up no doubt by Louise. A trick to frighten her into leaving the château . . . If she was ever allowed to leave it alive. Gilles was away, but in view of their situation he would not be entirely surprised to return and find her gone, her clothes packed and taken away somewhere by Louise and her ally. It would be a simple matter for them to invent a phone call, and a taxi. No one would ever be any the wiser . . . until it was far too late.

Lee stifled a small sob. For all she knew the woman could be on the other side of that door, listening for signs that she was giving way to her fear. Something scuttled past her feet, and she jumped up with a terrified scream. Shaking and trembling, she backed away from the door, stopping only when she felt the cold roughness of the stone wall behind her. She was going to die, alone in this black prison which embodied all her worst nightmares.

Suddenly the baby kicked, and as she covered the

small movement instinctively Lee felt her terror die away. She was being foolish, Louise might want Gilles, but she would hardly go to the lengths of committing murder to get him. No, all she probably intended to do was to give Lee a fright; force her into fleeing the château, preferably before Gilles returned. The phone call and the taxi were probably very much a part of Louise's plan, but real and not fictional. All she had to do was keep calm and simply wait. The darkness which was so terrifying could not hurt her. It held no horrors; no fearsome creatures waiting to destroy her. Forcing herself to keep calm, she made her way blindly round the small room, touching the cold stones, and dismayed at one point to find them damp, running with a trickle of water. The room was about six feet square. She paced it slowly, telling herself that any small creatures she might disturb would be far more terrified of her than she needed to be of them.

It was growing colder by the minute and she forced herself to keep walking, swinging her arms to try and keep warm, and trying not to remember all the appallingly sad stories she had ever read about people imprisoned in the Bastille, sometimes for an entire lifetime.

She licked her lips. They were dry. She felt very thirsty—and hungry. How long had she been down here? One hour? Two? She had no way of knowing; no means of discovering how long Louise intended to draw out her torture. Remembering the look on the Frenchwoman's face at the end of their last interview, Lee reflected that she would not be inclined to be merciful. The baby moved again, and she was filled with a fresh fear.

All the growing love she had felt for Gilles' child during the months she had been carrying it crystallised in a surge of protective fear, and she suddenly realised what high stakes Louise was gambling for. If she did not leave as Louise must hope, and told Gilles what had happened, it must surely mean an end to Louise's chances of reinstating herself in Gilles' life? Gilles might not care what happened to *her*. But he did care about his child—passionately!

Fresh tears welled, as the panic she was trying to bank down welled up and her hands reached convulsively for the locked door. She banged on it frantically, waiting in a silence that tortured her eardrums for some sort of response, shouting until she was hoarse, in the forlorn hope that someone might actually venture down here and be alerted to her plight. Not for nothing did Madame Le Bon carry all the household keys, and now, when it was too late, Lee remembered that she had actually had to unlock the door leading to the passage—something which surely would not have been necessary were the cellar in constant usage. Her thoughts rushed backwards and forwards, tormenting her until her head ached with the effort of trying to think. She stopped pacing for a moment and realised that she was shivering with cold, her fingers already almost numb. She reached for the door again and then slumped back forlornly. What was the use? No one was going to hear her. Tears welled and she sank to the floor, curling up into a small ball, listening for the longed-for sound of another human being, until exhaustion claimed her and she fell into an uneasy sleep.

'You say Lee is missing, but where can she have gone?' Marie-Thérèse was puzzled. It was true that she had not warned Lee that she might visit her, but with Gilles away in Paris she had thought Lee might be lonely, but now the housekeeper was telling her that Lee was not in the château.

'Not gone, but missing,' the cook protested fiercely. All three of them were in the kitchen, where Marie-Thérèse had gone thinking she might find Lee. 'Madame was not in her room when Claire took up her tea,' she told Marie-Thérèse. 'Always she lets me know if there is to be any change, but today, nothing. She is missing Monsieur le Comte and has perhaps wandered away from the château. Every afternoon she walks, but always she has returned by this time.'

'Have you looked for her?' Marie-Thérèse demanded worriedly. The cook's words had reactivated her own fears that Lee had something on her mind, and might have been less careful than she would normally be. Anything could have happened to her.

The housekeeper shrugged sourly.

'Madame la Comtesse is mistress here, it is not for us to question her whereabouts.'

'But she did not tell you she was going out,' Marie-Thérèse insisted, 'and now she cannot be found?' When the housekeeper did not answer she walked purposefully towards the door. 'I am going to telephone Monsieur le Comte and my husband. We must search the house and land for Madame.' She held out her hand to the housekeeper. 'I shall take the keys and go through every room. You will organise the men to search the gardens and fields.'

Marie-Thérèse nearly lost her temper when the woman appeared reluctant to part with her keys. Her manner was so surly that she did not trust her to search the rooms herself. It was almost as though she wanted some misfortune to befall Lee, she thought anxiously, her heart missing a beat.

Jean-Paul managed to get hold of Gilles by telephoning first his hotel, and then the Ministry, who eventually tracked him down at a reception.

When he came to the phone his voice was curt, but when Jean-Paul outlined the position, he announced that he was returning immediately.

When he had hung up Gilles did not immediately leave the luxurious study of his host, but instead stared unseeingly out on to the wide, gracious Faubourg, his face taut and white.

'Gilles!' The Minister stopped dead as he observed his face. 'Is something wrong?'

'A personal matter.' The words were terse. 'I must leave immediately, but first, may I use your phone? I have a couple of calls to make.'

The Minister agreed instantly and when he had gone Gilles picked up the receiver. There was only one taxi firm in Chauvigny, and the Paris train stopped there twice a day. When he had assured himself that Lee had not made use of either of these escape routes, he took a taxi, to his hotel, and within half an hour of receiving Jean-Paul's call was on his way back to Chauvigny, driving down the long, straight roads at a speed which—even for a Frenchman—bordered on the suicidal.

The moment he pulled up in the courtyard the door opened, his drawn face illuminated in the beam of light as he demanded curtly, 'Have you found her?'

Jean-Paul shook his head. He had been dreading this moment, trying to put himself in his friend's place. Gilles' self-control was phenomenal, but maintaining it had drawn grooves either side of his mouth and thrust into prominence the bones of his face, making it all planes and angles.

'We have searched everywhere. I have sent Marie-Thérèse home, but the men and I have combed the fields, the wood, the house, even the wine cellar.'

'Madame would never go down there alone,' Pierre interrupted positively. When Gilles frowned he shrugged apologetically. 'Forgive me, but I could not help but notice her reaction when she came down once with Jean-Paul. She tried to hide it, but she was frightened. It is being underground—it affects some people like that.'

'And no one has seen her? No one at all? Summon all the staff,' Gilles instructed Pierre tersely. 'She cannot have simply disappeared. Someone must have seen something.'

'We have talked to them already, Gilles,' Jean-Paul said gently. 'The last time she was seen was during the afternoon. She was walking in the garden with Madame Le Bon.'

Gilles turned to the housekeeper.

'What time was this?'

She replied as calmly as she could. When she locked Lee in the cellar all she had intended to do was to frighten her into leaving the château as Madame Louise had planned, but Marie-Thérèse had taken the keys from her and now Jean-Paul had them, and she was too terrified to admit that she had.

'We will search again,' Gilles decided. 'The château is a large house and it is possible that something may have been overlooked on the first occasion.'

Jean-Paul shook his head compassionately. 'Do you not think it would be wiser to alert the police, *mon ami*?' he suggested, but Gilles shook his head.

'If you will go through the château, Pierre and I will search outside. I see you already have the keys.'

Jean-Paul nodded. 'Yes, but Marie-Thérèse could not find doors to fit these.'

He held up two keys, and Pierre stepped forward, examining them frowningly.

'These open the door to the cellar where we keep the old wines, and the small one beyond it that is no longer in use.'

'Has anyone searched them?' Gilles' voice was clipped. No one noticed Madame Le Bon pale and shake visibly at his question.

Pierre scratched his head. 'But she cannot be down there! There is no reason . . .'

Gilles strode out before he could finish, Jean-Paul hot on his heels.

In her haste Madame Le Bon had neglected to lock the door to the wine cellar behind her, and it swung open at Gilles' touch, the solitary light bulb which had cast such horrifying shadows for Lee clearly illuminating the dusty bottles.

'Someone has been down here.' Gilles was studying the bottle Lee had leaned against when the mouse frightened her. 'Give me the keys for the store-room,' he demanded tersely.

Jean-Paul and Pierre hung back as Gilles unlocked the wooden door. How on earth could Lee be down here? The door swung open and in the darkness they could see nothing, except Gilles' back as he bent down and slowly lifted something into his arms. 'Call the doctor,' he commanded curtly.

Lee was cold. Not just cold, but frozen. She had been warm, drifting in a soft safe world, but someone was trying to drag her away from it. She protested soundlessly, twisting away from the hard fingers on her shoulder, and then all at once the reality she had been trying so hard to forget burst upon her. She cried protestingly, blinking in the electric light as she opened her eyes, relief flooding through her as she realised that she was no longer locked up in that terrifying dark prison from which she had thought she would never escape.

'Gilles!'

The man carrying her stopped and Lee realised for the first time that the arms holding her so securely were those of her husband. Weak tears rolled down her cheeks, making fresh tracks on her dusty skin.

'Madame Le Bon locked me in,' she tried to say, but her throat was too sore and the words would not come.

'Hush, *chérie*,' Gilles soothed. 'You are quite safe now. I am taking you to your room, and we have sent for the doctor. We will talk about it later when you are rested.'

Lee needed no second bidding; it was a relief to relax and close her eyes, listening to the reassuring thud of Gilles' heart. She felt no inclination to move away from him, or demand that he set her free, and when he placed her on their bed and closed the door behind him, she watched him with eyes still dark and shadowed with suffering, making no protest when he started to remove her filthy clothes, with hands so gentle that his touch brought fresh tears. Her skin was scraped where she had bumped into the rough stone walls, dried blood matted with the dust that cover her flesh.

From a distance she heard Gilles swear and when she opened her eyes his face was bone-white.

'Lie still,' he commanded softly. 'I am just going to get some water to bathe your cuts, and then we will let the doctor look at them.'

In the event there wasn't time. The doctor was ushered into the room before Gilles had returned from the bathroom. His matter-of-fact attitude did much to alleviate Lee's sense of unreality. She had suffered no apparent injury, he told Gilles, who explained that she had been trapped in the cellar, but he would prescribe something for shock just in case.

'No drugs,' Lee protested, the effort of speaking taxing her slender store of strength. There was one question she had to ask the doctor, and her eyes appealed to Gilles for help.

When he bent down over the bed, his ear close to her lips, she managed to whisper tremulously, 'The baby.'

Tears shimmered in her eyes as she thought of the small, helpless life inside her, and for a moment Giles' profile wavered, an expression she found it hard to interpret in the grey eyes. She could almost have described it as bitter, haunted even, but she was too exhausted to dwell deeply on it.

'Your baby is fine,' the doctor assured her with a beam. 'Indeed he has come off far better than his mother, although you must rest properly for a couple of days.'

Gilles turned to follow the doctor as he left the room, snapping off the light, and Lee could not prevent herself from calling out in a panic as the blackness engulfed her. Gilles was at her side instantly.

'Your wife has had an unpleasant experience, *monsieur*,' the doctor commented, 'but better than any medicine I can prescribe is the presence of her husband at her side. I shall see myself out.'

When he had gone a curious silence seemed to fall over the room.

'Are you feeling well enough to tell me what happened?' Gilles asked. He was sitting on the edge of the bed, his shoulders broad beneath his thin silk shirt, his eyes shadowed.

Haltingly, her voice almost failing her at times, Lee described what had happened without implicating

Louise. That was for Gilles to discover, if he wished, and she thought it significant that although his eyes darkened ominously when she described how Madame Le Bon had left her, he made no comment as to why the woman should have acted in so dangerous a fashion.

A knock on the door heralded the arrival of a maid with a supper tray, and when she had put it down, Lee became conscious of her grubby bedraggled state.

'I should like to wash . . .' she began hesitantly.

'I'll go downstairs and get one of the maids to come up and help you.'

He moved towards the door. In a moment he would be gone and she would be alone. Lee shivered, swept by the terror which had engulfed her in the cellar.

'Don't leave me!'

Gilles stared at her, but Lee was beyond wondering what her words might reveal. Her fingers curled into small desperate fists as he watched her. 'Don't leave me, Gilles,' she begged. 'I'm so frightened!'

The tears she had tried to stem during her imprisonment ran unchecked down her face, her shoulders shaking soundlessly. With a muffled imprecation Gilles crossed the space dividing them, lifting her up into his arms and carrying her into the bathroom.

'I won't leave you,' he promised soothingly, 'but we must clean these wounds. Shall I do it for you? I have never been a lady's maid before, so you will have to be patient with me if I am clumsy.' Lee recognised dimly that the gentle even pitch of his voice was deliberately adopted to stem her hysteria, and that if she had any pride she would banish him and wash herself. She was not helpless, after all, but every time she opened her mouth to do so she would remember the cellar and a fresh surge of weakness would rob her of the ability to do anything but gratefully accept his tender ministrations.

'Lee, be truthful with me,' he said at one point, kneeling in front of her while he applied antiseptic to her scraped knees. 'Just then when you asked the doctor about the baby, I got the impression that you genuinely cared about the child.'

Lee bit her lip. How blind he was! Of course she cared about her baby. After him it was the most important thing in her life.

'Lee, I know the circumstances of our marriage have not been ideal, but we are married, for better or for worse, and we have a joint responsibility to the child we have created jointly.' He paused as though searching for the right words, and Lee, who had never seen him at a loss before, felt her heart melt with tenderness. He was so close—close enough for her to reach out and touch—and yet so remote. She could touch his flesh, but not his heart.

'For the child's sake cannot we call a truce? I give you my word that I shall not force my . . . attentions upon you, nor will I embarrass you with liaisons such as the one I had with Louise, and in return . . .' He stood up abruptly, grasping her hands and looking into her eyes. 'In return I ask only that you love our child. Well, Lee? Do we have a truce?'

What could she say? That it was unfair of him to ask this of her now, when her defences had crumbled, when her heart ached for tenderness and her body for his protection?

Her heart cried out that what he was suggesting was not enough, that one day there would come a time when she could no longer endure the sterile relationship he was advocating; a day when she would either have to beg for his love or remove herself from his life, but she was too exhausted to wage war against her own clamouring senses, who demanded that she take whatever crumbs he was prepared to offer.

'We have a truce.' The words were so low; so painful that Gilles had to bend his head to catch them. She leaned against him like an exhausted child as he wrapped her in a soft, fluffy towel and carried her back to the bedroom.

A glass of wine was presented to her and she took a few cautious sips.

'It will help you sleep,' Gilles told her, coaxing her to drink a little more. 'Try to eat a little of this salad while I make a phone call.'

There was a phone in the room, and listening to him apologise for his unscheduled departure from the Ministry guilt washed over her.

'I've caused you a lot of trouble.'

'Indeed you have.' The enigmatic smile hurt more than the words, because she had the feeling that there was some meaning behind it that was hidden from her.

'I would have returned tomorrow anyway,' Gilles assured her. 'Lee, before you go back to sleep there is something we must talk about. Although you have not mentioned her I recognise Louise's hand behind your imprisonment.' His mouth tightened and Lee knew that there would be no compassion for the woman who had once been his mistress. 'It is unfortunate that circumstances prevent me from taxing Louise openly with her infamy, but you may rest assured that she will not be left in doubt as to my feelings, and I shall suggest strongly to her father that it is time she returned to Paris—for good.'

'And Madame Le Bon?'

'She left, apparently, while we were down in the cellars. Do you wish to have her pursued?'

Lee shook her head.

'What would be the point? I don't think she meant to leave me down there.' She would not tell him of her foolish imaginings—it was over now, and she suspected that Madame Le Bon had been punished enough by the realisation that she had almost caused a tragedy. It was Louise who was really to blame—not the woman she had used as her tool.

'Try and sleep now,' Gilles told her, when she had finished picking at her food. 'I shall only be in the dressing room. I shall work for a while and then go to bed, but I shall be here all the time if you need me.'

Gilles had been sleeping in the dressing room ever since the night of the ball. No one had commented on it, and Lee assumed that if the staff were aware of it—and they must be—they would put it down to her pregnancy. Pregnant women were notorious for their strange fancies.

The wine helped to relax her tensed muscles, the sounds of Gilles moving about in the dressing room soothing her into sleep.

She was dreaming . . . She was shut in a dark room, and although she called and called, no one came to set her free. The darkness seemed to press in on her, and although she begged Louise to let her out, the other woman only laughed callously. 'I'll go away,' Lee promised. 'I'll never come back.' But the Frenchwoman took no notice. She came closer and closer, her red hair curling round her face like flames, her mouth cruel as she told Lee that she would never, never be free.

The dream faded as Gilles shook her awake, and it came as a shock to realise that the sobbing she had heard so dimly in her dream had been her own. Her body was drenched with perspiration and yet she still felt dreadfully cold. Her teeth were chattering, and even in the darkness she could see the grim anger in Gilles' eyes. She flinched beneath it, apologising huskily for wakening him.

'I wasn't asleep,' he told her abruptly. 'Lee, did you think Louise intended you to stay down there for ever?'

She passed her tongue over her dry lips, not wanting him to think her hysterically stupid.

'It did cross my mind, but not very seriously. I think she just wanted to frighten me.'

'Into leaving the château? That's what you said during your nightmare.'

'It wasn't just because of Louise, I've always been frightened of the dark.' She shuddered suddenly, remembering the cellar, and as though he read her mind and saw the horror etched there, Gilles took her in his arms. As she felt the dampness of his skin against her, Lee realised that she must have disturbed him while he was having a shower. Her eyes went to his hair, dark, and still wet, sliding lower to his shoulders, his skin gleaming like oiled silk, and longing rose up inside her like spring floods after the thaw.

His hand smoothed the tangled hair back off her forehead, his eyes searching her face.

'Will you be all right now?'

His voice was faintly husky, his hands withdrawn from her body, and she shivered again, her fingers trembling yearningly against his chest as she reached towards him.

'Gilles, don't leave me.' The words were a repeat of those she had murmured earlier, but this time with a different meaning, and Lee could not bring herself to look at him, as she realised what she had said. 'I'm so cold,' she temporised, 'and frightened.' Neither were lies, but overriding them both was the need to have him beside her, his arms around her, even if it was only to protect her from her own childish nightmares.

'You want me to stay?' His eyes probed her shadowed features. 'You're very trusting, Lee. Or are you testing me to see if I can keep my word? Don't worry, you're quite safe.'

But did she want to be? Lee thought drowsily as he slid into the bed beside her, turning her into the warmth of his own body, the touch of his flesh sending her pulses out of control, flooding her with a desire more powerful than all her earlier fears.

There was a moment when, on the edge of sleep, she thought she felt the light brush of Gilles' lips against her hair, but the caress was not repeated and she thought she must have imagined it, until she felt Gilles' breath stir her hair.

'We haven't sealed our bargain,' he reminded her, and her heart pounded heavily at the sensual undertone to the words. 'Trust will be the cornerstone of our relationship, Lee. Do you trust me?'

Her mouth had gone dry, and as his touched it lightly she had to take a deep breath to prevent herself from shaking. His lips moved softly over hers, brushing them with a sensual expertise that left her longing to prolong the kiss.

'Trust me, Lee,' he murmured against her skin. His hands stroked the soft skin of her shoulders, sliding into her hair to tilt her head back, as his lips touched hers again. There was no force, no passion, just gentle warmth, and although Lee knew he had intended to reassure her, her predominant feeling was one of intense disappointment. What had she expected? That the moment he touched her desire would flare into life and that he would not be able to stop himself from making love to her? She smiled wryly. That was the stuff of romances, not life.

When he released her she veiled her eyes from him automatically, not wanting him to read what she felt must be reflected there.

'You see?' There was a smile in his voice. 'I can behave in a civilised manner!'

But it was the pagan in him that called to her, Lee acknowledged; the Gilles who had possessed her beneath a canopy of trees, while the rain drummed into the parched earth, and for a moment they had been at one with the universe, elemental and almost divine. If only she could stay within the haven of his arms for the rest of her life, feeling the powerful beat of his heart against her flesh, breathing in the warm male scent of his body, and feeling her own relax gradually from fear.

She closed her eyes hesitantly, but Gilles' arms held at bay the nightmares which had tormented her earlier.

This time, when she slept, it was dreamlessly.

CHAPTER TEN

LEE examined her reflection nervously in the mirror. She would have given anything to avoid going to this party. Gilles had watched her closely when he told her about the invitation. It was from Monsieur Trouville rather than Louise, but all the same the Frenchwoman would be there. And if they did not go, Louise would know why; she would know that Lee still remembered her ordeal in the cellar, and Lee was determined not to give her that satisfaction. And besides, she knew that Gilles was extremely fond of Louise's father. Although he had sold most of his land to Gilles, he intended to remain in the area, and they could not spend the rest of their lives pretending that he did not exist.

The worst thing would be facing Louise as though nothing had happened; pretending that the whole thing had merely been an unfortunate accident, which was the story Gilles had allowed to circulate locally. Madame Le Bon had completely disappeared; she had relatives in Paris and Lee suspected she must have gone there.

One good thing to come out of the incident was Gilles' changed manner towards her. Lee never had to sleep alone in the huge bed now, and if she woke up during the night, Gilles always seemed to be aware of it, drawing her next to the protective warmth of his own body, sometimes without even opening his eyes— but that was all. He might have been a father indulging a small child for all the interest he took in her sexually.

They had driven into Nantes for her check-up the

previous day and the doctor had been very pleased with her progress, although he warned her that she was still a little underweight. Gilles had insisted on buying her a new dress, a rich burgundy velvet, gathered gently at the front from a curved yoke, with a cream lace collar and cuffs. It suited her, bringing out the rich colour of her hair, which she was just twisting into a smooth chignon when Gilles opened the bedroom door. He halted and watched her, an expression in her eyes she found hard to define. He had been working hard and looked tired, and she longed to walk into his arms and smooth the frown from between his eyes.

'Are you sure you want to do this, Lee? You don't have to, you know.'

'I know.' She had to swallow hard on the tears which had gathered at the back of her throat in a hard lump, forcing herself to say gaily, 'But have you ever heard of a woman refusing to attend a party?'

It was being held to celebrate the New Year, and as they drove through Chauvigny, Lee couldn't help wondering exactly what that year might hold for her. She looked at Gilles. His hands held the wheel firmly, his attention concentrated on the road. His hair brushed the collar of his burgundy velvet jacket and she had to stifle an impulse to touch it, burying her fingers in its thick softness. His shirt glimmered palely in the dark, and a melting weakness invaded her stomach. If only this was a real marriage; the sort of marriage where she could turn to him and tell him to stop the car and take her home, where they could be alone to welcome in the New Year in the only way she really wanted to—held fast in his arms. Her small half sigh caught his attention and he glanced towards her.

'Are you sure you want to go?'

Lee smiled wryly. 'Not really, but it's something I

must do, Gilles. Louise isn't going to simply disappear because I want her to. Sooner or later I shall have to face her.'

The hands gripping the steering wheel tightened perceptibly. 'When I think of what might have happened . . .' His face had gone white. For a man of such self-control his feelings for his unborn child never ceased to amaze her, Lee thought a little jealously. Their child would never lack a father's love. Nor a mother's, she promised herself, and yet in her heart she knew for her own sake that she ought to leave before she betrayed herself and changed Gilles' kind tolerance into contempt for her unwanted love.

Louise welcomed them enthusiastically, her eyes on the emerald earrings Gilles had given to Lee with her Christmas present.

'Somewhat premature, surely?' was her only comment, but there was a hard challenge in her eyes that made Lee glad of Gilles' lean bulk between them.

'On the contrary,' Gilles replied smoothly, 'I had intended to give them to Lee before.'

'You are a very lucky woman. They must be worth a fortune. Aren't you frightened something might happen to them?'

The gloves were off with a vengeance, Lee reflected, trying to appear unmoved by Louise's enmity. Hatred had gleamed in her eyes as she looked at the emeralds, and it was all Lee could do to prevent herself from trembling visibly when she remembered the cold darkness of the cellar.

Gilles answered for her, his arm curved protectively round her body, the look in his eyes tender and reassuring. He was an excellent actor, she thought, not for the first time.

'What could happen?' Gilles asked evenly. 'Surely

you aren't suggesting that some of your guests are . . . dishonest?'

Louise shrugged, but her eyes were hard. She knew and they knew that they were not merely discussing the emeralds. They were soon swallowed up among the other guests. Someone found Lee a chair, and she found that her French had improved sufficiently for her to be able to hold her own in the conversation. When Gilles murmured that he wanted to have a word with Louise's father, she felt a momentary pang of fear, but she quelled it immediately. Gilles could not be at her side every moment of her life, and Louise could scarcely harm her here!

She ought to have known better. A buffet had been set out in the dining room, and Lee waited until most people had eaten before going to fill her own plate. She passed Gilles, who was still talking, and he acknowledged her presence with a small smile. His attentive care was becoming more of a burden than his indifference had ever been. So many times she had been dangerously close to allowing herself to believe he genuinely cared about her; dangerously close to deceiving herself that his touch was that of a lover and not merely a man concerned for the life of his unborn child.

Louise walked into the dining room as Lee was on her way out and they met by the door, Lee clamping down on her instinctive fear. Louise smiled cruelly.

'Ah, there you are—I was looking for you. Lee, we have another guest—an old friend of yours who has only just arrived.'

For the first time Lee noticed the man standing in the shadows behind her, his fair hair catching the light.

'Drew!' Shock stifled her, her eyes dilating as she

stared up into the cold features of the man she had
once thought she loved.

He stared back at her, grimacing distastefully as his
glance lingered on her body.

'Wh-what are you doing here?'

Lee realised immediately that the question was a
foolish one, smacking of guilt, and Drew's expression
mirrored her fears.

'I came because I thought I might be able to per-
suade you to come to your senses,' he began angrily.
'When I got your letter breaking off our engagement,
I thought you were simply having second thoughts.'
His mouth went tight with distaste, and he turned to
Louise, who had been watching gleefully.

'I have to thank you for your warning.' His lip curled
faintly as he looked at Lee. 'A little previous, weren't you,
or were you hoping to persuade your lover into marrying
you? My God, and to think I kept my hands off you
because I thought you were different! If I'd known . . .'

Lee had listened to him in growing disgust and fury,
and now it overwhelmed her.

'If you'd known, you would have what?' she
demanded angrily. 'Had a brief affair with me instead
of "buying" my virginity with an engagement ring?'

She felt sickened by the realisation that Drew had
simply wanted her because he had thought her a rare
commodity. Her innocence had been something he
thought he could buy and parade proudly in front of
his family. Had she admitted to any previous affairs he
would never have contemplated becoming engaged to
her, she realised with hindsight, remembering their
earlier conversations, his questions about her back-
ground and past, which she had answered guilelessly
merely thinking that he was as interested in her as she
had been in him. Now she knew better, and looking

into his face she felt only relief that she had been spared marriage to him.

'At least you had the decency to break off our engagement, although I suppose you thought you'd left it a bit late to pass the child off as mine.'

Lee's face went white. She couldn't believe that this was the same man who had only a year before had professed to love her. She swayed and closed her eyes, catching her breath as she felt a hard arm supporting her.

'Gilles!' He must have seen them from the drawing room.

Drew was looking at him with cold dislike. 'I wish you joy of her,' he said maliciously. 'Although by the looks of her, you've already had it.'

Louise screamed as Gilles' fist connected with Drew's jaw. For a moment he didn't move, staring at Gilles in stunned surprise, before crumpling slowly to the floor.

'Gilles, how could you!' Louise protested. 'He was within his rights. Did you know that Lee was engaged to him at the time she married you?' Her voice suggested that she thought he had not.

'I knew,' Gilles said grimly. 'Why do you think I was so anxious to tie her to me? But what I don't know is what he is doing here.' He glanced curtly down at Drew's unconscious figure. 'However, I can guess. This is the last time you interfere in my affairs, Louise, and much as I respect your father, I am inclined to tell him exactly what sort of woman he has for a daughter. Your husband did not leave you very well off, I believe,' he said pleasantly, 'and your father is extremely generous. Take care, Louise.'

Drew had come round and sat on the floor nursing his swollen jaw, his expression belligerent.

'I'll sue!' he threatened Gilles, allowing Louise to help him to his feet.

'Try it,' was Gilles' grim rejoinder. 'There isn't a court in France that will support your action. A man is entitled to defend his wife's honour.'

'His wife?' Drew stared disbelievingly at Lee, and then turned accusingly to Louise. 'You didn't tell me he'd married her!'

Lee didn't need to ask how Louise had obtained Drew's address—or why. She must have seen the letter Lee had written to him, and had perhaps thought when her earlier plan failed that Drew's arrival might turn Gilles back to herself. Louise had no way of knowing that Gilles knew all about Drew, and was hardly likely to be jealous of the other man, even had Lee had an intensely passionate relationship with him.

'Well, you're welcome to her,' Drew sneered, glowering at Gilles. 'Personally, I'm not very keen on other men's leavings.'

'It is just as well that I'm not a violent man,' Gilles replied smoothly. 'And that I know your remarks spring purely from jealousy. As I have every reason to know, your insults are entirely unfounded, and even if they weren't . . .' The look in his eyes made the colour come and go in Lee's cheeks. 'I have loved Lee since she was sixteen,' Gilles said softly, 'and nothing anyone could say about her could lessen that love.' He turned to Louise. 'It doesn't take much imagination to guess what you had in mind. I'm sorry to have to say this, Louise, but even if you had succeeded; even if Lee had left me, there is no place in my life for you.'

As he guided her out, Lee had time to feel almost sorry for Louise.

Gilles opened the car door and saw that she was comfortable before taking his own seat. He started the engine without a word, and when Lee looked at him she saw that there was a hard white line round his lips as though he was in the grip of some intense emotion.

'I'm sorry you had to go through that,' he said abruptly. 'Louise is a first-class bitch.'

Lee shrugged tiredly, 'It doesn't matter.' All at once reaction set in and to her shame, tears started to roll down her cheeks. Gilles swore and stopped the car, proffering an immaculate handkerchief, but the tears would not stop. They were only a few miles from the château and Gilles re-started the car, driving faster than usual, his expression withdrawn as he brought the Mercedes to a halt in front of the house.

Lee didn't wait for him to open her door. All at once the insults Drew had thrown at her broke through the calm she had exercised in his presence, and she felt almost unclean. This was the man she had once thought she loved and intended to spend her whole life with; a man so shallow and vindictive that he had wanted to destroy her rather than let her find happiness elsewhere; a man who wanted her only because of what she represented.

She could hear Gilles calling her name, but she did not stop. She wanted to be alone, to let the cleansing tears flow and wash away the memory of Drew's words.

Pierre stopped Gilles in the hall, and Lee escaped to the privacy of their bedroom, flinging herself down on the bed and giving way to the emotional storm she had been damming up ever since her release from the cellar. Gilles' kindness to her had meant that her emotions had had to be kept strictly under control, her senses alert for every danger to the fragile peace which existed between them.

'Lee.' She let Gilles turn her over, and survey her

tear-damp face. 'I could kill him for this,' he told her harshly. 'And Louise. I suppose there's no point in telling you that he wouldn't have made you happy, that he wanted you only as a possession.'

His arms were hard and warm. He had removed his jacket and Lee burrowed instinctively against the warmth of his chest, murmuring an inarticulate protest, as the thin silk shirt prevented her from achieving the closeness she craved. She clung blindly to Gilles as he rocked her gently, all her good intentions forgotten as longing swept her and her fingers moved of their own accord to the small pearl buttons, unfastening them and laying bare the moist heat of the flesh beneath. Her hands spread out feverishly, feeling the steady beat of his heart, the faint rasp of his body hair beneath her sensitive fingertips. She closed her eyes, trembling with the need she could no longer deny, her lips dry as she pressed them lightly against his throat.

His arms tightened; he pulled her on to his knee, his fingers stroking her softly.

'Gilles?' She lifted her face in mute invitation, no longer caring what she was revealing, pressing her body against him as she sought the possession of his kiss.

'Lee, don't make it harder for me,' he begged harshly. 'Leave me at least some dignity. If I don't leave now, I'll never be able to let you go, and although I promised you I'd never force myself on you again, I'm dreadfully close to breaking that promise. Oh God, *Lee!*'

There was a raw hunger in his voice that brought her from bitter despair to disbelieving incredulity. He groaned suddenly, finding her mouth with his own and possessing it with an urgency that swept aside all barriers. Lee clung to him with an abandon she was barely aware of, murmuring soft, incoherent cries of delight as his mouth moved from her lips to the soft creamy flesh his trembling fingers had exposed.

'Stop me, Lee,' he groaned at one point, his face flushed with the desire he was making no attempt to conceal. 'Stop me before it's too late.'

'I don't want to.'

The whispered confession stilled his questing hands. He looked at her for a moment, breathing as though the effort pained him, and then cupped her flushed cheeks, his voice unsteady as he muttered huskily, 'I told myself I'd never do this; never sink to emotional blackmail; that I'd never burden you with my feelings, but I didn't know then how desperate I would become. Stay with me, Lee. Let me teach you to love me. Perhaps you'll never be able to love me the way I love you, but you aren't indifferent to me.' His fingers tilted her chin upwards, the look in his eyes making her heart lift on a cresting wave of delirious happiness.

'That day when we made love for the first time was the most memorable of my entire life. I had convinced myself that you were just another woman—desirable, but nothing more. I kept reminding myself that you had disillusioned me once, that you were no different from any other woman. I had forced you into marriage, but it wasn't enough. I was tormented every time I touched you by the thought of all the other men who had known you before me. I wanted to possess you completely, an illogical desire which I could not equate with common sense. And then when I discovered that I had been wrong! I cannot describe to you how I felt, how much I loathed and despised myself, and yet even knowing what I had done didn't stop me from wanting you. I hated myself and I swore I wouldn't force myself upon you again, but every time I remembered that evening—and I remembered it constantly—I wanted you more. I couldn't believe it had actually happened. You were a virgin, innocent and inexperienced, and yet with you I experienced something I had known with no other woman—a total blending of minds and bodies. You'll never know how many times since then I've wanted to make you respond to me, to take the physical satisfaction I knew we could have together and pray that love would come, but I couldn't. I told myself I would have to set you free, and then I found out you were carrying my child. Will you hate me if I tell you that I was glad, fiercely glad because it gave me an excuse to hold on to you . . . Just as Louise gave me an excuse to force you into marrying me.'

'Will you hate me if I tell you that I was glad, that I wanted your child only a little less than I wanted your love?' Lee murmured tremulously.

For a moment there was silence, and then Gilles lowered his head, brushing her lips delicately, running his tongue over them, like a blind man exploring by touch alone, and then as Lee reached up for him he held her away, his eyes searching her face.

'Be very sure, my darling,' he said softly. 'There is nothing to be ashamed of in admitting that I arouse you physically. I am the first lover you have ever known, and you have a deeply passionate nature. I say this because my own love is such that physical passion alone will not be enough to satisfy my burning need for you. I want all of you, Lee, and I warn you now if you stay with me, I will possess you completely, and never set you free.'

'It isn't merely physical,' Lee told him softly. 'I love you, Gilles. Living with you like this has been torture. Every time you touch me I . . .' She flushed and broke off, her emotion still too tender to be put into words.

'You what?' Gilles prompted softly. 'Or shall I say it for both of us? Every time I look at you, I am consumed by the need to touch you, and when I touch you I want to go on touching you, and have you touch me in return. Like this.'

He drew her into his arms and kissed her tenderly before drawing slightly away, but as he had said, it wasn't enough, and Lee reached urgently for him, her eyes begging him mutely not to let her go. As though he still doubted her love he hesitated, watching her, and Lee knew that there must be no more misunderstandings or doubts. Sliding her hands over his shoulders, she lifted her head, her fingers delicately tracing the smooth muscles of his back as she pressed kisses against the warm column of his throat. She felt him tense and swallow, and her lips parted on a sudden aching wave of love. There was no need for words. His kiss blotted out everything but their mutual need.

A long time later Gilles released her, laughter gleaming in the depths of eyes no longer cold but warm with the intensity of their love.

'If I didn't know better, I might question exactly how you learned to arouse a man so thoroughly.'

'Ask me.' Lee dimpled back at him. 'I'll tell you anyway. I learned from my husband—whom I love very much.'

'And who loves you, but dares not show it at this precise moment in time.' His eyes lingered on the swelling curves of her body, and he smiled humorously. 'For the first time I find myself resenting the presence of our child, but later, after he is born . . .' His eyes darkened suddenly and he got off the bed.

'I fell in love with you when you were sixteen, that summer I spent at my aunt's. You were a rose in the bud, so perfect, so unawakened. I knew you were attracted to me, but I was a man of twenty odd, and it would have been criminal to put into practice what I was thinking—almost literally,' he added pointedly. 'But I couldn't stop thinking about you, about how it would feel to teach you all about love, to feel your first shy responses, and later the ardour I knew you were capable of—and then I got that letter.' He glanced at her and grimaced. 'I nearly went out of my mind! You caught me on my most vulnerable spot. I thought of myself as a man of the world, but here I was deceived by a sixteen-year-old girl, who looked like a child and had the knowledge of a woman of the streets. I had to leave. If I'd stayed I would have taken you—I couldn't have stopped myself. It was like an illness, and even though I loathed you, or what I thought was you, I still wanted you. Years passed, and I told myself I'd forgotten, but I hadn't. And then I saw you again, and it all came back, and I still wanted you.'

'I never wrote the letter,' Lee told him drowsily. 'It was Sally. When I read it I didn't understand half the things in it, but later, when you'd gone, I tried to learn, and when I had learned, I was so sickened, so bitterly hurt that you could believe I was like that that I told myself I hated you; that you had destroyed my innocence and opened my eyes to degradation and obscenity.'

Gilles groaned and took her back in his arms.

'Forgive me? It was because I loved you. My love blinded me to the truth. Perhaps I even wanted to think the worst of you, as though in some way that made my desire for you more understandable. What a fool I've been! When you gave yourself to me with such innocent abandon I nearly went out of my mind. When I found you there in the copse I wanted to punish you for frightening me so badly. I thought you had left me, and then when we started to make love my anger possessed me, and I wanted to obliterate from your mind all those men who had known you first. By the time I realised that they were entirely fictional it was far too late to draw back . . .'

'And I didn't want you to,' Lee said dreamily. 'I thought you were disgusted, shocked by my response . . . And then you accused me of experimenting . . .'

'Because I thought you were. I couldn't believe that you might actually care for me, and had you but known it, giving yourself to me like that was the worst punishment you could have devised. I had possessed you, yes, but it wasn't enough, and I knew that no matter what happened in my life those moments would always be my most precious memory. I love you, Lee,' he said huskily, 'far too much to ever let you go. You'll never know what I went through when I heard you were missing. I thought I had lost you, that you had left me, and then when I discovered the truth I wanted to squeeze Louise's throat until there was no breath left inside her. Today when I saw you with Drew, I thought you must love him. I watched him talking to you and saw you go pale. When I heard him insulting you I wanted to tell him what a fool he was, and yet I felt glad. I knew you had too much pride to plead with him, and I thought that knowing that he had never loved you might make you turn to me . . .'

'And I thought all your tenderness was because you felt sorry for me, and because you wanted our baby. I never dreamed you loved me. I keep thinking I'm imagining it all and that I'm going to wake up—alone . . .'

Gilles lifted her hand to his lips, pressing a kiss in the soft palm and closing her fingers over it. 'You're never going to wake up anywhere except in my arms,' he promised huskily, his mouth stifling her response as passion flared insistently between them and he lowered her gently on to the bed.

Six months later Lee stretched languorously beneath the hot Greek sun. They had been at the villa for three days and already she had slipped into a carelessly lazy routine. She rolled on to her stomach and watched Gilles swim another length of the pool. Corfu was a beautiful island, but so far they had seen little of it, content in their own private world—just the three of them. A small smile curved her lips as she glanced towards the pram beneath the shade of the olive trees. Philippe was still asleep. With any luck they would have another hour before he woke up. The baby was the image of Gilles, and they had called him Louis-Philippe. If she sat up Lee would just be able to see the fluff of black hair covering his scalp. His eyes, at first blue, were now turning grey.

'Wake up, sleepyhead.' Gilles hauled himself out of the pool, dripping water on her heated skin. He grinned down at her, and although she teased him by closing her eyes, Lee was aware of him with every nerve-ending. The villa had a private beach and last night they had swum together from it. The memory of how they had made love afterwards tinged her lips with a smile. Gilles was a pagan, no matter how he might deny it. He had insisted that they swim nude, and although Lee had at first demurred she had given in and delighted in the cool, silky feel of the water against her sunwarmed flesh; later to be replaced by the hard urgency of Gilles' body.

'Do you think he will make a good *vigneron*?' Gilles asked her, peering down at his son.

Lee rolled on to her back and smiled provocatively. 'Of course he will. It's in his blood . . .'

Gilles looked at her, and Lee knew they were both remembering the night Philippe had been conceived. There had been many other nights of love since then, but none quite so elemental, and Lee knew that Gilles had been holding back a little. The birth had not been an easy one, but this holiday was already restoring her strength and she knew that there would not be many more nights when Gilles would have to temper his passion.

He came and lay down beside her, and she felt his fingers on the hook of her bikini top. She pretended to be asleep and gasped when he suddenly bit her earlobe.

His arms tightened round her and she opened her eyes, loving the feel of his skull beneath her fingers, his hair still wet from his swim.

'What shall we do tonight? There's supposed to be quite a good nightclub down the road, and we could ask the maid to look after Philippe.'

Lee shook her head decisively, touching her tongue delicately to his throat and tasting the salt from the pool.

'I'd rather stay here.'

Gilles smiled at her, and there was devilment as well as comprehension in the smile.

'Didn't the doctor say something about you resting during the afternoon?'

Lee laughed. 'Call that resting?' she teased. 'And besides, Philippe will need feeding soon.' But Gilles' hands were stroking her skin, and she knew as well as he that her protests held no meaning.

'I love you,' Gilles murmured between kisses, 'more than life itself, Lee.'

She could feel the passion throbbing in his body, and knew instinctively that this time there would be no holding back. When he lifted her in his arms and carried her to their bedroom she felt her own desire rise up to match his, their mutual need engulfing them both in a tide which could not be stemmed.

The passion Lee had experienced the day Gilles had taken her virginity had overwhelmed and exalted her, but it was overshadowed now by the knowledge of Gilles' love and the way that knowledge coloured her own reactions to his passionate possession. Outside Louis-Philippe awakened and cried, and then fell silent, as though comprehending that for the moment his parents were oblivious to his hunger.

THE CAGED TIGER

THE CAGED TIGER

BY

PENNY JORDAN

MILLS & BOON LIMITED

15–16 BROOK'S MEWS

LONDON W1A 1DR

First published in Great Britain 1982 by Mills & Boon Limited

© *Penny Jordan 1982*

Australian copyright 1982
Philippine copyright 1982
Reprinted 1982
This edition 1986

ISBN 0 263 75603 3

Set in Monophoto Plantin 10 on 11½ pt
19/1286-53903

Printed and bound in Great Britain by Cox & Wyman Ltd, Reading

CHAPTER ONE

IT would be evening before the plane landed in Seville. It had been the only flight she had been able to get at such short notice and during the height of the season. It had been cheaper too, because of a sudden cancellation, but it had been a long day—all that hanging around at Heathrow to make sure they got the seats. She pushed a slim pale hand through her silver-blonde weight of hair, her amethyst eyes clouding as she shifted Jamie's baby weight from one arm to the other. Baby . . . She stifled a small smile. At three he considered himself a very grown-up young man. She often had difficulty convincing people that she was actually his mother—not just because she looked younger than her twenty-four years. Her small, slender body looked far too fragile to ever have carried a child. But it had. She wasn't a fool; she knew that despite the plain gold wedding ring she wore people wondered if she had actually ever been married—if Jamie was not simply the result of a youthful indiscretion. They were wrong, though. She had most emphatically been married; had had a husband . . . There were still faint traces of his orange juice round Jamie's mouth, and as she reached into her pocket for a tissue the letter crackled ominously.

She didn't need to take it out, to look at the heavy, expensive crested paper again. Every word written on it was engraved upon her heart, and had been agonised over ever since the letter arrive a fortnight ago.

Only a fortnight? It felt more like years. The letter

was brief, couched in words as dry as dust, making it impossible for her to think it had been written with any feeling. But then it hadn't. Any feeling that had ever existed between Jamie's father and herself had long since turned to ashes.

So what was she doing on this plane, flying back to Spain, taking her son to his unknown father?

She glanced down quickly at the sleeping child. Under the baby plumpness lay even now the signs of his recent illness. Enteritis was so frightening in a child—one could do nothing but hope and pray. He was over it now, the doctors assured her, but she was haunted by the fear that another poor summer would lower his resistance to the point where he would be ill again come winter. In Spain he would thrive in the warmth and luxury which were his birthright; his skin would take on the mahogany hue of his father's, his hair would gleam blue-black as a raven's wing in the strong sunshine . . . Hair that reminded her unbearably at times of Ruy . . . She stroked it back from his forehead where it had fallen in unruly curls. Even in sleep his profile had a subconscious arrogance inherited from a long line of Spanish hidalgos . . .

She had done her best for him, but it could never come anywhere near to matching what Ruy could give him. She was lucky in that she had been able to work from home, but her illustrations for children's books and cards did not bring in enough to keep them in luxury, nor to provide the winter away from the English climate which the doctor had suggested might be as well.

Jamie stirred in his sleep, the almost purple eyes which were what she had passed on to him remaining tightly closed. She had always been honest with him.

When she thought he was old enough to understand she had explained that his daddy lived far away in another country, without going into too much detail. He had been curious, but had accepted her matter-of-fact explanations without evincing any surprise or distress. At play-school several of the other children lived alone with their mothers, and he saw nothing odd in their own aloneness. Which was wrong, something inside her told her, as she remembered her own parents' happy marriage. If a child did not grow up knowing that love could exist between adults of both sexes then how could he in turn pass that knowledge on to his own children?

She was being sentimental, she warned herself. Jamie was unlikely to learn anything good about human relationships from observing hers with his father. Which brought her thoughts back full circle. Why had Ruy written to her? Why did he want his son—now?

She had been so sure when she left that he would find some way of having their marriage set aside—it had been a Catholic ceremony in accordance with his religion, but his family were influential and rich, and there were always ways and means . . . His mother had never liked the marriage. 'Liked!' She almost laughed. It would have been truer to say that her mother-in-law detested her, if one could apply such a word to the ice-cold contempt the Condesa de Silvadores had evinced each time their paths had crossed—and they had been many. The Condesa had seen to that. In the end a million tiny pinpricks could be more fatal than one crippling blow.

The plane landed, and a smiling stewardess helped her with Jamie. 'He's gorgeous,' she commented as she held him so that Davina could collect all their possessions, 'but not a bit like you.'

'No, he takes after his father,' Davina answered briefly, trying not to let her voice falter.

The stewardess could not know what the words had cost her. How much it always cost her to admit how much Jamie resembled his father—the father who had never wanted him, who had never seen him; never once sent him a birthday or Christmas present, made no attempts whatsoever to see him—until now. And even now he had left it to his mother—the woman who had always derided and scorned her—to write the letter summoning her back to the Palacio de los Naranjos— the Palace of the Orange Trees—the home of the Silvadores family set amongst the orange groves from which the family's fortune was derived and whose scent hung sharply and sweetly on the early morning air.

A shiver trembled through her, and mistaking it for coldness, the stewardess touched her arm, motioning her towards the airport building. Despite the huge number of people who passed through her life daily, something about Davina intrigued the other girl. She looked so frail, spiritual almost, her beauty tinged with a contemplative acceptance that touched the heart far more than any more overt signs of grief. What had happened to her to give her that look? She might have posed for some great painter of the Renaissance. Her expression told of great suffering and resignation, and yet surely she had all the things any woman could want? Youth, beauty, this adorable baby, and somewhere the man who had loved her enough to give her his son.

When they emerged from the Customs hall it was dark. Davina walked out into the soft silkiness of the

Spanish night, Jamie in her arms. Spain! How the scents of the night brought back memories. Herself and Ruy wandering hand in hand through the orange groves during their honeymoon, and later, when the moon had risen fully and he had taken her so paganly in that shadowed garden, teaching her and thrilling her until her passion matched his. She had been happy then—deliriously happy, but she had paid for it later. She had thought Ruy loved her, had never realised that to him she was merely a substitute for the girl he had really loved; that he had married her to punish that girl.

In the shadowed garden of his home she had thought she had found Paradise. But every Eden must have a serpent and hers had held Ruy's mother, the woman who hated her so much that she had deliberately opened her eyes to the truth.

And now Ruy wanted her back—no, not her; it was his son. The only one he was ever likely to have, or so the letter had told her. Jamie was his heir, and his place was with his father, learning all that he must learn if he was to take it successfully. And Davina could not deny it, although she could not understand why Ruy had not been able to get his freedom— Freedom to marry the girl he had loved all along, the girl he had really wanted to be the mother of the son who would succeed him, as Silvadores had succeeded Silvadores in an unbroken line from the sixteenth century onwards.

The letter had said that she would be collected from the airport. A porter brought her cases and she smiled as she tipped him. His eyes rested appreciatively on her face, and her hair, like spun silver, and so very different from the girls of his own race. Her features were patrician and perfect, her lips chiselled and firm, her complexion as fine as porcelain, her huge amethyst eyes fringed with luxuriously thick dark lashes.

She was the most beautiful thing he had ever seen, Ruy had once told her. But he hadn't meant it.

'Davina?'

She hadn't heard the opulent Mercedes drive up nor seen its driver emerge to come and touch her lightly on the arm, and she spun round, startled, her eyes widening slightly as she found herself looking into a face she remembered as being a boy's.

'Sebastian?'

'Let me take the boy. He looks heavy.' Her brother-in-law lifted Jamie from her arms with a competence which would have amused her four years ago. Then he had been nineteen, and still at the university studying viticulture in preparation for taking over the family's vineyards. Now, at twenty-three, he had matured considerably. Although superficially he resembled his brother, Sebastian lacked Ruy's totally male grace. Where Ruy was lean and muscled Sebastian showed a tendency towards what would develop into plumpness in middle years. He was not as tall as Ruy, his features nowhere near as tautly chiselled, but for all that he was still a very handsome young man. Especially when he smiled—which he had been doing as he held his small nephew. However, the moment he turned towards Davina the smile was replaced by cool formality. She was ushered into the expensive car as though she were a complete stranger, her luggage stowed in the boot, and then Sebastian was sliding into the driver's seat and starting the engine. It surprised Davina that if one of the brothers had to meet her, it had not been Ruy. Surely he must be anxious to see his son to permit his mother to write demanding their presence?

She voiced her opinion of her husband's lack of manners as they drove out of the city. In the driving mirror Sebastian's eyes met hers, before moving away evasively. She remembered that he had always hero-worshipped his elder brother. Twelve years separated them, and Ruy had already been a man while Sebastian was still a child in school.

'He was unable to meet you,' was all the explanation Sebastian would vouchsafe, and Davina was glad she had played down the meeting with his father to Jamie. The little boy would have been sadly disappointed had he been expecting him at the airport. In point of fact Davina was surprised that Sebastian had come for them. She had half expected to be collected by the family chauffeur, rather like a piece of unwanted luggage.

Before her marriage to the Conde de Silvadores Ruy's mother had lived in South America, the only daughter of a wealthy industrialist, and had been brought up very strictly. She had never learned to drive and was always taken wherever she wished to go by a chauffeur. That had been yet another cause of dissent between them. Davina had found it very hard to adjust to being the wife of a rich nobleman without having to behave like some Victorian heroine, not permitted to put a foot out of doors without an escort. Used to running her own life and relatively untrammelled freedom, she had rebelled against the strictures Ruy's mother had wanted to impose upon her.

Her small sigh brought Sebastian's eyes to her face. She was very beautiful, this silver-haired girl who had married his adored brother—even more beautiful now than she had been when they married. Then she had been merely a girl; now she was a woman . . . His eyes rested on his brother's child. Madre would be well pleased. The boy was all Silvadores.

Unaware of her brother-in-law's covert inspection, Davina stared out into the dusk of a Spanish evening, forgotten memories surfacing like so many pieces of flotsam, things she had vowed never to remember filling her mind, like the vivid beauty of the sunset, the subtle smell of oranges on the evening air, peasants trudging contentedly homewards after a day in the fields, donkeys with panniers laden. She sighed.

The Palacio lay between Seville and Cordoba, and this journey was the very first she had taken with Ruy after their marriage. They had left Barcelona straight away after the ceremony and flown to Seville . . .

More to bring a halt to her errant thoughts than out of any real curiosity, she questioned Sebastian about his life since she had left.

Yes, he had now left the university, he answered politely, and was running the family's vineyards. Davina had a hazy recollection of a young Spanish girl whom his mother had wished him to marry, and when she mentioned her Sebastian told her that they had been married for two years. 'But, alas, without any little ones,' he volunteered sadly. 'The doctors say that Rosita will probably never have children. An operation to remove her appendix caused some complications . . .' He shrugged philosophically, and Davina's heart went out to his young wife. She knew all too well what importance was placed on the bearing of children—especially sons—in her husband's family. Hadn't she had it drummed into her time and time again by her mother-in-law that Silvadores had been linked with the history of Spain for hundreds of years and how important it was for the name to continue?

Now she could understand why the family were so anxious for Jamie to be brought up in the full knowledge of what his role would one day be, although previously she had always expected, when Ruy had their marriage set aside so that he could marry Carmelita, that Jamie would be disinherited in favour of the sons she would bear him. She was not au fait with the Spanish inheritance laws, nor had she made any attempt to be. She had left Ruy swearing that never would she ask him for a single penny towards his son's upbringing, and she had stuck rigorously to that vow, and at the first suggestion that she had come to Spain with any thought of material gain, she would leave at once. They were the ones who wanted Jamie. All she wanted for her son was his restored health, and had there been any other means of achieving it she would have gladly taken them. She had no wish to be indebted to her husband or his family, but as the solicitor she had gone to see in England had gently pointed out, there was a possibility that Ruy might appeal to the Spanish courts to have custody of Jamie given to him, and as the child was his heir they might very well grant it.

With that threat hanging over her Davina had had no choice but to comply with the terms of the letter. That way at least she would still be able to be with her child.

They were starting to climb, driving towards the Sierra de los Santos. High up in those mountains was a monastery which had once belonged to the monks of the Inquisition, and she shivered as she remembered Ruy telling her about the ancestor of his who had been to England with Philip of Spain and fallen in love there with one of Queen Elizabeth's ladies in waiting. He had married his English Rose, as he had named his bride, and carried her back to Spain with him, but despite the fact that Jane Carfax was of the same religion as himself, the priests of the Inquisition had insisted that in reality she was an English spy. They had demanded that Cristo hand over his wife so that she could be questioned, but the Spaniard knew too much about their torture chambers to relinquish his wife. Instead he had made secret plans to leave his country with his bride and start a new life far beyond the reach of the burning fires to which the priests wished to sacrifice his love.

On the very night they were to leave for the coast the house had been surrounded and they had been taken to the monastery. Their secret had been betrayed by Cristo's brother, and the two young lovers had perished together in the flames. The brother himself had died shortly after, after an agonising illness— punishment from God, the villagers had called it. The story had haunted Davina. And now, as she raised her eyes to the black bulk of the mountains she shivered, holding Jamie tightly.

'Soon be there,' Sebastian told her over his shoulder. 'Everything is in readiness for you. Madre has given you your own suite of rooms. She has engaged a nurse for the little one. She will help him to learn Spanish, although he is not yet old enough for formal lessons, but he must learn his father's tongue . . .'

How much they took for granted, these arrogant Spaniards! Davina thought resentfully. Already her mother-in-law seemed to be usurping her place. Well, she would soon learn that Davina was no shy, awkward girl now, eager to please and terrified. Jamie was her child, and she would be the one to say what he would and would not learn.

And yet half an hour later when the Mercedes stopped in the courtyard of the beautiful Moorish house which had been the home of her husband's family for centuries, and Sebastian took the sleeping child in his arms, she had to admit that when it came to loving children, Englishmen could learn a good deal from their Spanish counterparts. As they walked towards the house Jamie stirred, and half frightened that he would think she had left him, Davina darted forward to take his hand. Two dimples appeared in his chubby cheeks as he smiled, his arms extended towards her. As she took him from Sebastian, she buried her face in the small baby neck, suddenly overwhelmed by dread, by the fear that she had done the wrong thing.

Too many memories that were best left dead had been stirred already. She might be able to close her heart against her husband, but she could not close her mind to her memories . . . Memories of the very first time she had seen this house; of how she had been entranced by Ruy's casual explanation that it had once been the home of a Moorish prince and that much of the original architecture remained. Even now she could hear the music of the fountains playing in the courtyard which had once been the sole property of the ladies of the harem, and even before the massive wooden doors opened, already in her mind's eye she could see the gracious hallway with its mosaic-tiled floor and elegant Moorish architecture. Everything was the same—but different. Then she had arrived with a husband she had thought loved her as totally as she loved him. This time she arrived with her son—the product of that union.

The doors opened, and in the light from the chandeliers Davina saw her mother-in-law waiting to greet them, regal and feminine in one of the long hostess gowns she always wore in the evening—always black, always elegant. How intimidated she had been on the first occasion! But not this time. Oh, definitely not this time.

Her head held high, she stepped past Sebastian and into the house. Her mother-in-law's eyes flickered once as Davina greeted her and then went straight to Jamie with a hunger no amount of sophistication could hide. She held out her arms, but Davina did not place Jamie into them. He was busily staring around his new surroundings.

'So this is Ruy's child.'

Davina ignored the other woman's emotion, her eyes hard as they probed the shadows of the room, as she forced herself to damp down the feeling nothing would make her admit was disappointment.

Sebastian had walked into the *salón*, plainly expecting that they would follow him. Her mother-in-law indicated that Davina should precede her into the room, and with her legs trembling a little Davina did so.

The room was much as she remembered. Rich Persian carpets glowed on the floor, the antique furniture was still as highly polished as it had always been, the room looking more like a film set than someone's home, and her heart sank at the thought of condemning Jamie to a house where his inquisitive little fingers would be forbidden to touch and explore.

A small, slight girl in a demure cotton dress stood up as they walked in. Davina guessed at once that she was Sebastian's wife, Rosita, and this was confirmed when Sebastian introduced her. Like her mother-in-law, Rosita's eyes went immediately to the child in Davina's arms, and she turned to her husband whispering something huskily in Spanish.

'She says that the child very much resembles Ruy,' Sebastian explained to Davina.

'I know.'

Davina could see that the dry words had surprised them. She had not been able to speak Spanish when she married Ruy, and as he spoke excellent English he had only made a halfhearted attempt to learn. But during the lonely weeks after her return to England she had bought herself some foreign language tapes, partially to pass the time, and partially because then she still hoped that it had all been a mistake and that Ruy loved her and would come to take her home. To her own surprise she had shown quite a facility for the language, and could now speak it reasonably well. She could tell by her mother-in-law's expression that the older woman thought her knowledge of her language had been gained purely to impress them, and to show her exactly how little she cared what they thought about her she lifted her chin proudly and said coolly:

'I was given to understand that Ruy was anxious to see his son. Where is he? Out somewhere with Carmelita?'

Rosita paled and started to tremble. Sebastian gripped her hand, his mouth white, and only the Condesa appeared unmoved by her question. What was she supposed to do? Pretend ignorance? Pretend that she didn't know that her husband loved someone else?

Before anyone could speak Davina heard an unfamiliar sound in the hall. For a moment it reminded her of her own days spent pushing Jamie's pram, which was quite ridiculous, for who would push a pram through the immaculate rooms of this house?

The *salón* had double doors, both of which stood open. All three members of the Silvadores family were staring towards them with varying degrees of tension evident in their faces. Only Davina's expression was openly puzzled. Sebastian walked towards her, his hand touching her arm, as though he wanted to say something, but before he could do so Davina knew the reason why her husband had not met her at the airport but had sent his brother instead. For the sound she had heard was made by a wheelchair and in it, his face drawn in tight lines of pain, was Ruy.

CHAPTER TWO

'RUY!'

His name burst past her lips of its own volition in a shocked gasp, *his* expression going from sheer incredulity to bitter anger as he stared from her slender body, half hidden by the child in her arms, to the faces of his relatives.

'*Madre de Dios!*' he swore angrily, his nostrils pinched and white with the force of his rage. 'What kind of conspiracy is this? What is going on?' he demanded harshly. 'What is *she* doing here?'

If she had felt shocked before, it was nothing to what she was feeling now, Davina admitted, her face going as white as his, but before she could say anything, Ruy's mother was speaking.

'She has come because I requested her to,' she told her son, holding his eyes coolly.

Davina wasn't paying much attention to them. She was still too stunned by the fact that this was actually Ruy, the proud and strong, in a wheelchair, to appreciate the full enormity of what her mother-in-law had done.

'*You* requested it?' The thin nostrils dilated further. 'By whose authority?' he demanded softly. 'I am still master in my own house, Madre. I can still say who may and may not rest under its roof, even if I can no longer walk as other men, but must needs propel myself about like a babe in arms.'

With his rage directed at his mother, Davina was

able to study him properly for the first time. What she saw shocked her. The Ruy whom she had known had walked tall—a veritable god among men, and if she was honest she would have to admit that she had thrilled to the arrogant grace; the hint of ruthless mastery cloaked by modern civilisation like velvet covering tempered steel. Now there were deep lines of pain scored from nose to mouth which were new to her, and a bitterness in the dark eyes that made Jamie cry out protestingly as her arms tightened round him unthinkingly.

His cry brought Ruy's eyes to them in scorching denunciation; a look that stripped her of everything and left her aching with a need to escape from it.

He turned his chair abruptly so that she was faced with the sight of his dark head.

'Get her out of here,' he told his mother emotionlessly. 'I never want to set eyes on her again.'

'And your son?'

His mother said the words so quietly that Davina couldn't believe that he had heard them, never mind stopped. But he had, and he turned his chair again, his eyes going slowly over the small form held protectively against Davina's breast.

'My son, or your grandson, Madre?' he asked sardonically. 'Tell me. If I were still man enough to father children, if Sebastian could provide you with grandsons, would you still want *that*?'

The use of the derisive word, the look he gave them, all combined to arouse within Davina the anger the sight of him, stricken, had tempered. Quivering with the pent-up force of it, she advanced on the wheelchair, her eyes blazing almost as darkly as his, unaware of the arresting picture her erect carriage and pale face made.

'*That*, as you call him, just happens to be your son,' she told him, barely able to form the words coherently. 'The son you've denied from the moment of his birth, but he is your son, Ruy, and he will live here as is his birthright . . .'

'How you have changed your tune,' he sneered bitterly. 'When I married you, you told me that you wished I were a poor man; that we could live an "ordinary" life. What went wrong, Davina? Or is it just that with age has come the realisation that you will not be young for ever, that there will come a time when men cease to desire your body; when you will have nothing but the dead ashes of too many burnt out love affairs . . . My son! How can I be sure of that?'

The sharp crack of her palm against his lean cheek split the silence. Behind her Davina heard someone gasp, and she felt faintly sick herself as she stared at the dull red patch against the tanned skin. What had prompted her to behave so outrageously? In her arms Jamie stirred again and whispered, opening his eyes properly for the first time to stare at the man who had fathered him. How could Ruy so coldly deny his own flesh and blood? she asked herself. It was obvious that Jamie was his child . . .

'I apologise for striking you,' she said shakily, 'but you did provoke me. Did you think I would have come here for one moment had Jamie not been your child?'

'I know only that you disappeared out of my life, only to reappear now, at the command of my mother. I am not a fool, Davina, no matter what I might have appeared in the past. It must have been a tempting prospect; a useless cripple of a husband whose presence need not disturb you, and the rest of your life spent in luxury waiting for your child to step into his shoes.'

'Stop! That is enough, Ruy,' his mother commanded. 'If you must have the truth, I allowed Davina to think that *you* had written to her.' She shrugged when he stared frowningly at her. 'Enough of this foolish pride. Jamie is the only son you are likely to have, the only son this house is likely to have. It is only right and fitting that he is brought up here where his place will one day be . . .'

It was at that moment that Jamie decided it was time he took a hand in the proceedings himself. Struggling against Davina's guarding arms, he demanded to be put down on the floor. When she did as he requested he toddled solemnly over to the wheelchair, while Davina, her heart in her mouth, darted forward to hold him back. It was only the pressure of her mother-in-law's fingers biting into her wrist that prevented her from wrenching Jamie away, her grasp restricting her for long enough for Jamie to reach his goal. Once there he stared up at his father, his eyes, so like Davina's, staring perplexedly at this man who looked back at him with such cool haughtiness.

'Is he my daddy?'

The question was addressed by Davina, over his shoulder, the shrill, piping treble baby voice filling the tense silence.

Davina tried to speak and could not. She had a photograph of Ruy at home which she had shown to Jamie, and although she doubted that he could have recognised the man pictured there, she was not going to lie to her son merely to spare the feelings of the father who denied him.

She cleared her throat, but her voice was still husky as she answered his question, going down on her knees to draw him back from Ruy, as though she feared that he might harm the child.

'Then why doesn't he talk to me?' Jamie demanded, turning towards her. 'Doesn't he like me?'

Such an innocent question! It brought a lump to Davina's throat and moisture to her eyes. This was a moment she had faced over and over again in all her worst nightmares, trying to explain to Jamie why his father had rejected them, but she had never, even in the very worst of them, guessed that she would be called upon to do so in Ruy's presence.

It was the Condesa who came to her rescue, her voice for once almost gentle as she placed her hand on Jamie's shoulder and smiled down at him.

'Of course he likes you, *pequeño*. Is that not so, Ruy?'

'What man can deny his own flesh and blood?' Ruy drawled sardonically, and Davina wondered if she was alone in remembering the accusation he had just hurled at her about Jamie's parentage. She had come to Spain reluctantly, and only for Jamie's sake, and if anyone had told her that if Ruy had repudiated them that she would insist on remaining she would have denied it most emphatically. It was not in her nature to be mercenary or grasping, wealth and position mattered little in her book when balanced against love and happiness, but something in Ruy's cold condemnation and lack of feeling for both of them had aroused all her fiercest maternal instincts; and for the sake of her child she was prepared to suffer indignities she would never have tolerated merely for her own gain. Jamie was Ruy's son, he had every right to be here at the Palacio, but one thing was going to be made quite clear to both Ruy and his family.

'Jamie is your child, Ruy,' she told him calmly. 'Oh, I know why you would prefer not to believe it. I'm surprised you haven't already had our marriage set aside. Had you done so and married Carmelita, she might have had a son of your own to displace Jamie, and then none of this would have been necessary.'

His harsh laughter jarred, shocking her into immobility. 'Nothing is quite that easy. Jamie would still have been my heir, whether he is my child or not, simply because he bears my name . . .'

'And knowing that Carmelita refused to marry you?'

She didn't know what prompted her to goad him like that; perhaps it was the nagging ache deep down inside her, a wound which refused to heal; the memory of how she had felt when she first discovered that Ruy did not love her and was merely using her instead to be revenged upon the woman whom he did love.

'Carmelita had no place in her life for a platonic relationship with a man,' he told her cruelly, 'and since I can no longer give her what she desires, she has found it elsewhere.'

'Carmelita has recently married and gone back to Argentina, with her new husband,' Sebastian interrupted, and as he said the words, Davina felt the full picture falling into place. Ruy's mother had always wanted him to marry Carmelita, but now, knowing that her plans must come to nothing, she had decided to fall back on what was left to her . . . Jamie. Only he would never be allowed to become cold and uncaring like his father, Davina told herself. He would not be brought up to think himself lord of all that he surveyed, to walk roughshod over anything and anyone who stood in his way, to ruthlessly and remorselessly crush underfoot the dreams and hopes of others . . . as Ruy had crushed hers.

'It has been a long day, and Jamie is tired,' she told her mother-in-law. 'If someone could show us to our rooms . . .'

'Motherhood has taught you courage, little white dove,' Ruy mocked. 'So cool and brave. I wonder how deep it is, that cool façade . . .'

'Just as deep as it needs to be to protect my son,' Davina told him with a calm she was far from feeling. How long could she endure the sort of mental and verbal torment he was handing out and not crack under it? Hard on the heels of the thought came the comforting knowledge that she was unlikely to see much of him. He was, after all, hardly likely to seek her out . . .

'So you intend to stay?' The hooded eyes watching her were unreadable, but guessing that he had hoped to frighten her into running away, for a second time, Davina lifted her chin proudly to stare back at him. 'For Jamie's sake—yes. Personally I wouldn't touch so much as a peseta of your money, Ruy, but Jamie is your son and . . .'

'And you have no objection to touching what will one day be his?' her husband mocked savagely.

At her side Davina's hands turned into minute angry fists. That hadn't been what she had been going to say at all. She had been about to explain to him that Jamie had been ill, that he needed building up, despite his robust appearance, and that for her child's sake she was willing to endure the torment and insult of knowing herself unwanted in this house.

'Which rooms . . .' she began, ignoring Ruy and turning to his mother, but Ruy forestalled her, his face cruel and malevolent as he too turned towards the older woman, anticipating Davina's question. 'Yes, Madre, which rooms have you given my delightful wife and child? The bridal suite, which we occupied before?' He shook his head and the sneer was clearly visible now. 'I think not. This wheelchair might be able to perform miracles, as Dr Gonzales tells me, but it still cannot climb stairs.'

Davina wasn't the only one to gasp. Even the Condesa seemed to go a little paler, her mouth nearly as grim as her son's as she addressed him.

'What nonsense is this, Ruy? Jamie and Davina will have a suite of rooms to themselves.'

'They will share mine,' Ruy corrected softly. 'I will not have the servants gossiping about my wife who leaves me and then returns only when I can no longer act the part of her husband. Well?' he demanded, turning to Davina. 'Have you nothing to say, no protests to make? Are you not going to tell me that you will return to England rather than suffer the indignity of sharing a room—a bed—with a crippled wreck?'

Davina knew then what he was trying to do—that he was attempting to frighten her into leaving, and how close he had come to succeeding. The mere thought of sharing a room with him, of suffering the intimacies such proximity would bring, had started her stomach churning protestingly. He might not be able to act the part of a husband, as he put it, but he was still a man— the man she had loved, and although her love had died her memories had not.

'You won't drive me away, Ruy,' she told him quietly. 'No matter what you do, I intend to stay, for Jamie's sake.'

A servant had to be summoned and instructed to prepare a room for Jamie. Davina could feel the girl watching her as Ruy spoke to her, and although she could not quite catch what was being said, her skin prickled warningly. When she had gone Sebastian and Rosita excused themselves, and as Rosita hurried past her, Davina thought she glimpsed compassionate pity in the other girl's eyes.

'My poor timid sister-in-law,' Ruy mocked, correctly interpreting Rosita's look. 'She sincerely pities you, but you have nothing to fear—unless it is the acid tongue of a man who has drunk ambrosia only to find it turning to acid gall on his lips.'

'Acid burns,' Davina reminded him coolly. Her heart was thumping with heavy fear, and she longed to retract her statement that she intended to stay. Jamie, who had returned to her side, clutching at her for support, suddenly abandoned her to walk across to Ruy for a second time, eyeing him uncertainly.

'I have a pushchair too,' he told Ruy conversationally, while Davina listened with her heart in her mouth. 'Mummy pushes me in it when I get tired. Who pushes you?'

'I can push myself,'Ruy told him curtly, but nevertheless, and much to her surprise, Davina saw him demonstrate to Jamie exactly how he could manoeuvre the chair. Something in her mother-in-law's stance caught her attention, and as she glanced across at her the other woman looked away, but not before Davina had seen the sheen of tears in her eyes.

How would she feel if that was her child confined to that chair? The sudden clenching fear of her heart gave her the answer, and for the first time she began to feel pity for the older woman. It was a dangerous thing she had done, summoning them here, and one which could alienate her completely from Ruy. She glanced across at him, her breath constricting in her throat as she saw

the two dark heads so close together. Ruy had lifted
Jamie on to his lap and the little boy was solemnly
examining the controls of the chair.

'He is Ruy's mirror image,' the Condesa said quietly.
All at once she looked very old, and Davina had to
force herself to remember how coldly this woman had
received her in this very room when Ruy had brought
her here as his new bride. The trouble was that she
had not been prepared for the hostility that greeted
her. But then she had not been prepared for anything,
least of all falling in love with Ruy. It had all happened
so quickly—too quickly, she thought soberly. She had
fallen in love with Ruy without knowing him. He had
married her for . . . For what? Revenge? For punishment? She shuddered suddenly, reflecting on the
harshness of a nature which could enable a man to turn
his back on the woman he loved and put another in
her place, merely as a means of punishment for some
small peccadillo. And yet the first time she met him
she had thought him the kindest man on earth—and
the most handsome.

It had been in Cordoba. She had gone on holiday
with friends—or more properly acquaintances—girls
she knew from her work at the large insurance offices
in London. Their main interest in Spain lay on its
beaches; flirting with the dark-eyed Spanish boys who
gave full rein to their ardent natures in the presence of
these Northern girls with their cool looks and warm
natures, so different from those of the girls of their own
country whose chastity was carefully protected until
marriage gave their husbands the right to initiate them
into the ways of love. Davina had felt differently. She
had come to Spain to explore its history—a history
which had fascinated her since her early teens, when

she had fallen in love with the mystery of a land ruled for centuries by the aristocratic, learned Moors, who had bequeathed to it not only their works of art, but also their colouring and fire.

She had been half way to falling in love with Ruy even before she met him, she acknowledged wryly, for her head had been stuffed with foolish dreams of handsome Moorish warriors astride Arab horses, flowing white robes cloaking lean bronzed limbs, glittering eyes softening only for the women they loved. A sigh trembled past her lips. That was how Ruy had first appeared to her—a heroic figure who seemed to spring suddenly out of nowhere, rescuing her from the gang of teenage boys who had been harassing her as she left the Mosque. His curt words had cut through them like a whiplash, dispersing them to the four winds, and her trembling gratitude at his timely intervention had changed to worshipful adoration when he had insisted on sweeping her off to a small café to drink coffee and tell him what she had been doing in Spain. He, it appeared, was in Cordoba on business. His family owned a hacienda where they bred bulls for the bullfight, and it was in connection with the annual *corrida*—the running of young untried bulls through the streets—that he was in Cordoba.

Davina had listened fascinated, held in thrall to the magnetism of the man; to the sheer pleasure of hearing him speak, his English perfect and yet still possessing something of the liquid gold of his own language.

She had agreed almost at once when he invited her to accompany him to watch the gypsies dancing the flamenco—not, as she discovered, the polished empty performance put on for the tourists, but the real thing; as different from the other as tepid water to champagne.

They had left before the climax; before the black-browed gypsy claimed his partner in the culmination of a dance so sexually explicit that merely watching it had brought the blood surging to her veins, her expression unknowingly betraying as she watched the dancers, and the man seated opposite her watched her. He had not lived his twenty-nine years without learning something of women, and what he saw in Davina's face told him, more surely than any words, the extent of her untutored innocence.

Davina hadn't known it, but it was that knowledge which had sealed her fate—as she later discovered.

When Ruy had proposed to her she had been robbed of words, dizzied and humbled by the sheer gratitude of knowing that the love she had come to feel for him in the short week they had been together was returned. She had had no knowledge when she accepted him that he was merely using her as a tool to torture the woman he really loved—the fiery Spanish beauty who could give him so much more than she herself could offer.

They had been married quietly—a church ceremony in keeping with Ruy's religion—and that had been the first time she realised that her husband possessed a title—that she had a title. It shouldn't have surprised her. He had about him an ingrained arrogance which should have warned her that here was no ordinary mortal. He had been a little amused by her stammered concern that she might not be able to match up to his expectations, that nothing in her life had prepared her for the role of Condesa; wife of a Spanish grandee. It was only when his amusement gave birth to bored impatience that Davina learned fear of her new husband, but this had been swiftly banished by the brief, almost tormenting caress of his lips against hers.

Prior to their marriage he had made no attempt to seduce her, and in her innocence she had mistaken this lack of desire for her as respect. She had often wondered, since her return to England, if she had not gone to him that first night after their arrival at the Palacio, had not let him see that she wanted him . . . and if he had not been in such a blazing rage of anger against his mother, whether he would not have made love to her; whether in fact it had been his intention to have their marriage annulled when Carmelita had been suitably brought to heel. But above all else Ruy was a man of honour. Once he had in actual fact made her his wife there was no going back—for either of them. Until she had conceived his son, and learned exactly why he had married her. With that knowledge how could she have remained? She might have suspected that all was not well between them, but until she was brought face to face with the truth she had been able to delude herself. When that was no longer possible she had escaped to London, taking Jamie with her, and leaving her mother-in-law to convey to her son the good news that he was now free . . .

Free . . . Her eyes were drawn irresistibly to the man in the wheelchair and for a brief moment pity overwhelmed her bitterness. Ruy would never be free again. Ruy, whose superb, physical, *male* body had taught her the full meaning of womanhood, never to make love, ride, swim or dance again.

'Look at her!' His words cut through her thoughts. 'She cries. For what, my lovely wife? For having to share my bed and being perhaps tormented by all that we once knew together, or have other men, other lovers, obliterated the memory of the pleasure I taught you?'

'Ruy!'

His mouth twisted bitterly at the warning tone in his mother's voice. 'What is it, Madre?' he demanded savagely. 'Am I to be denied the pleasure of speaking about love as well as that of experiencing it, or does it offend you that a man in my condition should have such thoughts? You who brought me the news that the woman I loved had left me . . .'

So the Condesa had been the one to tell Ruy that Carmelita was leaving him . . . Davina repressed a small shudder. She couldn't understand how the other girl could have done it. Had she been in her shoes, she thought with a fierce stab of pain, had she been the recipient of Ruy's love, nothing would have kept her from his side. He might be physically restricted, but he was still the same man; still very much a man! Her wayward thoughts shocked her, widening her eyes as purple as the hearts of pansies with mingled pain and disbelief. She was over Ruy. She had put the past behind her. All the love she had now was focused on Jamie. As though to reinforce the thought she reached out for the child, and her hair brushed Ruy's chin as she did so.

His withdrawal was immediate and unfeigned, and as she lifted Jamie from his lap, Davina was dismayed to discover that she was trembling. What was it about this man that had the power to affect her like this even now—so much so that his rejection of her was like the stabbing of a thousand knives?

Grateful that Jamie gave her an excuse to look away from the contempt she felt sure must be in his eyes, she busied herself with the little boy, listening to his informative chatter.

A manservant appeared, silent-footed and grave-faced, and positioned himself behind Ruy's chair.

'This is Rodriguez, my manservant,' he told Davina sardonically. 'The third member of our new *ménage à trois*. You will have to grow accustomed to him, since he performs for me all those tasks I can no longer perform for myself. Unless of course you wish to take them over for yourself . . . as a penance perhaps . . . and a fitting one. You took pleasure from my body when it was physically perfect, Davina, so perhaps it is only just that you should endure its deformity now.'

'Ruy!'

Davina thought her mother-in-law's protest was on account of the indelicacy of her son's conversation, but she ought to have known better, Davina decided, when she continued angrily, 'The doctor has told you, the paralysis need not be permanent. Much can be done . . .'

'To make me walk like an animal, used to moving on all fours—yes, I know.' Ruy dismissed the notion impatiently, disgust curling the corners of his mouth. 'Thank you, Madre, but no. You have interfered enough in my life as it is.' His glance embraced both Davina and the child held in her arms. 'Rodriguez, you will take me to my room. Davina.'

When her mutely imploring glance at her mother-in-law went unheeded Davina followed the manservant reluctantly down the long passage leading off the hall, to a suite of rooms she dimly remembered as being what Ruy had once described as a 'bachelor suite'. It had been the custom for young male members of the family to live apart from their sisters and mothers after a certain age, he had told her. The custom had originated from the days when his Moorish ancestors had

been jealous of their wives, and any male eyes which
might look upon them.

From what she could remember the suite was quite
large, built around its own patio, and as Rodriguez
opened the double panelled doors leading into the *sala*
Davina heard the sound of fountains playing outside
and knew that she had not been mistaken.

In contrast to the rest of the house the room was
furnished almost simply, with clean, uncluttered furniture that combined the best of antique and modern.
The dark blue azulejo tiles were covered with a Persian
carpet—a rich mingling of blues and scarlets, touched
here and there with gold and pricelessly expensive. On
a marble coffee table placed strategically next to a
cream hide chesterfield were some magazines, and
again Davina felt her heart twist with pity that Ruy
was reduced to finding his pleasure in such a passive
way.

'You remember this part of the house?'

She refused to look at him. He had brought her to
this *sala* after that dreadful scene with his mother,
when the older woman had accused her of trapping
him into marriage, of forcing him to make an honest
woman of her. It was in here that he had dried her
tears before leading her out on to the patio, where she
had flung herself despairingly into his arms and they
had walked into the orange grove and . . .

'I'm hungry!' Jamie eyed her crossly. 'Mummy, I'm
hungry!'

'You hear that, Rodriguez?' Ruy demanded with an
upward lift of his eyebrows. 'My son is hungry. He is
not yet used to our way of life.'

A smile glimmered across the other man's sombre
features.

'Maria shall make you a paella, and you shall have oranges picked fresh from the trees,' Ruy promised him. 'Only be patient for a little while.'

Davina was a little surprised at Jamie's immediate response to the authority in his father's voice. Perhaps it was true that all boys needed the firmness of a father's hand. But would Ruy let his obvious bitterness against her spill out to sour his relationship with his son? Had she known that the invitation to come to Spain was not from him she knew she would never have ventured here to the Palacio, and yet having done so, she was strangely reluctant to return again to England.

The courtyard outside was all in darkness, but the patio doors had been left open to allow the scents of the night to drift in—the spicy, sharp smell of the oranges, a constant reminder of that night when Jamie had been conceived; the sweetness of night-scented stocks, those timid, almost insipid flowers that only revealed their true beauty during the hours of darkness when their perfume filled the night air.

If she remembered rightly, beyond the patio was a swimming pool. She had swum in it once with Ruy. She pushed the thought aside, unwilling to remember the warmth of Ruy's arms around her as he pulled her down beneath the silken water, only releasing her when her lips had been subjected to a masterful, demanding kiss. Then she had thought that he loved her. She had not known about Carmelita.

The *sala* connected with a smaller room which had been turned into a tiny kitchen, presumably so that Ruy could be completely independent of the rest of the household if he wished, and Davina sensed intuitively that there must be many times when his pride could no longer bear the lash of enduring the silent pity of the rest of his family; when he must prefer to be hidden from the world to suffer alone. And yet he had insisted that she and Jamie were to share his suite, to share his torment . . .

Beyond the kitchen was a room which had been converted into a bedroom, opulently rich in its furnishings, but it was the huge double bed which drew Davina's eyes, fear hidden in their amethyst depths as she stared at it.

'Where's my bed?' Jamie demanded suddenly, breaking the silence. 'And where's my mummy's bed?'

'Your mummy's bed is here,' Ruy said silkily, turning aside to murmur something to Rodriguez, who disappeared in soft-footed silence through a door at the far end of the room.

'Through that door is the bathroom,' Ruy told Davina when he had gone, 'and beyond that a dressing room. Jamie shall sleep there for the time being.'

'And I shall sleep with him,' Davina said bravely. At home she had only a very small flat, and Jamie's small bed was in the same room as hers. It would frighten the small boy to find himself sleeping alone, but when she attempted to explain this to Ruy he cut across her explanation, his voice harsh as he said cruelly, 'You will sleep here in this room in my bed, Davina, otherwise Jamie will be banished to another part of the house. Do you understand me?'

'Why?'

His eyes searched her face, and for the first time she saw the true extent of his bitterness.

'Why? Because you are my wife,' he said softly. 'Because I will not endure the pitying glances of my servants and my family when it becomes known that my wife has returned to me only because she knows she will no longer be expected to undergo the degradation of sharing my bed. That was what you once called it, wasn't it?' he continued unmercifully. 'Degradation of the very worst sort? You don't even begin to know what it means, but you will learn, sharing this room with me, being forced to witness all the thousand and one indignities that my . . . my disability forces upon me. In fact . . .' his eyes roamed her set white face, 'I think you *should* take the place of Rodriguez.'

His fingers snaked out, grasping her wrist and making her gasp with pain, unable to believe that their hard, vibrant warmth belonged to a man who was no longer fully in control of his own body. 'It hurts? You should be grateful that you can feel pain,' he concluded grimly. '*Madre de Dios*, I wish I could!'

Davina swallowed a lump in her throat. Despite his desire to hurt and wound her, she could not prevent pity welling up inside her. Dear God, what torment he must be in, this man who had always taken for granted his male power. To find it cut off like this must surely be the worst blow fate could have dealt him. She knew she ought to feel some sense of satisfaction, some pleasure in knowing that he was now suffering as he had once caused her to suffer, but all she could feel was an overwhelming desire to reach out and brush the silky black hair off his forehead, to hold and comfort him as she might have done Jamie . . . The thought stunned her, rooting her to the spot as she stared blindly around her, not seeing the elegant room with its rich furnishings, the carved bed, the Persian carpets, the antique furniture, the elegant graciousness of a house that had been inhabited by Ruy's family for generation after generation; children brought up in a tradition, children of whom her son was the latest.

The door opened suddenly, and Rodriguez appeared with her luggage. Without looking at Ruy Davina followed him through the bathroom with its sunken bath in jade green malachite, the taps in the same material, azulejo tiles adorning the floor.

Beyond it was a small plainly furnished room overlooking the courtyard, with a single bed and a carved chest of drawers. When they were alone Davina undressed Jamie, before taking him back to the bathroom to wash his hands and face before she put him to bed. He chattered continuously, and she answered his questions almost mechanically, her mind still in that other bedroom with the man whose child Jamie was.

As though on cue, the moment Jamie was installed in bed the door opened again, and this time a woman came in carrying a tray, steaming fragrantly.

Jamie was not a fussy eater, and he tucked into the paella with such obvious relish that Davina had to repress a small smile. Contrary to her expectations Jamie seemed to be adapting very well to his new surroundings—far better than she was likely to do herself.

Only when she was quite sure that he was asleep did she return to the other room, unable to repress her feeling of relief when she saw Sebastian in the room, talking to Ruy.

'Ruy, will you not reconsider?' Davina heard him saying in a low voice as she re-entered the room. 'Surely you wish to spare Davina the . . .'

'The sight of my crippled limbs?' Ruy said harshly. 'Why? Am I spared them? Am I spared anything? No, it will do no good to plead for compassion for my wife, Sebastian,' he added cruelly. 'Or is it guilt that brings you to this room, little brother? After all, had you provided Madre with her grandson, there would be no need for Davina to be here, would there?'

A small sound must have betrayed Davina's presence, for both men turned at the same time.

'Ah, there you are,' Ruy drawled in a false parody of tenderness. 'Just in time to help me change for dinner.'

'I don't want any dinner,' Davina began, but her protest was overruled by Sebastian's angry protest.

'You cannot do this!' he told Ruy. 'You cannot mean to subject your wife to such indignity . . . Have you no compassion, Ruy? How is Jamie?' he asked Davina, turning to her. 'Has he settled down all right?'

'Better than I expected,' Davina told him. There was guilt and embarrassment in his eyes, and she thought she knew now why he had been so offhand with her at the airport. It was obvious that his mother had told him to say nothing of Ruy's condition to her, and now he felt guilty about the way his brother was treating her.

'Rosita had better be careful,' Ruy commented sardonically when Sebastian had gone. 'My little brother's concern for you is most touching. I trust you have something better than that to wear for dinner,' he added, giving her slender figure a disparaging glance. 'You will not have forgotten that we observe the formalities here at the Palacio.'

She hadn't. Since Jamie's birth and her flight to England there hadn't been any money for luxuries like evening dresses, but she still had the clothes Ruy had insisted on buying for her after their marriage—when he had realised that he was irrevocably tied to her, and had tried to make the best of their mesalliance. Her mouth twisted a little bitterly and for the first time she realised that she had been handed a weapon which she could use to gain reparation in full for all the hurt Ruy had caused her, if she chose to use it. She was to take the place of his manservant, or so he had commanded, and if she chose, she could make the performance of those small intimate tasks which would be required of her as humiliatingly agonising for Ruy as he had once made her life for her!

'You will go and prepare yourself for dinner,' Ruy commanded her curtly, frowning when she made no attempt to move.

'Don't you want me to help you first?'

Something in the soft tone of her voice must have made him suspicious, because he frowned darkly, manoeuvring his chair past her. 'Not tonight,' he said abruptly. 'I am hungry, and I don't propose to wait all evening for you to perform the tasks Rodriguez can perform in half the time.' He glanced at his watch, pushing back the cuff of his shirt, and Davina felt her stomach constrict painfully at the sight of his lean, sinewy wrist, and the dark hairs curling against the gold mesh of his watch-strap. All too vividly she could remember how that hand had so arrogantly caressed her yielding flesh, had turned her from girl to woman and taught her pleasure . . .

CHAPTER THREE

SHE had endured many formal dinners during her days at the Palacio, but none which had tautened her muscles to breaking point as this one was doing, Davina reflected, as the long meal seemed to drag on interminably.

On the table her glass of sherry still stood barely touched. It was Silvadores sherry, matured in their own *bodega* near Cadiz; the very best *fino*, dry and clean to the palate. The first time she had tasted it Davina had found it too dry, but habit had accustomed her taste-buds; all those long, lazy afternoons whose end had been signalled by the serving of sherry and tapas on the patio. She clamped down on the thought. On too many thoughts.

'You are not hungry?'

It was Rosita who whispered the words understandingly, but Ruy who answered them for her, even though they were separated by the length of the polished table, gleaming with silver and crystal. The Silvadores had no need to parade their wealth ostentatiously, and Davina knew that the fine china plates and silver cutlery they were using were nothing compared with the exquisite Sèvres and Meissen china locked away with the gold plate which was a legacy from the Conde who had sailed to the Americas. The family's wealth derived from many sources—from the sherry business, from land they owned all over Spain, from the young bulls raised on the *estancia*; from busi-

ness ventures involving the development of exclusive
holiday resorts—but it was here in this ancient
Moorish castle that they had set their deepest roots.
And Ruy was the sole ruler of this empire. How had
his accident occurred? By what means had he been
robbed of his independence? Davina glanced down the
length of the table. Seeing him seated no one could
guess that the powerful muscles moving smoothly beneath his dinner jacket were all that remained of his
old physical perfection.

As the meal dragged on images as sharp and crystal
clear as the day they were formed imposed themselves
relentlessly on her mind; Ruy swimming in the pool;
Ruy riding at the *estancia*, training the young bulls
destined for the arena; Ruy dancing . . . making love
. . . She shuddered deeply and wrenched her thoughts
back to the present, trying to tell herself that it was
divine justice that Ruy, who had cruelly and callously
used her to get back at the woman he really loved,
should now be deserted by that woman. Why had
Carmelita done it? Davina wondered. She had been a
bride of a matter of weeks when the sultry Spanish
woman had sought her out at this very house, reinforc-
ing what Davina had already heard from her mother-
in-law—that Ruy loved her; that there had been an
understanding between them for many years; that they
were on the point of announcing their betrothal when
they had quarrelled, and Ruy in a fit of pique because
she, Carmelita, did not choose to run to his bidding
like the milk and water English miss he had married
had chosen a bride as different from the seductive
Spaniard with her night-dark hair and carmine lips as
it would have been possible to find. She would get him
back, Carmelita had told her. A milksop like her could

never hold a man like Ruy, whose lovemaking demanded from his partner a deep-seated understanding of the complexities that went into the making of a man whose blood combined the fiery fanaticism of early Christianity with thousands of years of Moorish appreciation of the sensual arts—a woman such as Carmelita herself.

And yet now Carmelita had abandoned him. Because he was no longer the man he had once been; no longer capable of outriding the wind, of making love until dawn tinted the sky, or because her pride would not allow any child she bore him to come second to the son his English wife had given him? Under the polite mask of Spanish courtesy lay deep wells of passion that were a legacy of their Moorish ancestors, as Davina already knew. Who could say what had prompted Carmelita to desert Ruy and make her life with another?

At last the meal drew to a close, but instead of feeling relieved Davina felt her nerves tighten still further, the implacable determination in Ruy's eyes like the fiendish threat of a torturer ready to turn the screws that final notch which separated excruciating pain from oblivion by the mere hair's breadth.

All through the meal she had answered her mother-in-law's questions about Jamie's upbringing as politely as she could. Once she might have been intimidated by this woman whose ancestors had numbered kings and queens among their intimates, but where Jamie was concerned she would allow nothing to stand in the way of what she considered right for her child, and this she had been making coolly and firmly clear to Ruy's mother throughout the meal.

By the time she realised she was carrying Jamie she

had been too numbed by pain to care, for by then she had known exactly why Ruy had married her, and why too he spent so many hours away from the Palacio— away from her bed. The baby she had been carrying had been incidental to her pain, but after his birth she had been overwhelmed by such love for Jamie that that pain had started to recede, if only minutely. As she held him to her breast and felt him suckle strongly she had known that whatever the cost to herself Jamie would not be brought up in a house where his mother was despised. And her mother-in-law had aided her in her flight. She had been the one who had brought those damning photographs of Ruy and Carmelita together at the *estancia*, while she, his wife, bore his child alone. She had left the hospital one cold, grey winter afternoon, taking a plane for London, not knowing what path her life would take, but only knowing that she must get away from Spain and Ruy before her love for him destroyed her completely.

She had been lucky—very lucky, she acknowledged wryly. The chance entering of a competition in a women's magazine had led to a contract for illustrations for a magazine serial and from there to her present work on children's books. She was not rich, but she had enough to buy a small flat in a Pembrokeshire village; enough to keep Jamie and herself in modest comfort, but not enough to give the little boy the warm winters he needed until his strength was built up.

After dinner while Rodriguez served coffee in the *sala* Sebastian came and sat beside her.

'You must try to forgive Ruy,' he told her awkwardly in a low voice while his brother was speaking to the manservant. 'He has changed since his accident.' He shrugged explicitly. 'Who would not, especially a man like Ruy who was always so . . .'

'Male?' Davina supplied wryly, watching the blood surge faintly beneath Sebastian's olive skin. 'Oh yes, I can guess at the devils that torment him now, Sebastian, but what I can't understand is how your mother dared to conceal from him that she was sending for me.'

Sebastian shrugged again, this time avoiding her eyes completely. 'You have seen how Ruy reacted. Just as she knew that you would not come if you knew the truth, so she knew that Ruy would not allow you to be sent for. He has his pride . . .'

'And was deserted by the woman he loves,' Davina supplied.

Sebastian looked surprised and uncomfortable. 'That is so, but my brother is not the man to enforce his emotions on a woman who does not want them. You need have no fears on that score, Davina.'

'I haven't,' she told him dryly. 'I'm well aware that the only reason I'm tolerated here is because of Jamie; the son Ruy has always refused to acknowledge . . . the son who even now he tries to pretend might not be his . . .'

The telephone rang and Sebastian excused himself hurriedly, leaving her alone. Stifling a yawn, she closed her eyes, meaning only to rest them for a few minutes.

Whether it was the faint hiss of the wheelchair, or some sixth sense alerting her to another's presence that woke her, Davina did not know. When she opened her eyes the *sala* was in darkness apart from one solitary lamp casting a pool of soft rose light over the ancient Persian carpet.

'So, you are awake. I seem to remember that you had difficulty before adjusting to our hours.'

'You should have woken me before.' A glance at her wristwatch confirmed that it was late—nearly two in the morning. They were the only occupants of the room, and her sense of vulnerability increased as she realised that Ruy had watched her as she slept, observed her in her most unguarded moments. No, not her most unguarded, she acknowledged seconds later; those had been when they made love. She shivered involuntarily, the light shining whitely on Ruy's teeth as he bared them mockingly.

'Why do you shake so, *querida*?' he asked dulcetly. 'Can it be that you are afraid of me? A man who cannot move without the assistance of this chair? You fear the caged tiger, where you would not fear the free?'

It was on the tip of her tongue to point out that caged tigers could be unmercifully lethal, driven to scar and wound by the very virtue of their imprisonment, and so it was with Ruy himself. In him she sensed all the dammed-up power and bitterness of a man for whom life has lost its sharp sweetness and turned to aloes on his tongue.

'What is it you fear most, my little wife?' He was close enough for her to smell the sherry on his breath and to remember with contracting stomach muscles the taste of his lips on hers. 'That I shall exact payment for your desertion of me; for depriving me of my son?'

'You could have come after us,' Davina reminded him levelly. 'If you'd really wanted us. . . .'

He made a harsh, guttural sound in his throat, his eyes darkening to anger. 'Is that what you wanted in a husband, Davina, a man who would prove himself to you over and over again? And the man you left me for? The Englishman who meant more to you than your marriage vows—what happened to him, or did he no longer want you when you stopped calling yourself the Condesa de Silvadores?'

Davina had never been able to think of the title in connection with herself, but she was too bewildered by what Ruy had said to pay too much attention to his reminder that she had stopped using his name when she left his house. There had been no man in her life since the day she met Ruy, apart from his son, and it infuriated her to think that he dared to berate her about some imagined lover when he . . .

'There was no one!' she started to protest angrily, but Ruy's expression said that he did not believe her.

'No?' he sneered. 'You are lying to me, *querida*. You were seen with him in Seville. And it is known that you left Spain with him, taking my child with you.'

From the past Davina conjured up the memory of a bearded, fair-haired fellow-Briton she had met in Seville. He had been an artist, and with this common bond between them they had started talking. Davina dimly remembered that her mother-in-law had found them chatting enthusiastically to one another in a small pavement café, and she, innocent that she was, had assumed the older woman's contempt sprang from discovering her drinking coffee in such a shabby little place, but now, with the benefit of hindsight, she realised that the Condesa must have thought she was having an affair, perhaps as a means of getting back at Ruy. So now she knew why Ruy had been so reluctant to believe that Jamie was his—and she hadn't helped. Although she had known of her pregnancy she had said nothing for several months, trapped in the bitterness of knowing herself unloved and keeping the knowledge of Jamie's conception to herself as though

she could use it as a talisman to ward off the threat of
Carmelita.

'At least you now acknowledge that Jamie is your
child,' was all she said. No matter what else might lie
unspoken about between them, she was not going to have
any aspersions or doubts cast on Jamie's parentage.

'So everyone tells me,' Ruy agreed bitterly. 'He must
have been conceived during our honeymoon,
before . . .'

'Before I discovered the real reason why you married
me?' Davina demanded proudly. Once she had known
about Carmelita she had steadfastly refused to share
Ruy's bed, even though by doing so she was causing
herself the utmost pain. There hadn't been a single
night when she had not lain awake until the early hours
remembering how it had felt to drift off to sleep in
Ruy's arms, feeling the strong, reassuring thud of his
heart against her ear, knowing herself held secure
against all the dangers the world had to offer, but she
had not been safe; Ruy's arms were not a haven, and
he had never intended them to be. He had taken her
because he felt sorry for her; because she had made
her desire for him so plain that he could not in all
compassion do anything else. Even now it made her
writhe in self-torment to remember their 'honeymoon'.
Until the marriage ceremony was over she had known
nothing about the Palacio, or Ruy's family. He was
taking her to his home, was all he had told her in
answer to her excited questions; to the house built in
the protective lee of the Sierras where Silvadores
brides had come since the Moors first settled this part
of Spain.

She had been excited and tremulous; excited because
this handsome, sophisticated man had chosen her as

his bride, and tremulous because she was stepping out of one world and into another. She knew next to nothing about men, having experienced only the chaste, fumbled kisses of the boys she had known at home. Her parents were both dead and she had been brought up by a grandmother who adhered to the moral code of her own generation, and thus Davina had not had the same licence permitted to her school friends. She remembered that Ruy had laughed when she tried to explain that he would not find her experienced in the ways of love, as were her contemporaries. Did she think he was blind? he had mocked tenderly. Did she honestly think he could not recognise an unblemished bud, still unopened? and she had been content to leave it there, not knowing that beneath the words lay the bitter thread of self-mockery, for the woman he should have married in her place was of his culture and sophistication, and knew all the ways there were of pleasuring a man, while she . . .

She grimaced slightly to herself. Was she so very different now? She might have borne a child, but she was no more experienced now than she had been when she left Ruy. All her body knew of pleasure had been imparted to it by him; and while he had not loved her he had been a courteous teacher, leading her gently into the paths of sensuality.

She hadn't realised that Ruy had crossed the room until the scent of oranges filled the air and she realised that he had pushed open the patio doors and was sitting with his back to her staring out into the night.

As the delicate fragrance filled the room, her thoughts were dragged unwillingly to the past; to her arrival at the Palace of the Orange Trees, that first dreadful dinner when the Condesa had unleashed upon

her unprotected head all her chagrin and fury at her
son's choice of bride, and Ruy had found her prone
upon the bed in the room she had been given—quite
separate from his—crying as though her heart would
break. She had been too engrossed in her own misery
then to be aware of the undercurrents eddying strongly
all about her; of Carmelita, whose dark passionate
beauty had repelled her, like an overblown flower with
the touch of decadence already upon it, or of why the
Spanish girl had looked at her with such hatred in her
eyes.

Ruy had dried her tears, had told her that all would
seem better in the morning. Davina had begged him
not to leave her alone, half hysterical at the thought of
staying in her room, separated from the man who was
now her husband, and she had been relieved when he
suggested that they walk through the orange grove, to
give her time to calm herself.

The evening had been mild, stars spangling the sky,
the scent of the oranges drifting all around them. Ruy
had taken her arm—more out of courtesy than desire,
she now realised, and if she had not stumbled over a
tussock of grass who knew what might have happened,
but she had done, and Ruy had bent to catch her,
causing them both to overbalance, and there beneath
the orange trees she had looked at him with her heart
in her eyes and mutely begged him to make her his
wife in deed as well as thought.

He had seemed to draw back from her, but she,
without shame, thinking that he returned her love and
was thinking only of propriety, had flung her arms
round his neck, pressing small agonised kisses to his
throat, drinking in the taste of his warm male flesh.
The outcome was inevitable. Ruy was a very male man

after all, and even if she was not the woman he loved she was there in his arms, and very, very available. He had been tender with her and careful, she could not fault him on that, and it was only later that she realised had he loved her more he might have found it hard to be quite so temperate. Even so, despite his care, his possession had caused her to cry out, the soft sound silenced by his mouth, and later, when she had slept a little, he had made love to her again, and this time there had been no pain. They had returned to the house, the scent of his flesh mingling with the perfume of the oranges, the two inextricably linked in her mind for all time, so that since she had left the Palacio she had been unable to touch the fruit.

After that they had been given adjoining rooms, and no matter how late it was when Ruy retired Davina had padded through to his room, begging him mutely to take her in his arms and reassure her that he still loved her. Dear God, what a crass fool she had been! He had never loved her at all. He had felt pity for her, that was all.

She had discovered the truth while he was visiting the bodega in Cadiz. She had wanted to go with him, but he had told her he would not be gone long. He wasn't, but it was still long enough for her world to come toppling down over her ears when her mother-in-law and then Carmelita opened her eyes to the truth. When Ruy returned she had had her things moved to another bedroom. He had never questioned her about her decision and she had never told him. The first few nights had been sleepless, while she listened in vain for the sound of him coming to seek her out, but why should he, when he had Carmelita, who could offer him so much more than she ever could? Carmelita, in

whose veins ran some of the proudest blood of Spain.
Carmelita, who could match him skill for skill, passion
for passion; Carmelita, whose vivid beauty paled her
own to a violet next to a hybrid rose. It had been that
week while Ruy was away that Davina had met Bob
Wilson in Seville and had been seen with him by Ruy's
mother; it had also been that week that she first suspected she was carrying Ruy's child.

'Do you intend to sit there all night? Is the thought
of sharing a room with me so repellent that you would
rather sleep upright in a chair? How you have
changed!' Ruy mocked savagely. 'I can remember a
time when you couldn't wait to share my bed—didn't
wait, in fact.' He laughed without humour when he
saw her white face illuminated in the pale glow of the
single lamp. 'Do not look so afraid, *amada*, I can no
longer walk with you through the orange groves of my
home and give way to an emotion as eternal as
man . . .'

Tormented by the images conjured by his careless
words, Davina got to her feet. 'I'm surprised you can
remember,' she said bitterly. 'After all, it was a long
time ago and scarcely important.'

'You think not?' In the shadows his face seemed to
harden, pain mingling with bitterness in the eyes that
raked her from head to foot—a trick of the shadows,
she imagined, for there was no reason why it should
cause Ruy pain to think of their marriage, unless it
was because of all that that simple ceremony had
deprived him of. 'You think a man forgets the vows he
makes, so easily. I am not like you, Davina. I cannot
treat our marriage so lightly.'

There was a brooding quality to the words that made
Davina wonder if this was why he had not taken steps

to have their marriage set aside before. Marriage was something which was taken very seriously in Spain, but surely Ruy had thought of this before the ceremony that made them man and wife? But then he had never intended it to be more than just a ceremony, she reminded herself, suddenly overwhelmed by a terrible feeling of guilt. If it had not been for her, for her foolish belief that he loved her, he could have been free to marry Carmelita, to father children on the woman he loved, instead of which ... She turned towards him impulsively, the moonlight turning her hair to silver and her eyes to dark mysterious pools of darkest purple, her expression unconsciously pleading as she reached out to him.

'Ruy, I know ours isn't an ideal situation, but must we be enemies? For Jamie's sake can't we try to put aside our differences, to ...'

The explosive curse ripped from his throat froze her where she stood. When he turned to face her his face was white with held-in anger. 'You can say that so easily,' he said harshly, 'but then it would suit you, wouldn't it? A wife, but yet not a wife; secure in your position within this household and yet absolved from the duties that go with that position. Is that why you came back? Because you perceived how you could have the best of both worlds ... Because you knew you would not have to share my bed?'

'I knew nothing about your accident,' Davina told him, shocked that he could think her capable of such calculation and greed.

'So, what is it you are offering me? Your pity?' His face contorted savagely. 'Keep it, for I do not want it. You are here on my sufferance alone, and sufferance is the operative word, Davina. Be careful that I don't

decide to exact penance for my suffering. Come, it is
time we retired.'

She moved towards his chair, but he motioned to
her to precede him towards his own suite, which she
did, wishing her heart would not thump so painfully,
and that she had not been foolish enough to allow Ruy
to see her compassion for him. He was a bitter man,
and bitter men sometimes delighted in inflicting pain
on others purely to relieve their own anguish. But
could whatever pain he chose to force her to endure
now compare with the agony she had known when she
realised she did not have his love?

She had half expected to find the manservant
Rodriguez waiting for Ruy in his room, despite the
latter's comments earlier in the evening, but when Ruy
switched on the light and flooded the room with bright
colour she saw that it was empty.

She was just about to step out of the room to check on
Jamie when Ruy seized her wrist painfully tight. Whatever might have happened to his lower body the muscles
of his arms and chest were as hard and firm as ever.

'Oh no, you don't escape so easily,' he mocked her
softly. 'You elected to come back here of your own
free will, my dear wife, and now you must start to
perform those duties which fate has chosen to be
yours.'

On the bed Davina saw a towelling robe which was
obviously Ruy's, and one of the thin silk nightdresses
she had brought with her from home.

'I wonder what was in the mind of the maid who
laid out those things,' Ruy drawled, following her eyes
to the bed. 'Was pity there for you, do you suppose,
because you are condemned to share the bed of a man
who is no man at all?'

'Stop it!' Davina's hands closed over her ears to blot out the harsh sound of Ruy's bitter laughter, but he reached for her wrists, dragging them downwards, so that she was forced to listen to his hatefully cold voice as he told her unmercifully, 'I have wished many times to blot out the truth, but God has not yet granted me the ability to do so. Who knows, perhaps tonight, with you in my bed, I might discover some panacea for the nightmares which haunt me. Help me to undress,' he commanded abruptly. 'It has been a long evening—longer perhaps than any other I have ever known.'

Davina glanced wildly towards the door and wetted her dry lips with the tip of her tongue. 'Surely Rodriguez——' she began uncertainly, but Ruy cut her off impatiently.

'Rodriguez is asleep in his own bed, would you have me wake him because of your selfish revulsion about seeing my body? What is it you fear the most? Looking upon my useless limbs, perhaps? Being forced to touch the dead skin and muscle?'

He sounded so cool, but beneath the controlled sarcasm of his words Davina could sense the dammed-up bitterness, and knew she could not tell him that what she feared was his loss of control if he found the strain of torturing both her and himself too much. Because to torture her was to torture himself, to reveal his innermost scars. Wanting to bring his torment to an end as much for himself as for her, she hurried to his side and began to unfasten the buttons of his shirt. It was a task she had performed countless thousands of times for Jamie and should have meant nothing to her at all, but the smooth brown flesh beneath her fingers was not a child's but a man's; the heart beating steadily

that which had lulled her to sleep, the crisp mat of
dark hairs on the lean chest an unbearable reminder of
the strength and warmth of his body possessing her
own.

'Come,' Ruy jeered softly, when she trembled, 'I can
remember a time when you were swifter than this, although then too your fingers shook, but then you had
something to anticipate, did you not? Then it was
desire and not fear that shone from your stormcloud
eyes.'

She had his shirt completely unfastened, the taut
flesh of his chest rising and falling with the rhythm of
his breathing. Perspiration beaded his upper lip and
beneath her palms his flesh felt warm and moist. She
tried to force herself not to remember how on other
occasions she had touched her lips to his skin, drinking
in the feel and taste of him, running her tongue along
the hard bones of his shoulders, absorbing the scent
and feel of him with senses blind to everything but
him.

She was bending to remove his shoes when she heard
the cry from the other room. Jamie! She straightened
up, her eyes flying to the door, and Ruy's followed
them.

'He must be something special, this child I have
given you, for you to care so deeply about him. What
is it, I wonder?'

'He hasn't been well.' The words came jerkily from
between her lips, as she remembered exactly how ill
Jamie had been. 'Please, I must go to him.' She rose
to her feet in one lithe movement, hurrying to the door
and opening it.

Jamie was clutching his battered teddybear, his eyes
wide and frightened.

'Mummy, I wanted you and you wasn't there,' he reproached gently. 'I was frightened!'

'What of, darling?' Davina asked him, kneeling down to push the thick dark hair, so like his father's, out of his eyes. 'You're quite safe here. You've got Teddy to look after you, and Mummy will be sleeping in the next room.'

'I want it to be like it is at home,' Jamie protested. 'I want you to sleep in my room.'

Suppressing a sigh, Davina explained to him that this was not possible. His room was very small, she told him, and there was not enough room for another bed.

She could share his, Jamie said reasonably, and when Davina told him that it wasn't big enough he said that his daddy could have this little room and then there would be enough room for Jamie and Mummy in Daddy's bed.

Sighing again, Davina reminded him that mummies and daddies slept in the same bed, just like in his story books, reflecting that while Jamie seemed to accept the presence of his father without too much curiosity this matter of the shared bedroom promised to be more difficult. The doctor had told her during Jamie's illness that it was unwise for her to have him in her room. 'Pretty girl like you—bound to marry again,' he had told her gruffly, 'and my lad here isn't going to take kindly to that if this state of affairs goes on much longer.'

Only when she was quite sure that Jamie was deeply asleep did Davina return to Ruy's room. It was in darkness and for a moment she thought that Ruy had come to his senses and decided to leave her and Jamie alone, but this thought was speedily despatched when her eyes grew accustomed to the darkness of the room and she saw the humped figure in the large double bed. The wheelchair was neatly folded beside the bed, and she frowned, wondering how Ruy had managed to finish undressing himself and get himself from the wheelchair into the bed—unless of course his disability was less severe than she had thought.

'Are are you coming to bed, or are you going to stand there all night like a nervous virgin?'

She had thought him asleep, and jumped as he rolled over on to his side, his eyes piercing the darkness as they searched for and found her.

She was in half a mind to demand a separate room, but her eye was caught by the wheelchair and a wave of pity overwhelmed her, softening her animosity towards him. Besides, she could hardly get one of the maids out of bed at this hour of the night, and if Jamie should wake again he would wonder where she had gone.

'In a moment,' she told him, surprised to discover how calm her voice was. 'First I want to have a bath.'

The bathroom was a sybaritic pleasure all on its own. The bath was wide and deep enough for two, set into the tiled floor, so that she had to step down into it. How did Ruy manage? she wondered as she sprinkled rose-scented bath crystals on the water and lay back, luxuriating in its perfumed warmth.

Ten minutes later, feeling relaxed and refreshed, she stepped out of the jade green tub and reached for the towel she had left in readiness. A mirrored wall threw her reflection back to her, emphasising her pale slenderness; the narrow waist and hips and the curved fullness of her breasts with their rose pink nipples. Since Jamie's birth her figure had become more voluptuous and it seemed to her disturbed gaze that her breasts seemed to swell and tauten, anticipating the touch of a lover. Dragging her eyes from the mirror, she wrapped herself quickly in a towel, rubbing herself dry briskly before slipping on her nightgown. Only when the slip of soft pink silk concealed her body did she turn back to the mirror and smooth moisturiser into her skin.

In the bedroom she found her hairbrush already laid out on the dressing table. An antique set of silver-backed brushes and cosmetic jars adorned the polished wood, and Davina brushed her hair automatically, her ears alert for any sound from Jamie's room. Her hair curled naturally and needed very little care apart from conditioning and generous brushing. It floated on her shoulders like a silken net as she padded across to the bed, taking care not to disturb the motionless figure lying on the opposite half of it as she slid back the covers and slipped down inside the cool freshness of soft linen sheets. During the nine months of their marriage she and Ruy had never slept together for an entire night. He had had his room and she had had hers, and it struck her as incongruous that they should do so now, when they had never been farther apart.

Despite the good twenty-four inches between them, she could feel the heat emanating from his body, her own absurdly aware of the deep even rise and fall of his breathing, her mind tormenting her with memories of his smooth teak skin, laid like silk over bone and muscle, fragrant with the musky odour of masculinity. Her body was as tense as a coiled spring.

'Go to sleep, Davina.'

She had thought him asleep and the words startled her to the point of closing her eyes obediently, and cringing back to the edge of the mattress until she realised that he could not follow her across the space which divided them even if he wished to do so. He had hurt her more than any man had ever hurt her before or after; she should be rejoicing in his downfall, so why did she have this overwhelming urge to take him in her arms and hold him as she held Jamie after he had had a tumble, cradling him against her breast and kissing away the pain? As sleep stole over her she fought against the tide of knowledge that would not be denied. All the love she had once felt for Ruy was dead, completely dead, and nothing could ever resurrect it. But deep down inside her a small voice whispered softly, 'Liar', and there were tears on her face as she finally slid into oblivion.

CHAPTER FOUR

SHE awoke to brilliant sunshine streaming in through the uncurtained windows, and Jamie patting her gently but impatiently on the arm.

'Come and watch my daddy swimming,' he besought her impatiently. 'Quickly, Mummy, before he stops. He can swim even faster than Superman!'

The events of the previous day came rolling back. Blinking uncertainly, Davina stared at the dent on the pillow next to hers, where Ruy's dark head had lain. Was Jamie imagining things, or was she the one whose imagination was playing tricks on her? How could Ruy, confined to a wheelchair, be swimming?

'Quickly, Mummy,' Jamie demanded, imperiously tugging at her nightgown. 'Quickly!'

Her son was dressed, his hair brushed tidily and his shorts and tee shirt clean; his sandals properly fastened and the right buttons in the correct buttonholes, tasks of which Jamie was not quite capable as yet.

Someone had dressed him. She glanced round the bedroom and then gasped, pulling up the covers as Rodriguez walked in.

'Rodriguez, is my daddy still swimming?' Jamie demanded impatiently.

The manservant's smile for the little boy was particularly warm. Spaniards loved children, Davina acknowledged, and it was obvious from the unselfconscious manner in which Jamie was chattering away to him that they had become firm friends.

'Rodriguez helped me to get washed and dressed, after he had helped my daddy,' Jamie told her, explaining how it came about that he was up and dressed. 'You were still asleep, Mummy. I wanted to wake you up, but Daddy said to leave you. I'm going to have my breakfast on the patio with Daddy. We're having proper orange juice from real oranges, and then Rodriguez is going to show me where they grow . . .'

She should have been pleased that he was adapting so quickly, but she couldn't quite prevent the small stab of pain his words caused her. Almost overnight he had changed from her baby to an independent young man who preferred the company of his own sex to hers.

'Well, if we're having breakfast on the patio I'd better get up and dressed before I miss it,' she said with a cheerfulness she wasn't feeling.

'Yes, hurry,' Jamie instructed her. 'And come and watch us swimming. I'm going to swim too, Mummy. Daddy said I could if you were there to watch me. Rodriguez has found my ring . . .'

Swimming was Jamie's latest accomplishment and love. Davina had been taking him to the local baths for several months. The doctor had suggested that the exercise might help to build up the muscles which had become a little wasted during the long weeks of his illness.

She glanced at the manservant and as though he had read her mind he offered politely, 'I shall watch him for you, Excelentisima, until you are dressed and then I must get His Excellency's breakfast.'

The title fell unfamiliarly on her ears, even though she had grown accustomed to hearing it during the brief months of her marriage. No matter how close

Rodriguez might be to Ruy, Davina knew he would never dream of not using his title. It was a matter of pride—to them both. A Spaniard felt no sense of inferiority to someone of higher rank, Ruy had explained coolly to her when she had commented upon it, because in his eyes a man was measured in other ways, and had Ruy suggested that Rodriguez adopt a more familiar attitude towards him the manservant would have taken it as an insult; a suggestion that he considered himself inferior to his master and therefore in need of compensation for his inferior role, whereas in reality they were both men and equal therefore in the sight of God and each other.

Davina dressed quickly, pulling on a soft lilac tee-shirt which accentuated the colour of her eyes, and a pretty floral wrap-round skirt which emphasised her long slender legs and narrow waist. The outfit was simple and yet becoming, although she herself was unaware of it and pulled a slight face at her reflection in the mirror, remembering the couture gowns worn by her mother-in-law and Carmelita. Of course she could not hope to compete with them; but then why should she want to?

Head held high, she walked in the direction of the swimming pool. Although it was early in the day the air was warm, and the sun strong enough for Davina to find it necessary to perch her sunglasses on the edge of her nose as the clear, pure light bounced back off the surface of the water.

She could hear Jamie shrieking with laughter as she approached the pool, and as she rounded the corner she could see why. Ruy was playing with him, tossing him a huge brightly coloured beach ball, which Jamie's chubby, baby hands reached for impatiently whilst his inflated arm bands kept him afloat, Rodriguez's sharp eyes alert for the first sign of any danger.

Man and boy were both so engrossed in their game that at first they didn't see her. Watching them Davina felt her heart contract with an emotion she was reluctant to name. With the water running off the brown satiny skin, the thick dark hair plastered wetly to his skull, Ruy might have been the lover she had once known. Watching him cleave the water powerfully as he directed the beach ball towards Jamie she found it almost impossible to believe that he was actually paralysed; that those powerful brown limbs slicing the water were incapable of any feeling . . . of anything . . . She made a small choked sound in her throat, drawing the swimmers' attention to her. Jamie squealed excitedly. 'Look at us, Mummy, we're playing ball . . . Watch my daddy swim. He can swim faster than anyone else in the whole world . . .'

Darling Jamie. How readily he accepted Ruy's role in his life.

She could hear Rodriguez moving behind her, presumably going to get the breakfast now that she was here to watch over Jamie . . . and Ruy. In the water he had all the swift sureness of a fish, but out of it he was equally helpless. When she could see that Jamie was tiring she went to the edge of the tiled pool and leaned down, holding out her arms to him. His hair was as wet as Ruy's, plastered to a small skull which was an exact replica of his father's. He was beaming with delight when Davina lifted him out.

'Soon, I'll be able to swim as fast as my daddy,' Jamie told her as she started to towel him dry. She glanced over her shoulder, half expecting to see Rodriguez emerging from the house. When she had crossed the patio she had seen the table already prepared for their breakfast, and as she knew from experience Ruy normally breakfasted on crisp, fresh rolls and honey which did not take long to prepare. Her own mouth was starting to water at the thought of those rolls, fresh from the Palacio ovens. Jamie stepped out of his brief trunks and Davina looked round for his clean clothes before she remembered that he had come out with the manservant.

'You stay here for a moment,' she instructed him. 'I'll go and bring your shorts and a tee-shirt.'

When she returned there was still no sign of Rodriguez. Ruy was still in the pool, but as she walked towards them a very young maid came hurrying towards her holding a tray. On it was a bowl and a packet of cereal, and with smiles and gestures the girl indicated that it was intended for Jamie.

Requesting her to place it on the table Davina found Jamie sitting patiently by the side of the pool, still watching Ruy. In the strong sunlight his skin looked almost unnaturally pale—a legacy of his illness—and Davina covered his arms and legs with sunscreen before dressing him and pulling a canvas sunhat firmly down over his dark hair.

There was still no sign of Rodriguez. Ruy's robe was lying over his chair, and Davina glanced uncertainly from it to the seal dark head at the other side of the pool, wondering whether to go or stay. Watching him moving so smoothly and effortlessly through the water reminded her unbearably of those few brief days of happiness she had snatched from the grasp of fate before the truth had blotted out her foolish dreams for ever. She herself had not been able to swim before she married Ruy. She had always been slightly afraid of the water; timid and nervous of the rare occasions when there had been school outings to the local baths, but Ruy had insisted on teaching her the basic strokes and now she enjoyed her weekly visits to the baths with Jamie, who had taken to the water like the proverbial duck. A trait he must have inherited from his father, Davina reflected, watching Ruy float lazily on the blue green surface of the water.

He rolled over suddenly and swam leisurely to the side, shaking the water off his hair, and out of his eyes, before opening them and staring up at her. From the look in his eyes Davina realised that he hadn't been aware of her presence until that moment. It was as though a mask suddenly came down over his face, turning it into a hard implacable barrier.

She looked round again for the manservant, and not seeing him hurried across to the patio, hoping to find him there with Jamie. The little boy was eating his breakfast and chatting to the maid who was watching over him, and in answer to her query concerning Rodriguez's whereabouts told Davina that she did not know where he might be. For a moment Davina nibbled her lip indecisively. She was sure that Ruy could not manage to get out of the pool by himself, and remembering his threats of the previous evening wondered if she was supposed to help him. But how could she lift a grown man who must be half her size again? The only thing she could do was to go back and tell Ruy that she would have to go and find Rodriguez.

When she reached the pool, she saw by some super-human feat of strength he had managed to pull himself out of the water and was lying face downwards on the paving by the poolside, water streaming off his body. He was so inert that for a moment Davina feared that he might have lost consciousness and she approached him tremulously, her eyes unwillingly drawn to the mahogany breadth of his back tapering to the lean waist and narrow hips. He moved, causing muscles to ripple sinuously beneath his skin, reminding her of how it felt to touch the bronzed flesh of his back before sliding her fingers round to clasp the breadth of his shoulders.

'Well are you going to stand there all day staring at me, or are you going to help? Anyone would think you've never seen a man before,' he jeered, his eyes wide open and fixed contemptuously on her face. 'What's the matter?' he demanded. 'What were you expecting? Some obscene deformity?' He stretched upwards reaching for his chair and Davina rushed instinctively to help him, grasping the taut flesh of his waist, and receiving a shock like a jolt of electricity through her own body for her pains. Beneath her outspread palms his flesh felt warm and damp. She could feel a strange, almost forgotten heat rising slowly inside her, curling demandingly through her stomach and making her tremble with the knowledge it brought. Tears filled her eyes, and she blinked hurriedly to try and banish them. What was wrong with her? She had learned her lesson, hadn't she? She was over Ruy. Over all that nonsense about loving him. So why did she have this overwhelming urge to let her hands wander at will over the raw silk flesh beneath them, to take away his pain and humiliation, and make him feel for her the burning desire she had never stopped feeling for him? She forgot that she was half supporting him as he leaned between her and the wheelchair, and her hands released his flesh as though it burned as the enormity of what was happening dawned upon her. She still loved Ruy, had never stopped loving him, in fact. She stared dazedly into space for several seconds, coming back down to earth as she heard Ruy curse and she saw the lines of pain etched deep into his face as he slumped over the chair.

'Damn you!' he swore at her as she hurried to help him. 'Haven't you done enough already? Have you any idea of what it means to a man when the woman he loves leaves him? Keep your pity, Davina. I don't want it,' he told her brutally. 'Physically I might only be half a man but mentally nothing has changed. I can still feel . . . still desire . . .' he emphasised while she stared uncomprehendingly at the purple graze along his abdomen, the flesh raw and puckered where it had been torn and mangled by some primitive force, before disappearing beneath the top of the brief black swimming trunks he was wearing.

When she looked away she was white and trembling.

'So it sickens you, does it?' Ruy demanded harshly. 'You cannot feel desire for a man whose body is torn and mutilated. You prefer the smooth, pale skin of your Englishman. Get out of my sight,' he demanded bitterly. 'I have endured enough for one day, without being forced to endure any more.'

She went, on legs that threatened to give way beneath her. For a moment, after the first horror of his appalling scar had left her, she had longed to bend her head and place her lips to the ravaged flesh, to heal with the benison of her kiss the pain which she could only guess at, but it wasn't her kiss Ruy's heart and soul cried out for; it wasn't her love and compassion he desired. Hadn't he just accused her of pity?

She couldn't face any breakfast. She went straight to the bedroom, but the maids were working there, so she was forced to return to the patio, where she found

Jamie chatting to his grandmother, and Ruy calmly eating his breakfast, as though nothing untoward had occurred at all.

'This afternoon we are going shopping,' the Condesa informed Davina as the maid poured her a cup of coffee. 'As Ruy's wife you will have a certain position to maintain, and it is only fitting that you should be dressed accordingly.'

'It really isn't necessary,' Davina started to protest, but Ruy cut in cruelly, 'You can say that, when you are dressed in garments most of our maids would scorn—what manner of woman are you, Davina, that you conceal your body in such things? Or is it that you do not care how you dress when there is no man to impress?'

'That's a hateful thing to say . . .' There were tears in her eyes; tears of pain and tears of pride. Perhaps her clothes weren't elegant or expensive, but they were all she could afford.

'Next month we shall be entertaining visitors from Madrid—men connected with the wine business, and I shall want my wife to be dressed as befits her position. However, before that I must visit the *estancia*. The young bulls should be ready soon, and I must check on . . .'

'No, Ruy, let Sebastian go in your stead, *por favor*,' his mother begged, her face paling suddenly at his words. 'There is no need for you . . .'

'You would have me hide behind my little brother?' Ruy's face had darkened, his fist smashing down on to the table, making the crockery jump. 'Enough, Madre. I am still the head of this family, and if I say I shall go to the *estancia*, I shall go. Davina and Jamie will come with me. It is time my son learned how we derive a part of our income.'

Before his mother could protest further, he had turned away and was wheeling himself quickly towards his suite.

Giving her mother-in-law time to recover herself, Davina poured herself another cup of coffee, and assured Jamie that his daddy wasn't cross with him.

'It is my fault,' the Condesa said. She lifted her coffee cup and Davina was dismayed to see that her hand trembled. What had happened to the formidable woman who had seemed such an ogress such a very short time ago? All at once Davina was seeing her with her defences down, as a mother whose child was badly hurt and who was rejecting her. 'But he is so proud and I am so very worried. It was at the *estancia* that he received the wound and the fall which paralysed him. He was gored by one of the young bulls,' she told Davina quietly. 'An accident. One of the young boys ignored an instruction and the bull broke free. Ruy was only there by chance . . .' Her voice faded away, and Davina saw tears shimmering in her eyes. She felt like crying herself. Ruy, the proud and strong, to be reduced to dependence upon other human beings, and desertion by the woman he loved. If only he might have loved her! Her heart swelled with the intensity of her pain. Even without the bonds of physical pleasure she still loved him, and would have been proud to stand at his side. Ruy crippled was a thousand times more of a man than any other she knew; a thousand times more worthy of the name than others.

'You can see why I do not wish him to go to the *estancia,* but with you with him, and Jamie, he will not . . .'

She could not go on, and Davina turned to her with

shocked disbelief in her eyes. She could not believe
her mother-in-law was actually suggesting that Ruy
might be driven to making an end to his own life, but
the words lay unspoken between them and she knew
that this was the fear lying heaviest upon the other
woman's heart—and now upon her own. If necessary
she would stick to Ruy's side night and day to prevent
such a thing happening.

'I can never forgive Carmelita for deserting him
now, when he needs her the most,' Davina told her
quietly. 'To throw Ruy's love back in his face now . . .'

She was aware of a curious expression on the other
woman's face. 'Davina . . .' she began hesitantly, but
Jamie suddenly demanded her attention and when
Davina was able to turn back to her mother-in-law,
the latter commented that they had best hurry if they
were to reach Cordoba before the siesta. Sebastian and
Rosita, she explained, were to leave that afternoon on a
visit to Rosita's family, and if Ruy insisted on going to
the *estancia* then she would go to Cadiz to stay with
her sister for a short time.

'She has recently been widowed and very much
misses her husband . . .' She glanced at Davina. 'Now
that you have seen what has become of Ruy, Davina,
are you prepared to stay with him, as his wife, to bear
the brunt of his bitterness and anger, for the rest of
your life?'

Davina could not look at her. 'We are married,' she
said simply, and then holding her head high added,
'And I still love him, how could I not stay?'

Once admitted the truth seemed to release its crushing grip of her heart a little. Of course she loved him,
and had never stopped doing so no matter what she
might have told herself. In England's temperate clim-

ate her love might have gone into hibernation, deceiving her that it was dead, but beneath the warm, sunny
skies of Ruy's home, it was growing again, reaching
out to the warmth and sunshine. If she could persuade
Ruy that life was still worth living, that she loved him
paralysis or not, perhaps together they might be able to
rebuild something. She was not Carmelita and never
could be, but she was the mother of his child, and she
loved him—enough for both of them? That was
something she dared not ask herself.

Jamie was left with Ruy and Rodriguez while
Davina and the Condesa went on their shopping trip.
At first Davina had been reluctant to leave the little
boy, so soon after their arrival, but sensing her hesitation Ruy had sneered harshly, 'Don't worry. Rodriguez
will be here to watch over him, and unlike me he has
the ability to follow his every move.'

'He is very precious to me,' Davina said simply,
thinking but not saying that he was all she had of his
father.

'You surprise me,' Ruy threw at her over his shoulder as he wheeled round abruptly. 'In view of your
lack of feeling for his father and your marriage.'

She wanted to cry out that he was wrong, more
wrong than he knew, when he accused her of not caring
about him, but pride tied her tongue. How could she
admit her love to him now, knowing that all he cared
about, all he craved for was Carmelita?

Cordoba was much as she remembered it, enchanting dusty alleys where the sun turned the stone molten
gold and without too much imagination it was possible
to imagine these streets as they had been when the
Moors ruled here. Enchanting courtyards and grilled
gateways attracted the eye at every corner, a reminder

of the secrecy which was an inherent part of these people's legacy from the Moors. With a little additional effort Davina could almost believe that dark-eyed girls still sat behind those grilles awaiting the arrival of their cavaliers, even though Ruy had told her that nowadays most young Spanish girls longed more for tee-shirts and jeans and boys on noisy scooters than serenades in the moonlight and courtship conducted with wrought iron between themselves and their admirers.

The Condesa did not waste time glancing in the windows of the small shops they passed—to Davina's eyes entrancing treasure troves of antique silver work and beautiful hand-crafted leather. Ruy had a saddle which had been presented to him by the gypsies who travelled across his lands every year on their pilgrimage to the Shrine of the Virgin. It was made of the softest, most supple leather Davina had ever seen in her life, embossed with silver and so heavy that when Ruy had handed it to her she had all but collapsed under its weight.

Every year during the annual Feria in Seville Ruy used the saddle when he took part in the horseback parade. The year of their marriage Davina had gone with him, and even now she could remember quite clearly the thrill of pleasure it gave her to see her husband dressed in the traditional Andalusian riding costume—the black Cordobes hat, frilled white shirt, short frogged jacket, red sash and narrow dark trousers. She had felt colourless against the Spanish girls in their beautiful dresses, riding pillion behind their menfolk, their flamenco dresses cascading in vivid rivulets against the sleek sides of their mounts.

Davina remembered that they had ridden down an avenue beneath scented white flowers of the acacia trees lining the streets. And after the parade there had been dancing—and what dancing! It went on without cease for three days and nights, Ruy had told her. She had not been able to join in because she did not know the steps, but Carmelita had been there to dance with Ruy, her scarlet skirts living up to her name as they danced breast to breast in the shadows.

She came back to the present with a sudden start as Ruy's mother directed her down a narrow flight of stone stairs to a small, enclosed patio, ornamented with pots of tumbling scarlet geraniums and bright blue lobelia. Elegant shutters kept the harsh sunlight off the windows, a gaily striped awning in black and gold throwing welcome shadows over the ground floor window, which the Condesa indicated that Davina was to examine.

'Concepcion is the daughter of an old friend of mine,' she told Davina. 'Her mother is disappointed because her daughter chooses to design clothes rather than marry, but girls these days do not heed their mothers as we had to. I have brought you here to see if perhaps we can find some clothes to suit your English colouring. Concepcion has travelled widely and this is reflected in her designs, so we shall see.'

Davina knew what the Condesa meant the moment they stepped into the small shop. Concepcion herself stepped forward to exchange lengthy greetings with the Condesa, leaving Davina free to examine the racks of clothes covertly—and acknowledge that her mother-in-law had chosen well. Here were all the colours of the rainbow, to suit her English fairness as well as the more olive-tinted Spanish skin. A pure silk dress with a tiny cinched-in waist and raglan sleeves piped in silver caught her eye and Concepcion smiled as they were introduced.

'That is one of my favourites too,' she told Davina. 'But pink is not often worn by my countrywomen. They prefer black even now. However, I am fortunate in having built up a clientele more modern minded than my mother's generation, and despite my parents' doubts since I opened this salon I have done quite well for myself.'

Davina could see why. The clothes a young salesgirl was discreetly displaying for her were mouthwateringly tempting. There was an evening dress in swirls of misty grey and lavender chiffon, which she knew the instant she saw it was made for her, elegantly simple day dresses in fabrics which whispered seductively against her skin when she tried them on. She would have been more than content with just a couple of items, but her mother-in-law insisted that she needed a completely new wardrobe. When Davina would have protested, she murmured in a brief aside,

'It is for Ruy. He is still very much a man, and it is only natural that he should want to be proud of his wife, that he should want to say to other men, this is my wife; she is beautiful and she dresses to complement her beauty for my appreciation. Continue to wear the clothes you brought with you from England and you might as well tell all Cordoba that you feel nothing for him. No woman who truly desires a man would dress for him in clothes such as you wear.'

By the time Davina had recovered her wits, two more evening dresses had been added to the steadily growing pile, and in her heart of hearts she knew that nothing would give her greater pleasure than to be able to wear these seductive, feminine clothes for Ruy's appreciation. Even though she knew that it would be

Carmelita he would be thinking of? a tiny cruel voice asked her.

'My parents are giving a party to welcome my brother and his wife home from South America,' Concepcion told them as they were on the point of leaving. 'I know they would be delighted to see you all there, and to make the acquaintance of Ruy's wife. It is good when all misunderstandings are past,' she added simply. 'Sometimes it takes a tragedy such as Ruy has experienced for us to realise the true importance of other people to us.'

It was only when they had left the small boutique that Davina realised that Concepcion thought that she had returned to Ruy because of his accident; and she wondered exactly how her absence in the intervening years had been explained away to their friends. For some reason she had thought that their marriage was something which would not have been discussed amongst their acquaintances—as far as Ruy was concerned it had been a mistake, and all he had wanted to do was to put the whole thing behind him and start again with Carmelita, or did his pride prevent him from admitting to outsiders now that the woman he loved had left him, and so he was obliged to fall back on the woman who was tied to him by law.

A chauffeur-driven car was awaiting them in the small square appointed as a rendezvous. It was extremely pleasant to settle back against the leather upholstery amidst air-conditioned comfort and be swept back towards the Palacio. Behind them lay Cordoba, the city of Abderrahman, the one-eyed red-haired giant, who had won a throne in the West for the Omayyad family of Damascus, and who had built around it a city of a million inhabitants, with a drainage system that could not be rivalled today, and street lighting a thousand years before any other European city, and of course, its Mosque.

The men who had fought with Abderrahman for the rich prize of Andalucia were the same men whose blood flowed through the veins of Ruy, neither tamed nor subdued by a thousand years of Christian rule and intermarriage with their Spanish captives.

Jamie was just waking up from his afternoon sleep when they got back to the Palacio. He already seemed to have wound the household round his little finger and when Sebastian and Rosita came to say goodbye to them, Davina thought she saw tears in the younger girl's eyes as she kissed Jamie on the forehead.

'You are lucky,' she told Davina softly. 'I would give much for such a son . . .'

'*You* are lucky,' Davina countered with a smile. 'I would give much to be loved as you are, Rosita . . . to have a husband who cares for me as Sebastian cares for you.'

When Davina went to her room to change for dinner, she found Ruy already in the room, lying back against the pillows of the double bed, his torso darkly tanned against the linen sheets. His eyes were closed and when Davina looked more closely, she could see the lines of pain etched beside his mouth and across his forehead and she had an almost overwhelming desire to reach out and stroke away the frown lines.

It was just as well she hadn't given way to it, she thought seconds later as the black lashes fluttered upwards and the dark eyes raked her assessingly, completely wiping out the impression of vulnerability she had had only seconds before.

'Aren't you coming down to dinner?' She knew it

was a stupid question the moment she uttered it. It was quite obvious that Ruy was in some sort of pain. Beneath his tan his skin had a faintly grey cast and now that she was looking at him properly she could see the tight white line of physical strain round his mouth, his knuckles gleaming whitely through his skin as his fingers clenched on the bedclothes.

'Why? Will you miss me?' he taunted. 'You could always stay here with me, if you really cared one way or the other, but we both know that you don't give a damn, don't we, Davina? If you did you'd never have walked out on me in the first place, would you?'

'You know why I did that,' Davina choked, turning her back on him, so that he couldn't see her expression and guess at the agony that decision had caused her. She still had her pride—for what it was worth.

'Yes, of course.' All at once he sounded oddly tired, defeated was the word she would have used in conjunction with another man, but it was unthinkable to use it for him. 'And we both know the folly of trying to preserve a marriage where one loves and the other merely . . . endures . . .' he added cruelly. 'So why did you come back?'

She took a deep breath, trying to steady her nerves. 'Because of Jamie,' she told him steadily. Well, it had been the truth after all. When she had decided to return it had been for Jamie's sake. She had honestly not known then that she still loved him so completely; or if she had, her subconscious had craftily kept the knowledge from her until it was too late for her to do anything about it. 'He was very ill last winter—enteritis, with complications, and the doctor told me that he needed to live somewhere warm . . . to build up his reserves. I couldn't afford to take him abroad . . . I earn enough to feed and clothe us but . . .'

'If you were so short of money, why have you never touched the allowance I make you?' Ruy demanded harshly.

He sounded so close that for a moment she had almost believed that he was standing behind her, but when she turned swiftly, he was still lying on the bed, his eyes burning into her like living coals. She hadn't touched the money because she had told herself that she wanted nothing of his, nothing at all, except his love.

'I couldn't,' she said simply.

'I see.' The effort of controlling his breathing showed in his tense muscles and dilated nostrils. 'But yet you were willing to return here and live on my charity . . .'

'I was frightened that if I didn't come you would try to take Jamie away from me. He is your heir after all. And . . .'

'You have talked to him about me?' he demanded abruptly, startling her. 'He knew I was his father . . .'

'He knew that we were coming to see his father,' Davina corrected. 'I've never lied to him about you, Ruy, nor tried to pretend you didn't exist, but neither have I told him a great deal about you. I thought it best, after all . . .'

'You never expected that I would play a significant part in his life, that's what you're trying to say, isn't it?' he goaded.

What could she say? That she had not wanted Jamie to endure the humiliation of knowing his father preferred the children he had given to another woman; that he hadn't been wanted; that his father had never even come to the hospital to see him; that he had been too busy making love to his mistress to bother about his wife and newborn son? These were not things you could tell a child, not even an adult, and if she had not talked to Jamie about his father, it had been from a desire not to taint his mind and heart against him, rather than with any thought of maliciously concealing Ruy's existence from him.

'I thought you would marry Carmelita,' she said quietly. 'After all, it was what your family wanted.' And what *you* wanted! The words trembled on her tongue, but she could not utter them, could not remind him of all that he had lost. Loving someone was an agony that made their pain your pain, only intensified tenfold, and she knew that if by some means it were possible to restore Ruy to full health and give him back Carmelita's love, she would have done so.

'Ruy . . .' Her voice faltered as she turned and saw that he was lying with his face turned away from her, the high cheekbones thrusting through the bronzed flesh, his eyes closed in total rejection of her.

She changed in Jamie's room, reading the little boy a story, before tiptoeing through the room where Ruy lay asleep to go and eat a meal she did not want, with her mother-in-law.

CHAPTER FIVE

THE bedroom was in darkness when Davina returned, Ruy a motionless shape in the vastness of the bed that had been designed generously to hold a couple who would and laugh and cry together all their lives. She averted her eyes from it and from the man lying there, the sheet pulled down to reveal the muscular darkness of his back, the broad shoulders tapering downwards to the narrow waist.

Quickly Davina hurried into Jamie's room. The little boy was curled up beneath the bedclothes still clutching his much beloved teddy. She bent to kiss him, straightening with tears in her eyes as she tried to blot from her mind the man lying in the bedroom opposite.

Not even the stinging spray of the shower dispelled the emotions that had surged up inside her when she looked at Ruy. She had had an insane desire to go to him and curl up against the protection of his body willing it to respond to her presence. Such wayward thoughts could cause her nothing but agony. There was no place in Ruy's life for her as a lover; indeed, it seemed that he could barely tolerate her there in any capacity. Sometimes when he looked at her she thought she glimpsed hatred in his eyes. The towel with which she was drying herself fell to the floor unregarded. Did he hate her? She pulled on her robe blindly. She had left her nightgown in the bedroom, but it didn't matter. There was no possibility that Ruy might inadvertently look upon her nakedness—even if he were to wake up she felt sure he would feign sleep as he had done before dinner.

With a small sigh she walked through into the bedroom, her unslippered feet making no sound on the cool tiles. Beyond the huge windows lay the gardens with all their fragrant intoxication, and her heart rebelled at the knowledge that she would never again walk in them with Ruy, never again lie with him beneath the stars never ... A sob rose in her throat, ruthlessly silenced by the small white teeth biting so deeply into her lip that it bled. Who were her tears really for? she asked herself. Ruy, because he would never walk again, or herself because she would never know his love?

There was no sign of her nightgown, and rather than risk disturbing Ruy by searching through her drawers for a clean one, she decided to sleep without. The cool crispness of the linen sheets stroked her naked skin like the hand of a lover. Sleep had never been farther away. Light from the crescent moon filtered through the windows, touching gentle silver fingers to Ruy's face, and clearly revealing the lines of suffering marked on it. An impulse which would not be denied had her reaching out trembling fingers to trace the path of the moonlight over the hard warmth of his skin. Surely it wasn't just her imagination that told her that the high cheekbones were sharper than she remembered, the skin tauter. Ruy moved and she withdrew her hand quickly, dismayed by the reaction of her flesh merely to the touch of his. Even her bones felt as though they were melting in the fierce heat of her hunger for him.

For nearly four years she had lived the life of a nun and never once after the first initial agony of parting from Ruy had she allowed her physical hunger for him to disturb her, and yet now, within forty-eight hours of her entering his house, her heart and body craved the close communion she had once known with him, to such an extent that merely to lie motionless at his side was almost a physical pain, and that was knowing that he did not want her; that he did not love her. There was neither rhyme nor reason to it; no sense in loving someone who loved elsewhere, and lying next to him, with her senses alive to the proximity of him, Davina found herself praying for the self-control not to reach out and touch him. Not to betray to him how she felt.

In the darkness she felt him move, tensing every muscle against her own involuntary reaction. His eyes opened, and he thrust back the sheets, muttering something under his breath, obviously unaware that she was there.

He rolled over on his side, reaching for the carafe of water by the bed. Davina heard the telltale rattle of pills as he picked up the bottle and then a bitter curse as he tried to pull himself upwards and knocked over the water jug.

Davina was out of bed, and at his side almost immediately, pulling on her robe as she hurried towards him.

'Mind the glass!' he warned her savagely. 'Don't come any nearer. Send for Rodriguez.'

'It's nearly one o'clock in the morning,' she told him calmly, 'and there's no need to disturb Rodriguez.'

In the kitchen she found a small brush and pan with which to clean up the mess. When she hurried back into the bedroom Ruy had switched on the bedside light, but its soft glow could not hide the pain in his eyes and the deep lines of strain etched on his skin.

The bottle of pills had crashed to the floor with the

water, and as she bent to pick them up Davina glanced at the label.

'Painkillers,' Ruy told her abruptly, as she replaced them on the cabinet. 'My wound still sometimes bothers me.'

Davina remembered her mother-in-law telling her that the wound had not healed as quickly as it should and that Doctor Gonzales had left a special cream to be applied to it when it proved especially painful. A quick glance at Ruy's face told her that now was one of those occasions, and when she had cleaned up the splintered glass and water from the floor, she went into the kitchen and quickly made a hot milky drink which she took back to Ruy and handed to him in silence.

'What is this?' he jeered. 'Have you discovered some long-buried desire to play the nurse?'

'I thought it might help you sleep,' Davina said quietly, adding before he could guess at the feelings which motivated her, 'If you're restless it keeps me awake too.'

'Meaning that if I were a gentleman I would allow you to have your own room, I suppose?' He looked bitterly angry; so angry that Davina couldn't help wondering if he was remembering that Carmelita had refused to share his bed.

'Well, I'm not going to, Davina. You're my wife, and you'll sleep in my bed, and that's an end to the matter. Where are you going?' he demanded sharply as she walked past him towards the bathroom.

'To find the cream for your wound.'

If she said it very matter-of-factly he would never know what it did to her insides to think of touching his body, even in the most clinical of ways, but the bitterness in his face undermined her resolution, and she had to look away from the hatred she saw in his eyes. Did he hate her so much that even the thought of her touching him could affect him like that?

She found the cream without difficulty, and although Ruy protested that he did not need it, the pain evident in the tautening bones of his face, and the eyes he closed against her, said otherwise.

'*Por Dios*, then get it over with if you must do it,' he gritted at her when he realised that she was not going to be swayed. As she reached for the sheets, he suddenly switched off the lamp, plunging the room into darkness again.

It was easy to find the ridge of the scar even without the benefit of the light, but her fingers trembled uncontrollably as she spread the cream lightly over the flesh which felt hot and burning to her touch, willing herself not to be betrayed into turning the action into a caress as her fingers so longed to do. His stomach was as lean and taut as ever, but she might as well have been touching alabaster for all the reaction she evoked, but her fears that his paralysis was such that he was unaware of her touch were banished when he pushed her away with a muffled curse and said harshly:

'You tremble like a captive dove. Why? Does my torn body revolt you so much? Does your imagination relay to you the full horror of my wound even though you cannot see it?'

'It doesn't revolt me,' Davina said softly.

'Liar. I saw it in your eyes before.'

Very slowly but determinedly, like someone in a trance, Davina pushed back the sheet until the moonlight touched starkly upon the jagged pulsating scar, and then deliberately bent her head and placed her lips to it, moving gently along the angry length of it, until

Ruy's fingers bit deeply into her shoulders, dragging her upwards.

'*Por Dios!*' he groaned huskily, staring incredulously at her. 'What are you trying to do to me? Would you humiliate me still further?' He pushed her away with a rough movement, and she half fell against the bed, her robe parting to reveal the full curve of her breast, silvered where the moonlight stroked it. She felt Ruy's indrawn breath, the sudden tensing of his muscles as his hand reached out and touched her flesh. Her mouth was dry with mingled tension and anticipation as his fingers brushed her breast. She was shaking uncontrollably and so was Ruy, his face dark and tortured as though he struggled under some terrible burden. Davina could have moved away, but she didn't. For a moment the silence stretched between them, and then with a hoarse groan Ruy reached for her, pulling her down against him, his face buried in the silky curtain of his hair as his mouth sought and found the betraying pulse beating in her throat, before moving upwards to capture her lips, parting them with a savage hunger to match her own.

Carmelita, the past, were both forgotten. Her arms slid round the hard warmth of his back, clasping her to him, her lips parting willingly under the assault of the passion she could feel rising up inside him.

'You have driven me to insanity!' she thought she heard him whisper against her skin, as his hands cupped the full warmth of her breasts. 'God has taken so much from me, surely he will not deny me this.'

The words were lost, smothered beneath the intense pressure of his mouth as it closed over hers, blotting out everything by the ferocity of their mutual desire. Thought was a slow, painful process obliterated by the instant communication of lips upon lips, flesh upon flesh. His accident and its results were forgotten, swept away in the sheer joy sweeping through her at the mastery of his touch.

'*Dios*, I have denied myself too long,' Davina heard him say thickly as he stared down at the unashamed nakedness of her body. 'I have fasted and thirsted; deprived my soul and flesh, but no longer.' His eyes lingered on her soft curves, making her pulses race in answering passion, her body mutely pleading for his touch.

His tortured groan filled her with a fear that he meant to withdraw from her, and she reached up towards him, gasping in pleasure as his mouth found her breast, his touch piercing her with exquisite sensation which seemed to run like quicksilver through her body, building up into an excruciating ache at the pit of her stomach.

His name whispered past her lips in aching surrender, lips which she pressed in mute supplication to the warm flesh above her.

She could hear Ruy's harsh breathing in her ear, feel the tremors that shook his body, sweat beading on his skin as he suddenly wrenched himself away from her, grasping her wrists as he stared down into her pale face with tormented eyes.

'Physically I may still be a cripple, Davina,' he told her hoarsely, 'but I can still feel . . . I am still capable of acting the part of your husband.'

The coldness of his tone made her wince, and his fingers tightened cruelly round her flesh, the look in his eyes reminding her of the primitive blood that still flowed through his veins.

'You cringe,' he said savagely. 'And well you might.

I am not a child to be petted and cossetted with kisses
of pity, Davina. I am a man with all a man's reactions.
Do you understand what I am saying to you?'

Even if she hadn't understood the words, those
moments in his arms had already communicated the
knowledge to her, and her heart filled with love and
despair. Carmelita's desertion must have hurt him
bitterly. He was still a man, she knew that beyond any
shadow of a doubt, but when she tried to tell him so,
he pushed her away and said sardonically, 'I don't want
your pity, Davina. And I don't think I need to tell you
what I did want. Next time you feel like pampering
me like a small child, you might remember that—or
does it give you some sort of perverted enjoyment to
know that you can arouse a man like me; a man who
ought to be revolted at the thought of a woman touching his rotting carcase of a body.' He moved violently
to one side of the bed, and winced in pain.

Davina wanted to tell him that he was wrong. That
she was the one who needed pity, because she had
actually wanted him to continue making love to her
even though she knew that he felt absolutely nothing
for her, but he was already reaching for his bottle of
tablets, and he swallowed two quickly, lying back with
his eyes closed, exhaustion a pale grey shadow beneath
the dark skin,

'If I were Carmelita . . .' she began hesitantly, but
he silenced her with a look as cold as ice and a cruel
smile as he told her softly, 'But you are not, and she at
least is honest about her revulsion for a man confined
to a wheelchair instead of trying to conceal her feelings
with mawkish sentiment—a grave fault of the English,
and one to which they are much addicted. Witness
their outrage at the corrida. The bulls do not want

their pity. They go to a noble death. And I do not want yours.'

It seemed like hours before she could get to sleep. Those moments in his arms remained vividly etched on her mind, and even though she told herself that she was glad Ruy had stopped when he did, she knew it was a lie. She had wanted him to possess her, wanted to feel again the magic she had first experienced as his bride.

As before when she awoke she had the bedroom to herself. She found Ruy and Jamie already eating their breakfast on the patio.

'My daddy is going to take us to a place where they grow bulls,' Jamie told Davina as she sat down. 'When are we going?' he asked Ruy.

'Soon,' the latter promised him. 'You will enjoy it at the *estancia*, *pequeño*. There are other children there for you to play with.'

Jamie seemed pleased by this observation. He had few friends in the small village where they lived, and she remarked unthinkingly to Ruy, 'It is a pity he is an only one. I think it tends to make children too precocious,' blushing furiously as his eyebrows rose mockingly.

'Is that an observation or an invitation?' he asked coolly. 'If it is the latter, I thought I made my views clear to you last night.'

'Meaning that I could never hope to take Carmelita's place, I suppose,' Davina said bitterly, not caring how much she might be betraying.

'Carmelita is a sophisticated woman of the world who knows how to let a man down gently. I scarcely think that description fits you.' He was about to leave the table when his mother approached them, a stiff white invitation card in her hand.

'It is from Concepcion's parents,' she told Davina. 'An invitation to their party as she promised. You will go, Ruy?'

'Of course,' he agreed smoothly. 'I am sure they must all be longing to see the freak I have become, and of course the beautiful woman who has so nobly chained herself to me.'

'If only he could learn to accept!' the Condesa sighed when he had gone. 'I had hoped having you here . . .'

'Me?' Davina tried to smile. 'I'm afraid I'm more of a nuisance than a help. Having me here must constantly remind him of Carmelita, and all that he's lost . . .'

Her mother-in-law seemed deep in thought. She glanced up at Davina and was about to speak when one of the maids hurried towards them.

'Dr Gonzales is here,' she told the Condesa. 'He asks to see the Conde.'

'Dr Gonzales brought Ruy into the world,' the Condesa told Davina as they walked towards the house. 'He is a friend as well as our doctor, and I should like you to meet him.'

The Condesa introduced them, and then had to hurry away to the kitchen.

Left alone with the doctor, Davina found herself being studied by a pair of shrewd, button bright black eyes.

'So you are Ruy's wife,' he announced at last, with a smile. 'I did not make your acquaintance before because at the time of Ruy's wedding I was away in South America, visiting my son. However, I have heard much about you, and I confess to being . . . surprised . . .'

He took Davina's arm and led her on to the patio. 'You do not strike me as the sort of girl who would desert her husband to run off with her lover. You do not have the eyes for it. Yours are far too vulnerable.'

Was that what he had been told?

'I left Ruy because . . . because I could no longer endure a marriage which was not founded on love. But there was no lover . . .'

'So . . . But now you are back to take your place at your husband's side. Tell me, do you find him much changed?'

'A little. He is very bitter, but that is only natural. To have lost the use of his legs, and the woman he loves . . .'

'So you admit that love, or the lack of it, can have a profound effect upon our behaviour? That is good. Has Ruy told you much about his condition?'

'Only that he's paralysed,' Davina said, feeling a little puzzled. 'And of course I've seen the scar . . .' She bit her lip, not knowing quite how to phrase the question she wanted to ask. 'Doctor, surely when one is paralysed there's no feeling . . . no . . . sensation, and yet Ruy experiences pain. 'I've seen him take pain-killers, and I know . . .' she blushed, and fumbled awkwardly for the words. 'I know he's not totally without . . . without physical feeling.'

To her relief the doctor did not press her to explain herself, merely pursing his lips and patting her hand reassuringly. 'You strike me as a sensible young woman. If you think Ruy can experience sensation, then I am sure you have excellent reasons for doing so.' His eyes twinkled and he added teasingly, 'I am very glad to hear that you do. Ruy is a very proud man, and the fact that you have been able to break down his barriers sufficiently for you to discover that his paralysis is not what it at first seems reassures me considerably. Men are men, Condesa, whether they are in wheelchairs or not. The simple fact of being deprived of the ability to walk does not deprive them of the curse of feeling. I confess when I heard that you had returned my first feeling was one of concern—for Ruy. A woman who turned from him in disgust, who refused to accept that he still had great need of her— more now possibly than at any other time, for when else can a man—any man—truly transcend the physical bonds that constrain us than at that moment of consecration to love which sets the soul free? A small foretaste of heaven, or so the poets would tell us, and I sometimes wonder if they are not right—— Such a woman would have destroyed him, and it was such a woman that I feared you to be. Instead I find you are exactly the opposite.'

All this had been said on a much more serious note, causing Davina to stop and stare curiously at her companion.

'Let us sit down and talk together, you and I,' Dr Gonzales suggested, indicating a stone seat set into a low wall next to a circular pool where light and shadow played unceasingly on the water, and koi carp basked indolently beneath the lily pads.

'You have thought that perhaps another child might do much to lift Ruy from his despondency?' the doctor suggested. 'Oh, I know his mother persists in the belief that there will be no more children, fed, I am sure, by a certain person, who I am glad to say no longer holds any sway in this household.'

'You mean Carmelita?' Davina smiled sadly. 'I would love to have another child, but I doubt I shall be granted the opportunity,' she said bluntly. 'Ruy has already told me that I can't take Carmelita's place . . .'

'Take her place? But you have your own,' the doctor said vigorously. 'Come, you are letting Ruy's depression infect you. Has he discussed his accident with you at all?' he asked, changing the subject.

Davina shook her head.

'So. You do not know, then, that it is my opinion that this paralysis is psychosomatic—that is to say it is of the mind rather than the flesh, but exists physically nonetheless.'

Davina stared incredulously at him. 'You mean Ruy is not really paralysed?'

Dr Gonzales shrugged. 'Who is to say? Certainly there is no organic reason why he should not walk. The spinal column is still intact; the muscles were torn but are now repaired, but it is the mind that controls our will. In Ruy's case there is what you might call a mental block, a refusal to accept that he is unharmed. The goring by the bull, the fall from his horse, all these are shocks to the system. A similar shock—a traumatic experience, as you would perhaps call it, this might sweep away the block that prevents him from walking.'

'And Ruy knows this?'

The doctor spread his hands expressively.

'I have told him, yes, but he does not choose to believe me. It is quite common. As I have said, Ruy is a proud man. He does not care to think that his subconscious is the master of his body, although it is so with all of us. And forgive me for saying so, but Ruy has more reason than most to suffer in this way. Has he not already lost the woman he loves—his child?' he demanded, when Davina looked puzzled.

He was, she realised talking about her; attributing at least a part of Ruy's condition to her absence!

'A proud man, who cannot tell the wife who has left him how bitterly he misses her, and the child she had borne him, what could be more natural than that he should find a more subtle means of telling her that he wants her to return?'

When Davina stared at him, he smiled. 'You do not believe me, I can see, but think about it. It worked, did it not? Subconsciously Ruy called to you, and you responded.'

'As any woman would have responded,' Davina began helplessly, unbearably tempted to allow herself to believe that he was right, that Ruy had wanted her, even while she knew in her heart of hearts that it could not be so.

'Not any woman,' Dr Gonzales corrected her. 'A very special woman. One who appreciates that her husband is still a man . . . still has a very great need of her.'

'If you were right, surely now that I have returned Ruy would recover,' Davina pointed out logically, but the doctor only smiled again and shook his head.

'If only it were as simple as that! These deep workings of our subconscious are something even modern medicine cannot totally understand. We know that it does happen, we know how much power the subconscious can exert over the body, and even in what circumstances that power can be reversed, but what we do not yet know is how! We cannot simply tell the subconscious to release its hold of the body—or of the mind in the case of amnesia—we can only provide it with the right sets of circumstances and hope that they will act as a trigger. Either Ruy's subconscious will not heed the trigger or he still fears deep down inside that perhaps you will leave him again. To his subconscious it might appear that you will stay with him only while he is helpless, and thus he will remain.'

'And the other thing you were telling me about,' Davina questioned him, 'the traumatic experience which might free the mental block?'

It was pointless telling the little doctor that she could not be the cause of Ruy's paralysis, simply because he did not love her, for she was sure he would not believe her.

'Ah yes ... So much danger surrounds such a method of treatment that we doctors are reluctant to advocate it. In Ruy's case, for instance, such a shock treatment might require him to be gored by a bull for a second time.' He shrugged and grimaced slightly. 'If he did not die from the goring there is no guarantee that it would work, and so you can see that as a cure it is not particularly reliable.'

Davina could well appreciate why. She had read of such cases, especially where amnesia was concerned, where people had lost complete decades of their life only to find them returning after some chance meeting with someone from that previous, forgotten, life. She had even read once about a deaf man suddenly recovering his hearing after standing too close to a jet aircraft preparing for take-off, but as Dr Gonzales said, the risks of such hit-and-miss treatment were too great for any professional man to suggest that a patient take them.

He came every other day, he told her a few minutes later, but she declined to accompany him to Ruy's room, knowing that Ruy would not want her present when the doctor examined him.

She could not understand why Carmelita had turned away from Ruy and married someone else, unless it was as she had suspected before, that the other girl's pride would not allow any child of hers to take second place to Jamie, and so she had used Ruy's accident as an excuse to put an end to their relationship. Despite her comments to the contrary, Davina had never thought that Carmelita truly loved Ruy—not as she loved him—and she longed to go to him and tell him that no matter what might happen in the future, he would always have her love to call on should he need it. But that was the point, wasn't it? He didn't need it. All he wanted was Carmelita!

CHAPTER SIX

HER skin was beginning to tan already, Davina noticed appreciatively as she slid on one of her new dresses. She was changing in Jamie's room, ostensibly so that the little boy could see her in her new finery, but in reality she hadn't been able to endure the feel of Ruy's critical eyes on her, nor his own torment as he waited to be dressed as helplessly as any child.

Only that lunchtime he had thrust her away from him when, unable to watch him struggling any longer with the shirt he was endeavouring to pull over his shoulders, she had run to his side to help him. It would be a long time before she forgot the raw fury in his eyes as his fingers locked on her wrists in a grip that had left purpling bruises on her smooth flesh. She glanced down at them now, a tiny frown creasing her forehead as she touched the swollen flesh. Why did he insist on tormenting both of them in this fashion? It was plain that he hated her witnessing his disability, and yet when she had tentatively suggested that they have separate rooms after all, he had told her in a cold fury that as long as she remained under his roof she would share his bed, adding cryptically that it was a penance for them both.

Davina had dressed for tonight's party with special care, remembering what the Condesa had said about their hosts being importantly placed in Cordoban society.

The dress was one of Concepcion's creations, a misty

froth of chiffon in pearl greys and soft lilacs, the boned
bodice emphasising the taut thrust of her breasts before
hugging her narrow waist and falling to the floor in
graceful folds. There was a matching jacket to go with
it, with a tiny stand-up collar and tight sleeves, and as
she applied a hint of pearlised lilac eyeshadow to
deepen the amethyst of her eyes, she had to admit that
she had never owned a dress which became her so
well.

'Mummy smells nice,' Jamie commented when she
touched perfume to her pulse points before slipping
into her high-heeled evening sandals.

As she bent down to give the little boy a last-minute
hug she heard the bedroom door open. When she
straightened up Ruy was behind her, looking immaculate in a crispy laundered white shirt and narrow hip-
hugging black pants. Not even being confined to a
wheelchair could really rob him of his vitality, Davina
thought, suppressing a longing to reach and cradle his
dark head against her breast as she had done Jamie's.

'Mummy smells nice,' Jamie repeated for his father's
benefit.

'So I notice. They say a man can learn a good deal
about a woman by her choice of perfume.'

Davina wore Chamade. The first time she had ever
worn it had been on the day they got married. Ruy
had given it to her as a present, and her face flamed at
the thought of what her wearing of it now might
betray.

'In your case it betrays a lack of sensitivity which is
staggering,' Ruy continued bitterly. 'Or don't you
think a woman should feel sentimental about her first
lover and the gifts he gives to her?'

'Why should she?' Davina demanded before she

could stop herself. 'When he intends those gifts for someone else?'

She turned back to the mirror and busied herself applying her lipstick, firmly ignoring the trembling of her hands and the uneven pounding of her heart. Why did he insist on torturing her in this fashion, or was he using her as a substitute for Carmelita, taking out on her all the bitterness he could not give vent to elsewhere?

She didn't see him again until she went into the main *sala*. His mother was talking to one of the maids, and as she walked into the room Ruy beckoned her over, his face still grim.

When she was standing in front of him he flicked open a small black velvet box to reveal, embedded in white satin, a pair of diamond and pearl eardrops.

Davina knew at first glance that they were a family heirloom. The pearls were huge, the setting old-fashioned.

'It is customary for these to be presented to the wife of the Conde on the birth of their first child,' Ruy told her emotionlessly. 'Madre was kind enough to remind me that our friends would expect to see you wearing them tonight.'

The look he gave his mother was no kinder than the one he had given Davina, but the Condesa seemed better able to withstand it, for she shrugged carelessly and asked him if he was not going to put the earrings on for Davina.

'But of course. Provided she doesn't mind kneeling on the floor at my feet so that I can do so. It would be best for us all, Madre, if you ceased this folly of pretending that I am as other men, when the very evidence that I am not stands before you in the shape of my oh, so beautiful and faithless wife.'

'Ruy!'

The warning in his mother's voice was ignored, and for the first time Davina saw the older woman quail before his anger.

'You take too much upon yourself,' he said harshly. 'And I have said nothing—but listen well, Madre. I will no longer tolerate your interference in my life. Yours or anyone else's,' he finished pointedly, his eyes on Davina.

Davina could only admire the other woman's superb self-control. Not so much as by a flicker of an eyelash did she display any emotion, but Davina was sure she had seen the betraying glisten of tears in her eyes before she calmly turned away.

There was a gilded rococo mirror in the *sala* and Davina stood almost on tiptoe to see into it as she clipped the heavy earrings on to her ears. As she moved her head the diamonds flashed blue-white fire, the pearls reflecting the subtle lilacs and greys of her dress, but magnificent though they were, Davina would much rather not have worn them. She was terrified that she might lose one or damage them in some way, and as she followed the others out to the car her fingers strayed constantly to her ears to make sure that they were still in place.

'Before the winter Ruy must buy you some furs,' the Condesa commented as the chauffeur opened the rear doors of the car. 'I still have the sables his father bought for me.'

'What are you trying to do, Madre?' Ruy asked cynically from the shadows. 'Persuade Davina to stay with the promise of a reward for good behaviour? Perhaps already she grows tired of her life sentence and looks forward to the time when she may be free of it.'

'No . . . that's not true!'

Ruy turned to stare at her, his lips twisted in a mocking smile.

'I think I preferred you when you were indifferent to me, Davina. At least then you were being honest. I cannot see what the point is of this pretence of caring about me, unless it is that you enjoy torturing me . . . causing me pain. Get in the car, Madre, we are already late, and we do not wish to keep the other guests waiting, especially when we are the star turn.'

There had been a grain of truth in Ruy's sardonic statement, Davina acknowledged an hour later, making polite small talk with the gentleman seated to her left. From the moment they had entered the *sala* Davina had been subject to courteous but thorough inspection.

'Pay no heed to them,' Concepcion had murmured gaily to Davina just before they went into dinner. 'They have nothing else to occupy their minds. Whenever my mother bewails my unmarried state, I point to the daughters of her friends and ask if she would really want such an empty featherbrain of a child. Now I can see that I shall have to marshal fresh arguments. Now that she has seen you I fear my days of convincing her that marriage equals intellectual death are at an end!' She had smiled to show that her words had not been meant to be taken seriously, but nevertheless they had warmed Davina's heart, making her feel welcome in a house where everyone else seemed to be viewing her slightly critically.

Ruy was obviously a great favourite with the other guests, but beneath their kind questions Davina sensed

the well-meant pity that she knew must be like salt in
Ruy's unhealed wounds. She glanced across the table,
where he was deep in conversation with Concepcion.
The other girl was laughing up into his face, and Ruy's
mouth was curled in the teasingly mocking smile she
remembered from their first meeting, his eyes crinkling
at the corners, and all at once she was overwhelmed by
a fierce rush of jealousy—jealousy that Concepcion
should be the recipient of his smiles, when for her, his
wife, he had nothing but harsh words and contempt.

After dinner Ruy disappeared with their host into
the latter's study—'To discuss business,' Concepcion
told Davina. Her father and Ruy had a joint interest in
a new development of holiday apartments in a select
part of Marbella and this was what they were discussing.

While Concepcion was telling her how charming she
looked in her new dress, Davina became aware of a
tall, darkly handsome man watching them. She glanced
up quickly, flushing a little when he smiled, uncoiling
his lean body from the wall and strolling across to join
them.

'Ah, Carlos, you are making good use of Ruy's absence to make yourself known to his lovely wife,'
Concepcion told the intruder. 'Davina, allow me to
introduce you to my cousin Carlos. At the risk of
swelling his over-large head even more I must tell
you that Carlos is one of Ronda's most famous bull-
fighters.'

Davina smiled shyly at him. He was about Ruy's
age, and built in much the same mould, although he
had a devil-may-care air that made her think that here
was a man who lived from peak to peak, tasting only
the sweet things of life. When he raised her fingers to

his lips with old-fashioned courtesy and then lingered over their pink tips with a meaning that was decidedly modern, Davina gave him a reproving look.

'Ah, I can see that Davina has your measure, Carlos,' Concepcion, who had intercepted the look, chided. 'I must also tell you that Carlos is a terrible flirt . . .'

'You malign me,' her cousin contradicted, still holding Davina's fingers. 'It is just that I have not yet found the woman to make me forsake all others, and so, like a busy bee, I must flit from flower to flower, tasting them all . . .'

'Well, don't try any tasting on Ruy's preserves,' Concepcion warned him, much to Davina's embarrassment.

Far from being disturbed, Carlos merely laughed wickedly. 'A man may only trespass on private property when the fences are down and the gates left untended, is this not so, *señora*? Ruy does not strike me as a man careless enough to leave his property in such an uncared-for state.'

'My mother tells me that you and Ruy are shortly leaving for the *estancia*,' Concepcion interrupted firmly. 'You will enjoy it, I am sure. I remember visiting it once with my parents. In our cities we Spanish preserve formality with rigour, but in the country, life is more relaxed, more as you are used to in England. And best of all, you will have your husband and son to yourself, for Ruy's mother does not go with you, does she? A second honeymoon, yes?'

Davina managed a rather strained smile.

'Ruy wants to check on the young bulls,' she said hesitantly.

'And you fear another accident such as the one which has put my poor friend in that wheelchair?' Carlos suggested, misreading the reason for her hesitation. 'Ruy is a brave one, *pequeña*, but not, I think, a foolish one.' He smiled suddenly to someone behind Davina. 'Speak of the devil, is that not what you say in your country? Ruy, we were just talking about you,' he said to the man coming towards them. 'You are shortly to leave for your *estancia*, I hear? May I take the liberty of inviting myself to visit you?'

Ruy must be in pain, Davina thought worriedly. She had not seen his face looking so grey since last night. She was just wondering if she could discover discreetly if he had brought his painkiller with him when he said brusquely, 'If it is the bulls you come to see, Carlos, then you are welcome as always.'

A small smile played round Carlos' lips.

'Ah, that is one of the penalties of having a beautiful wife, *amigo*, it causes one's friends to break the tenth Commandment!'

Other members of the family joined them and the conversation became more general, but before they left Concepcion drew Davina to one side and said awkwardly, 'Forgive me if I presume, Davina, but I like you and think we could become good friends. I must admit at first I was prejudiced against you, but having met you ... If you will take a little advice. Do not provoke Ruy's jealousy. On the surface I know he is all urbane sophistication, but this is just the covering, the velvet which clothes the steel; inside there is a man whose ancestors defied convention and law to obtain their desire. Ruy may not show it, but he is a deeply passionate man; to compare him to Carlos is like comparing a babbling brook to a bottomless lake, if you take my meaning. I would not what you think I am meddling,' she added hastily. 'Sometimes it is good for husbands to think they have a rival, this is something all women know, but there are other times . . .' She shrugged as though unable to find the words, and Davina said quietly,

'Ruy need fear no rival, Concepcion. Neither your cousin nor any other man.'

'So. You and I know this . . . but does Ruy?'

There was silence in the car on the return journey. Davina felt drained of all energy, exhausted by the effort of continually smiling and answering questions.

'So Carlos is to visit the *estancia*,' the Condesa commented when the car drew to a halt in front of the Palacio. 'A charming young man . . .'

'Who has slain as many women with his *piropos* as he has bulls with his sword,' Ruy said dryly.

The Condesa shrugged. 'He is young, handsome and famous, it is natural that girls should admire him—do you not think so, Davina?'

'Yes, Davina,' Ruy goaded, 'do tell us what you think, or can we guess? I believe my delightful wife was quite blinded by the light of admiration shining in Carlos' eyes.'

'Nonsense,' Davina said as lightly as she could. 'I'm not a fool, Ruy. Carlos was doing nothing more than passing a few idle moments. I've lived long enough to recognise flirtation from any stronger emotion.'

'And to recognise love when you see it?' Ruy said softly. 'But of course you can. How many men have loved you, Davina? Have been deceived by that air of outward purity and innocence?'

It was so unfair, Davina thought resentfully, when he had deliberately and coldbloodedly deceived her, letting her think that he actually loved her when all the time . . .

Rodriguez was waiting for Ruy in the *sala*, but he dismissed him. 'I have work to do before we can leave for the *estancia*. You need not wait up for me. The Condesa will do all that is necessary.'

'He must be in pain,' Ruy's mother confided to Davina when Ruy left them to go to his study. 'Often then he cannot sleep and works to ward off the agony of his wound. If only I could turn back the clock!'

'To before his accident,' Davina said, understandingly.

'And earlier still. Davina, perhaps you would be kind enough to pour us both a glass of *fino*. It has never been my habit to drink sherry before I retire, but tonight I am in need of courage, and perhaps a glass of the sherry matured in our own *bodegas* might help me to find it. But first, let me ask you a question. Why did you come back to Spain? Was it just for Jamie?'

Davina poured them both a glass of the pale dry *fino* and handed one to the Condesa before taking a chair opposite her. Only the lamps illuminated the room with its carved furniture and rich rugs. On the wall hung a portrait of Ruy's father, and she glanced up at it before speaking. He had died when Ruy was still at school, and from being a boy he had been forced to grow up almost overnight to assume the responsibilities that went with the title.

'No,' she said honestly at last. 'Oh, I told myself it was. I told myself that Jamie needed the mild climate; that it was his right ... I had a thousand and one reasons why I should come here, but none of them entirely the truth, and even when I discovered that Ruy had not written to me, that he didn't want us, I couldn't go home. I couldn't find the pride to turn my back on him ...'

'Because you love him . . . still?'

'Yes.' The sighed admission fell into the silence of the room. 'Yes, I love him, even now knowing that he cares nothing for me; that he truly believes me capable of passing off another man's child as his . . . that he didn't even care enough to come and visit me after Jamie's birth . . .'

'That wasn't his fault, Davina.'

'No? I saw the photographs of him at the *estancia* with Carmelita, remember? He was making love to another woman while I was bearing his child!'

'No.' The Condesa had gone pale. It seemed to Davina that she was steeling herself to speak. 'I took those photographs, with Carmelita's conniving. You see, Davina, I bitterly resented you for marrying my son. It had been an understood thing that he would marry Carmelita since they were both children, and then suddenly in one week all that was changed and he was married to you. I was very proud in those days and had yet to learn that man is no match for God. I was determined to break up your marriage. It could be set aside, I told myself. The Church would look favourably on a petition from a man of Ruy's standing—but then you conceived Ruy's child.

'It was Carmelita who thought of the plan. She encouraged Sebastian to gamble heavily at a casino in Marbella. All he had was his allowance from Ruy, and we timed it carefully so that Ruy would discover his brother's misdemeanours when you had to go into hospital. I assured Ruy that I would tell you why he could not be with you, why he had been called away. I had also let slip to him, as though by accident, that you were meeting an Englishman behind his back. My son has a jealous nature, although he conceals it well.

It was easy to drop the poison into his ear. Insecurity is an excellent breeding ground, and it wasn't hard to convince him that you had a lover—a man to whom you turned in his absence.

'It was Carmelita's suggestion that we show you the photographs. They had been taken the previous summer, but you too were uncertain and hurt because in your eyes Ruy had deserted you when you needed him.'

And hadn't loved her, Davina reminded herself. She mustn't lose sight of that; mustn't think just because the Condesa was telling her this now that it meant that Ruy felt any differently towards her. He still loved Carmelita.

'Thank you for telling me, but you must see that it can't make any difference now, although it does help to explain why Ruy seems to think that I've had a chain of lovers in and out of my life since we parted.'

'And why he did not show any interest in Jamie, although to look at the *pequeño* is to know that he is a Silvadores . . .'

But if Jamie had taken after her in looks, what then? Davina couldn't help asking herself. Still, it was pointless to speculate.

'It has lain on my conscience since your return,' the Condesa continued. 'You are Ruy's wife—a far better wife to him than Carmelita could ever have been—and Jamie is his son. I hope you can forgive me, Davina.'

'For what?' Davina smiled bleakly. 'What happened would probably have happened anyway. I'm only sorry that Ruy had to be disillusioned about Carmelita. Her defection must have hurt him.'

'You are a generous child,' the Condesa said softly, replacing her glass on the table. 'Perhaps now that I have sought absolution from you I can start to forgive myself. Will you tell Ruy?'

Davina shook her head.

'No. The past is dead, and as you say, no one looking at Jamie could doubt that Ruy is his father.'

Even so as she prepared for bed it was hard to tell herself that nothing could be gained from telling Ruy now what had happened all those years ago. It was true that the Condesa and Carmelita between them had done much to break up her marriage—had Ruy come to the hospital after Jamie's birth she would probably never have left him, and it was inarguable that Carmelita had deliberately made sure that he would not be with her, just as the Condesa had deliberately fostered the impression that she was having an affair with another man, but both of them had believed these deceits without question.

Hadn't Carmelita had enough with Ruy's love, without stooping to destroy whatever feeling he might have had for the wife he had taken in retribution? She could still remember how she had felt that day when Carmelita had told her that she and Ruy were lovers— had been lovers for some time, and were on the point of marriage until they quarrelled—facts which were borne out by the Condesa's information that there was an 'understanding' between the two families. Knowing that had robbed her of the ability to respond to Ruy with the passion his lovemaking had aroused inside her. She couldn't forget when he touched or held her that he loved another woman, and so eventually he had withdrawn from her and she had told herself that she was glad; that it was impossible for her to endure the degradation of being made use of merely because she was there.

She had just stepped out of the bath and was reaching for a towel when the bathroom door was suddenly pushed open. Knowing she was alone in the bedroom, she hadn't bothered to lock it. For what seemed like aeons she and Ruy stayed at one another and then, suddenly becoming aware of her nakedness, Davina grabbed for the towel, flushing furiously as his eyes made a slow appraisal of her body, lingering on the full roundness of her breasts. The effect was exactly the same as had he actually touched her. Her breath seemed to be lodged somewhere in her throat, her nipples hardening in immediate aroused enticement. She tried to cover her nudity with the towel, but Ruy was too quick for her. For all that he was confined to his chair he could manoeuvre it deftly, and when it came to a struggle she was no match for him. In seconds he had removed the towel from her grasp, placing it on his lap as he drawled savagely:

'Why should I not look at you? Why should I deny myself the pleasure you give so freely to others? Your body tells me that your thoughts were not those of an innocent. Of whom were you thinking? Carlos? Does it excite you to think of him coming to you with the blood of his bull still scarlet upon his hands?'

'Stop it! I won't listen to any more!' Davina clamped her hands to her ears, her face pale with shock and pain. 'I wasn't thinking of Carlos.'

'No?' The soft word was accompanied by a smile that sent chills down her spine. 'Then who were you thinking of—and do not tell me "no one".' He was moving towards her, forcing her backwards into the corner, until the walls brought her to an abrupt halt and she had no defences against the cruel stroke of his fingers along the thrusting outline of her breasts. 'I know well what this means,' he told her, caressing her erect nipple with his thumb. 'So, who were you thinking of when you looked in the mirror and saw the reflection of your own body; whose caresses were you imagining?'

'My lover's!' Davina flung at him, goaded beyond endurance, and after all, it was true. The person she had been thinking of had been him, and although he did not know it he had been her only lover.

'*Por Dios!*' A fury she had never seen before glittered in his eyes, and, thoroughly frightened, she tried to escape, but he was too quick for her, and her bare feet slipped on the tiles, causing her to fall against him.

'Your lover, you say?' Ruy ground out furiously against her ear. 'Well, as your husband, I must just see if I cannot give your wayward thoughts another direction, must I not?'

The moment he touched her Davina knew that she was lost. She could not fight his anger and her own desire. His touch kindled a fire that spread through her veins like melted honey, rendering her mindless and able only to obey an instinct which went deeper by far than reason or logic. With her body crushed against his, the buttons of his shirt tiny pinpoints of pain against her skin, she allowed him to explore and plunder as he wished, finding in her surrender a sweet agony which blinded her to everything but the need to prolong the pleasure of feeling his hands on her skin arousing feelings she had thought long dead, his lips sending spirals of pleasure through quivering nerve endings as they moved languorously along her throat and shoulders.

'You want me, Davina,' he said slowly, cupping her

face and forcing her to stare at her own aroused expression.

'And you want me . . .'

It was a statement of fact and one he didn't choose to deny. Instead he released her slowly and then started to remove his shirt, manoevring the chair forward.

Davina followed him. An intense ache built up deep inside her. The next move, if there was to be one, would have to come from her. Did she have the courage to openly solicit his lovemaking, knowing his desire was merely physical?

She had convinced herself that she had not when she remembered Dr Gonzales saying that another child might help to release Ruy's mental block. Like a sleep-walker she walked towards him, kneeling to unfasten the cufflinks gleaming palely gold in his cuffs.

He had gone completely still and when when she looked up at him his face might have been carved out of a block of stone.

'Make love to me, Ruy,' she said huskily. 'I want you.'

It was almost a relief to say the words, although what she should have said was that she loved him, but love was a word which must never be uttered between them.

When still he made no move towards her her heart plummeted downwards. Perhaps she had misjudged the extent of his need. It was hard to pull on her nightgown and pretend that nothing had happened, turning her back and closing her ears against the sound of him preparing for bed. His chair lifted to the height of the bed, enabling him to get from one to the other without help, and she felt the mattress depress as he rolled on to it.

His hands on her waist made her stiffen in shock.

'So you want me to make love to you? Why, so that you can add it to your lengthy list of "experiences"? Damn you to hell, Davina!' he swore suddenly, his mouth closing over hers. 'Well, if it's an "experience" you want, I'll make damn sure this is one you'll never forget!'

And neither would she, Davina thought pain-hazed seconds later as the clamped hands on her waist prevented her from moving and the oppression of Ruy's mouth forced the tender inner skin of her lips back against her teeth until she could taste blood. The full weight of his body held her pinned to the bed as the restricting nightgown was rent destructively from neck to hem to make way for hands which seemed to know exactly where to touch and torment, bringing her to the very edge of pleasure and then withholding it until her breath was a sobbed rasp in her throat. Time and time again his hands stroked across her stomach and beneath her ribcage, causing her to press herself against him in a frenzy of desire, her lips leaving moistly pleading kisses in the hollow of his throat and the breadth of his shoulders while her fingers curled protestingly into the muscles of his back, and her breasts ached for his possession.

As though he knew exactly what it was doing to her his hands cupped their heavy warmth and he lowered his head. Her stomach muscles tensed defensively, but it was no use. Even the merest touch of his breath against her skin betrayed her need, and when his tongue tormentingly circled first one tautly erect nipple and then the other she could barely prevent herself from crying out loud.

'I hope you're enjoying this experience, Davina,' she heard him mutter thickly as he lowered his full weight on to her and the ache in her stomach became a tormenting fever. 'I should hate to be in any way mediocre.'

She didn't want him to talk to her. Hearing him speak ruined the dream she had spun for herself that he actually loved her as she loved him; that the burning pressure of his lips was conveying more than mere desire and that the sudden tremors shuddering through him were not merely caused by physical desire.

She wound her arms round his neck, forcing herself not to beg him to give her his love.

'Please, Ruy . . .' It was near as she could come to an admission, but instead of complying with the soft plea, Ruy suddenly thrust her away, swearing savagely.

'No,' he said bitterly, 'I cannot do it. I will not compete with your other lovers, Davina. I may be a useless cripple, but I am still a man and not an animal!'

'But you wanted me . . .'

'For a moment, until I remembered how many other had also "wanted" you.'

'Ruy . . .' She reached out tremulously, intending to tell him the truth and that there had been no other man but him, but he thrust away the hand resting lightly on his chest as though it had burned and said thickly:

'*Por Dios*, do not touch me, or are you determined to drag me down to your gutter?'

Her tears soaked steadily into her pillow, making her throat ache with the effort of suppressing them. Never again would she allow Ruy to hurt her as he had done tonight. She had offered him her body out of love and desire, and he had turned that offer into something sordid and hateful. From tomorrow they would sleep in different rooms no matter what Ruy might say to the contrary; it was one thing to accept his bitterness and contempt, it was another to allow him to humiliate her as he had done tonight and for the sake of her sanity she could not allow it to happen again. He had quite deliberately aroused her—she was sure of that—she was even sure that he had intended to make love to her, but to be told that he could not do so because she disgusted him was something she would never recover from.

CHAPTER SEVEN

As he had business in Marbella, they would break their journey there and have lunch at the Yacht Club, before going on to the *estancia*, Ruy told Davina over breakfast.

There were still lines of pain etched heavily on the taut flesh of his face and she was worried that the long journey, plus the strain of sitting through an arduous business meeting, might be too much for him, but when she ventured to suggest that they dispensed with lunch and that instead he rested, his eyes darkened to the colour of obsidian, glittering with the anger which found an outlet in the ice-cold-voice with which he demanded if he was expected to believe that her 'concern' was truly altruistic.

'If you are ashamed to have lunch with me then you can always remain in the car. I will not be reduced to the life of a hermit simply because I no longer have the use of my legs.'

His twisting of her words infuriated Davina. When Jamie had toddled off with Maria to help 'pack his clothes' she rounded on Ruy, ignoring the implacable set of his mouth and the warning glint in his eyes.

'*You* are the one who insists that the loss of the use of your legs diminishes you as a man,' she told him, anger overcoming caution. 'From the first moment I arrived here you have insisted that in some way I relished your pain and disability, but this is just not so. You're the one who's enjoying it, Ruy. Dr Gonzales

says there's nothing wrong organically; you could walk
. . . but you refuse. If you want my view, I think you're
deliberately trying to make me feel guilty, to make . . .'

She faltered to a standstill, horrified by what she
had said. Ruy's face was as grey as the paving beneath
their feet, and she longed to take back her impulsive
words and tell him that they had been said in the
heat of her anger, but she was not granted the opportunity. Struggling to pull himself out of his chair,
supporting his weight on the table, he towered over
her, his eyes raking her trembling body from head to
foot.

'To make you what?' he grated. 'Fall in love with
me?' His harsh laughter filled the enclosed space of the
patio. 'Is that what you honestly think of me? That I
am so weak-willed, so cowardly, that I am reduced to
such stratagems?' Numbly Davina shook her head,
trying to conceal her tears. 'So our good doctor has
told you that he *believes* my paralysis to be caused by a
traumatic shock—and it is only a belief; it cannot be
proved. Has he also told you of the odds against that
mental block being removed?'

'Yes.'

'I suggest you examine your own motives a little
more closely before you delve into mine, Davina. For
instance, what motivates a woman to stay with a man
without love existing between them?'

What answer could she give? A love so strong that it
overrode common sense and pride?

When she and Jamie emerged from the Palacio an
hour later, Ruy was already seated in the driving seat
of a sleek Mercedes coupé.

His mother would be using the chauffeur-driven car,
he explained as Jamie begged to be allowed to sit in

the front passenger seat, and this car had been especially adapted for him to drive, he added suavely when Davina suggested to Jamie that it might be best if he sat in the back.

'I wasn't doubting your driving ability,' Davina began defensively, but Ruy's raised eyebrows said that he did not believe her.

'No? Then in that case you won't mind sitting beside me yourself, will you? That way Jamie can sleep in the back if he gets tired.'

It was so obviously a sensible suggestion that Davina found herself sliding reluctantly on to the cream hide seat while Jamie climbed into the back.

The car smelled of expensive hide and the thin cigars Ruy sometimes smoked. There was a box of them in front of him, and he lit one as they waited for Rodriguez to finish loading the luggage. Davina had been surprised that the manservant was not to accompany them, but Ruy had explained that he would go straight to the *estancia*. Blue smoke from the cigarillo curled lazily upwards, the smell of the tobacco reminding her evocatively of that first meeting in Cordoba when he had bought her coffee and listened to her pouring out her story.

The boot was closed. The Condesa was waiting to wave them off. Ruy switched on the engine and they started to move forward, the car coming to an abrupt halt that threw her against the padded dashboard as Ruy stopped suddenly when they had gone no more than a few yards.

'Seat-belt,' he reminded her sharply, when she turned to him. 'That was a small sample of what can happen when a driver has to brake suddenly.'

She had been so concerned about Ruy and Jamie

that she had forgotten this simple safety precaution. Her finances at home did not run to such luxuries as a car, and she had got out of the habit of thinking of herself as a passenger.

Shakily she reached for the strap, pulling it across her body, as she tried to push the metal tag into the holder. The fitting was tight and although she exerted as much pressure as she could, it was not sufficient to drive the tag home.

'Let me.' Her hands were pushed unceremoniously out of the way as Ruy's lean brown fingers deftly manipulated the belt. His knuckles brushed accidentally across the soft curve of her breast—completely impersonally—but she withdrew immediately nonetheless, not wanting him to think she had deliberately fumbled with the belt to engineer the brief contact. For a moment his fingers seemed to tremble—probably because of the pressure he was having to exert, but when the belt was securely fastened and adjusted he merely glanced remotely at her before re-starting the engine.

Davina had never been to Marbella before. The business venture which Ruy had entered with Concepcion's father had been started more recently. They were financing the building of a small number of select villas on a holiday complex, Ruy told her in answer to her queries.

The powerful Mercedes made light work of the long miles, the air-conditioning mitigating the effect of the heat outside, just as the tinted windows kept out the harsh glare of the sunlight.

Riding in a car was still a novelty to Jamie and it was easy to keep him amused by encouraging him to count all the different coloured cars he saw, and after a few miles even Ruy joined in the game, making Jamie laugh with triumph when his father occasionally missed seeing a car, allowing him to add to his score. But even while making allowances for his youth Ruy in no way patronised the little boy, correcting him firmly but quietly when he made a mistake or when his exuberance led him to attempting to cheat.

'Soon we shall have to make arrangements about his schooling,' Ruy commented to Davina when Jamie was engrossed in the new game.

Cold fingers touched her heart. Of course she knew that Jamie was growing up and would soon be leaving babyhood behind and entering the world of men, but mother-like, she wanted to hold off the evil day as long as she could.

'What had you in mind?' she asked steadily, feeling that to betray her pain would only give Ruy a weapon to use against her. 'Boarding school?'

'Later, perhaps. There is an excellent school in Cordoba which he could attend. I do not believe in forcing children into a mould for which they are not fitted by nature, although in Jamie's case, as my son he will naturally, one day, have to step into my shoes. At the moment he is constantly among adults, and I think he would benefit from companions of his own age.'

Davina could find nothing to argue with in this statement. She turned her head and looked at Jamie's absorbed features.

'You love him a great deal.'

It was a statement rather than a question, but nevertheless she replied to it.

'Did you expect me not to? My own child?'

'And my child?' Ruy reminded her, his mouth compressing. 'Truly mother nature is wonderful, that she can cause a woman to love the child of a man for whom she feels nothing.'

They were driving along the valley of the Guadalquivir past rich cereal fields tended by peasants who worked tirelessly on the crops. This land had been under cultivation from the time of the Moors, and they had bequeathed to it the irrigation system which made it so rich and fertile. Groves of olive trees, their leaves silver-grey in the sunlight, bowed beneath the weight of their fruit. Jamie, to whom they were still new, demanded to know what the olives were used for, and patiently Ruy explained, 'To the Spaniard the olive is the symbol of prosperity. It was first brought to Spain by the Moors, along with peaches, pomegranates, medlars and many other fruits. At one time Seville had a reputation second to none for its learning and scholars. People came from all over Europe to consult its doctors and lawyers, so you have much to be proud of in your heritage, my son, and much to live up to.'

Jamie nodded his head in solemn agreement and then smiled sweetly and said vigorously, 'When I grow up I want to be just like my daddy. Can I learn to ride a real horse when we go to the *estancia*?'

Ruy glanced at Davina.

'I don't see why not. We shall find a small pony for you, and Rodriguez will teach you, as his father taught me.'

And as Ruy would have taught Jamie had it not been for his accident. Davina had to make a pretence of studying the landscape so that neither pair of male eyes would see her tears.

'Perhaps he'll teach me as well,' she said when she was sure that her voice would not betray her. 'I've always longed to be able to ride.'

Ruy made no comment. He was concentrating on overtaking a farm cart pulled by a small donkey wearing a straw hat threaded with faded pink roses, and Davina did not like to repeat the request. On their wedding night, after the culmination of their love-making, he had whispered huskily that there was much he would teach her, and that they would derive mutual pleasure from the lessons, but it was well known that men said many things they did not mean in the aftermath of physical satisfaction. With painful clarity she remembered how he had held her close within the circle of his arms, kissing the tears of pleasure from her damp cheeks.

The Yacht Club had its own extensive grounds and had once been a private house. Balconied verandas overlooked the harbour, which was crammed with craft of all sizes and origins, the one thing they all had in common being their luxurious splendour.

His meeting should not take long, Ruy announced as he parked the car. The driver's seat had been removed to accommodate the wheelchair, and there was an electrical device to lift it from the car to the ground which retracted back inside the Mercedes once the manoeuvre was completed.

A steward appeared almost immediately to conduct Ruy to the room where he was to meet his business associates. They had an hour, he had told Davina, warning her that it would not be wise to stray too far, or stay overlong in the hot sun.

Bearing this in mind, she insisted on Jamie wearing his white linen sunhat. His chubby legs were already turning healthily brown. The Condesa had insisted on buying him some new clothes and as they set off hand

in hand for the harbour, Davina was amused to hear a
passerby comment loud enough for her to hear. 'Just
look at that darling little boy! So Spanish!'

The quayside bustled with activity—people coming
and going from the various craft; men with skin like
leather and eyes fanned by a network of lines, dressed
in jeans and tee-shirts; girls in brief shorts and tops.
Everywhere except for the half dozen or so yachts
which to Davina's uneducated eyes more resembled
full-scale liners, the accent was on casual clothes, but
Davina smiled to see two men dressed in navy pin-
striped suits and carrying briefcases gingerly going on
board one of the larger yachts.

'The boss's private secretaries,' the seaman standing
by the gangway told Davina cheerfully with a wink.
'Keeps 'em busy, he does.'

The two men had looked very hot and uncomfortable. She wouldn't like to be at the beck and call of a
rich boss, Davina thought. Jamie drew her attention to
a speedboat circling the bay, a girl on water-skis behind
it, wearing the briefest bikini Davina had ever seen in
her life.

'I want to do that,' Jamie insisted, tugging on her
hand, and when Davina told him that it was very, very
hard, he replied cheerfully with the sublime confidence
of the very young, 'I bet my daddy can do it. I bet he
can do it a hundred times better than that lady!'

Davina squeezed his hand, too moved to speak. She
had never seen Ruy water-skiing, but she knew that he
could. Sebastian had told her that he had won a shield
for it, and she knew that he was practically a cham-
pionship swimmer. That pleasure at least had not been
taken away from him.

Jamie insisted on having an ice-cream although,

knowing that they would shortly be having lunch,
Davina prudently bought him a very small one.

An eye-catching outfit in a harbourside boutique
drew her attention. It was a female version of the traditional male Spanish riding costume, and on impulse
she went in and asked if she might try it on.

It fitted perfectly. She had lost a little weight since
coming to Spain and the narrow black trousers emphasised her slender waist.

'It might have been made for you,' the girl told her.
'It is one of our most popular lines.' She wrinkled her
nose despairingly. 'But you try telling a size sixteen
tourist that it really isn't their style!'

By the time it was wrapped up and the bill paid
Davina realised that they ought to be heading back to
the Club. When she stepped outside into the bright
sunshine a wave of dizziness swept over her. It was
gone almost instantly. Hunger, she told herself firmly,
grasping Jamie's hand, but as they got closer to the
club, the noise and bright light of the quayside seemed
to heighten in intensity to a point where it was making
her feel physically ill.

Once inside the shady, cool foyer of the club, the
nausea seemed to recede. A waiter came to conduct
them to a table discreetly placed in a small alcove, per-
mitting the maximum degree of privacy but still allowing an excellent view over the harbour and of the other
diners.

Ruy was there already, talking to two other men,
who smiled and bowed as she approached.

'Ah, there you are, darling!'

Was that really Ruy talking to her in a voice like
warm brown velvet, reaching for her fingers to curl
them round inside his own and brush them tenderly

against his jaw? A tug on her arm brought her down towards him, the light kiss he placed against her lips making her stare at him in bemused wonder, her cheeks still flushing.

'My wife is still very English,' Ruy laughed. 'She believes that all gestures of affection should be conducted in privacy.'

Both men were eyeing Davina appreciatively. In fact although she was unaware of it her entrance had created quite a stir. Slim blonde girls with eyes the colour of amethysts, and a shyness that aroused the hunting instinct in the essentially male Spaniard, were a rare find in such modern times.

Sensing that something was expected of her, Davina leaned forward and brushed her lips against Ruy's skin. It felt hard and warm to touch, sending tiny electrical impulses through her own body, and making her long for the right to touch him as a lover.

The two men did not linger. Business must not be allowed to interfere with such a serious matter as eating lunch.

Davina let Ruy order for them. Their first course was tiny fried prawns in a delicious sauce accompanied by crisp rolls, but Davina could not finish it. The nagging headache which had begun outside the boutique seemed to have taken over her entire head. She made a pretence of picking at the salmon salad Ruy had ordered for them, hoping that Jamie's excited chatter would distract his attention away from her. Whether it was the sudden change of temperature from the harbour to the air-conditioned club, she did not know, but she suddenly felt chilled, almost to the point of shivering.

'What's the matter?' The coldly incisive words cut

through her pain. 'Was it the effort of pretending to be a loving wife that makes you look so pale? My associates have naturally heard about our marriage and expect to see us at least making a show of being happy together. They tell me that I am fortune to have such a loving wife. Fortunate!' He grimaced slightly. 'Would you agree with them, Davina? Would you say that I was "fortunate"—a man who cannot move without the assistance of others; a man whose wife turns from him in horror and disgust?'

You're wrong, she wanted to shout, but the words remained unsaid. Ruy was using her as a means of venting his wrath, that was all, but the cruelty in his probing expression as he added so softly that only she could hear, 'A wife whose body I can still arouse nonetheless, though . . .' deprived her of the ability to fight back.

Let him think of her what he wished, she decided dully, pushing away her meal barely touched, as long as he stopped tormenting her.

The road to the *estancia* went through the city of Ronda—traditional home of the bullfight, Ruy explained to Davina as they turned away from the coast and towards the Sierras, divided in two by the chasm that sliced it in half as neatly as a sword-slash.

Hairpin bends like a switchback track carried them up into the mountains, each swerving curve increasing Davina's nausea to the point where it was all she could do merely to remain upright in her seat. At one point she unwisely obeyed Jamie's excited command to 'look out of the window, Mummy!' and immediately wished she had not when she saw the drop below them, the remains of cars driven more carelessly than theirs rust-ing away in the gorge below.

'This is reputed to be one of the most dangerous roads in all Spain, and he wants to overtake me!' Ruy gritted at one point, glancing into his mirror. The shrill blare of a horn behind them confirmed his words, and as Davina glanced over her shoulder she saw a small scarlet sports car on their tail, its hood down, and four young people crammed into a space intended only for two.

'Crazy fools!' Ruy swore succinctly. 'Do they want to kill themselves! *Loco! Turistas!* They are a menace to other people's safety!'

A glance at the speedometer showed that they themselves were travelling at some speed, although the expensive engineering of the car nullified some of its effects, but the driver of the red sports car seemed determined to pass them, even though the road was busy and barely wide enough for two cars.

'*Cristo!*' Ruy swore at one point, when he was forced to brake and they could hear squealing tyres behind them. 'I should like to give those young fools a piece of my mind. Do they know how many people have lost their lives on this road, I wonder?'

They reached a point where the road started to climb steeply, and to Davina's relief the powerful Mercedes soon pulled away from the overloaded sports car.

'If I were not confined to this damned chair, I would have stopped and spoken to them,' Ruy said bitterly. '*Por Dios!* I could just see their faces had I done so—a cripple . . .'

His anger seemed to fill the car like a dense cloud, silencing Jamie and making Davina long for the ability to shrug aside the pain-filled sickness which seemed to keep coming and going in ever-strengthening waves.

She lifted a hand to her head, trying to ease the agonising throbbing, but even that movement was sufficient to make her shiver with the effort of suppressing her nausea.

'What's the matter? Are you car-sick?' Ruy demanded, lifting his eyes from the road to follow the betraying gesture.

Davina could only shake her head, even that small motion excruciatingly painful.

'I don't know.' Her voice was merely a thread of sound. 'My head aches. I feel sick, and dizzy . . . I feel so cold . . .'

'Heatstroke! Did you not have the sense to cover your head when you were out this morning?'

Davina was beyond replying. She merely wanted to curl up and die, but rather than admit that Ruy was right she sat bolt upright in her seat and stared out of the car window.

They were driving through mountains of rust red sandstone, sprinkled with moss and alpine flowers. She remembered reading somewhere once that the Garrison at Gibraltar used to spend the dog days of summer at Ronda where the air was cooler.

Beneath them lay the plain and the coast, but mindful of her nausea Davina refused to look back. Ronda itself was all narrow, winding streets and ancient buildings. Ruy pointed out to her the bridge across the chasm of red sandstone from which its designer had fallen to his death, dizzied by the depth of the gorge.

The *estancia* lay beyond the town and had at one time served as a summer residence for the family. It was Ruy who had built up their herd of bulls, all carefully bred for the arena. Bulls came in two classes, he explained to Jamie as they drew nearer the *estancia*; either young bulls three to four years old or older ones of four to five which were used in the *corrida* proper. The bulls had to be bred to an extremely exacting standard. Their weight must fall within certain limits; their age must be correct, and most important of all, they must be brave. 'A cowardly bull disgraces a brave *torero*, just as a cowardly man disgraces a brave bull,' he told a round-eyed Jamie, who was listening with awe.

A narrow road with cattle grids across it led to the *estancia*. Davina could see no sign of the bulls as they drove past flat paddocks. This was because during the heat of the summer the animals were kept where there was most water, Ruy told her. Thousands of pounds were invested in these animals and nothing could afford to be left to chance.

'It seems pointless, when they are going to die anyway,' Davina commented. She had never witnessed a *corrida*, although Ruy had once told her that it was not for the spectacle of a blood sport that his countrymen flocked to the bullfight; it was something that went far deeper than that; left over from the days when man worshipped the goddess of fertility, and the male fortunate enough to be chosen as her mate reigned as king for a year before being sacrificed for continued prosperity. Gradually as cultures evolved the bull had come to take the place of man, as depicted in the Minoan culture, and it was from this that the bullfight had evolved. To the Spaniard the experience was an ennobling and uplifting one—almost religious, and the death of a good bull was mourned almost as much as the death of a good matador.

At last they reached the hacienda. It was a double-storey house with a long low frontage and a delicate veranda running its full length, wrought iron balconies ornamenting the upper windows, the entire façade smothered in the purple flowers of the bougainvillea through which the delicate white-painted tracery of the wrought iron gleamed softly in the late afternoon sun.

As the dust from the car tyres settled doors opened and Rodriguez, accompanied by a small, plump woman with eyes like raisins, her hair in a neat bun, came hurrying out to meet them.

Jamie was lifted from the car and snatched to an ample bosom, a torrent of excited Spanish engulfing them as Davina struggled to extricate herself from her seat. Where she had been cold she was now hot; her dress was sticking damply to her back, perspiration beading her forehead. Her body ached with fatigue and she longed to lie down somewhere quiet and cool.

'Dolores says that Jamie is a true Silvadores,' Ruy told her wryly as the Spanish woman continued to hug the little boy. 'She has seven children of her own, three of whom are living here on the *estancia* with their parents, so Jamie will not lack company. Between them Dolores and her husband, who is my manager, have been running the *estancia* since my father died. They look upon it as their home, and Dolores will have gone to a great deal of trouble to ensure our comfort.'

What was he trying to suggest? That she might find the hacienda wanting in some way? As she followed Dolores into a large, comfortably furnished *sala*, its shutters closed against the bright sunlight, Davina could not imagine why he should think so.

It was true that the hacienda lacked the elegance of the Palacio, but the house had a comfortable, family air, which appealed to her instantly. Here small children would be able to run about and touch to their hearts' content. The furniture was no less well cared for than that in the Palacio, but somehow it was less intimidating. Sturdy, cushion-filled settees and chairs invited one to sit on them; brightly woven carpets overlaid the coolly tiled floors. There was a jug of flowers on the coffee table, and along one wall ran shelves which housed books and magazines that seemed to relate to farm management. The room could have been that of a comfortably off farmer rather than a Spanish grandee, and Davina was not ashamed to admit that she liked its ambience; the smell of leather and beeswax mingling with the hot, dusty scent of the land.

'I have given you the bedroom of the *patrón*,' the woman explained as she led Davina up the gracefully curved stairs to the upper storey. Ruy had already warned her that here at the *estancia* they dispensed with titles. To these people he was simply 'the *patrón*'. The title had a patriarchal air which suited him. Davina found herself imagining him as an old man surrounded by his family. Her heart gave a small thump; she must not give way to such foolish visions.

The bedroom she was shown was large. Floral wallpaper adorned the walls, the theme continued in the curtains and bedspread. The bed was a fourposter, the furniture Spanish provincial. Off the bedroom was a bathroom and small dressing room, both showing signs of having been recently modernised. The bathroom fittings reflected the same country style as the bedroom, the white porcelain painted with flowers and leaves.

'You like?' Dolores beamed up at her. 'It is all new since the *patrón* marries, for his *novia* . . . *si* . . .'

Davina's stomach plummeted downwards and she

stared round the room with new eyes. All this had been
done for Carmelita. She touched the pastel wallpaper
tentatively. Somehow the room did not strike her as
suitable for the other girl's vibrant personality. She,
on the other hand, loved it. The moment she walked
in the room she had felt her taut muscles start to relax.
The sheets smelled of crushed lavender, and the scent
hung evocatively on the air. Lavender. She smiled to
herself. Such an English scent! Surely carnation or
something equally exotic would have been more suitable for Carmelita?

Rodrigues came upstairs with the luggage. Both her
cases and Ruy's were placed on the floor, Davina
noticed, remembering her vow that on their removal
to the *estancia* she would tell Ruy that she wanted her
own room.

'The *pequeño* grows anxious for his dinner,'
Rodrigues told Dolores.

'He has been ill,' Davina found herself confiding to
the other woman—a mother herself, after all. 'The
damp climate . . .'

'But here he will grow tall and strong, you will see,'
Dolores beamed.

The sickness Davina had experienced on the journey
returned over dinner. Dolores had prepared a dish of
crisply fried chicken served on a bed of peppers and
sweetcorn. Jamie tucked into it with every evidence of
enjoyment. Apart from during his illness he had never
been a fussy eater, and Davina was relieved to see that
he seemed to be adapting to a changed diet without
too much trouble. She herself could barely force down
a mouthful. They were eating early because Ruy
wanted to spend the evening in discussion with the
estate manager.

'The bedroom is to your satisfaction?' he enquired as he poured her a glass of wine.

'It's very attractive.' Her voice sounded listless. 'Dolores told me it has been decorated quite recently—for your *novia*, she told me.' It was impossible to prevent the hint of bitterness from creeping into the words. 'I shouldn't have thought it in accord with Carmelita's personality.'

To her amazement Ruy's jaw clenched in anger, a pulse beating warningly beneath the skin as he drank his wine before saying curtly, 'That room was not decorated for Carmelita. It was decorated for my wife—for you. I arranged for it to be done while you were carrying Jamie. I had thought after his birth that we might spend more time out here. Its atmosphere is more conducive to family life than the Palacio's.'

Davina didn't know what to say. The thought of Ruy going to all this trouble on her behalf stunned her. She remembered the lavender perfumed sheets, and the furnishings which now that she thought about them closely resembled those to be found in an English country house. No wonder she had had such a nostalgic sense of coming home!

'Ruy, I just don't know what to say . . .' she began weakly, but he brushed aside her words, shrugging as though he had grown bored with the matter.

'It no longer matters,' he drawled, confirming his actions. 'The room was prepared in vastly different circumstances from those we now find ourselves in.'

What he meant was that now he no longer needed to ease his conscience by providing her with pleasant surroundings as compensation for not being able to give her his love.

He left the table before she could tell him that she

did not want to share a room with him. With Jamie to be bathed and put to bed, his excited questions all answered, and the pain in her temples to contend with, Davina herself was on the point of crawling into the comfort of the cool sheets before she remembered that Ruy was still downstairs and she had not been able to speak to him.

She bit her lip and glanced to the other side of the bed where his robe had been carefully laid out. She could scarcely demand that he find another bed tonight.

She could talk to him tomorrow, she decided sleepily, reaching out to switch off the lamp. She had gone very cold again, the cool sheets now felt like an Arctic wasteland, and her body longed treacherously for the warmth of Ruy against her.

CHAPTER EIGHT

DAVINA woke up feeling cold, taking several minutes
to remember where she was. Her head ached and there
was a sour taste in her mouth. She reached for the
bedside lamp and then realised that Ruy was asleep at
the other side of the bed. Rather than risk waking him
she pushed back the sheets and tiptoed towards the
bathroom.

Her head hurt, and her face looked flushed. Ruy was
right, she reflected as she studied her reflection. She
ought to have worn a hat when she was out in the sun.
She had forgotten how strong it could be. Cleaning
her teeth dispelled the unpleasant taste in her mouth.
She had some aspirins in her handbag and she resolved
to take a couple before going back to bed.

The windows to the balcony stood open, allowing
the hot night scents to drift into the bedroom. Davina
knew that the temperature had not suddenly dropped
ten degrees, but as she crossed to the bed the breeze
from the window brought out tiny bumps of gooseflesh
on her arms—the aftermath of too much sun. Below
the windows the darkness was full of the sound of
crickets, petals from a jacaranda carpeting the balcony
floor.

As she slid back into bed Ruy moved and muttered
something under his breath in Spanish, his features
for once relaxed. Asleep, he looked more like the man
she had married. A sudden fit of shivering seized her,
making her teeth chatter.

'*Amada* . . .'

Ruy didn't open his eyes, but his arm came round her, pulling her against the warmth of his body, the heat from his skin bringing hers tinglingly alive, his warm breath fanning across her temple.

Chiding herself for giving in to the demand of her senses so easily, Davina allowed herself to luxuriate in his proximity. His action had been no more than a simple reflex, she warned herself; and meant nothing, except perhaps that he was dreaming that he held Carmelita in his arms. The thought made her move slightly away from him, but his arm tightened possessively, dragging her against him, his lips teasing tender kisses against the vulnerable skin of her throat and shoulders.

'Ruy . . .'

She tried to push him away, but his arm only hardened, his husky, '*Querida?*' turning her bones to water. She looked at him and saw that his eyes were still closed even though his fingertips were making a delicate exploration of her body.

She was a fool, she told herself when Ruy pushed aside the thin cotton of her nightdress and buried his head in the shadowed hollow between her breasts, holding her to him as though he never wanted to let her go. This time his touch held tenderness—worship almost, the soft Spanish lovewords whispering past his lips, punctuated by seductive kisses, weakening her shaky resolve. It would be so easy to respond to him, to encourage him even, but she was convinced that he was not aware who she was. His lovemaking held a quality she remembered from their honeymoon; sensual and lazy, that of a man who touches for the tactile pleasure of doing so. There was no sense of urgency, no driven furious anger, and never once did his eyes open as he stroked and caressed her body into melting surrender, murmuring to her in Spanish, husky words of passion intermingled with the moist warmth of his mouth as it touched her body in tender worship.

'*Amada* . . .'

Davina heard him whisper it on a satisfied sigh as his lips brushed hers, and he begged her to tell him of her love.

Tears stung her eyes. How gladly she would have complied, if she thought for one moment that he might have wanted it. But the soft words and sweet kisses falling from his lips were not for her.

She held her breath and prayed that he would not wake up, and soon the even rise and fall of his breathing told her that her prayers had been granted, although when she tried to move away from him to her own side of the bed he refused to let her go, and she slept, as she had dreamed of doing for so long, clasped in the arms of the man she loved, his heart beating beneath her cheek, her palms spread against the satin warmth of his skin.

'Kiss me, *amada* . . .' The sleep-drugged words penetrated, and Davina's eyelids fluttered open. She was lying in Ruy's arms, his lips feathering light kisses along her jawbone.

'Ruy?'

'*Dios*, I want you!'

She could feel his heart thudding beneath her palms, his face pale in the morning light. He bent his head, parting her lips with the mastery she remembered, coaxing her mouth to give up its sweetness. Beneath her hands his heartbeat accelerated, his body tautening with the desire that throbbed pulsating through him, making plain his need. Her own body was half crushed beneath his superior weight, the powerful muscles of his thighs contracting in sudden urgency as his hands slid her nightgown from her shoulders, his lips plundering the creamy curves bared to his burning gaze, and playing on her body like a master drawing a response from a carefully tuned violin.

'Ruy . . .' Her protest was lost beneath the warm pressure of his mouth, draining her of the will to resist, his fingers tangling in her hair as he held her head pinioned to allow his lips to rove freely where they wished.

She managed to drag her lips away for long enough to whisper his name again. His body crushing her to the bed, his hands either side of her face on the pillow, he raised himself slightly to stare down into her pale face.

'You are my wife, Davina,' he said broodingly, 'and you have brought home to me the fact that I am a man. Sharing a bedroom with you has reminded me of all that I have been missing. Your skin is like silk beneath my hands and you tremble at my slightest touch like a shy virgin who has never known a man. You taste of roses and honey and your hair is the colour of moonbeams. A man would have to be made of stone to resist your beauty, and I am only flesh and blood. See,' he said softly, taking her hand and placing it against his body. 'Can you not feel what you do to me?'

'Ruy, this is madness!' Davina protested, more shaken than she wanted him to see by his words. He thought her beautiful! He desired her, but desire was not love.

'Of a certainty,' he agreed with a mocking smile, 'but it is a madness that mortals need to keep them sane. Why deny me, Davina, when you have permitted so many others? I am your husband . . .'

'And because of that I'm supposed to allow you to treat me like . . . like a harem slave?' Davina demanded bitterly. 'I thought better of you, Ruy. I didn't think you would take a woman without love, purely to satisfy a sexual appetite.'

'Neither did I, but needs must when the devil drives, as he is driving me.'

He lowered his head and knowing that he wouldn't be swayed, Davina sought wildly for time. This wasn't how she wanted him to make love to her, as a substitute for Carmelita.

'Think . . .' she begged him despairingly. 'We'll only end up hating each other—hating ourselves . . .'

'Perhaps.' The word grazed her skin like a kiss. 'But in the meantime we would have known a shared sweetness; an oblivion that brings its own recompense. Will you not taste that oblivion with me, sweet Davina?'

As his mouth closed over hers Davina fought its insistent pressure like a drowning man fighting water. Beneath his hands her body turned to pure flame, betraying her even while she resisted.

'Davina.' Her name was a thick plea on Ruy's tongue, overturning all her determination, like a spring tide crashing through a sea wall, carrying her back with it to a place where nothing mattered but the feel of Ruy's skin beneath her hands, the harsh warmth of his mouth as he filled her senses to the exclusion of everything but the driving need in the lower half of her body, prompting her to arch imploringly beneath the heated thrust of the thighs imprisoning her, Ruy's

name a soft moan of desire-laden protest as his lips left
the vulnerable hollows behind her ears to torment the
throbbing pulses of her neck and lower still, while her
own lips fastened on the tanned column of his throat,
her teeth biting sensually into the sunwarmed skin.

'*Dios . . . querida*, but I want you!'

The tormented groan seemed to shiver right through
her, finding all her most vulnerable corners, making
her flesh quiver with a yearning need which could only
find appeasement in Ruy's complete possession.

'Ruy . . .' All her longing for him was in that one
word and he lifted his head to survey her with eyes
black as night and burning with desire.

'Ah, now you do not talk of hating one another, do
you, *querida*? Do you feel as I do? Does your body
long to be united with mine, no longer separate, but a
part of one enticingly perfect whole? Does your need
for fulfilment overcome all your moral scruples? Do
you want me as I want you?'

'Yes.' The shamed whisper could not be held back.

'So . . .'

He turned abruptly as someone knocked on the bedroom door, and then frowned as he glanced at his watch
on the bedside table.

'*Dios!*' he swore softly. 'I had forgotten. I asked
Rodriguez to wake me early so that I could go down to
the bull pens. What shall I do, *amada*? Send him
away?'

Davina flushed at the openly sensual tone.

Those few seconds' respite had given her the chance
to allow common sense to reassert itself, and she shook
her head, moving away from Ruy's constraining
hands.

'Ah,' he mocked softly, 'I had forgotten that prim

English streak. You surprise me, *querida*. A woman of your experience should not be embarrassed because it is known that your husband would rather lie in bed in the mornings and make love to you than visit his livestock.'

'Lovemaking without love,' Davina said tiredly.

'So! But very enjoyable nonetheless,' Ruy said cruelly. 'Do not deny it. One only has to look in the mirror. Your face is that of a woman who has recently been aroused.'

'Desire is not enough—at least not for me, Ruy.'

All at once his face seemed to close up and grow cold.

'I think you are deceiving yourself, *querida*,' he said harshly. 'But now is perhaps not the time to prove the truth of my statement.' He called out something in Spanish to Rodriguez, and Davina turned away from him in despair. How quickly she had plummeted from the heights to the depths! It was pointless telling herself that he wanted her physically; to allow him to possess her in such circumstances would be an act of insanity which would eventually destroy them both.

'You were going to allow me to make love to you, Davina,' Ruy said evenly from behind her, 'however much you try to deny it. Was it only desire?'

Her cheeks burned as she realised how close he had come to stumbling upon the truth. No matter what happened he must not guess that she still loved him.

'Yes,' she lied bravely. 'And besides, I've already told you—I don't think it's good for Jamie to be an only one.'

'Damn you, Davina!' Ruy ground viciously in the silence that followed. 'Damn you to hell!'

'I'm sorry I'm late, Dolores,' Davina apologised as she sat down at the table. 'I'm afraid I . . . overslept . . .'

For the life of her she could not prevent the colour running up betrayingly under her skin. She was quite sure that the entire household knew exactly why she was late for breakfast—and she shot Ruy a bitter look as Dolores beamed cheerfully and chuckled, '*De nada* . . . It is the second honeymoon, *si*?'

She laughed again, while Jamie looked uncertainly from Davina to Ruy as though he sensed the bitter undercurrents between them.

'Have you thanked Dolores for making you such a lovely breakfast?' Davina asked him to distract his attention.

'*Gracias*, Dolores,' the little boy said solemnly. He had already picked up quite a few words of Spanish and unlike Davina was not shy of showing off his new achievement.

'*De nada, pequeño*,' Dolores assured him. 'It is a pity your *madre* does not eat more, *no*? But then love steals away the appetite, is this not so?'

Davina dropped the roll she had been crumbling absently as though it were red hot, not daring to look at Ruy. She could hardly believe that the calmly remote man sitting next to her was the same one who had whispered such tender words of love such a short time ago.

Half asleep and still dreaming of Carmelita, Davina reminded herself. No wonder his manner was so icily distant now! He obviously wanted to leave her in no doubt about his lack of feeling for her.

'Today I'm going to learn to ride,' Jamie confided importantly as he drank his orange juice. 'Rodriguez has already promised that I might. Papa is going to take me to see the bulls afterwards. They're very big and I'm not to go near them on my own.'

Davina glanced at Ruy for confirmation that he did actually intend to take the little boy down to the bull-pens, but he was engrossed in his mail, reading a long letter written on lavender-coloured paper, and scented with carnation—a letter quite obviously from a woman.

'Will you come with us when we go down to the stables?' Jamie asked her.

'Your mother will not want to risk getting her clothes dirty, I am sure,' Ruy answered for her, briefly lifting his head to glance warningly at her.

'Oh, I can change into my jeans quickly enough,' Davina replied, pinning on a false smile. Ruy had made it quite obvious that he didn't want her to accompany them, but she was not going to be deprived of her son's company simply because his father could not bear the sight of her.

Ten minutes later the three of them were making their way down to the stables, Jamie's excited chatter covering the silence between his parents.

They were within easy distance of the house, but remembering the effects of being out in the hot sun-shine the previous day, Davina had taken the precau-tion of wearing a large-brimmed sun hat to protect herself from the strong rays. Likewise Jamie was wearing his hat, but Ruy was bareheaded, the sun turning his dark hair blue-black as it emphasised the tanned column of his throat and the fine sprinkling of dark body hair beneath the thin white silk shirt.

There were half a dozen loose boxes, but only three of them were occupied. The animals in the first two were used for work on the *estancia*, so Ruy told Jamie, explaining that this had two advantages. Firstly the horse could go where it was impossible to take a Land Rover, however stoutly constructed, and secondly it prepared the bull for the sight and smell of horses in the bullring. He went on to explain to a wide-eyed Jamie that there was a tradition connected with the bullfight, dating back to the days when this had been conducted not on foot, but on horseback, and that although nowadays matadors fought on foot at every bullfight there was still an exhibition of the traditional Andalusian horses and their riders, performing manoeuvres which in their way were as spectacular as those of the Lipizzaner stallions of the Spanish Riding School in Vienna, whose forebears had been pure bred Andalusian horses.

Davina had only witnessed it once, at her one and only bullfight, but the memory of the white horses and their darkly handsome riders in their traditional costumes had stayed with her. Such riding was now the sport of rich young men, Ruy had told her, because they alone could afford the costly horses. He himself had owned an Andalusian stallion, named Cadiz, and it had been this horse which had carried Davina to the Fair in Seville.

She mentioned him to Ruy, wondering at the tiny warning shake of his head Rodriguez directed towards her.

'A highly bred stallion is not an animal for a man who is a cripple,' Ruy told her harshly. 'Cadiz only owned me as master as long as I had his respect.'

For one horrified moment Davina had wild visions of Ruy ordering the animal to be destroyed, as she had heard of Caliphs doing in those long-ago days when the Moors brought their Arab steeds to Spain, but to her relief, Ruy told her that Cadiz was now lodged at a stud farm owned by a friend of his.

'Where he longs for the green pastures of his home,' Rodriguez commented, with the first sign of disapproval Davina had ever heard him express.

'Cadiz, like the rest of us, must learn that life cannot always be just as we would wish it,' Ruy said harshly. 'In many ways I am a fool to keep him. I should have sold him. I shall certainly never ride him again.'

'Where's my pony?' Jamie demanded plaintively, bringing a welcome interruption to the conversation. Davina could imagine what anguish it must have caused Ruy to part with his horse. She remembered how on that one occasion when Ruy had held her up in front of him, horse and man had seemed to move with one mind, both supreme in their own individual ways.

'See, *pequeño*, here is your pony,' Rodriguez told Jamie, lifting him up so that he could see the soft muzzle just peeping over the top of the box.

Davina, who had been watching them, chanced to glance across at Ruy and surprised such a look of aching longing on his face that she looked away almost immediately, shaken by the feeling that she had just witnessed a man with all his barriers down and intruded upon an essentially private moment.

'What is the matter?' Ruy demanded of her, seeing the look. 'Am I not allowed to have emotions, to wish that I were the one to hold my son up to his first mount, to feel his body in my arms and know the wonder of touching a part of my own flesh?'

'I didn't think you cared,' was all Davina could find to say. 'He's nearly four years old, and never once . . .'

'Because I knew I could not look at him and then

turn my back on him,' Ruy said fiercely. 'A clean cut and a quick one is always far preferable to an aching wound that festers and eventually kills.'

What was he trying to say? That he had wanted Jamie? Then why had he never made any attempt to see him? Even though they might have remained estranged there had been nothing to prevent Ruy from building up a relationship with his son. Unless, of course, Carmelita had demanded that he did not do so.

'You told me you couldn't even be sure that he was yours,' Davina reminded him, touching a wound which still had the power to hurt.

'And so I told myself. It made it easier for me to keep to my decision, but to look at him is to know his fathering, is this not so?'

'Look at me, Papa!' Jamie crowed triumphantly from the back of the placid pony. 'I'm riding!'

Rodriguez was walking him quietly round the yard, keeping within an easy arm's distance in case of any mishaps, but Jamie seemed to have no sense of fear, his face alight with pleasure as he held on to the reins.

Davina felt her heart swell and lift as she looked at her son, and tried to quell the bitter ache Ruy's words had aroused. All this time she had thought that Ruy was ignoring Jamie's existence simply because he had no interest in the little boy—because Jamie had not been born to the woman he really loved—and yet now Ruy was trying to tell her that his indifference had sprung from the belief that Jamie might not have been his son.

'His paternity, yes,' she agreed proudly, hoping that Ruy wouldn't see the tears in his eyes, 'but it takes more than mere conception to be a father.'

She fled before Ruy could answer, unable to bear

the sharp scrutiny of eyes which she felt must surely probe the secret lying deep in her heart.

Davina was in her room when she heard a car draw up outside the house. Ruy was still down at the stable yard, and she was hurriedly pulling on the skirt she had removed before lying down on the bed when Dolores knocked on the door.

When Davina opened it the first thing she noticed was the air of suppressed excitement about the other woman.

'It is Señor Carlos,' she told Davina breathlessly. 'He has come to see the bulls. It is many, many months since he was last here. He is *muy hombre, si*?'

Davina laughed. Even Dolores was not proof against Carlos' charm.

'Once Señor Carlos spend much time here,' Dolores told her as she waited for Davina to finish brushing her hair, 'but that was before the Conde's accident.'

'Condesa!'

The warm pressure of Carlos' lips against her fingers belied the formality of his greeting, and Davina had to fight to prevent herself from snatching her hand back in adolescent confusion.

From the twinkle in Carlos' eyes she suspected that he was by no means unaware of her reaction, and soft colour washed over her cheeks.

'Please bring us some *fino* and almond biscuits, Dolores,' she requested, trying to appear calm. 'Ruy is down at the stables,' she added to Carlos. 'Jamie is having his first riding lesson and . . .'

'Naturally the proud papa wishes to be there,' Carlos finished for her. 'As I would myself had I such a fine son, although I confess my loyalties would be divided.'

When Davina looked confused, he smiled and leaned forward so that she could see the thick darkness of his eyelashes brushing the warm olive of his skin. 'With such a beautiful wife as yourself, *querida*, I should want to spend every minute with you, and yet the bond between father and son is also very precious. Ruy is an extremely lucky man.'

Dolores returned with the sherry and small almond biscuits before Davina could remonstrate with Carlos for flirting with her. They were sitting on the patio sipping the fine dry liquid when Davina heard the soft hiss of the wheelchair and Jamie came running towards her.

'So this is your son, Ruy,' Carlos said carelessly when Ruy was within earshot. 'He is a fine boy.'

'Carlos. What brings you here?'

The question was terse and for the life of her Davina could not prevent her eyes from sliding to Carlos' face to see how he took Ruy's less than enthusiastic welcome.

He affected not to notice it, shrugging lightly.

'I am to fight in the ring at Ronda this week and so I thought I would come and see your bulls—and of course your beautiful wife. Also, I was hoping I might be able to beg a bed overnight.'

'I have prepared Señor Carlos' favourite paella,' Dolores announced, arriving with a glass of milk for Jamie. 'It is good that he visits us again, *si*?'

'I am sure my wife agrees with you, Dolores,' Ruy said heavily, turning to his manservant. 'Rodriguez, I wish to go to my room—help me, will you? Dolores will prepare a room for you,' he added.

Davina was on her feet automatically, reaching for the chair, but to her chagrin Ruy pushed her away roughly.

'You must forgive Ruy,' she said huskily when she and Carlos were alone. 'He finds it hard to accept the help of others . . .'

'And so he takes pleasure in humiliating you?' Carlos asked softly. 'You are very loyal, *pequeña*. Ruy is one of my oldest friends, but for the way he behaved towards you just now I could willingly have knocked him to the floor. Why do you endure it?'

'Because I love him,' Davina admitted jerkily. 'But it's no use—he doesn't love me.'

'No?' Carlos asked softly. 'I know jealousy when I see it, *querida*.'

'If Ruy is jealous it's only because he considers me to be his possession—there can be no other reason— you see, I know who he does love.'

The moment the words were uttered Davina wished them unsaid, but it was too late to recall them, and Carlos was watching her with compassionate understanding.

'So . . . Who is this woman?'

'Carmelita,' Davina said huskily. 'He married me only to spite her.' She couldn't think why she was confiding in Carlos like this. Perhaps it had something to do with the fact that she could no longer tolerate the burden of her thoughts alone.

'If he does, then he is a fool,' Carlos said savagely. 'To put a woman like that above you! I cannot believe it. I know Carmelita well. The man she has married was the fiancé of Concepcion—nothing had been formalised, but it was understood that there would be a marriage. He is extremely wealthy and I am convinced that it was purely because of his wealth that Carmelita seduced him away from my poor cousin, who, although she tries to hide it from us, has suffered badly over the

affair. In Spain it is still considered the utmost humiliation for a girl to be jilted. Ruy and I quarrelled over
it. Knowing him to be close to Carmelita, I begged
him to intercede with her on Concepcion's behalf, but
he refused.'

'Because he could not bear to deny her anything she
wanted,' Davina said bitterly. 'Oh, it's useless. I wish
I had never returned to Spain—never . . .'

Without any warning tears filled her eyes. She tried
to dash them away, but not before Carlos had seen
them.

'Poor *pequeña*,' he said softly. 'You must teach that
husband of yours that if he neglects you there are other
men who will not be so backward—myself included.'
He captured her fingers, raising them to his lips and
kissing them slowly. 'You are very beautiful, little
Davina, and if you were not so much in love with your
husband I would attempt to steal you away from him.
As it is . . .' His fingers tightened suddenly and before
Davina could divine his purpose his head bent swiftly,
capturing her lips in a brief kiss. Before he released
her he whispered softly against her ear, 'Ruy has just
come in and is watching us. I do not think he likes
what we are doing, *pequeña*.'

That was the understatement of the year, Davina
reflected as Carlos set her free and she turned round
slowly to see Ruy seated in his wheelchair by the door,
his face a frozen mask of rage.

At once she was on her feet, hurrying across to
him, but as she reached the wheelchair, he swung it
round abruptly, swearing as it collided with the
door.

'Ruy . . .' her protest went unheard as he pulled
himself upwards and with a superhuman effort held

himself erect before Rodriguez suddenly emerged on to the patio, his gasp of dismay coinciding with a sudden loss of balance as Ruy started to collapse.

Davina was nearest. Her arms went out to catch him, but he thrust her away with such violent force that the rough stonework of the wall grazed her arm, and it was Rodriguez who supported him back to the chair and wheeled him into the house.

'Oh, Carlos, how could you do that?' Davina protested when they were alone.

'How could I not?' Carlos said disarmingly. 'I like kissing lovely girls, and besides, I wanted to put a theory to the test. Ruy is not as indifferent to you as you believe, I am sure of it. All he needs is to be made a little jealous—to be forced to realise what you mean to him. You are, after all, his wife, and to a Spaniard marriage is sacred . . .'

When Davina shook her head, Carlos pressed, 'But did you not see the way in which he pulled himself to his feet? A man who is supposedly crippled? Does that not tell you something?'

It did! Davina remembered what Dr Gonzales had told her. Because he was furiously angry with her Ruy had got to his feet. Although she knew quite well that he did not care in the slightest about her, Davina could see how it would hurt his pride if he thought she was attracted to another man. But would it hurt it enough to make him overcome the mental block and walk? How angry did she have to make him to achieve that?

'I have an idea,' Carlos was saying. 'We shall conduct a little flirtation, you and I, and we shall see who is right. I am convinced that Ruy does care for you.'

Nothing Davina could say would sway him. All through dinner Carlos insisted on paying her the most lavish compliments and she could feel Ruy's eyes upon her. When the meal was over she excused herself, saying that she was tired. Carlos insisted on kissing her hand in the same intimate fashion as before. Davina dared not even look at Ruy.

As she prepared for bed she thought of what Carlos had said about Carmelita—how Ruy must love her—and her throat ached with suppressed tears. Carlos was so sure that Ruy cared for her, but she knew better, and yet for a moment he had been so furious with her that he had actually stood up without any help . . . If only she could give him back the ability to walk, but how?

CHAPTER NINE

'THESE are the bulls used in the *novillada*,' Carlos was explaining to Davina as they inspected the bullpens together, 'and these larger animals the ones used in the *corrida* proper. There is no difference in the length or style of the bullfight, it is merely that in the *novillada*, we use the young bulls and junior matadors. Ruy himself once entered the ring as a *rejoneador*—that is one who fights the bulls on horseback. It is very skilled— very difficult.'

It was his first reference to Ruy since Davina had joined him at the breakfast table, and Davina was glad that he had not pressed her concerning Ruy's reaction to his 'flirtation'. She knew that Carlos meant to be kind and that it was possible to fan a spark into a conflagration, but first one needed the spark, and Ruy felt nothing for her.

'*Si*, Ruy and Cadiz worked well together in the ring. You will see what I mean this afternoon in Ronda, although the *rejoneadores* you will see there before the fight proper come nowhere near equalling him.'

'Why did he give it up?' Davina asked absently, shuddering a little as she studied the hard, solid-packed, muscled bodies of the bulls grazing beyond the electric fence—a necessary precaution, Carlos had told her, for an excitable bull was not above charging and destroying a fence if the mood so took him.

He shrugged. 'I once asked him, he said he preferred growing things to killing them, but that as such a remark to a Spaniard comes close to heresy he did not wish it to be made public. In those days we were close friends and I understood his meaning. Between bull and matador exists a close communion, each knows he wins his life at the price of the other's, which is why in a good bullfight each feels respect for the other. I have never yet taken the life of a good bull without regret.'

Davina studied the bulls with a fast beating heart, feeling the primeval fear beat up inside her as the sunlight grazed the tips of the wickedly lethal horns, and she had a vivid impression of how it must have felt to be a Minoan bull-leaper and forced to grasp those horns and vault between them on to the bull's broad back. It made modern athletics, for all its rigorous training, seem tame in comparison, and she couldn't forget that it had been one of these animals who had gored and injured Ruy. As they watched, Dolores' husband and two young men on horses started to separate the bulls driving some towards them.

'Keep still,' Carlos warned her, even though they had the electric fence safely in front of them. 'A sudden quick movement is all it takes to distract their eye, I should hate to be obliged to demonstrate my skill with my bare hands and without my *trajes de luces*.' His droll comment made Davina laugh, as it had been intended to do, but fear still shivered through her. The bulls must cross the open courtyard before being penned to await transportation, and she made no demur when Carlos touched her arm and suggested that they leave.

'You were thinking of Ruy, were you not?' he said gently, as they walked back to the house.

Davina admitted it. 'Doesn't it frighten you?'

'Because his fate could so easily be mine?' Carlos

mused. 'One thinks of it, of course, but is that not half
of the appeal as it is always for those who engage in
danger; the thrill of the close breath of death; to feel
the dark angel's wings beating so close that one can
feel the draught, and then the exhilaration of knowing
one has cheated it—yet again. But to see Ruy as he is
is a sobering experience. I remember him when we
were at the university together in Seville. Such an
hombre . . . always the pretty girls!' He shrugged and
smiled reminiscently. 'It is different, of course, here
from England, but young people have their ways of
getting to know one another. Balconies are not always
inaccessible; our nights are warm and made for love,
and the moonlight a conspirator. But he was always,
behind his smile, serious. The weight of his responsibilities, you understand . . . He will be able to
spare Jamie much of those. His own father died when
he was fifteen and he was thrust into manhood while
still a boy. When I heard that he had married an
English girl with the shyness of a flower before it un-
furls and hair the colour of pale sand in the moonlight,
I was glad for him. For all his apparent self-sufficiency
he is a man who needs love more than any other. For
Ruy mere sexual satisfaction would not be enough.
Their feelings run deep, those of our countrymen who
have the blood of the Moro running through their
veins.'

Davina acknowledged that Carlos was probably
right, and her heart ached afresh to know that she
would never be the one to provide the love Ruy so
badly needed.

When they reached the courtyard Davina could hear
Jamie's voice raised in excitement.

'Look what Papa has given me!' he cried to Davina

when he saw her. On a chair was a beautiful handmade leather saddle of bright red to match the bridle Rodriguez had given him the previous day. Chased in silver and small enough for a very little boy, it had obviously been made especially for him. To his son Ruy could be generous, Davina admitted, giving him both love and care, but to her he showed another side of his nature, as he had done last night when she had tried to help him. She doubted that she would ever be able to forget the savage hatred in his eyes when he had pushed her away so violently.

'You must take care of the saddle yourself,' Ruy was telling Jamie firmly. 'Rodriguez will show you how.' As he spoke his eyes swept Davina's trim form in her jeans and the thin tee-shirt she had put on before breakfast. The thin fabric had shrunk a little with numerous washings and clung seductively to the soft curves of her breasts, outlining their tender peaks, and it was on these that Ruy's eyes lingered longest. Heat coursed through her, turning her legs to boneless agony, an ache in the pit of her stomach that made her colour up afresh as she was forced to accept the extent of her desire. Were Ruy even to attempt to touch her at this moment she knew she could not endure it without betraying her love. With a small cry she turned on her heel, desperate to seek the sanctuary of her bedroom.

She was lying on the bed staring at the ceiling when the door was suddenly thrust open and Ruy came in. His unexpected presence brought her bolt upright on the bed, her eyes widening with mingled fear and uncertainty.

'Dreaming of your lover?' Ruy asked sardonically. 'Imagining how it would feel to have his hands upon your body . . . is that why you dressed in such a revealing fashion? *Por Dios,*' he muttered, coming towards her, 'if it is the feel of a man's hands you long for so much that you must seek solitude up here to dream of it, then you shall have it. My hands at least are not crippled.'

Davina moved, but not quickly enough. She could see the stretch fabric of Ruy's cotton knit shirt tautening over the solid muscle of his back as he leaned towards her, his hands fastening on her arms and holding her helpless as they tightened into steel bands whose touch seemed to burn into her very bones.

'No . . .' The small word was a taut protest, cried instinctively as she saw the look on his face; reinforced by a frightened glance upwards from beneath eyelashes which fluttered betrayingly as his warm breath fanned her skin.

'No? You seem to have a habit of saying that word when you mean "yes",' Ruy taunted softly, pulling her off the bed with a strength she found it impossible to deny.

Half lying and half sitting across his lap, with one arm encircling her like a steel brace, she couldn't move, and was forced to endure Ruy's leisurely inspection of her sparkling eyes and flushed cheeks before it moved upwards, lingering on the betraying tremble of her parted lips and lower still to where her breasts strained against the thin tee-shirt, as though mutely imploring his possession.

'Is this that you dreamed of Carlos doing?' he murmured softly, as his tongue moistly caressed her throat, making her shake with the effort of not betraying how much the sensual movement aroused her; how much she longed to unfasten the buttons of his shirt and slide her hands inside it. She looked downwards, not daring to close her eyes in case blotting out their

surroundings made her even more vulnerable to the
desire storming through her, but that too was a mistake
because it brought into her line of vision the dark
brown vee of flesh exposed by the neck of his shirt, the
crisp tangle of hairs curling darkly there making her
stomach somersault weakeningly as she remembered
the provocative scrape of the rough hair against the
smoothness of her breasts.

'Or this . . .' Ruy suggested, still in the same soft
voice, driving her mindless with pleasure as his free
hand slid under her shirt to unclip her bra and close
over her breast while his tongue outlined the vee-
shaped neckline of her shirt, making her shudder with
the pleasure it evoked.

Against her will her arms lifted, her fingers curling
into the dark hair, revelling in the feel of it as she
strained instinctively against him, longing for closer
contact with his body.

'Or perhaps this,' Ruy continued, deliberately
heightening her torment as his thumb stroked leisurely
over her now hard nipple and his tongue lightly traced
the outline of her lips until they parted in a harsh moan
of surrender, her clasped hands tugging his head
downwards so that she could prolong the contact. She
made a small sound in her throat, a combination of
longing and despair, and as though he too were not
unaffected by their proximity Ruy's mouth at last
closed demandingly on hers, surprising her with its
sensual intensity where she had expected harshness.
Her lips parted on a sigh as gladly she abandoned herself to the magic of Ruy's touch, revelling in the heated
caress of his hands against her skin, and aching with
the need to prolong it.

'So . . .' he released her almost gently, his lips lingering for a tormenting moment before they were withdrawn. 'You see, Davina, there is no need to dream all alone of a lover's caresses. Any man, even a man such as I, can offer appeasement.'

While she was still trying to recover from the agony of the wound he had just inflicted, he continued in the same soft voice, 'And now we shall go downstairs. No . . .' he commanded when she slid from his knee and started to straighten her clothing, 'I want Carlos to see you exactly as you are, *querida*. He is a man of much imagination. He won't be required to tax himself unduly to know what has happened. Your skin is pale and bruises easily,' he added significantly, glancing at the mauve shadows already forming on her arms where he had grasped them. 'Now, we shall go downstairs, together, with your lips still swollen from my kisses and your body aroused by my lovemaking . . .'

A lift had been installed in the hacienda to make it easy for Ruy to go up and down stairs alone, and as she stood in trembling fury at his side Davina could hardly believe that she had actually heard him correctly. She knew now beyond any shadow of a doubt that he had deliberately come upstairs to seek her out, to make sure that he destroyed what he thought was a love affair between herself and Carlos. The lift came swiftly to a halt, and without stopping to think, driven only by a blind need to punish him as he had punished her, she said huskily:

'Carlos is not like you, Ruy. He's compassionate . . . understanding. Knowing that you have . . . touched me will not destroy what he feels for me.' And with her head held high she walked from the lift, refusing to look back. It was true, after all. Carlos would understand, but not for the reasons Ruy thought!

Carlos left the hacienda shortly before lunch for the drive to Ronda. He never ate before a fight, he told Davina when she exclaimed that he would miss lunch. He had given them tickets for some of the best seats, and had insisted that they come to his dressing room after the *corrida* was over.

'You are chancing fate, my friend,' was Ruy's only comment. 'I thought you never talk of "afterwards".'

'Perhaps not, in the past,' Carlos agreed with a secret smile for Davina, 'but then I did not have what I now have to look forward to. You will pray for me, *querida*?' he asked Davina softly, raising her fingers to his lips and lingering over the kiss he pressed to them.

'Yes . . .'

'*Bien.*' He turned her hand over and deposited a warm kiss in the palm, closing her fingers over it before releasing her. 'A small keepsake which I shall ask that you return, if I am successful.'

Greatly daring, Davina managed a smile. 'Then I shall have to pray doubly hard that you *are* successful.'

The expression in Carlos' eyes spoke—and promised—volumes, and so did that in Ruy's, only of a very different order!

Obeying some instinct which was only now asserting itself, Davina chose one of her prettiest dresses to change into, white silk chiffon overprinted with flowers in delicate lilacs and mauves. It had long sleeves and a wrapround skirt which left a seductive glimpse of long slender legs as she moved, the vee neckline drawing subtle attention to the swelling thrust of her breasts. High-heeled sandals in matching lavender kid and a hat to match the dress, trimmed with white ribbon, completed the outfit.

She knew that she had chosen well, when Ruy entered their bedroom and stiffened antagonistically.

'So . . . For Jamie and me jeans are good enough, but for Carlos you flaunt your femininity in a parody of innocence that would be laughable if it were not so grotesque. And do not think he will be deceived. Carlos is an astute Spaniard beneath that playboy exterior. His wife, when he takes one, will be pure and docile; until then it pleases him to amuse himself with *rameras* . . . coquettes,' he explained insultingly when Davina looked blankly at him. 'Women who exchange their virtue for tawdry trappings. Women such as you, *mi querida*.'

He said the last words with such savagery that Davina shrank under them, unable to force past her tight throat a single word in her own defence. Half blinded by tears, she stumbled from the room, busying herself with dressing Jamie until she had full control of herself again.

'Mummy cried,' the little boy told Ruy chattily when they were all assembled downstairs, much to Davina's dismay. 'But I kissed her all better, didn't I?'

Davina nodded, thinking in her heart that it was kisses of a far different sort she needed to soothe her lacerated heart. Even so, she could not prevent herself from glancing beneath her lashes at Ruy to see how he had received Jamie's innocent confidences.

His head was tilted to one side as he regarded the little boy. The white silk shirt against the tanned flesh of his throat emphasised his vigorous maleness. He was wearing dark trousers, the fabric clinging firmly to the muscled width of his thighs. An aching sensation began to spread through her lower limbs and she could not

believe that he could not rise from his chair and walk.
He looked so alive, so vital; she wouldn't accept that
he was chained to that chair for the rest of his life.
Something not unlike hysteria rose up inside her and
she had to fight to stop herself from dragging him out
of the chair and forcing him to walk. Only yesterday,
in the fierce heat of his anger, he had seemed to drag
himself upwards, the movement almost imperceptible.
Was rage the key which would turn the lock and free
his paralysed limbs? If so she knew that she could
gladly incite him to the point of murder, were she sure
that it would have the desired effect.

Now, looking at him, lean and dangerous like a panther at his ease, the firm lips softening as he listened to
Jamie, Davina had an irresistible urge to go to him
and beg him to love her.

Fortunately, before it completely overpowered her
Rodriguez arrived to announce that the car was outside.

Once again Ruy drove, Rodriguez giving Davina a
warm smile as he helped her into the front passenger
seat. As she turned her head to make sure that Jamie
was comfortable she glimpsed again a look of bitter
frustration on Ruy's face. Was he thinking that she
should have been Carmelita? That Jamie should have
been his and Carmelita's child?

The tickets Carlos had given them admitted them to
the very best seats—'*sombra*' it said on them, which as
his manager explained as he met them at the gate,
meant in the shade. Carlos' manager was a small plump
man with coal black eyes and a small moustache, who
never seemed to stop talking. He rather reminded
Davina of a character out of *Carmen*, but she blessed
Carlos for his thoughtfulness in sending him to them

as she saw how quickly the seats filled up, and how tactfully arranged their seats were, at the end of a row with ample room for Ruy's chair.

Señor Bonares had even thought to provide them with *almohadillas*, comfortable cushions to place on the wooden seats.

Ronda's bullring was among the oldest in Spain, Davina was told with pride, as Señor Bonares took a seat next to her.

'Don Carlos has asked that I explain everything to you,' he told her with a smile. 'And so, Condesa, you must consider me entirely at your service.'

Despite his somewhat comic opera appearance the Señor proved to be an excellent teacher. As a hush fell on the auditorium he directed Davina's eyes towards the President, in his box above them.

He made a sign, incomprehensible to Davina, but seemingly quite clear to everyone else, because the hush took on a tense expectancy, suddenly splintered by the strains of the *pasadoble*, as a procession advanced across the clean sand. In a muted whisper Señor Bonares explained to Davina that the two men leading the procession were *alguacillos*, or constables. They rode on horseback dressed in fantastic medieval costume. They took no part in the *corrida* itself, the Señor added; their appearance was merely a tradition.

Behind the *alguacillos* came the matadors; three of them abreast, all wearing their *trajes de luces*, the so aptly named 'suits of lights'—the most spectacular male dress in the world—the cloth coruscated with shimmering silver and gold and purple. In an aside Señor Bonares informed her that each suit weighed upwards of twenty-five pounds, and she hid a small smile as he pointed Carlos out to her proudly, commenting with a beaming smile, '*Esto muy hombre, si?*'

To the rear of the matadors were their assistants, and behind them again came the picadors on horse-back, the sun glinting on their metal leg guards, and finally the *monosabios*, the 'wise monkeys', as the ring servants were called, and the mules, whose purpose, Davina was told, was to remove the carcases of the bulls.

She shuddered a little at that, the words bringing home to her that she was here to witness the death. The other spectators seemed to be stilled by the same knowledge, because the crowd was momentarily silent. The procession disappeared into the *callejon* running alongside the ring.

Again the President's handkerchief fluttered in the afternoon stillness, and to the sound of drums and bugles the first bull entered the ring.

'He is small and timid,' Señor Bonares commented disparagingly, leaning behind Davina to say something to Ruy, who was holding Jamie on his knee so that the little boy could get a better view. 'The Conde agrees with me,' he announced, turning back to her. 'We shall not see much sport from this one.'

What he said proved to be true. The bull, to Davina's secret sympathy, was despatched well within the allotted fifteen minutes and the young *novillado* received a smattering of cheers from the crowd.

'The *novillados* merely whet their appetite,' Señor Bonares told her. 'It is Carlos they have come to see.'

This proved to be true. Carlos was the last matador of the afternoon. He came into the ring proudly at the President's command and bowed first to him, and then, quite deliberately, to Davina. While the crowd roared its appreciation Davina blushed, and caught Carlos' grin as he observed her embarrassmemt.

The bull was released. His name, announced over the loudspeakers, was 'Viento Fuerte', or 'Strong Wind', as Señor Bonares translated for her, and he weighed five hundred and forty kilos, slightly over half a ton.

Davina's throat was dry during the opening stages of the *corrida*. Although the sand had been freshly raked, the smell of blood hung sickeningly upon the air, mingling with the dry heat and the tense expectancy of the crowd to create an atmosphere which she had never experienced before, but which she felt sure must be the closest modern equivalent to that prevailing in the ancient Roman arenas.

The picadors were placing their darts with skilled precision, and Davina averted her eyes in horror as the wicked horns grazed past one pony's withers.

'Don't worry about it,' Ruy advised her drily. 'The pony is well protected by his *peto*. You are too squeamish.'

The picadors withdrew; Carlos advanced, placing the *banderillas* expertly and drawing a cheer from the crowd. They did not like it when the matador wasted time at this stage, Señor Bonares confided to her. 'Carlos was lucky today, he had drawn a bull *muy bravo*.'

Davina shuddered. The animal was pawing the sand, now streaked rusty red with its blood. The small eyes gleamed and the dark head lowered. . . .

'*Por Dios . . . magnifico!*' she heard Señor Bonares exclaim reverently as Carlos swung his cape over his head in a spectacular swirl and the crowd roared fresh approval.

'An *afarolado*,' the Señor breathed, 'the lighthouse.

See how the bull just scrapes past him. *Magnifico!*'

Silence descended yet again. Carlos made several more passes, each one seemingly more dangerous than the last. 'See with what *cargar la suerte* Carlos controls the bull,' her instructor commanded her. 'He has style, and the bull, he is a good one.'

The taut expectancy, the smell of blood mingling with the hot air, combined to make Davina feel dizzy. The bull charged again, suddenly swerving and almost catching Carlos off guard. The tip of the animal's horn grazed his suit, tearing it with a sound which could be clearly heard, and exposing his flesh. The nausea rose inside her. This was how Ruy had been torn, how his flesh had been savaged ... The crowd went wild, shouting out and applauding, and Carlos bowed to them audaciously before turning to face the bull once more.

The scene reminded Davina unbearably of Hemingway's *Death in the Afternoon*; the same atmosphere pervaded the arena. She saw the bull charging on Carlos and covered her eyes, not daring to look. The crowd cheered themselves hoarse, and Señor Bonares shouted excitedly, '*Por Dios*, that was *perfecto*! See, Condesa, the sword is in ... It is over, the bull is vanquished!'

The President made an announcement in Spanish and the crowd roared full-throated approval. Feeling sick and dizzy, Davina watched the mules, gaily caparisoned in green and gold, dragging the huge carcase away.

'Carlos has been awarded both ears and the tail,' Señor Bonares told her. 'It is good to kill the bull like that with one stroke.'

Davina nodded. Jamie was watching round-eyed

with wonder. The paganness of the scene seemed to have escaped the little boy and he was sitting as enthralled as though he had been watching a favourite television programme.

Children saw death so differently, Davina thought, having no conception of what it really was.

'Condesa. Condesa!' Señor Bonares' urgent whisper focused her attention upon him. He was gesturing to her with barely concealed excitement. 'See, Carlos wishes to present you with the ears.'

True enough! Davina saw a grinning Carlos coming towards her through a hail of shoes, handbags, hats, flowers, chocolates and sundry other items which the spectators were throwing at him in recognition of his skill.

Sickness welled up inside her. She tried to speak, to show the appreciation she realised was expected, but the words would not come; the world whirled round her in a coloured kaleidoscope through which all she could hear was Ruy's coolly firm voice saying sardonically, 'You forget, Carlos, my wife is English and not used to such expression of love. Cool English violets need careful handling lest they are crushed and spoiled.'

'Forgive me, *pequeña*,' she heard Carlos apologise. 'I had forgotten. Bonares, bring them all to my dressing room. After this afternoon I feel like celebrating. I shall take you to a restaurant where the food will make you forget everything and think only that you are in heaven,' he promised Davina as he strode off to the accompaniment of ecstatic cheers from the crowd.

'Why did Carlos want to give Mummy those ears?' Jamie enquired, puzzled.

'It is a sign of appreciation . . . a great honour which

does not come the way of many women,' Ruy explained tongue in cheek, his eyes sliding to Davina's pale face. 'Although perhaps in Carlos' case the latter statement is not strictly true,' he added unkindly. 'I believe it is a favourite practice of his to dedicate to his latest mistress the strongest bull. A Freudian practice, would you not say, *amada*?'

Davina hated it when he used words meant to be spoken with love in that coldly mocking tone.

'No more Freudian than your behaviour,' she felt compelled to point out, while Señor Bonares was still fussily engaged in arranging for them to go down to Carlos' dressing room.

'So impatient to reach your lover,' Ruy sneered as she stood up to follow the Spaniard. 'I am surprised you did not beg him to possess you physically on the sand where he killed his bull. Come, surely you are not going to pretend that there aren't women who find increased sexual enjoyment from that sort of thing, or that you are one of them . . . I was watching you,' he told her savagely. 'You were damn near close to fainting with wanting him . . . I am well aware of the effect the *corrida* can have upon those not brought up in its traditions, *querida*—and so, I can guarantee, is Carlos. No doubt he is expecting a warm reception from you later on and . . .'

'Stop it!' Davina pleaded, covering her ears, and glad that Jamie had gone on ahead with Señor Bonares. 'How can you say such things to me?' she asked sickly. 'None of it is true.'

But Ruy wasn't listening. He was propelling his chair away from her without even bothering to glance over his shoulder to see if she was following.

Crushed and battered by the crowd, she lost sight of

him scores of times as she tried to hurry after him, panic setting in when at one point she thought herself lost altogether, and in danger of being crushed by the crowds.

'*Idiota!*' Ruy abused her as he suddenly materialised at her side grasping her wrist and almost pulling her through the milling crowd.

Carlos' dressing room was full of flowers and gifts which had been sent to him by spectators. He greeted them with a smile. He had not yet changed and was sitting in his sweat-soaked shirt, his jacket thrown carelessly on a chair, from which he removed it to offer the seat to Davina.

She sank down on to it gratefully, caught off guard when Carlos suddenly slipped an arm round her waist and tilted her chin with hard fingers.

'Have you forgotten so quickly, *querida*?' he asked her huskily. 'You have not yet returned my token.'

Enlightenment dawned. He was referring to that kiss he had given her at the hacienda. She smiled uncertainly. Here in the confines of the small dressing room he seemed different, highly charged and somehow a stranger. Excitement glittered in his eyes, and Davina realised with a sense of shock that she had aroused him.

'If you will not give me my reward freely, I shall have to take it by force,' he told her in a low voice, bending his head to capture her lips and part them expertly.

Her hand went instinctively to his shoulder to push him away, but someone else beat her to it.

'*Bastante!*' Ruy grated. 'You forget yourself, Carlos, or is it that you think my infirmity gives you license to dishonour me without fear of reprisals?'

'A kiss ... you, who have so much, begrudge me that?' Carlos countered, once more the teasing young man Davina remembered and liked. 'You make too much of it, *amigo*. Come, I shall take you all out to dinner as a recompense, *si*?'

The meal was not a happy one. In spite of all Carlos' endeavours to lighten it a heavy, threatening tension seemed to infuse the air around them, rather like the oppressive calm before a fierce storm.

Davina could only pick at her food. She had noticed on the menu *filete de toro*, and seeing it had immediately robbed her of what scant appetite she had had.

Carlos was not to return to the hacienda with them. He was dining later with his manager, he explained, and would stay the night with him. As he bent to open the Mercedes' door for Davina he whispered contritely,

'Forgive me, *querida*, I think I have awakened the slumbering tiger in Ruy, and you will have to pay the penalty of my foolhardiness. I meant only to tweak his tail,' he confided ruefully, 'but I had forgotten that today I would be drinking the blood of the bull, and that it makes men foolishly over-confident. I shall visit the hacienda again before I leave Ronda.'

'To make sure I'm all in one piece?' Davina asked ruefully, allowing him to kiss her lightly on the cheek.

Not once during the drive back did Ruy speak to her. He seemed to have retreated behind a wall of icy hauteur, his expression on the rare occasions when he chanced to glance at her contemptuous to the point of shrivelling her with its arctic distaste.

Jamie was asleep when they reached the hacienda. As she stepped out into the scented warmth of the

darkness Davina turned to lift him out of the car.
There was no point in waking him up to bath him.
She would let him sleep on.

The chirruping of the crickets was the only sound to
break the sullen silence that seemed to hang over her
like a threatening cloud.

By the time she had put Jamie to bed, the sleepiness
which had come over her in the car had gone, and she
was wide awake but reluctant to go down to the *sala*
and face Ruy.

Feeling restless, she changed into jeans and a tartan
shirt, picking up a jacket in case she got cold. An overwhelming desire to see again the scene of Ruy's accident had come over her, as though by seeing it she
could find the means to free him from the silken bonds
that held him fast. Dr Gonzalas had said that modern
medical men did not know how the processes of the
subconscious worked, but thinking of voodoo and the
spells of witches during the Middle Ages, Davina
wondered if there might not, among more primitive
civilisations, exist those who could penetrate its secrets,
even if the tiny kernel of that knowledge was wrapped
in mystery and fear, perhaps even a legacy from civilisations more wise in these matters, like the Egyptians
who had known the secret of brain surgery and had
the ability to hypnotise their patients to a state where
they felt no pain, might still exist.

She stepped out into the darkness, shivering a little
as it encompassed her, and stood for a moment on the
steps trying to steady the frantic beating of her heart.
Her senses, alive to the living silence surrounding her,
caught the faint sound of wheels. She glanced back
into the hall and saw Ruy bearing down upon her, his
expression one of livid fury.

'So . . . You leave my house like a thief in the night. Going where? To your lover?'

His hands gripped her wrists, and for a moment Davina felt real fear. He reversed the chair, dragging her along, refusing to release her aching wrist, his grip so tight that it manacled her to his side like a captive prisoner.

The lift was all in darkness. There was a light inside it, but Ruy did not switch it on. The darkness seemed to press down upon her, smothering her, and Davina was relieved when it eventually came to a stop.

Her relief was shortlived when Ruy threw open their bedroom door and dragged her inside, locking it behind him and throwing the key on to a chair.

'So . . . If your lover comes looking for you, he will have the pleasure of knowing that his tardiness has not deprived you of the caresses your body so plainly craves, even if they are bestowed by hands other than his.'

'Ruy, you don't understand . . .' Davina began, but her protests were ruthlessly silenced by the hotly merciless pressure of his mouth forcing her lips apart and stifling all rational thought. His free hand sought the tender curve of her breast, roughly pushing aside the material and exposing the pale gleam of her skin.

Davina gasped as his mouth descended like that of a predator, determinedly seeking the tenderest flesh. She heard her skirt tear as his mouth and hands grew impatient, and then all rational thought—all will to exist apart from him—was suspended as her bones melted to liquid heat, her body a pliant wand in the arms that held her prisoner. The bed was behind her. Ruy pushed her on to it, pinning her to it with his weight so that she could feel every taut muscle; the sharp angles of his hips beneath the thin trousers, the hard flatness of his stomach, the harsh sound of his breathing filling her ears as her jeans were discarded and she was held fast beneath the merciless scrutiny of eyes the colour of night as they slid in silent assessment inch by inch over her body.

When at last his eyes returned to her face they were both breathing unevenly.

'So you want a lover . . . Then you shall have one,' Ruy told her softly. 'A lover whose image you will carry imprinted against your bones until the day you die. *Por Dios*, I have fought against this,' Davina heard him mutter, 'tried to play the part of a saint; to remember that desire is not love and should never contaminate love's sweet fulfilment. But there is fulfilment of a darker kind to be found just in looking at you.'

What was he saying? That although he loved Carmelita he desired *her*? Even though he despised himself for doing so?

He moved restlessly, cupping her face, a smothered groan forced past his lips.

Answering desire flooded her, hotly tempestuous and sweet. She glanced downwards in confusion, not wanting Ruy to see what was in her eyes. One arm encircled her, holding her slightly away from him, her skin pale against the bed. She could see his chest rising and falling unevenly, the dark material encasing his thighs straining sensually as he moved closer.

'For tonight forget that there is no love between us,' Ruy muttered thickly. 'Look at me and know that I desire you, and can make you desire me, and let that be enough. I want you, Davina,' he emphasised softly. 'Is it not possible that we can find solace together?'

His words weakened her resistance. If she was

honest with herself this was what she wanted, after all.
To be held in his arms, to know that he desired her
. . . and loved her, a stubborn voice protested, but she
refused to listen to it. Her hands reached towards him
in trembling supplication and encountered the hard
breadth of his shoulders. She heard him mutter
something unintelligible and closed her eyes like a child
trying not to see something unpleasant.

'Undress me, Davina.' The thickly spoken command
unleashed her dammed-up feelings. Her hands moved
slowly over his shirt, unfastening the buttons slowly,
and were pushed aside with an impatient oath as Ruy
completed the task with surer hands before grasping
hers and placing them on the taut warmth of his skin.
In the past shyness and uncertainty had always
tempered her desire, but tonight everything within her
urged her to accept what the gods had so casually given
her. Her eyes delighted in the tanned maleness of Ruy's
body against her own, marvelling at the clean, hard
lines of his body, still that of an athlete despite his
accident. The moonlight touched his scar and she
frowned, running compassionate fingers along its
puckered length. This time Ruy did not demur, his
'*Dios, querida*, how I long to feel the cool benison of
your lips against my flesh!' freeing her to place their
pink softness to the scar much as she had done before,
but this time she was allowed to linger over each tiny
caress—not merely allowed, but encouraged, her exalt-
ing heart rejoiced.

'*Adorada* . . . love me,' Ruy begged huskily, drawing
her against his body and removing the tiny briefs which
were all that separated her from the heated intimacy of
his thighs. His rough breathing filled her ears, the
burning pressure of his hands on her body inciting her

to move beneath him in answering response. His skin seemed to be on fire, burning fiercely beneath her palms, his muttered words of love interspersed with the hot kisses tormenting her flesh, urging her senses to clamour for his complete possession even as he withheld from her, as though he wanted to drive them both to the edge of oblivion before granting her body the satisfaction they both craved.

The first time when he had aroused her to the point where nothing mattered but the slow sweet surrender of her body to the domination of his, and then withdrew, Davina had thought it an accident, but when for a second and a third time he taught her body to betray her and brought it into trembling subjugation she knew his actions were no accident—and nor was he unaffected by them. His breathing was a ragged torture to his throat, his skin gleaming silkily with sweat as his lips moved down, over her shoulders to pause and bring shuddering pleasure to her body as his tongue stroked roughly first over one nipple and then the other, filling her with an aching need, which was left unappeased by the warm caress of his hand along her thigh, the soft seduction of his kisses on the quivering warmth of her stomach and lower . . .

His name was torn from her throat on a sob that brought an instantaneous response.

When she trembled uncertainly, wondering if this was just another teasing game, the fierce drive of his body as he slid between her thighs promised her that it was not.

This time was different. This time the aching need deep inside her was quenched by the completeness of a possession which carried her far beyond the barriers of any pleasure she had known before, his mouth muffling her small cries of exhausted pleasure, consuming her with an intensity that left room for nothing else.

'Now you will not dare to leave me again,' Ruy murmured in sleepy satisfaction when they were both at peace again. 'Tonight, *querida*, I have given you the child who will be Jamie's brother or sister. Carlos will not take you now. The state of motherhood is sacrosanct to a Spaniard. He will not take you while your body ripens with my child.'

Davina lay staring into the darkness, tears blurring her eyes. So that was why! So that she would not go to Carlos. If only Ruy knew how remote a possibility that had been! Had he done so he would have been spared the necessity of making love to her. She should have felt bitter, but she couldn't. She loved him. Her hands strayed to her stomach and she was unable to deny the faint thrill of pleasure she experienced at the thought of another child—his child. She glanced at his sleeping body. If only there were some way she could help him!

CHAPTER TEN

DAVINA was up early. She hadn't been able to sleep. Jamie was still in bed. All alone she had wandered on to the patio and received a shy smile from the girl setting the table for breakfast. Accepting a cup of coffee, she drank it slowly, a plan beginning to form in her mind. What she had in mind was dangerous—fatal perhaps—but it was something she had to try.

On the pretext of returning her cup she wandered into the kitchen. Dolores was talking to her husband, and she beamed at Davina. 'Enrique is waiting for the *patrón*. At this time of the day he goes to see the bulls.'

Davina already knew this. She had just gone down to the kitchen to confirm it, but Dolores' comment saved her the necessity of asking outright. As she waited she heard the bell which Enrique confirmed was Ruy's summons to him.

When the manager had gone she sauntered out into the sunshine as casually as she could, her red blouse a vivid scarlet splash in the sunshine. She rarely wore red, and finding this blouse in her case had been quite a stroke of luck.

The bull pens were the centre of industrious activity. The animals' bellows reached Davina well before they came in sight, and her stomach contracted sharply as she saw the first one. Its coat was as black as night— as black as Ruy's hair, its small red eyes glinting wickedly as it tossed its horns. Shrinking, she tried not to look at it. She saw Enrique and Ruy approaching the pens and moved towards an olive tree. If they chanced to see her she could always say that she had merely come out for a stroll.

They didn't. Ruy seemed to be engrossed in something Enrique was telling him, his forehead creased in a frown.

Davina knew that the bulls to be shipped out that morning would be driven across the yard from the pasture to the pens. This, as Carlos had told her only yesterday, was the most dangerous part of the whole proceedings, because for several seconds the bulls were not actually confined, and only the skill of the horses and their riders prevented them from breaking free.

This was where Ruy had had his accident due to the momentary negligence of a young boy. Her palms felt damp, and the fingers she touched to her forehead came away stickily wet. The red blouse seemed to draw the heat; she was sure she could smell again the mingled odours of blood and hot, dry sand, as she had done in the bullring yesterday.

Out of the corner of her eye she saw that Ruy and Enrique had reached the pens. Enrique moved away, shouting a command to the men waiting by the gate to the pasture. It was a manoeuvre they conducted every morning.

Please, God, let it work, Davina prayed as she heard the men shouting to the bulls. Whatever happened, at least Ruy would be safe. And would she? She shuddered as she remembered those wickedly sharp horns and small mean red eyes. A bull marks out a man he will kill, just as a matador marks out his bull, Carlos had told her. Quelling her rising panic, she waited until she could see that the bulls were marshalled in the yard. There were four of them, but she only saw one, the huge black animal she had seen as she walked down.

Like a sleepwalker she started to move towards the yard. Behind her she could hear the sounds of the men getting the bulls on the move; the clatter of horses' hooves on the cobbles, the everyday sounds giving way to cries of concern as someone observed what she was doing.

Ahead of her was Ruy, and she clung on to that thought, her eyes finding and focusing on his face even while her mind blotted out the words he was shouting to her.

She knew he was telling her to go back. There was still time. The safety of the barrier was only three yards behind her; all that was needed to keep her from those razor-sharp horns and the half a ton of bone and muscle which would soon be bearing down upon her.

She had worn the red blouse deliberately, knowing the effect it would have on the bulls. They were between her and the men now; she could hear Enrique angrily chivvying them on to reach her, but she didn't hesitate. Out of the corner of her eye she saw the bulky black shape, but she didn't allow her concentration to waver; didn't allow her eyes to leave Ruy's face. Only when she knew that the bull had seen her, when she sensed from the shocked silence of the men that it was going to charge, did she start to run; not directly for safety but diagonally across the yard, changing direction when she heard the drumming of its hooves.

It was the bull and her now. The men had managed to herd the others away, but this one, this black harbinger of death, was pawing the ground behind her, snorting as he caught the scent of her fear.

'Davina . . . This way! Don't run, just walk

slowly . . .' She heard the words and ignored them, knowing that her frantic movements, the vivid splash of scarlet, were enticing the animal to destroy her.

Her heart thumped with dry fear. Behind her she could hear the men; someone was trying to distract the bull, waving a red cloth towards it, but it saw only Davina. In front of her was Ruy, sitting in his chair, his hands gripping the sides in white-faced agony. She had a moment to wonder a little at the agony, where she had expected anger, before her foot slipped on a cobble and she was falling . . . falling . . . If only she were a Minoan girl she might have vaulted to freedom over the bull's horns, was her half-hysterical thought as something gored her thigh, burning into it like red-hot steel, and the waves of pain beat upwards, engulfing her.

Her last thought was that she had failed, for Ruy had not moved, had not been provoked into rising from his chair as she had prayed . . . and she had given up her life for nothing.

It was dark and there was a pain in her leg. She tried to move and winced as it increased in tempo.

'Good, you are awake.'

Dr Gonzales was bending over her, shining a torch into her eyes and making her flinch.

'There is no concussion, that is good,' he said to someone standing behind him. For one wild moment Davina thought it was Ruy, but it couldn't be Ruy. Ruy could not stand. The doctor moved and she recognised the slender body of her mother-in-law, only the Condesa looked different somehow. It was several seconds before Davina realised why. The other woman was crying.

'Oh, Davina, how could you? To take such a risk! Have you no thought for Jamie, for . . .'

'She must rest,' the doctor was saying gently. 'The body has received a bad shock, and the heart also, I think, although I am not the one to mend that.' His eyes seemed to hold a knowledge which was denied to Davina. She had risked so much—everything—and now she had lost.

She was handed a glass and she drank thirstily from it, not realising until too late that it had contained a sleeping potion.

When she awoke again Ruy was in the room sitting next to her in his chair, Jamie perched on his lap.

'Naughty Mummy,' Jamie chided severely when she opened her eyes. 'Not to go near the bulls!'

'What were you trying to do?' Ruy asked evenly. 'Destroy yourself as well as my child?'

He was gone before she could make any retort, leaving her to escape back into sleep where she could ignore the pain in her thigh and that in her heart.

She remained in bed for three days. There was no sign of Ruy; but then why should he bother to come and visit her? she asked herself miserably. The Condesa remained at the hacienda. She came to see Davina every day and they talked together. At least they were drawing closer together, Davina reflected one afternoon when her mother-in-law had left with Jamie to take the little boy for a walk. Dr Gonzales was pleased with her progress. Another day and she would be able to get up, he promised her when he came to visit her. He had made no reference to what she had been doing crossing the yard, which surprised Davina a little, because she had expected him to guess what she had hoped to achieve.

Jamie returned from his walk with the Condesa; Dolores brought up her meal; both women seemed to share an air of suppressed excitement.

Davina was surprised when the Condesa did not offer to join her for dinner. She had been doing so lately, explaining that Ruy was busy. As she ate her omelette Davina heard a car door open, and Dolores' voice raised in excited pleasure. Who was their visitor? she wondered.

A knock on the door startled her. She watched it open and Ruy came in, in his chair. Her accident had achieved what her pleading had not, she thought miserably. They now had separate rooms.

'You are feeling better?'

Her throat closed up with pain. She could scarcely look at him, it hurt so much.

'Yes.'

'That was a foolish thing you did. You could have been killed.'

'Yes.' The word acknowledged the truth of both statements.

'So then why, *amada*, did you do it?'

The soft '*amada*' made her shake like a fragile aspen buffeted by an unkind wind.

'I . . .'

'Yes?' Ruy encouraged.

'I . . .'

To her horror two large tears welled and splashed down on to the hand Ruy had placed on the bed.

'Tears?' His voice was so soft that it was almost her undoing. 'Why, *querida*? Is it true that you love me?' he suddenly demanded arrogantly, changing tack.

When her heart had recovered from the shock she countered, 'Do you think I should do?' Lying down in bed wearing nothing but a scanty silk nightdress was not a good position in which to conduct her defence.

'No. But Carlos seems to think you might.'

Carlos? How could he have betrayed her? She looked

wildly into Ruy's face, trying to see if he was just testing her, but all she could see there was tender amusement, and something else—something she could remember seeing only once before, and that had been the day she had agreed to marry him. Men were selfish and impossible, she railed inwardly. Even loving another woman he derived satisfaction from forcing her to acknowledge her love. His hand captured hers, lifting her fingers to his lips and kissing them individually, his eyes never leaving her face. Her whole body tingled tormentingly; the pain in her thigh was forgotten, but not the pain in her heart.

'Well?' Ruy prodded softly. 'Is it true, do you love me, *adorada*?' Weak tears spilled down over her ashen cheeks on to their still interlocked hands. 'Now you cry! Why, I wonder? You crossed that yard deliberately, didn't you, Davina?' His voice was tender no longer, but angry. She could barely bring herself to look at him.

'I wanted to . . .'

'To what?' he asked softly from the wheelchair. 'To walk with me beneath the moonlight and make love under the orange trees, perhaps?'

Her heart stood still and she refused to look at him.

'*Bien*, and so we shall,' Ruy said huskily, as though unable to trust his self-control any longer, 'but for now you will have to be content with this, light of my heart.'

Her head jerked upwards. She could hardly believe her eyes. Ruy was standing up, leaning over her to lift her from the bed and cradle her in his arms as he sat down upon it.

His lips touched hers and she started to shake, unable to believe that it was not all a dream. Ruy moved away to look into her eyes and smiled wryly.

'Very well, *pequeña*, explanations first and then we

shall make love, but I warn you, they must of necessity be brief.' As he spoke he glanced ruefully at his body, and Davina flushed fiery red as she followed the look and witnessed the evidence of his arousal.

'First my apologies,' Ruy said sombrely. 'For my cruelty; for my grossly insulting behaviour I beg your forgiveness, *querida*. My only defence is that I was jealous . . .' He saw the disbelief in her eyes and laughed harshly.

'Oh yes, it is true. Jealousy is a tame word to describe the hell I have been through, first when you left me, and then through all the long years we were apart, and since then, more recently, the agony I have endured thinking you in love with another—but the blame is not all mine, *adorada*. When I telephoned my mother about your accident she insisted on coming straight to the hacienda. She was on the verge of hysteria. You had restored to me the use of my legs, willingly risked your own life, and she had wronged you badly. You see, *pequeña*, my mother had this idea that I should marry Carmelita. I confess there was a time when I considered it—before I met you. But the moment I set eyes on you I knew there was only one woman I could make my wife; only one woman who could fill the aching emptiness of my life.'

'But I thought you loved Carmelita and had only married me to make her jealous,' Davina interposed.

Ruy's smile was tenderly amused.

'Such an innocent, to think a man—any man—would take such a drastic step to court the attention of another woman! No, I married you because I dared not let you out of my sight in case I lost you. You were so young, so innocent . . . I told myself I would teach you to love me as I loved you.'

'You mean a man of your experience didn't realise that I already did?' Davina marvelled, dizzy with the happiness creeping over her.

'Ah, experience flies out the window when love comes in the door,' Ruy retaliated sagely. 'Between them my mother and Carmelita have caused us much unhappiness. I have had the full story from my mother. How she allowed you to believe I was with Carmelita when you were having our child, when in reality I had been called away to an unavoidable meeting—I drove all night to reach the hospital, only to find you had left and taken the baby with you. I was like a man deranged. You had gone with your lover, Carmelita told me, reinforced by my mother. What could I do? I knew if I went after you I was in danger of killing you. I told myself I would get over you . . .'

'How could you believe Carmelita?' Davina murmured. 'You must have known . . .'

'I knew only that you melted like honey in my arms,' Ruy said simply, 'and that your eyes shone like the hearts of pansies, but your heart was a secret to me and one dared not look closely into lest I discover it barred to me.'

'When all the time it already stood open,' Davina said dreamily.

'When I saw you in the Palacio and realised what my mother had done I wanted to die. The last thing I wanted was for you to pity me. Your presence tormented me. I wanted you so badly I couldn't sleep or eat. I told myself it was the act of a man not worthy of the name to force myself upon you, but yet I couldn't help myself.'

'Oh, Ruy!' Her tremulous mouth was kissed into submission, her arms going round his neck as he strained her against him. 'We have a lot of lost time to make up.'

'And you have a lot of reassuring to do,' Ruy announced mock-severely. 'Carlos called to see you. I think he thought I had deliberately allowed you to risk your life for me. He threatened to beat me into a pulp until I told him that I wasn't a helpless cripple any longer. Then he told me that you loved me. For that I have promised him that he shall be godfather to our next child,' Ruy said. Laughter glinted in his eyes as he waited for her to take up the challenge, but Davina was too happy to take exception.

'You can walk? Oh, Ruy!'

'More tears,' he commented, mock-horrified. 'Yes, I can walk—thanks to you. When you ran from that bull, I was filled with helpless rage. I could do nothing. Your life was in danger and I could do nothing. Then I remembered the gun we keep on hand in case of such emergencies, and the next thing I knew I was on my feet walking towards it. I don't know which of us was most surprised when I shot him—myself or the bull.'

'Oh, Ruy . . .'

'Can you say nothing else! Do you realise what you have cost me? That bull was a valuable animal. You will be required to make due recompense.'

'Very well, as long as I can make payment in kind,' Davina agreed, entering the spirit of the game.

Ruy pretended to consider, his head one one side.

'*Si* . . . just as long as the payment you have in mind can be measured in kisses, and long nights spent in your arms, *querida*. We have much to catch up on. I am taking you away for a short time—a true *luna de miel* this time. I own a villa on Menorca, and we shall go there. Madre will look after Jamie, it is all arranged. All that is required is for you to say yes,' he finished huskily.

'Yes . . .' Davina whispered the word against his

throat, delighting in the sudden clenching of his muscles, the dark colour running up under his skin, as he held her away for a few seconds.

'*Madre de Dios!*' he commented feelingly. 'Is this how you treat a man not long out of hospital?' When she gasped he smiled reassuringly into her face. 'No, nothing is wrong. Doctor Gonzales wanted me to have a full check-up, but I am assured that everything is in order.' A brief smile touched his lips. 'I'm afraid the nurses found me impatient, but they understood when I told them that I was anxious to get back to my wife. That is why I haven't been to see you before . . . That, and because I thought perhaps you had taken such a drastic step to . . .'

'Kill myself and our child,' Davina reminded him with a wan smile.

'*Dios*, forgive me for that,' Ruy groaned. 'No, *querida*, what I really feared, knowing your tender heart, was that you might have tried to free me in order to free yourself. For a moment I was tempted to pretend that I was not healed. Carlos reassured me on that point, as did your face when I came in here tonight. How could you ever think that my life was of any value to me without you in it?'

'Doctor Gonzales said it might work . . .' was all she could think of to say.

'*Dios!* I am sure he said no such thing. He would no more have wanted you to take such a risk than I did. But he has given me some food for thought, I admit. I would not believe him when he told me the paralysis was of the mind. I was too proud to admit that it might, as he said, be a way of pleading with you to return, as though my body knew what my heart refused to admit, that you were too kind, too compassionate to be as I stubbornly kept telling myself you were. And now, *querida*,' he said, with a glint in his eyes that brought the colour to Davina's cheeks, 'I think it is time that I showed you my gratitude with more than words, *sí*? What would you prefer?' he teased. 'For us to dance, perhaps, so that you may be assured of how fully recovered I am? Or . . .'

Davina's insistent tugging on his shirt brought his face level with hers. Her lips parted, mutely pleading, but refusing to take any further initiative.

'*Adorada*,' Ruy muttered throatily, closing the small space between them. 'Beloved Davina . . .' She winced involuntarily as the pressure of his hands on her body affected the wound on her thigh. In time the scar would fade, Dr Gonzales had told her kindly. The wound was clean and not very deep, but for now it sometimes ached painfully.

'What is it?'

If she hadn't believed Ruy before, she did now. The look in his eyes melted her heart with tenderness.

She touched her thigh and his eyes followed the betraying movement. '*Sí* . . .' he breathed jerkily, tenderly pushing her back on the bed and moving aside the thin silk.

His lips caressed the scarred tissue, and she shuddered in mindless delight.

'Yes, it is a little touch of hell, is it not?' he agreed huskily, taking her in his arms, 'this touch of the one we love against our wounds. Tonight each of us will be balm to the other's heart and soul, *amada*, and you shall greet the morning in my arms—as you shall greet it for the rest of our lives.'

His name was lost beneath his kiss. Happiness flooded her. She was here where she wanted to be, locked safe in the haven of Ruy's protective embrace.

Loving

Little Heather Fraser had everything she could possibly want, except the love of her father, Jay.

His callousness shocked the tiny Cotswold village, and most of all Claire Richards, whose daughter Lucy was Heather's friend.

When Jay accused Claire of encouraging the girls' friendship so that she could see more of *him*, nothing could have been further from the truth.

A freak accident suddenly put paid to Claire's cherished independence. Would she be able to swallow her angry pride and reluctantly share the Frasers' roof?

After 25 million sales worldwide, best-selling author Penny Jordan presents her 50th Mills & Boon romance for you to enjoy.

Available January 1987
Price £1.50.

Mills & Boon

TAKE 2 MILLS & BOON BEST SELLER ROMANCES ABSOLUTELY FREE

Having just enjoyed a Best Seller Romance from Mills & Boon, here is a special introductory offer that is guaranteed to appeal to you. Two top-selling Best Sellers **absolutely free** – plus a unique Mills & Boon tote bag with our compliments. It's our way of introducing you without commitment to our regular reader service. All we ask is that you take your 2 free Best Sellers (the most successful Romances republished by popular demand) and tote bag. Then, if you enjoy them (as we're sure you will) take out a regular subscription. Now turn the page and see the other benefits a subscription brings you...

▶ ▶ ▶